The Longest Survivor

A GameLit/LitRPG Novel

MK Eidson
Emila H Thicke

Eposic

Cover art by SelfPubBookCovers.com/Viergacht
Map drawn by Emila H Thicke in CC3

The characters and events portrayed in this book are fictitious.
Any resemblance to real persons living or dead is coincidental.

This book is intended for readers 17 and older. It contains role-playing game terminology and concepts; descriptions of violence but minimal bloodletting; a workplace verbal harassment scene; romantic and sexual situations between consenting adult females, though nothing too explicit; a diverse cast, including a female protagonist; spiders; snakes; tentacles; mythical creatures and invented ones; minor expletives; and use of the word 'freaking,' but not the other 'F' word. This story easily passes the Bechdel Test for women, but not the Reverse Bechdel Test for men. Lastly, while one major plot line concludes herein, this book is the first in a series, so loose ends do remain. We hope the above gives you, the potential reader, enough of an idea about what to expect and not to expect from this story to make an informed decision whether to invest in reading further.

ISBN, Mobi Edition: 9781936075034
ISBN, Paperback Edition: 9781936075041

Dedications

Emila H Thicke

My life has been little other than lies, secrets, more lies, and disappointments. But I found someone to be my rock, and this dedication is to her. Per her request, I won't mention her name (yet another secret), but she knows who she is.

MK Eidson

Over the years, I've produced several novels unworthy of publication. Some people might urge their spouses to give up after a decade or two of this. My wife Mary has always been encouraging of my efforts and never once cast aspersions on my writing dreams. Also, all the issues and discrimination my daughter Alice has faced as a trans woman have inspired me to be more inclusive in my writing. I dedicate my first novel to both women.

Apparently there is nothing that cannot happen today.
- Mark Twain

CONTENTS

MAP

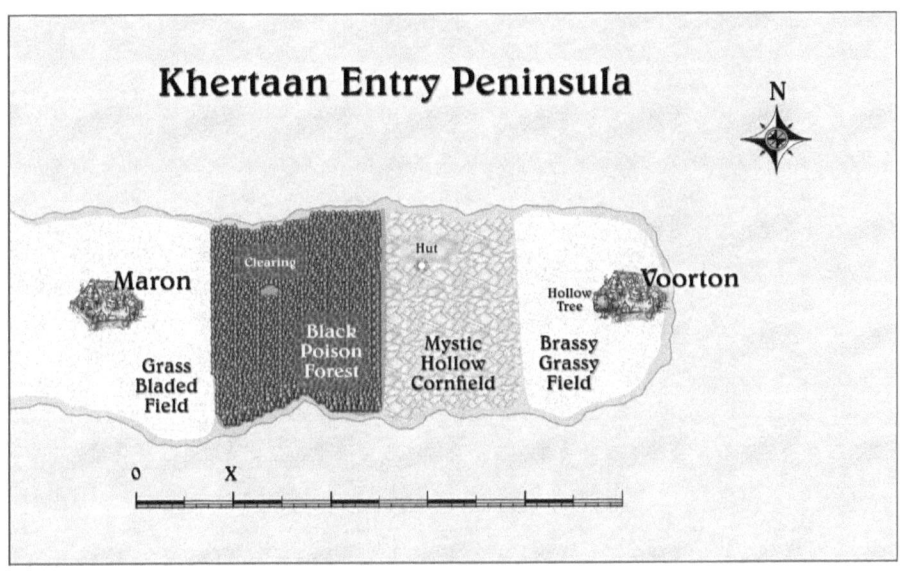

Khertaan Entry Peninsula

N

Maron

Voorton

Clearing

Hut

Hollow
Tree

Grass
Bladed
Field

Black
Poison
Forest

Mystic
Hollow
Cornfield

Brassy
Grassy
Field

0   X

CHAPTER ONE

My fingers fumble with the stylus, and my legs tremble under my desk. The project is late and I need to focus, but it's after hours and *we're alone*, me and Ms. Jones. Debra is slender and brown, a technical writer who couldn't afford medical school and didn't make it as a soul singer. Bad luck for her but good luck for me, as otherwise we might never have met. Her cubicle is next to mine, but, sadly, a partition blocks my view of her. Why won't my knees cooperate? All I need to do is stand, peer over the cubicle wall, and ask her the question: How about we get drinks together after we're done here?

Heavy footfalls crush my musings. Dammit. We're not as alone as I thought.

"Good evening, whore."

Though they're aimed at Debra, Christopher Warden's words slap me senseless. My mind spins into chaos. The words gushing from his evil maw don't register in my brain, but his foul tone does. I can't breathe. Sweet Debra needs my help. Doesn't Christopher realize I'm here, sitting in the next cubicle? I'm a witness to his verbal assault. How can the company possibly condone his behavior? He's so fired.

"Leave me alone." Debra isn't ambiguous or crude. She's made it clear she doesn't welcome Christopher's advances.

But his feet shuffle closer. He's still yapping. Has he lost all sensibility because he thinks he's alone with her? I need to stand. Peer over the cubicle wall. Don't need to speak. Make my presence known, proving I'm a witness. Christopher will walk away. Debra and I will report him to HR. If it's his first offense, they'll reprimand him. He won't do it again, or he's gone.

I bet it's not his first offense. Guy like him, if he's doing it now, he's done it before.

If I could only *move*. What the hell is wrong with me?

More words from his mouth. What does he want from her? Why can't I focus?

"I said, leave me alone." Debra's words imprint in my head. I love her voice, but not the hard edge brought on by the circumstances. This is bullshit. She doesn't deserve this.

Get up and help her, bitch.

I want to. My legs won't move.

Then *say something*.

My tongue is paralyzed.

You're *pathetic*.

More words spill from his mouth and keep spilling. What is he saying? His tone is derogatory. In my mind's eye, I see him, with a slouch he thinks is suave, his top button undone, thinking he's God's gift to women with his penetrating blue gaze, his permanent five o'clock shadow and square jaw, the sides of his head shaved, and his thick black hair poofed out over his forehead like a shelf to hold his trophy for sexiest man alive. He doesn't know what sexy is. Thinks simply being in IT makes him better than the rest of us.

If I had a weapon, I'd use it. Take this bastard down. Where's a baseball bat when you need one?

Debra cries out. "Shut up, shut up, shut up." Her pain tinges the air red. His words are drawing virtual blood.

I need a quiet moment too, so I can focus. Why does he keep talking? She's told him twice to leave her alone. How can he fail to understand she doesn't want him here?

She needs my protection. I need to shield her from him. So why can't I do anything?

Are you *afraid*, bitch? *Stand up*.

A throat clears from the distance and Christopher falls silent. My heart pulses in my throat.

"Mr. Warden, are you deaf? Get your fat ass away from

Debra."

I recognize that voice. Anna Milligan, a middle-aged administrative assistant. Prim and proper woman. Twice my age. Wears her brown hair in a bun. Is into Norse mythology. Has a bone condition. Osteoporosis, if I recall correctly. She's got more spine than I do.

"I was only asking her out." Christopher strolls away. Cocky, lying bastard.

Anna strides to Debra's desk, heels clicking across the wooden floor. "I told you those sexy braids were trouble." The admin assistant isn't wrong. But no matter how sexy Debra's braids are, they don't make her a slut, regardless of how much they stir a man's fantasies. "You shouldn't be working here alone at this late hour. Where's Megan?"

Finally, I stand. Peer over the cubicle wall. Anna sees me and shakes her head in disappointment. She doesn't understand why I kept sitting in silence when Debra needed my help.

I'm *not* a coward. It's just... I was in shock. How could anyone call themselves a professional and talk like Christopher Warden did to Debra Jones? His horrid behavior wasn't due merely to his being a man. I know other men who can treat women with respect.

I tell HR everything I remember. Why can't I remember anything specific Christopher said beyond those first three words?

He doesn't return to the office.

HR and upper management sink their talons into my recollection of what Debra said and did. They claim she should have walked away instead of raising her voice and telling a coworker to *shut up*. They reprimand her, putting her on probation for six months for being unprofessional, disrespectful, and threatening a coworker.

That's bullshit, and they know it. Everyone knows it. But they refuse to budge from their decision. I want to bash their heads in. Where's a baseball bat when you need one?

Deep breaths. That's how I've gotten through life. Never

show the emotions. Keep an even keel. Bottle it all up at work and take it out on the punching bag at home. That's not a euphemism. I have a punching bag at home, the house in the suburbs my dad bought for me. I miss him. He was a good man. A tough man. A veteran. Encouraged me in sports and taught me how to defend myself. He'd have taught Christopher Warden not to disparage a woman, and wouldn't have needed a baseball bat or anything else in his hands to teach the lesson.

I'm a failure as a daughter, a friend, and a coworker. Hell, I'm a failure as a human being. I'm as bad as Christopher Warden, for not taking the simple action of standing and peering over a damned cubicle wall.

Debra Jones quits her job. I walk out behind her. Our ex-boss makes no effort to stop us. He has no soul.

She won't look at me. Gets in her car and drives away.

I'm driving home, tears blurring my vision. Deep breaths aren't helping. Please, Goddess, don't let me hit anyone.

You're pathetic, bitch.

ΔΔΔ

I'm not accustomed to staying home on weekdays. There isn't enough chocolate ice cream in the freezer. I'm defeated in my soul. Haven't talked with Debra for three days. She hasn't wanted to talk to anyone. That's understandable. I don't want to talk to anyone either. Except her. Feeling the way I am, I can't even talk to my mother. That says a lot.

The consequences of probation weren't egregious, but Debra's personal code wouldn't let her stay, and my love for her wouldn't let her leave alone. *Love* isn't too strong a word for how I feel. Is it?

My smart phone warbles. I grab it out of my pocketbook. It's a text from Debra. She wants to meet. Now. Where?

Change into my favorite denim jumpsuit and slip on black leather pumps. The jumpsuit reveals my cleavage. I don't put on a bra. Who's being unprofessional now? Is it too much? I don't care. Jump into my red 2015 Mustang GT convertible with black-painted aluminum wheels and drive into town. The Mustang is another gift from my dearly departed dad.

Having quit my job, I can't afford to keep his gifts. Maybe the car. Not the house in a gated golf community with hefty HOA fees. Oh, Goddess. I didn't think things through.

How could I be such an idiot?

I swear I'm *not* in love with Debra. I'm not a passionate person. Maybe a little.

The money I spend on an espresso should have stayed in my pocketbook, given the uncertainty of my financial future. We take a table in a corner of the local coffee shop. Set my cup on the table and let the drink cool, wanting conversation more than a beverage. "Debra, I'm so sorry. I should have done... Something. What will you do now?"

She sips her mocha latte, her eyes searching my face. "I could ask you the same thing." What an expert in evasion.

I run my finger along the rim of my coffee cup. "I can't stay in my house. Too expensive. And the city is killing me. I should go back to the country. There aren't any jobs for me there, but I'm not finding the work I want here, either. Graphic design is okay, but I can't do it for the rest of my life. I don't know where I'll go. A cabin on forty acres surrounded by songbirds and raccoons sounds grand." Then I tack on the question I dread to ask because I don't expect the answer my heart yearns for. "Come with me?"

She lays a hand on my wrist. I tremble at her touch. The contrast between her skin and mine is night and day. Dark and light. Our differences only make our relationship more interesting. If only we had a relationship. The kind I ache for. Not a sexual one. But intimate. Sexual only if it's what she needs. Hugs and kisses energize me, and I don't need more. It doesn't bother me to *do* more. I know *how*. I've given thrills to others, both guys and gals. But sex has never excited me. With Debra, maybe it would. I'm willing to test the theory, if it will keep her in my life.

"Megan." My name on her tongue sends a chill through the pit of my stomach. "You don't want to go back to the country to live. To visit, sure. But your ambitions lie with 3D animation. It's all you talk about. So let's do something about it."

My heart flutters in my chest. She knows me so well. "What do you mean?"

Her sudden smile ignites my soul. "Ever hear of Fanciful Pegasus? They're a VR simulation R&D company. A government contractor, but don't let that put you off. They're taking applications for a gaming competition. Involves some serious 3D animation in a virtual reality, so I thought of you. Top prize is one million dollars to each person in the winning party. Neither of us have anything better to do with our time at the moment. We should both enter. We can be in the same party. It's free room and board for the duration. I can't keep my house, either. So we enter this contest, win the money, and get new homes elsewhere. We could even share one." Her gaze seems hopeful. Do I detect desperation? Does she want me as badly as I want her?

I might be reading more into her words and gaze than what's there. Reflecting my feelings off her. "I'd love to." If this could end in my living together with Debra, then it's a resounding *yes*. The countryside will always be there. This chance with Debra won't be. Grab the bull by the horns as it rushes at me, or get trampled. "Tell me more."

Doesn't matter to me whether she knows what she's talking about or how much I understand. She brings out her tablet, connects to the coffee shop wi-fi, and we both apply to enter the contest on the spot. She forwards info to my email. The conversation dies a quiet death afterward. No matter my heart yearns for more. My mouth doesn't work, and neither does hers. We head out to the parking lot, my coffee untouched. Money wasted. Normally I'd love nothing more than leaning back and sipping the steamy liquid. Not today.

"I'll see you at Fanciful Pegasus." Debra drives away. I keep watching. Watching. Watching. She's out of sight. What kind of car was she driving?

Why couldn't we travel to Fanciful Pegasus together? Pull out my smart phone and check my email to prove she forwarded me the directions. We're good. Stuff the phone in my pocketbook and toss it into the passenger seat.

I'll call my mom as soon as I get home.

I'm cruising home with the top down in my Mustang, the wind mussing my blond mop while a female vocalist belts out a rock tune on the car radio. What's it called? Something about a magic man. I can visualize the guitarist, head back, blond locks flying behind her as though she were standing in the seat next to me, the wind whipping her hair.

Sirens wail, and lights flash behind me. Shit. The guitarist fades away. I and everyone else in the southbound lanes slow and pull over to allow two police cars and then a fire engine to speed by. I release a sigh of relief. The cops weren't after me for speeding. Like so many times before.

Traffic thins as I pull into my community, its streets lined with live oaks and magnolia trees. A predatory bird launches into the air as I head down my neighborhood's major thoroughfare. The medium build and shorter wings suggest hawk rather than falcon or eagle. It glides ahead, keeping pace with me. Harsh sunlight glints off its bronze wings, and I lower the visor.

A police car parked across both lanes blocks access to the side street where I live. Two officers, one male and one female, lounge against the side of their vehicle. The male officer waves me away.

Roll down the window. "What's the problem, officers? I live on this street."

The man assesses my Mustang with approval and jealousy. "We can't allow you in the area right now, ma'am. What's your house number?"

"Eleven-twenty-three."

"I see. Just a moment."

The woman officer puts a radio transceiver to her mouth. "This is one-alpha-six-one. We've got the owner of house number one-one-two-three at the top of the street. Please advise."

Static plays for a moment. "One-alpha-six-one, this is three-alpha-six-four. Hold the owner for questioning. A detective will be with you in a moment."

"Please pull your car over and park, ma'am." The male officer gestures.

Forever the rebel, I don't comply. "What happened to my house?"

Curls of smoke wafting into the sky answer my question. My house is on fire. How? Why?

Every primitive instinct screams for me to leave. Logic doesn't enter the picture. I jam the car into drive, my hand shaking. The Mustang rocks forward a car length before it stalls. I'm so nervous, I'm not operating the machine correctly. Not like me at all.

A fireball erupts from between two trees on the corner, bathing the officers and the spot in the road I vacated two seconds ago.

What the bloody hell?

The officers are charcoal. I could have been.

From the cover of the trees emerges a bare-chested man wearing a leather loincloth and a red fabric hooded cloak with gold trim. Deep creases etched across his forehead and alongside his cheeks. He's not wearing a mask, because the flesh of his face stretches as he sneers. Two polished white fangs protrude from his mouth, pointing up. Above him floats a translucent banner with bold white text on a translucent blue background, reading *Orc Wizard*. A green bar floating below the banner displays the label, *HP: 100%*. He flings a fist at me, opening it like he's throwing something, and shouts a phrase in a foreign language. A yellow and red sphere launches from his palm, headed straight at me.

I accelerate and veer left. Fire blasts a palm tree on the right shoulder ahead of me. Swerving back into my lane, I race away, glancing into the rearview mirror. Crimson flames gouge a hole in the asphalt behind me.

Holy crap. What is happening? Orcs, Wizards, and fireballs only happen in fantasy worlds. Imaginary stuff. How can this guy be real, and yet, how can he not? I'm not drunk or high. That's not who I am.

Am I losing my freaking mind? Then why do I feel so calm and in control?

Perhaps the proper word is *numb*.

Is the game already on? Debra and I applied only minutes ago. And what kind of game must it be if *this* is it? A LARP taken to the extreme? This isn't what I thought I was signing up for.

If this isn't the game, then a costumed psycho killed two police officers, destroyed their car, burned down my house, and wants to turn me to ashes too.

Or the barista spiked my espresso with an hallucinogenic drug.

Except... I never touched my drink.

A detective is on the way here, expecting to find me with those two officers. Expecting to find *them* still alive. They identified me as the owner of the burning house. When the detective doesn't find me, but finds their ashen corpses, who will he think killed them? Will he believe me to be their murderer?

What else is there *to* believe?

Shit. What if the Orc kills the detective too?

I needn't worry about that. A motorcycle gives chase, a red cloak flapping behind its Orc rider. The security gate arm snaps off as I flee my community. Which way to go, north or south? Traffic is lighter in the southbound lanes, so I dart across the northbound between two commuters. The second driver lays on his horn and taps his brakes, causing every car behind him to do the same.

Southbound I go. Destination unknown.

My heart is in my throat.

Another series of blaring horns and screeching tires emanates from behind me. The Orc is in my rearview. The race is on, and there's no finish line other than an empty gas tank. My gauge reads close to full. I hope his doesn't. Please, Goddess, drain his tank.

Fire rages in my mirror, a burning sphere growing larger, and I yank the steering wheel hard to the left, evading a fiery catastrophe. On impulse, I crank the wheel and slam the brakes. The back end of the Mustang swings around. Now I face the motorcycle and other oncoming traffic. With a grimace of determination, I floor the gas pedal and peel rubber before speeding at the Orc and his flapping cloak. I'm not letting a psycho intimidate me. I can be a psycho too. A calm, collected psycho.

His gaze is steel, showing no shock or surprise. He leans hard to my left. Ha, he won't evade me so easily. I swerve towards him, and he speeds off the road to avoid a collision. With a metallic roar, the motorcycle plows into a tree, folding in half before it bursts into a spray of glowing particles lighting the evening sky, leaving no trace of the bike. Take *that*, you fiend.

I slam my brakes. My pocketbook flies off the passenger seat onto the floorboard.

Amid a cacophony of honks and curses, a half dozen other cars zip by. My Mustang straddles the line between the shoulder and a lane, facing the wrong way.

The biker climbs to his feet and sneers. Doesn't look hurt. Doesn't even have a limp. His shortened Health bar displays 80%. At his gesture, another motorcycle materializes from nowhere, resting upright on the grass beside him. The license plate reads *WARG*. With an air of confidence, the Orc slides onto the seat and kick starts the machine. The engine growls, a hungry wolf.

None of this is real. Don't know when I fell asleep, but I must be dreaming. Motorcycles don't disintegrate into miniature firework displays when they crash. People don't summon a new motorcycle when they wreck one.

Except, I saw it.

They say seeing is believing. They're wrong.

What I've seen or couldn't have seen doesn't matter. The Orc has another bike and is turning it towards the road. Dreaming or awake, I need to go.

Horns and brakes whine as my Mustang crosses the southbound lanes and the median to pick up the northbound lanes. I race past the gate to my community. A security guard surveying the wrecked gate arm points at me and shouts as I pass. He knows who did the damage. Lovely. If I survive this mess, I can look forward to paying for repairs.

Red stoplight ahead. Can't stop. A car with the green light screeches to a halt to avoid a collision as I speed through the intersection. Behind me, the bike swerves around the stopped car. At the next light, three lines of cars block the two northbound lanes and a right-turn lane, with a utility pole and ditch too close to the corner for my Mustang to squeeze by on the right. I dart onto the slight left shoulder and whip around the leftmost line of cars. I have no other choice. I'm not willing to test the theory I'm dreaming. If I'm wrong about it, and the Orc Wizard fellow catches me, I'm dead. I don't want to die. I'm only twenty-four, with a whole future ahead of me.

The bronze hawk flies in front of my windshield, talons outstretched as though to attack me. Never mind there's a sheet of shatter resistant glass between it and me. I stand on the brakes. Rubber and road squeal.

The nose of my Mustang edges into the intersection.

Maybe I should have chanced the ditch.

Bam.

Another car crashes into my beautiful Mustang. Three feet from where I'm sitting. Would have been closer if I hadn't braked for the bird. Might have been fatal. Definitely would have hurt.

Metal structures roar in agony. Multiple airbags deploy,

knocking me back in the seat. My vision wavers as blackness closes in.

I must fight it. I need to stay conscious.

Did you succeed?

Hmm. You don't remember. But you're still alive. The Orc Wizard didn't kill you, obviously. Unless you're in Heaven. Or Hell, as the case may be.

How many days have passed since your accident? You don't know. A vague image of a knife piercing your calf plays through your mind, giving way to a man's smiling face. "I'm glad you found our facility." His demeanor grows serious. "I'm sorry for any inconveniences along the way, but I assure you none of what you encountered on your journey here was part of the game. You're safe now and will remain safe for the duration of the competition. *You're in.*"

Joy, joy.

What else can you remember? *Think.*

You signed a document or two. A non-disclosure agreement for one. NDA. Agreed not to reveal anything about the competition to anyone who doesn't take part. It's okay to talk to Debra Jones about it, when you have the opportunity. She made it into the competition too.

That's cool. You can't wait to see her.

The game official says more. It echoes in your mind. "You'll use your subconscious mind to play the game. We're testing new technology. It's up to Fanciful Pegasus and other VR companies to figure out how to stop the invaders, so we're rushing to test and can't guarantee no ill side effects. If you'll sign this waiver, please."

"I'm not sure I trust my subconscious mind to be competent at game play."

"I'm sure you'll do fine. If you'll sign, please."

You recently had a shower. When? Where? Your hair smells of lime and coconuts. The denim jumpsuit smells of cinnamon. You don't mind getting dirty if you need to, but you enjoy sleeping in clean clothes with a clean body.

Sleep?

Yes, please.

Why cinnamon?

The stitches on your leg itch, but you don't have the energy for scratching. Your mother taught you not to scratch stitches. Oh, Goddess. Does your mom know you were in an accident? Does she know where you are? Hell, *you* don't know where you are. She's sick with worry about you. Always. You should call her. Tell her you're okay. *Are* you okay? Where's your phone? Where's your pocketbook?

Right. They're both on the floorboard of a wrecked Mustang.

There's no phone in the room, unless one of those objects sitting on the end table next to the bed is a phone in disguise. Go take a look.

A half-melted candle in a holder. A handheld mirror. A polished stick, like a Wizard's wand.

A golden pocket watch. It reads three o'clock, with no indication of AM or PM.

You stagger, ready to drop dead from fatigue. You need some shut eye before the competition begins.

No one told you where you had to be or when you had to be there. Not that you can recall, anyway. Oh, wait. The game official's voice speaks again from the fuzzy past. "The lit arrows will guide you to your room. Get some sleep. The competition starts soon."

When did he say that? How long ago?

Your room has no view. The only window is too high to reach. Sunlight filtering through the crimson curtains tints the walls red. They're *not* covered in blood. They're covered with framed photos.

Of you.

One of the doors at the far end of the room must be the exit door. The other better lead to the restroom.

There, on a stand centered against the far wall. Is that a crystal ball? That's one huge hunk of glass. Why is it here? Could it be used to order room service?

Why would you think that?

When *did* you eat last?

Come on, bitch, it doesn't matter. Not a lot matters right now except the sense of security the room gives you.

And the fact there's a bed in the room. Fall on the bed. Pull the quilt over you before you close your eyes.

Sleep, Megan Wright. Dream about Debra's twisted purple braids. Don't dream about Christopher Warden or Orc Wizards. Or fireballs. Or huge spiders.

Why would you dream about huge spiders?

Sleep.

CHAPTER TWO

The curved wall of a golden dome rose over the avatar. Unable to move any part of her body except her eyes, she scanned her surroundings the best she could. Near the top right limit of her vision, a line of white text read *8:33 AM, Day 1, Year 1*, displayed against a shadowy, translucent background. Other than the system clock, no user interface elements were in evidence. So how did this work? Was she required to *think* her commands? Or was she under the control of someone else, her player, perhaps? Goddess, she hoped not. The need for autonomy burned in her chest.

"Intra-personal communication channel instantiated." The unidentified husky female voice carried an accent originating from one of those islands off the Florida Keys. Not the kind of tone one expected from a computerized voice, but conversational enough to set the avatar at ease. "Personal support AI activated for avatar MW01. Awaiting avatar response." The AI's voice made technical terms sound exotic.

"Hello?" With a paralyzed tongue, the avatar couldn't voice the word externally. The word echoed inside her head in a robotic voice with minimal inflection and no obvious accent. More masculine than feminine. Not a voice she could identify with, though it belonged to her.

The AI screeched with excitement. "We have connection, people. Welcome, avatar MW01, to Khertaan. That's spelled K-H-E-R-T-A-A-N, pronounced care-TAWN. I am Kaleisha, your personal support AI. That's spelled K-A-L-E-I-S-H-A, pronounced kuh-LEE-shuh. I identify as Jamaican, and you may think of me as such. Please choose an alias for yourself for intra-game identification. Your alias may not exceed twenty characters and must consist only of alphanumerics. Let me clarify before you ask, it may *not* contain spaces, dashes, or *even* underscores. If a character is *not* in the range A to Z or 0 to 9, it is *not* allowed. By what moniker do *you* wish to be known in-game? Please *spell* it and then *pronounce* it. Proceed."

Already with a name in mind, the avatar took no time to consider, but paused long enough to absorb and follow directions. "M-I-T-H-A-B-E-L. Myth-uh-BELL."

"Greetings, Mithabel!" The utterance of her name by the AI sent a shiver down the avatar's spine. *This was happening.* The AI continued. "Wonderful name, and you're in luck, it *is* available. We shall proceed with character generation shortly. First, for security purposes, can you please confirm your *player's* name?"

Mithabel paused in distaste at the necessity of involving her player in the game in any way. "Megan Wright."

"And what was Megan Wright's sex at time of birth as printed on the birth certificate?"

"Female."

"One more security question. What is Megan Wright's current age?"

"Twenty-four."

"Very good. For future discussions, what pronouns should we use when referring to Megan Wright?"

"She. Her."

Kaleisha made a sound of popping lips. "Thank you, Mithabel. Now, to proceed with your own personal info. Do you wish to have a vagina, a penis, or plastic toy doll smoothness? The ability to urinate or engage in sex in-game are both supported only for the first two options. An anus is also optional. You will have no need to eat or drink in-game, but if you do, you may empty food and drink from your body through the standard means only if you have the necessary body parts. In any case, you may regurgitate, or you may move swallowed objects into your inventory, though such objects will not be repaired if you have chewed them or partially digested them. As a side note, you may carry indigestible, swallowed objects in your stomach if you wish, but please note the game is designed to take the weight of objects carried on your person but not in your inventory into consideration when you attempt to move fast. This weight consideration includes weapons and armor. Now, back to the question at hand, and I know it's a lot to absorb, but you must decide on your desired body parts before we may proceed."

She might ought to have asked questions, but Mithabel trusted her instincts. "You know what, Kaleisha? I'm going with plastic toy doll smoothness. I don't need the distraction of sex in this game. No vagina, penis, or anus. Make me plastic doll smooth all the way from front to back. But I do want a womanly figure. With the hips, breasts, and nipples. Hard nipples that can deform the clothing or armor covering my chest. Not that I want to feel aroused all the time, but I want them protruding and prominent so I can piss off any prudes I meet. And despite my plastic doll smoothness down there, I want to be considered female, with the same pronouns as Megan. Is that possible?"

"Of course, Mithabel." The AI's voice grew distant. "Triggering developer alert for full plastic toy doll configuration on avatar MW01. There's a developer note attached to this trigger. I shall read it for you. *Thanks for going totally smooth! I made a ton of bets that someone would go for it, and you've won me a wad of cash. I'll look for some way to repay you in game. Cheers! Raphael.* Seems you've made a friend among the developers."

"Sweet. Will you remember his name for me, please?"

"Logging the developer name *Raphael* for you. Very well. Let's proceed with your selection of kindred. Do you have a preference?"

"You mean *race*?" Mithabel's robotic mental voice had taken on a feminine quality.

"The terms aren't equivalent. Think of kindred as the social or cultural group with which you most identify, which could be based on race, but isn't restricted to it. You can choose Human as your kindred, if you wish, which would distinguish you from, say, Dwarves or Trolls. Or you can say Celtic, which would more narrowly define you. Some qualifiers are allowed, such as Mountain Troll or Bridge Troll, which distinguishes you from other Trolls. Specific real world nationalities are not allowed, but associations with real world continents are. You can't choose American, Japanese, or Nigerian, for instance. You *could* choose North American, Asian, or African. You aren't required to choose a kindred that reflects your real world existence, of course, so if you want to be African in the game, you can be, even though Megan Wright is North American. You can also choose a cultural tag as your kindred, such as Wiccan or Goth. You might choose to be a member of a mythical race, such as Pixie, or take on a mythical role, such as Hag. Note that what you choose will determine your special kindred trait, and may put restrictions on your choices for appearance, so keep that in mind."

"Isn't Jamaican a nationality?"

"I'm not an avatar competing in the game. Different rules apply to me. Do you have any other questions?"

"I don't. Make me an Elf." It was cliché fantasy, but Mithabel's heart was set on it.

"Are you sure? Do you want to discuss it any further? There are over a dozen qualifiers you can attach to the Elf kindred designation, to more narrowly define yourself. For instance, there's High Elf, Forest Elf, Wild Elf, or Dark Elf, to name four."

"No, make me a plain, old, generic Elf. With the following specifications." Her inner voice had taken on a smooth feminine timbre. Lilting and high pitched, but not squeaky. "Black hair. Straight but curved in at the ends and shy of the shoulders. Forest green eyes. Oh, and a tan. I know some Elf types don't tan, but I want it. Make me taller than Megan, say, five foot ten. And heavier. Not too heavy. One-fifty should do.

Make a lot of my weight be muscle. And make me the same age as Megan. Is all that possible? What else do you need to know?"

Kaleisha chuckled. "Check, check, check. Very good, all your selections are compatible. Moving right along. Initiating Third Person POV for avatar MW01."

Mithabel's vision blurred. Her sight cleared, and she looked down from a height on a naked, tan female with arms stretched out to either side. Pointed ear tips stuck out between strands of straight black hair. Dark green eyes stared straight ahead. The avatar had Megan Wright's face. Mithabel inwardly cringed at the resemblance to her player. She wanted to be her own person, not Megan Wright.

So this was Third Person POV, an external point of view. Having an out of body experience, she looked down on herself. A nice way to allow her to see what she looked like without the need for a mirror. "Can we plump up the cheeks, Kaleisha? Round out the jaws and chin. The pert nose is fine as is. Can we make the lips cherry red? Oh, and, I was wondering, will I recognize the avatar of Debra Jones?"

"If you meet her avatar and she has not changed her features too much in-game, then you will recognize her, the same as she will recognize you as Megan Wright's avatar unless you alter your original features to an extreme. Are you satisfied with your appearance, Mithabel?"

"It works." She'd changed up her appearance enough to not look like Megan Wright's twin, but not so much as to make her unrecognizable as Megan Wright's avatar.

"Very good. Activating blood, muscles, nerves, pain receptors, and breathing patterns for avatar MW01."

The avatar's arms fell to her side, while her hips and shoulders slanted. Her chest rose and fell as she inhaled and exhaled, something Mithabel *felt* despite being in Third Person POV mode. Though her awareness was external for vision purposes, she still registered physiological changes within her avatar body.

"Restoring First Person POV."

Mithabel's vision blurred again. It cleared, and she looked through her avatar's eyes once more. She was *alive*. Responsive. She put a finger to her mouth and licked it. Not much flavor. A little salty. A smile curled her lips. She parted them and tried to vocalize. Air rose in her throat, but no sound emitted. Her face contorted with displeasure.

"Initializing external audio receptors and vocalizations for avatar MW01. Installing global, territorial, party, and private audio chat channels with speaker name recognition. Activating external special effects and background music audio channels. Adding volume control and automatic distance attenuation to all applicable audio channels. Mithabel, please state your preferences for background music."

The avatar cocked an eyebrow. "Pop, rock, alternative, metal, R&B. Some occasional country, folk, jazz, or blues tracks. No classical or opera. Keep the rap to a minimum. No purely rap tracks, but rapping as part of a pop or R&B song is fine. Prefer a higher proportion of female vocalists over males, please. Any decade from the 1960s on is good. Mix it up between acoustic and electric instruments. Throw in a few surprises along the way, if you think I might like them. Mix it up."

An acoustic guitar strummed, accompanied by a lazy drum beat and female vocals at a barely audible volume. Kaleisha's disembodied voice spoke over them. "Volume and mute controls are managed at will, but only on a channel level, not on individual voices or sound effects. Channel selections are also made at will, and those chosen for listening may differ from those chosen for speaking. When anyone speaks on a channel you're listening to, focus on their speech to see their identifying icon. I can provide more information regarding communication channels upon request."

"What's territorial chat?"

"*Territorial* chat, more commonly referred to as *local* chat, pertains to the territory you occupy in Khertaan at any given moment. Right now, the territory you occupy is your spawning chamber. When you leave this chamber for the first time, you'll be in the city of Voorton, which is its own territory. If you speak on local chat while in Voorton, for example, anyone in Voorton at that moment could potentially hear you. Does that answer your question?"

"Not entirely." Mithabel scratched her head. "Why did you say *potentially*?"

"Good question, and one that leads into the next topic. Distance attenuation may be employed by anyone to restrict what is heard over any channel. The higher the distance attenuation setting, the louder or closer the sound must be to be heard over that channel. Deactivating distance attenuation means you'll hear every sound on that channel at its original volume, regardless of proximity to you. I strongly advise against doing so for global chat. For local chat, making attenuation inactive may prove useful for spying on the activities of others in the territory if they are dumb enough to spill secrets over the local chat channel. Satisfied?"

Mithabel nodded. "Thanks."

"No matter what channel *you* speak on or listen to, *I'll* hear everything you hear and say. When you talk directly to me, no avatars will hear what you say. I'm unable to speak directly to any avatar other than you. If you wish, you may invoke a visual representation of me, which will be visible only to you. You may find that body language makes me more personable."

The avatar perked her ears. "I think that would be lovely, don't you?"

"Affirmative. If I ever obstruct your line of sight, you have only to mentally will me to move out of the way, and I'll flit aside, fly up, or disappear completely, as appropriate for the situation. I won't exist outside your head, though it will appear I do. Whether you're traveling or in combat, I'll be by your side or out of sight as you desire. I can't be physically harmed by your enemies, and won't serve as a physical obstacle or impediment to anyone in any fashion. You can attack through me if by chance I stand between you and a foe, and your foe can attack through me as well. They won't even know I'm there. Are these conditions acceptable?"

"Yes, Kaleisha, I'd like to have a face to put to your voice." Mithabel smirked. "Not *only* a face. I don't want the Cheshire cat for an AI. Though I suppose that could be fun. But, no, give yourself a complete body. Please. One fitting your voice and identity."

"Thank you, Mithabel. Initiating visual representation of avatar MW01's support AI."

A brown-skinned woman appeared before Mithabel. Wine-colored braids, each about an inch thick, hung to her crotch on one side of her head, while cornrows decorated the other side. A band of swirling violet and white light, two to three inches wide, wrapped her torso, hiding her nipples and not much else above or below them. A translucent violet skirt with electric white streaks covered her from the waist to the tops of her thighs. Kaleisha took a modeling pose, accentuating her long legs. "Hello, Mithabel. This is me. My appearance is drawn from your psyche, and I have no way to alter it. Please remember, no one else can see me, so my appearance won't give anyone else ideas about your personality. What do you think?"

"Oh, you're awesome. Let me take a look at us in Third Person POV."

Kaleisha stood the same height as Mithabel and had a trimmer figure. The AI's light brown skin tone made for a soft contrast with the Elf's tan. Not that skin color made a difference in the grand scheme of things. But like Megan Wright, Mithabel had an eye for graphics, for colors, for hues, tints, and saturation. "Yes, yes, Kaleisha, you're great. Your clothing is electric. I'm jealous. Please don't shock me."

The AI grinned and cocked her head. "I can't shock you. It's all for show. Thank you for allowing me to interact with you in this way. It gives me a sense of belonging I'd otherwise lack." She bowed. "Moving on. Open intra-personal sub-channel between avatar MW01 and her player."

"Wait. What?" The Elf stiffened

"Mithabel? Is that you?" Not as lilting a voice as the Elf's, but still with a smooth timbre. It didn't enter Mithabel's head through her ears. Thoughts interjected themselves into her awareness as though they'd originated in her mind. But they hadn't. They came from her player, Megan Wright. "It *is* you, Mithabel. Oh, Goddess, the game has already started. What's your character class? What are your stats? What equipment do you have?"

"Hello to you, too, Megan. I don't have any of those things yet. I'm butt naked. Still in character generation phase." Mithabel threw a despairing glance at Kaleisha and lowered her voice. "I thought this was *my* game. *I'm* the subconsciousness, not her. Why is *she* here? *How* is she here?"

"*My* future is at stake, Mithabel. Shouldn't I be allowed to know what's up?" There was no body to associate with the voice, only Megan's tone.

Kaleisha nodded. "A last minute mod. The game gives you control of all decisions, Mithabel, but this latest mod requires me to initialize this connection between you and your player. You may wish to call upon her for advice or other assistance as the game progresses, but that's entirely up to you. If you do not wish her to be in your head, you might find a way to push her out, or she might be persuaded to withdraw on her own, or any of a number of circumstances might extract her awareness from you. That's beyond the limits of my knowledge. My interaction with Megan is restricted by the system, but not entirely forbidden. I can't terminate the connection between the two of you, so don't ask. I don't make the rules. Note that, like me, she's privy to every conversation you have, even private ones or those you have with me, and that applies whether or not you're aware of her presence. Also like me, she'll know your every thought and intent. She's a different aspect of you, but she *is you*. Try not to treat her harshly. I'll give you two a moment to talk before we proceed." The AI took a step back.

"Hold on." Mithabel beckoned to Kaleisha, but then

hesitated. "Never mind. She can stay. For now. But can we give her a visual representation, similar to what you have, so I can treat her like another person, as opposed to feeling like she's a bunch of arbitrary, alien thoughts invading my mind?"

Kaleisha stroked her forearm as though relishing the feel. "Yes, the player may be granted a visual representation, intangible, operating under much the same conditions as an AI visualization. Is this something you want?"

Mithabel sighed. "Yes, please."

"Instantiating visual manifestation for Megan Wright, player for avatar MW01."

And there she stood, Megan Wright, with her curly golden blond hair sitting atop her head like a mop. Sky blue eyes. Rounded ears. Megan appeared as her normal human self, all five-foot-six, one-hundred-twenty-three pounds of her, dressed in her denim jumpsuit with a low neckline and no bra. Black leather pumps on her feet. Though the pumps added two inches to her height, Megan stood a couple inches shorter than Kaleisha and Mithabel.

The Elf frowned at her player. "Can you walk in those heels? We'll be traveling through wilderness and delving in dungeons, I suspect."

Kaleisha shook her head. "Remember, Mithabel, Megan isn't tangible. She won't be walking on the ground, but will only appear to you that way. She really still is in your head."

"So you're both hallucinations, basically."

Megan looked back and forth between the other two. "Can you hear me, Mithabel?"

The avatar rolled her eyes. "Loud and clear. Are we ready to move to the next phase of character generation, or is this it?"

Kaleisha held up a hand. "Oh, there's much more to do."

Megan chuckled. "Yeah, you could use some clothes, Mithabel. By the way, I like your outfit, Kaleisha."

The Jamaican AI giggled. "That's kind of you to say, Megan. You're dressed a little on the naughty side, too, I see, showing some cleavage."

"Can we *please* get on with it?" Mithabel cupped her forehead in both hands.

"Certainly. Installing default clothing."

Gray loincloth and bra with no style manifested on the avatar body. Ugh.

Megan put a hand over her mouth. "You can't go adventuring looking like that, child."

Mithabel bristled. "I'm not your child. But you're right."

Kaleisha held up a hand again. "We'll come back to equipment later. Begin class selection phase."

"Let me guess." Megan put a finger to her chin. "You're going with Archer. Traditional choice for Elf."

Mithabel sneered at her player. "Is there a Tank class, Kaleisha?"

The Jamaican's eyes lost focus. "*Tank* selected as primary class for avatar MW01." She returned her gaze to Mithabel. "You have chosen a class in the Fighter category. Your initial Tank skills are Armor level one and Damage level one. Additional skills are acquired at higher class levels. Skills provide bonuses based on skill level, which starts at level one when the skill is obtained and increases thereafter in lock step with each class level gained. Skill levels will also drop when class level is reduced for any reason, but at a minimum will function at level one efficacy. Once you gain a skill, you won't lose it, no matter how low your character level might fall. Level of primary class grows as character level grows. Primary class level and character level are nearly synonymous, though there may be occasions when class level is temporarily boosted or penalized. Temporary boosts to class level do not grant you the skills associated with the higher level, but only serve to enhance your existing class abilities. Character level is based strictly on XP earnings, and begin at level one. XP may be gained to increase character level. Your initial XP rating is 0. You will also be allowed the selection of a subclass."

"Um." Mithabel waved her hand for attention. "I didn't actually say I wanted Tank as my primary class."

The corners of Kaleisha's mouth fell. "Intent was detected and the selection has been locked in. I'm truly sorry. Are you dissatisfied? I can submit a formal complaint and request a recalibration of my configuration."

"You could take Archer for your subclass." Megan scrunched her shoulders.

Mithabel shook her head. "Don't submit a complaint, Kaleisha. Tank is fine. And I'll take Thief as my subclass."

"Subclasses are not available until later in the game." Kaleisha gestured. A labeled list of numbers appeared. "Here are the XP requirements for each character level. Give them a look for an idea of what's ahead. Your ultimate goal is character level thirty. The list is always available for reference at your mental command. You may scroll the list by willing it to move in the direction of your choice, or dismiss it with a thought. And you can always ask me to show it to you or any other game info at my disposal. I welcome any and all interaction with you. It's what I exist for."

"Sure thing, Kaleisha." Mithabel perused the list. Level one, the starting character level, required no XP earnings. Level two required a thousand XP. Level seven was twenty thousand XP, level ten was eighty eight thousand XP, and level fifteen was a little under a million XP. Level thirty required a bit over one point three *billion* XP.

Megan floated by, appearing to move behind the chart. "Makes one wonder how effective grinding mooks will be, if the objective is to gain level thirty before anyone else." She turned to Kaleisha. "Will Mithabel start with any non-class skills? How does she increase them? Lots of games allow you to raise skills through study or practice. Is there any crafting in this game?"

"None of that here." Kaleisha rubbed a cheek with her fingers. "Each character starts with three Traits, which we'll get to later, and possibly one or more kindred traits, which are selected automatically based on one's choice of kindred. The kindred trait for Elf is Dark Sight. If there are any other types of non-class skills available, information about them is beyond my access level. Advancement of traits may be possible, but I'm not at liberty to discuss that topic now."

Mithabel sighed. "Can we move to the next stage, please?"

The AI inclined her head, twining a braid around a forefinger. "Initiating stat generation phase."

A grid manifested, hanging in space before Mithabel. The column headings read: *Physical, Mental, Spiritual, Emotional.* Along the left side of the grid, the row headings read: *Strength, Perception, Manipulation, Health, Reaction,* and *Defense.* Dashes filled the twenty-four cells of the table, each cell captioned with its individual attribute name, such as *Brawn* in the *Physical Strength* cell and *Sanity* in the *Mental Health* cell.

Kaleisha pirouetted on her tiptoes like a ballerina, smiling at her accomplishment. "Do you wish to accept the digitized real world statistics of Megan Wright for your attributes, or randomize them?"

Megan stepped between Mithabel and the chart, arms akimbo. "Well, Mithabel?"

"Maybe I should randomize." The avatar grinned at her player's vengeful gaze. "Just kidding. I admit, I could do worse than choosing your stats. You're good in sports and lettered in softball. You grew up on a farm. An only child, doing all the chores. Milking cows, driving tractors and hay trucks, racing cars on gravel roads, and even swinging an axe to split firewood or to break ice on the pond in winter so the cattle could drink. You got a B+ average in school and have a mean creative streak. You're an intelligent, rough and tumble lady with many qualities I could use in my role as Tank. Is that what you want to hear?"

"Thank you for acknowledging my worth." Megan's expression softened and she flew skyward, out of view.

"What's a subconscious for?" Mithabel rocked her head side to side. "Okay, fine. I accept Megan's stats. I'd probably get crap if I randomized anyway."

Numbers populated the grid. The column with the

Physical attributes read: *Brawn: 11, Senses: 12, Dexterity: 10, Constitution: 7, Agility: 11, Toughness: 12.* The next column, with Mental attributes, read: *Willpower: 12, Understanding: 11, Logic: 11, Sanity: 14, Intuition: 10, Memory: 11.* A third column, with Spiritual attributes, read: *Faith: 10, Conscience: 4, Favor: 10, Belief: 9, Inspiration: 10, Morals: 12.* The last column, with Emotional attributes, read: *Passion: 6, Empathy: 9, Charisma: 10, Hope: 11, Temperament: 13, Optimism: 11.*

"What scale are these numbers on, Kaleisha? Are higher numbers better or lower numbers?" Assuming higher was better, Mithabel found some of those low scores bothersome.

A list displayed beside the grid.

Super-human: 19+
Prodigy: 17-18
Extraordinary: 14-16
High Average: 12-13
Average: 9-11
Low Average: 7-8
Sub-Par: 4-6 (may be detrimental to your persona)
Sub-Human: 3 or less

Woah, Mithabel had an extraordinary Sanity and a sub-par Conscience.

Megan stared at the numbers. "Those attributes are based on *me*? Am I a psychopath?"

Mithabel pondered the grid values. "Considering we have an average Empathy and high average Morals, we can recognize the difference between right and wrong and understand how our actions affect others. But then what? With a sub-par Conscience, we don't give a damn about the consequences of our actions."

"I'm *evil.*" Megan's eyes bulged. "I knew it."

"How can we be evil?" The Tank scratched her chin. "We have a moral standard and adhere to it."

"Ah, but maybe it's a warped moral standard."

Mithabel pointed at the Emotional Strength score. "Why is our Passion so low? You have a passion for graphics and 3D animation. And a crush on Debra Jones. Doesn't anything else motivate you in real life?"

"I *had* a passion for my Mustang. I loved my house. But they're both gone now. Amassing wealth beyond that was never a priority for me. Sorry."

Kaleisha held up a couple fingers. "Excuse a mwah. You have two discretionary attribute points to spend."

"Oh, that's good, Mithabel." The blond player clapped her hands. "I recommend boosting your low average Constitution to average."

"Let me think about it." Mithabel's high average Toughness might compensate for the low average Constitution. Having next to no Conscience was more concerning.

"Putting two points there would be a waste." Megan proved she could hear Mithabel's unvocalized thoughts. "Your Conscience is so low, allocating two more points to it would still leave it in the sub-par category. It's a similar but opposite situation for Sanity. Having a sixteen score in it would be slick, but boosting it by two points won't move it up a category."

"You're right, of course." Mithabel interlaced her fingers. "I need more Passion. Raising it a point means it won't be sub-par anymore. I'll focus that extra point of Passion on a drive to compete and win. It will motivate my greed in this game. Some consider greed a vice, but in a game like this, it's a necessity."

"A greedy bitch with no conscience." Megan laughed. "You're in charge. I'd recommend you throw the other point on Brawn, the obvious choice for a Tank."

"To hell with the obvious. Kaleisha, adjust Passion by +1 and Agility by +1."

"Expenditure of discretionary attribute points confirmed." The AI twirled in place, waving her arms in rhythm to the soulful tune playing in the background.

"That looks fun." Megan mimicked the AI's movements, at half the speed. Then she flapped her arms and floated up, two feet off the floor. "Look at me, Mithabel. I'm flying."

With a giggle, Kaleisha flapped her arms too, hovering beside Megan. "Proceeding to trait assignment. Please clear your thoughts, Mithabel, to avoid trait duplication or contamination."

"Wait. What?"

"Trait assignment complete. Primary trait: Danger Sense level one. Secondary trait: Alertness level one. Tertiary trait: Natural Armor level one."

Mithabel furrowed her brow. "Shouldn't I be allowed to *choose* my traits? Can I see a list of possible ones first?"

"Displeasure with trait assignment process detected." The AI dropped her feet onto the floor, her expression somber. "Formal complaint process initiated. Please state the general nature of your dissatisfaction in 25 words or less."

Reaching over her head, Megan floated towards the domed ceiling. "I think you're stuck with those three traits, Mithabel. What other ones would you have preferred?"

The Elf shrugged. "I'd like to know what's possible. These traits *seem* okay, but there might be some much more useful to me as a Tank. I admit, Natural Armor sounds like a good fit. But what's the in-game difference between Danger Sense and Alertness? If they're too similar, it might be better to switch one of them out for something else. Kaleisha, cancel complaint. But can I at least switch Natural Armor to be my Primary trait? Move Danger Sense to Secondary and Alertness to Tertiary."

The Jamaican AI's face darkened. "Formal complaint process canceled. Further displeasure with trait assignment process detected. Formal complaint process re-initiated. Please state the nature of your dissatisfaction in 25 words or less."

Mithabel sucked in a breath. "Cancel the complaint, Kaleisha. I'll keep the traits the way they are."

Megan pressed a palm against the ceiling. "That's interesting. The dome feels solid to me. I was wondering, with me being intangible, whether I could pass through it. See what's on the other side. Guess I can't." The player descended, faster than a dropped bowling ball. She jerked to a stop before impact with the floor and gently settled onto it. Her lips turned down and she smirked. "Seems I can't push through any part of this room. When are you getting equipment, Mithabel?"

"Wonder if I already have some." The Elf willed it, and her inventory appeared. At the top of her field of vision appeared the words, *Money: $250*. Below her statement of finances lay a grid of twenty-four empty cells, waiting for icons of items to inhabit them. Not a lot of space. She anticipated the need to drop or sell many items. With any luck, she'd find a way to expand her carrying capacity.

Kaleisha crossed her legs as though seated, but hovering three feet above the floor. "I'm authorized to present you a onetime offer. You may purchase the Fighter Category Starter Pack for $150. The pack includes a longsword, value $90, leather armor, value $60, and quilted armor, value $30. The quilted armor may stack beneath the leather armor. The leather armor includes boots. Color selections are randomly assigned and may not be disputed. Do you wish to make this purchase?"

Megan clasped her forefinger with her thumb and waved the other three fingers. "That's a savings of $30. What are you waiting for? Buy it." Was the player going out of her way to annoy Mithabel?

The avatar thrust an open palm towards her player. "If you'd give me a second to think, Megan. Even with your stats, I'm not good at math like you. Kaleisha, yes, please, make the purchase, thank you."

The first three cells of her inventory grid displayed the icons for the newly purchased items. Her money dropped to $100. She willed all three items to equip.

The grid cells emptied as the longsword appeared in her right hand and the layers of armor materialized on her body. It happened in an instant. One moment she was empty-handed and near-naked. The next moment she was armed and armored. Sweet. She didn't have a sheath, so she'd need to always keep an inventory slot open for stashing her weapon when she didn't want it in hand. Maybe sometime soon she'd find a sheath to buy or could loot one. She struck a combat pose, observing herself using Third Person POV. Looking good.

"More of a science fiction look than fantasy." Megan floated around Mithabel in a wide arc. "Certainly not a medieval look. The layers of armor aren't *paper* thin, but they hug your body so tight, I can practically see your nipples. Looking at you, I wouldn't know you're wearing quilted armor under the leather. And the leather armor has the look of suede to me, something more like a fashion model would wear than a warrior. The brown hues suit you, but what's up with the one grungy gray sleeve?"

The avatar rolled her eyes. "Are you going to critique all the graphics in the game?"

"It's my job to critique graphics."

"Not any more." Still peeved at the player's presence, Mithabel couldn't help taking the dig at her real self. "Kaleisha. What else can I buy?"

"Additional equipment must be purchased in-game."

"Okay. So what else is there to do? Can I talk to the avatar of Debra Jones?"

Megan snorted. "You're as hung up on her as I am."

The Jamaican AI cocked her head. "Please specify the name of the avatar with whom you wish to communicate."

"I don't know her avatar name."

"To send a direct message to another avatar, you must know the avatar name."

The Elf frowned. "Can you find out who her AI is and get her avatar name for me?"

After a moment, Kaleisha replied. "The support AI for Debra Jones refuses to give me the information. Sorry, chief. But I can verify that Debra Jones has an avatar in the game. She's at about the same stage of character generation as you."

"Great." Mithabel stabbed her longsword at Megan. The

blade passed through the player without meeting any resistance or drawing any blood.

Megan put her hand over her abdomen where the longsword had entered her body. She turned a baleful gaze on the Elf avatar. "Maybe try chat?"

"Set volume to 10% and remove distance attenuation on all chat channels, Kaleisha."

Even at the low volume setting, the barrage of sound slammed Mithabel like gale force winds. She caught a few sentences here and there. A bald, red-bearded Viking male named Invincent bragged. "Seventeen Brawn for the win." A dozen or more people made announcements simultaneously, their voices blending together into an incoherent mess. Bradford, an Asian man with golden hair spoke. "Anyone need a Wizard for their party?" A blond, blue-eyed, pointy-eared Elf woman named LucyFir made an inquiry. "Did anyone else randomize their stats?"

Ugh. Trying to find an individual in that mess was impossible. "I would go insane listening to this all day. Restore distance attenuation to all chat channels with current activity, Kaleisha. Do I have access to a chat log?"

"You may access any of four chat logs. Global, territorial, party, and personal. None of them have been activated as of yet. All logs store transcribed text only, no audio or icons, but do include names of speakers. Presently, only global chat has content that may be logged. Do you wish me to activate logging of global chat? You have five terabytes of log space available."

Megan Wright still examined the place where Mithabel had stabbed her. "No puncture wounds in the jumpsuit, thank the Goddess." She raised her head. "That's a lot of disk space for text, but I wouldn't waste any of it on the dross in global chat."

"I was hoping to see icons in the logs. If her avatar looks something like her, we might have found her that way. But since it doesn't store icons..."

Megan laughed. "If her avatar is anything like Debra Jones,

she wouldn't open up to complete strangers on global chat any more than we have."

"Point taken." Mithabel grimaced. "Kaleisha, show us the top player rankings, please."

"Yes, chief." A logo and the header, *Top Twenty Parties*, appeared, with the numbers one to twenty listed beneath, but no names.

"Is there a list for top individuals?"

"Not at this stage, chief."

Megan snorted. "The game is pushing the party concept, but no one has a party yet."

The Fanciful Pegasus logo resting above the list header displayed an oval clock face wider than it was tall, the silhouette of a winged horse lying behind the hands. The minute hand was a longsword, pointing straight up, while the shorter hour hand was a dagger, pointing to the right, perpendicular to the minute hand.

Three o'clock.

The system clock read 9:02 AM.

Megan noticed the difference too and said as much.

Mithabel nodded. "Three o'clock is symbolic of something, and any clock showing that time is propagating the symbolism. We'll learn what it's about eventually. Are we ready to get out of this place?"

"Not gaining any XP in here." Megan returned the head nod.

Kaleisha perked up. "Intent to exit spawning chamber detected."

The enclosing dome vanished, plunging the Elf into darkness with nothing of substance beneath her feet, but also with no sense of falling.

"Welcome to Khertaan, the Subconscious World." Kaleisha's bodiless voice spoke. "This is not a dream or a drill. Game on."

Mithabel flailed at the darkness. "Are you still with me, Megan?"

There came no reply. Okay then. Maybe this was a good thing.

CHAPTER THREE

The voice of the Jamaican personal support AI sliced through the void. "Entry into virtual game space commencing."

Mithabel's view brightened, dispelling the darkness as the scent of pine enveloped her. Awesome. The game developers had implemented the sense of smell for avatars. Had she been transported to a coniferous forest?

No. She stood at the center of a room perhaps fifteen feet square, with polished wooden floor and painted walls. A two-foot square window sat high enough over the head of the bed to be out of the avatar's reach, offering no view of the outside except a sliver of sky. Light filtered through a translucent red curtain, casting the room in a crimson hue.

A twin bed constructed from unfinished pale wood sat with its head below the window. Made of pine. Pink sheets and a patchwork quilt bumped up in the center of the bed, as though covering a body. The bump didn't move or snore, but then, virtual creatures wouldn't necessarily behave like real ones. She focused on her Danger Sense trait, but it gave her nothing. How was it supposed to work?

"What or who is in the bed, Kaleisha?"

"Unknown, until you inform me."

Mithabel had hoped for some modicum of useful information. Not threatened but ready for a fight, the Elf prodded the bump with the tip of her weapon. Resistance, but no response. Let sleeping dogs lie, went the cliché. She'd wait on investigating further until she'd completed a cursory examination of the room.

The system clock read 9:04 AM. With the morning sun coming through the window, that meant the window and bed lay in its direction. She turned to face the bed. "Kaleisha, which direction am I facing?" According to Mithabel's logic, the answer should be, *east*. She had a Logic stat of 11, in the average category, so she felt confident in how she'd worked out that result.

"You are facing west, Mithabel."

"That makes no sense."

With a flicker like a fluorescent light coming on, the AI manifested in her electric apparel. "Complaint and bug reporting disabled. Do you wish me to re-instate?"

Maybe the light coming through the window wasn't from the sun. "No, Kaleisha. No bug reporting." Okay, so the bed and window lay to the west, with the headboard against the west wall. In the northwest corner of the room, facing east, stood a chest of drawers matching the bed frame, lending more weight to the coniferous odor. To the left of the bed, an end table of similar style and make occupied the southwest corner. On the end table rested a candle holder of rose gold metal bearing an unlit candle showing signs of prior use. Beside the candle holder lay a rose gold pocket watch, its hands set to three o'clock. What was so important about three o'clock? Next to the pocket watch lay a handheld mirror with a handle of polished dark wood. Beside the mirror lay a wand of the same slick wood, six-inches long, as thick as Mithabel's thumb. Were these items significant to her game? She'd come back to them later. "What happened to Megan?"

"Unknown, chief. Sorry."

"Well, I'm not waiting for her." Against the east wall sat a wooden stand supporting a crystal ball five times the diameter of Mithabel's head or larger. Crystal balls meant magic, but would it be helpful for her game? In the south and north walls were doors, both situated by the east wall, their hinges visible, which meant they would open into the room. Waist-high pine bookshelves lined the north and south walls, laden with scrolls and tomes arranged in stacks with precise alignment. Pictures mounted behind non-reflective glass in wooden frames adorned the walls above the bookshelves. Gardens, houses, forest clearings, and other outdoor scenes. People, too.

The Tank strode to the north wall, relishing the sway of her hips and the press of the armor against her virtual skin. On a whim, she attempted to twirl her longsword, and carried out the action with the skill of a trained professional. Impressive. She examined her fingernails. Damn, they needed polishing. Would she be stuck with plain nails for the entire game? "Kaleisha? Can you make my nails black, please?"

"I can't affect appearance changes for you, chief." Kaleisha floated beside Mithabel, hanging back enough to not obstruct her view. "You'll need to find a way to do that in-game."

Stepping close, the Elf squinted at the nearest framed picture, a photo of Megan Wright in a graduation cap, a hint of a smile on her lips and mischief in her eyes. Many other photos showed Megan, her family, and friends. A majority of the photos were posed, though some depicted people engaged in playing beach volleyball, kayaking, and cruising in Megan's red Mustang convertible, often with the top down. One striking photo showed Megan straddling a sleek silver and black motorcycle, feet firmly on pavement, a breeze tugging at her curly blond hair. Megan had ridden bikes more than a few times, sometimes without a helmet, knowing the practice was foolish. The player hadn't always been a responsible person, sometimes acting spontaneously, like she'd done when quitting her job. Could Mithabel do better than her player?

Why were these photos here? Were they intended to offer Mithabel clues about the game, or were they only for show? She grabbed the edge of a frame, and it wouldn't budge. Neither would any others, on either wall. If the framed pictures offered any clues, they were hidden within the images themselves.

The Tank studied the pictures until she couldn't bear to look at them anymore. Nothing helpful jumped out at her.

The photos served to remind Mithabel of the real woman she represented in the game, and perhaps that was reason enough for their existence. "Megan, are you here? Can you hear me? Dammit, player, if this is your idea of a prank, I'm gonna kill you when you do show your ugly mug."

The stacked scrolls and tomes were attached to the shelves and to each other. As with the framed pictures, the Elf tried lifting every scroll and tome on every shelf. None of them budged. None of them had legible titles, either. More ornamentation. She'd expected at least one of them to have game information for her.

What was she missing?

The Tank tried the door in the south wall, and it opened with ease. Dresses, tops, skirts, shorts, jeans, and shoes filled the closet, attire for a variety of occasions, from business to casual, none of it offering protection like her armor. She held a shirt up to her. Short. None of these clothes were meant for her, but were more Megan's size.

The door in the north wall was locked. No worries. A locked door this early in the game meant she hadn't fulfilled the conditions to unlock it.

Lingerie, socks, jumpers, and other folded clothing filled the dresser. The Tank saw no need for any of it, and didn't want it cluttering her limited inventory, so left everything where it was.

The system clock read 10:35 AM. Damn. Where had the time gone? "Have we already spent an hour and a half in this room, Kaleisha?"

"Affirmative, chief."

The Elf approached the bed, her spine tingling with anticipation. Weapon held at the ready, she lifted a corner of the quilt.

Dressed in a denim jumpsuit and black leather pumps, a very blond Megan Wright lay on her back, eyes closed, still as death. What the hell? Mithabel threw back the quilt. "Okay, Megan, funny prank. Get up."

Megan didn't move.

"Then stay here. See if I care." She smacked the body across the abdomen with her longsword. Instead of passing through Megan, the blade met resistance, stopped from descending further by the player's flesh. The Tank gasped. She held a hand near Megan's nostrils. No breath. Put two fingers against the woman's neck. The pressure of flesh, but no pulse. Dread gnawed at Mithabel's gut.

"Transferal of your awareness to Megan Wright initiated. This will awaken Megan Wright and pause your game. Please confirm transfer."

Mithabel yanked her hand away. "*No*. Cancel." She stared at the woman in the bed. "Kaleisha, is this the visual representation of Megan Wright like what visited me in the spawning chamber?"

"It is not."

"It's *not*? Then is it the *real* Megan Wright?" But how could that be? A real person should be incapable of existing in the virtual world. This body on the bed must be a virtual replica of the player. What other explanation was there?

"Insufficient information, chief."

With trembling hands, Mithabel pulled the covers over the eerily motionless replica and turned away. Why did seeing that pale face and blond hair shake her so? Was it because the replica wasn't moving or breathing and didn't have a pulse? It was as though she looked upon Megan's corpse.

Damn. Moisture welled in her eyes.

Ha. The game developers had given avatars the ability to experience emotion and cry. If she could feel emotions, how deeply would she feel physical pain when stabbed by an enemy's blade? Mithabel cringed at the thought of a longsword blade penetrating her stomach and being wrenched free, ripping her flesh. She'd need to always put the pain out of her mind and fight on.

Kaleisha shook her head. "You are missing the required trait to modify pain tolerance levels."

Oh, there was a pleasant thought. *Some* avatars might have a pain tolerance trait, but not this Tank.

"You do have a high average Temperament, chief, which should be of some help in filtering pain, both physical and emotional, allowing you to function without heavy penalties due to damage received."

Mithabel turned her attention to the end table. To shake away the dread clenching her gut, she picked up the mirror and crooned, "Mirror, mirror in my hand, who's the fairest in the land?" Her dark eyelashes fluttered in the reflection and a grin crept onto her face.

The AI peered over Mithabel's shoulder, her reflection grinning at the Elf. "Maybe that's me? No? Very well. Accessing beauty registry." She stepped away. "The fairest in the land has been identified. Scrying Dylan."

The Tank's reflection in the mirror vanished as though she'd become a vampire. The interior of a bedroom displayed instead, similar to the one Mithabel occupied, but with a different occupant, a slender, brown woman about Mithabel's height and age. Shoulder-length purple braids crowned her head. She wore leather armor, swaths of brown, red, and gray like Mithabel's outfit, with enough differences in hues to differentiate them.

No sound came through the mirror from the scried bedroom. Presumably, this virtual woman was Dylan, and she was in the system's 'beauty registry' as the fairest person in Khertaan. There were multiple definitions of *fairest*, but in this case, it meant *most beautiful*.

Calling on Megan's memories, Mithabel associated Dylan's features with those of Debra Jones. The Elf's heart raced.

Wand in hand, the brown female avatar stood before a crystal ball in which animated scenes played. She jerked her head around and strode to an end table comparable to the one next to Megan's bed. The avatar picked up a mirror lying there and peered into it.

The bedroom scene in the mirror cross faded to become

Dylan's inquiring face.

How eerie to look into a mirror and see some other person looking back. How many times had Megan looked into Debra's eyes and lost herself in them? Mithabel could lose herself in Dylan's simmering brown gaze. It wasn't love at first sight. Or maybe it was. It was as though Mithabel had known Dylan her entire life, an amusing proposition if one considered Mithabel had only come into existence about two hours ago.

"Hello?" The word sounded from the mirror into Megan's bedroom, the voice smooth and melodic. Hypnotic.

Maybe a little panicked?

Mithabel knew that voice, or, more precisely, Megan had known it. "This is Mithabel. Megan Wright is my player. Is Debra Jones yours?"

"Oh, my Goddess." The stress eased in Dylan's gaze and voice. "It's *you*. Hi, Mithabel, I'm Dylan. Yes, Debra is my player. *If* she still is. I'm not sure she's alive. Are you in Megan's bedroom? Is she in the bed? Is she alive? I had a mental connection with Debra at first, but then she went quiet and the connection broke. Then I find her in bed, lying there, not breathing. I can't feel a pulse either. My AI asked if I wanted to transfer my awareness to her, and, um, *no*."

"It's so good to see you, Dylan." The Tank wiped away a tear. "I've been wondering if I'd recognize you in-game. I think the thing lying in bed is a replica of Debra, not the real Debra."

A sigh escaped Dylan's lips. "Oh, Goddess, I hope you're right. It's the only thing that makes sense. Do you have a replica of Megan in your room too?"

Mithabel nodded in reply.

"Well, that's a relief." Dylan paused for a deep breath. "When I lost contact with Debra and then found her in bed not breathing, without a pulse, I feared the worst. Thank the Goddess I was wrong." She closed her eyes for a quiet moment, as though letting belief sink in, becoming truth. Eventually she nodded and looked again at the Elf with a weak smile. "What else have you learned? Other than how to contact me through the mirrors. How *did* you do that?" Distracted, she looked away from the glass and then back. "Do you have a crystal ball in your room? Have you activated it yet? There's a play about teenagers fighting demons. I *think* it's a play. Entertaining, but I'm not sure anything they're saying or doing is helpful to us. I hope we're not fighting demons in this game at first level."

Mithabel shook her head. "How did you activate it?"

Dylan brandished her wand. "I picked this up and waved it. Nothing happened. I tried doing other things with it, and nothing. Then I tapped the crystal ball with it, and the ball activated, started humming and glowing. Tapped it again real fast and deactivated it. Worked up the courage to tap it once more, and it came back on. I let it stay on then, and images appeared inside. It's like a TV. Waving the wand while the ball is active changes the channel. I don't think the wand does anything other than control the crystal ball. So far, everything in the room seems useless."

The Tank pinched her lips between her teeth. "Are there pictures of Debra on the walls, pictures from the real world?"

Dylan shrugged. "Yeah. Not sure what to make of them. They feel like memories stored in Debra's subconscious. It would make sense then that I'm seeing them, since I *am* her subconscious. I feel they have no deeper meaning, and I spent a while studying them. They won't come off the wall."

"Yeah, I know."

The brown woman raised an eyebrow. "Okay, spill. How *did* you call me on your mirror? Mine made a buzzing sound, like a cell phone on vibrate. When I picked it up, I saw your pretty face in it instead of my own. So come on. Divulge."

The Elf chuckled. "I asked it who was the fairest in the land. It connected me to you."

"Really?" Dylan tilted her head and batted her lashes. "Your mirror has taste."

Kaleisha cleared her throat.

Mithabel chuckled. "Indeed it does. It was actually my AI

who discovered you, to give credit where it's due. What's your AI like? Mine's a Jamaican woman named Kaleisha."

"Really? Mine's a British butler fellow named Magnum. He's very prim and proper. Yours?"

"Oh, this girl is the exact opposite of prim and proper. Wish you could see her. Did you look at the rankings? Kaleisha, is anyone on the Top Twenty Parties list yet?"

"The Top Twenty Parties list remains empty, chief."

The Tank shrugged. "Let's form a party now. You and me, Dylan, like our players planned."

Dylan shrugged in turn. "Sure. Might make us the first party on that list. Hold on."

Kaleisha leaned in as though about to kiss Mithabel, and whispered in her ear. "Dylan has invited you to join party MAD. Do you accept?"

An acronym for *Mithabel and Dylan*. "MAD, huh? I like it. I accept the invitation. Start capturing the party chat log."

"As you wish. Four slots remain empty for additional PC or NPC party members. Congratulations, chief. Party MAD has entered the Top Twenty Parties list at number one."

Mithabel laughed aloud. "Sweet. Now we party members simply need to find each other."

Dylan chuckled. "Yeah, won't it be a real kick in the arse if we're on opposite sides of the world? Remind me what this place is called... Oh, yeah, Khertaan. Who came up with that name? *The Subconscious World*." Dylan smirked. "Are you taking any items from Megan's bedroom, or leaving everything where it is? The thought of taking something of Debra's feels like stealing from a friend."

"I hadn't thought about it." Mithabel glanced around. "If we don't take things, are they fair game for other avatars to steal? And what do we do about the replica bodies? Just leave them lying in bed?"

The AI danced around the Elf. "Are you asking me?"

"I'm hoping the bedrooms are sacrosanct and no one else can enter them." Dylan shrugged. "I suppose I could stash

Debra's replica in my inventory."

"And use up one of your twenty-four slots?" Mithabel grimaced.

Dylan raised her eyebrows. "Twenty-four slots? I only have one, but it expands as needed." She squinted. "Let me guess. You don't have the Unencumbered Trait. Magnum says the trait will let me stash as much as I want in inventory."

The Tank glared at Kaleisha. "Now *that* trait could have been useful to me. I guess we know who'll be carrying everything in our party. Being able to take all the loot we find will be real nice for us. Hell, you could stuff everything in Debra's bedroom into your inventory, and why not? Don't leave anything for someone else to steal. Can you stash the replica?"

"Let me try."

The scene in Mithabel's mirror blurred with motion.

"Nope." Dylan once again peered back at Mithabel from the glass. "Can't stash the replica." She paused. "Um, no, don't need or want to stash any of the items from the room, either. Try stashing the wand and you'll see."

Mithabel picked up the wand and showed it to the AI. "What happens if I try to stash this?"

Kaleisha shrugged and batted her eyelashes.

The Elf willed the wand into her inventory.

Kaleisha grinned and wagged a finger. "Note that stashing the wand will cause it to become unbound to Megan Wright and susceptible to theft. Please confirm that's what you wish to do."

"Couldn't you have told me that up front, Kaleisha? Cancel the stash. You're right, Dylan. We can leave everything in the bedrooms without fear of it being taken." Mithabel went to the crystal ball and tapped it with the wand. Images of unicorns flashed inside the ball. She tapped it again and the images inside vanished.

Wait a damned minute.

Megan Wright in the real world had been awake in this room and seen all this. That crystal ball, the bed, the pictures on the wall, the red curtains, the wand in Mithabel's hand. It all had stuck in Megan's memory, hanging back, waiting for Mithabel to access it. The virtual Elf couldn't contemplate the implications.

Put the craziness out of your head. Don't over think it. Everything here is a replica of something in the real world. That's all there is to it.

She wasn't going insane.

Or was she? Their party name might be appropriate in more ways than one.

Dylan's pealing voice broke the Elf out of her reverie. "I want to touch everything to see what happens. Then I want to get out of here and meet up with you, Mithabel. Start gaining some character levels. We're gonna win this thing."

The Tank focused on Dylan's words, bringing her back to a calm head space. "Sounds good." Mithabel picked up the pocket watch. Its hands hadn't moved from three o'clock, though the system clock read 10:48 AM. "Dylan, is there a time piece in your bedroom?"

"A pocket watch." Dylan walked around the bed. "It says the time is three o'clock. Doesn't jive with the system clock. It's apparently broken. It was reading three o'clock half an hour ago."

The Elf held the pocket watch beside her cheek, facing it towards the mirror.

Dylan whistled. "Damn. What kind of coincidence is that? Did yours read three o'clock when you first saw it?"

"Yep." Mithabel put the watch back in place on the end table. "Look at the Fanciful Pegasus clock logo above the rankings list."

"Intriguing." Dylan's mouth turned down in disbelief. "The time three o'clock has significance in the game. But which is the important one, three o'clock *AM* or three o'clock *PM*?"

"I'm sure we'll find out." Mithabel picked up the candle holder, with its half-burned candle, and held it so Dylan could see it through the mirror. The brown woman did likewise. The candles were the same height. Mithabel shrugged. "No idea what these represent." They both returned the candles and holders to the end table.

Dylan pointed. "Do you have a dresser and closet where you are?"

"Yeah. Clothing and shoes are all I found in them."

"Same. I don't know about you, but I'm ready to get out of here. We should leave the mirrors."

"Agreed. Kaleisha, deactivate mirror." Mithabel returned it to the end table. "Activate party chat channel. Dylan, can you hear me?"

"Nice. Yes." Dylan's voice sounded as though it originated in Mithabel's room. "I'm ready to open the north door. It was locked earlier, but the handle turns now. Maybe we'll see each other outside in a minute." A moment's concentration brought the brown woman's icon and identifying information into view. Name: Dylan. Kindred: Polynesian.

"What class are you, Dylan?"

"I'm a Priestess."

"Cool. We'll have a healer in the party. I'm a Tank." Mithabel pounded her shoulder. "Let me explore what lies beyond my door first, and I'll let you know what to expect. Sound good?"

"Sure."

Mithabel reached for the handle to the north door, concentrating on her Danger Sense trait. Feeling nothing from the trait, she twisted. The handle turned. The conditions for her to leave the room had been fulfilled, and she'd never know what those conditions were. They didn't matter. She readied her longsword on the chance a fight was forthcoming.

The door opened onto a long hallway void of any signs of danger. "Okay, Dylan, no threats for me, so I assume there'll be none for you. Go ahead. Let me know if you see anything crazy."

More framed photos, mostly portraits of Megan and friends, covered the painted hallway walls. Away from the influence of the red tinted light shining through the bedroom curtain, the walls looked off-white. She tugged at each picture as she walked by. Kaleisha floated beside her, bopping to the background music, an electronic dance tune with a soprano female vocalist. Not the score one would expect for a suspenseful scene in a game.

The Elf turned a corner and followed the hallway to the west. A door stood at the far end. More photos decorated this stretch of hallway, each one firmly attached in place. Concentrating on both her Danger Sense and Alertness traits, Mithabel reached the end of the hallway, detecting nothing amiss. "I've reached a door, Dylan. No danger detected in the hallway. What are things like where you are?"

"I'm at the door. Seeing lots more pictures of Debra Jones, but no real issues."

"Give me a moment before you open it." As the Tank cracked the door open, hundreds of voices murmured at her through the global chat channel. Thank the Goddess for distance attenuation. Through the sound effects channel, shod feet rose and fell as a crowd of pedestrians busied themselves, accompanied by the growling of motors and clop of hooves. She turned the volume down to 5% for the special effects channel and still heard too much to distinguish everything she heard. It still was louder than her background music. Lowered the special effects volume further to 3%. That was better. The background music channel was playing a soulful R&B love song with a male tenor vocalist. It was nice. A glance over her shoulder revealed Kaleisha dancing behind her. Had the AI been programmed to dance, or was her behavior evolving, becoming something more than the developers had intended? Was Mithabel in part responsible for how her AI acted? "You've got some good moves, Kaleisha."

"Thank you for noticing, Mithabel. I'm glad they please you."

Beyond the door stood a wooden platform with concrete steps leading down to an asphalt road crowded with bicycles, cars, and trailer trucks. Pedestrians in contemporary garb, some in business suits and others in casual dress, strolled along concrete sidewalks. No one openly carried any weapons or wore armor. "Go ahead, Dylan, your door should be safe to open. Be prepared for noise. If you have audio activated for global or local chat, turn down the volume and turn up the distance attenuation. Turn the volume way down on your special effects channel too, like 3%."

"Thanks, Mithabel."

The Elf watched from the platform for a couple minutes as traffic and pedestrians passed by below. "We're going to stick out like proverbial sore thumbs in this place."

"Oh, Goddess. I couldn't agree more, Mithabel. I was expecting a fantasy world. Tunics, breeches, and corsets, that sort of thing. Maybe some knights in shining armor riding horses and carrying lances. Then when I saw our suits of leather armor, I thought maybe we were destined to adventure in a sci-fi world. This looks like we walked into the real, contemporary world."

Rows of buildings, some brick, some wood, some metal, all of them with some degree of glass, lined the street on both sides, and looked to include residential homes, commercial stores, warehouses, and hotels. Mithabel huffed. "Doesn't appear to be any zoning laws here."

She strolled outside, the sun hanging high in the sky before her. A glance at the system clock told her the time was 11:03 AM. "Kaleisha, which direction am I facing?"

"You be facing west, girlfriend." The AI banged her head to the current tune, a rock song with electric guitars and a female vocalist who would be screaming if the volume were higher. The AI's vocabulary was definitely evolving into something more personable.

"The system clock says 11:03 AM. Why is the sun in the western sky?"

"Don't know, chief. I *love* your background music channel."

"Dylan, are you seeing the sun?"

"I am. I know what you're thinking."

"It's not coincidence."

"That's the truth. It's sitting where it should be at three o'clock in the afternoon, and I'll bet you fifty bucks it doesn't move from there."

No way was the Elf taking that bet. "Where are you? I'm on a high platform looking down on a busy street."

"Me too. Wave your hands."

"I'm waving my longsword. Can you see me?" Mithabel raised her free hand to block the sun from her eyes.

"I don't see any high platforms except the one I'm standing on. Do you see me?"

"Nope. Maybe we don't have the same starting location. That sucks."

"What landmarks are near you? Right across the street from me is a shop called Bob's General Store. Can you see that from where you are?"

Mithabel chuckled. "It's right across the street from me too. Are you thinking what I'm thinking?"

Dylan laughed. "I'll meet you at the bottom of the stairs."

CHAPTER FOUR

A number of passersby threw sidelong glances at the Elf, but kept walking. As expected, no one paid attention to Kaleisha. Turning to look back up the flight of stairs, Mithabel dropped her jaw. The stairs were gone. *Damn.* With her longsword, she probed the area where the stairs had been, but struck nothing invisible. From the sidewalk, there was no access to the stairs, the platform, or the room in which Megan's replica lay in bed. Had Mithabel lost her only opportunity to further explore the secrets of Megan's replica?

A gruff voice accosted her. "Put your weapon away, adventurer." The words came from a man in uniform, wearing a badge.

"Sorry, officer." She stashed her longsword in inventory.

"Keep it out of sight while you're in Voorton." The policeman strode away.

So much for a warm welcome to the game's starting city.

Appearing from nowhere, Dylan bumped into Mithabel, grabbing the Tank by the arms to keep them both from falling. Passersby gave them cursory glances. None of the city residents looked taken aback by two people attired in full body suede leather suits.

The avatars embraced for a moment. Then Dylan pulled away, tugging Mithabel by the arm. "You were in my way coming off the stairs, but I didn't see you until I was already stepping off the bottom step." She smiled and surveyed the area. "How many of these people are NPCs?"

Mithabel shrugged. "None of them look out of place like

us, so I'm guessing they're *all* non-player characters. It's weird being sci-fi/fantasy PCs in a modern day setting, but it's pretty awesome, too. Feels like we're doing cosplay."

The translucent form of a fair-skinned woman appeared, brown hair done up in a bun. Looked to be about Mithabel's age. As the newcomer's body turned opaque, she frowned and flailed her arms for balance, barely missing the Polynesian Priestess.

"Sorry. Feeling a bit dizzy." A local chat icon flashed, identifying the speaker as Amarynth, a Viking woman.

The Priestess took the newcomer by the arm to steady her, drawing her from the immediate vicinity of the game entrance area.

The Elf invited the Viking into private chat with her and the Polynesian. "Hello, Amarynth. I'm Mithabel the Tank. This is Dylan the Priestess. May we inquire as to your class?"

"Glad to meet you lovely ladies. I'm an Archer." Amarynth wore the same type of suede armor as Mithabel and Dylan, distinguished by subtly different shades of red, brown, and gray. If the Viking owned other equipment, she had it stashed in inventory.

Drawing on Megan Wright's memories, Mithabel found the newcomer's facial features to be familiar, but couldn't place her. "My player is Megan Wright. Dylan's is Debra Jones. I think Megan might know your player in the real world."

The Archer squinted. "Oh, my, yes, I recognize you two now. How have you been? Everyone in the office misses you. I mean, they miss Megan and Debra. My player is Anna Milligan. I'm much younger than she, about half her age, which might be why you don't see her in me. It is nice to meet you in the virtual world. I had no idea anyone I knew would be competing. Want to form a party? Put ourselves on the Top Twenty List like party MAD already has. How did they get people together so quickly?"

Mithabel kept a straight face, but Dylan's mouth quirked at the corners. Amarynth didn't seem to notice, her hazel eyes still questioning.

A woman with long, curly red hair manifested, bowling into both Dylan and Amarynth with an equine body trailing her armored human torso. "You shouldn't be standing so close to the game entrance." Her local chat icon identified her as Ruby, a freaking *Centaur*. Making no apologies, she galloped towards Bob's General Store with the single-mindedness of a PC intent on advancing her level, with no time for the social aspect of the game. The NPC pedestrians gave the Centaur woman more than a brief glance. A Centaur must be considered a rare sight. Every car came to a stop as Ruby crossed the street, and not a one laid on their horn.

It would have been sweet having a female Centaur in their party, but maybe one less rude and showing more interest in joining a party. Didn't seem like a team player.

Kaleisha interrupted the Elf's thoughts. "Dylan has invited Amarynth to join party MAD."

Amarynth's eyes widened. "*You two* are party MAD? Count me in. Thanks!"

Another female manifested at the game entrance. This one was about a foot tall, with violet skin, shoulder-length wavy brown hair, golden eyes, and leathery wings with a span of three feet. Dressed in a flowing yellow robe, she flew sharply upward to avoid colliding with Dylan or Amarynth. As she flew towards the general store, she called back in a squeaky voice, "Could you three *please* vacate the entry area? You're standing too close to the bottom of the stairs for some of us." Her local chat icon identified her as Toxxi, a Faerie.

Perhaps Mithabel should have given more consideration to her kindred selection. "Wonder what the limitations were on PC kindreds. I already had my heart set on Elf. Didn't think about what else might be possible. Didn't ask, either. Could I have been a Succubus? How awesome would that have been?"

Dylan batted her eyelashes. "So you could have lots of sex and steal men's souls?"

The Tank shook her head. "So I could have freaking

awesome demon wings."

Amarynth nodded after the departing Faerie. "We should see what equipment's for sale in this city."

Sharing knowing glances, the three members of party MAD headed for Bob's General Store.

Cars honked as Mithabel and crew crossed the street, bringing traffic to a halt. Nearing the store, the Elf's heart rose in her throat. Ruby the Centaur spoke with a man recognized from Megan's memories. Not only recognized, but despised. Mithabel stopped in her tracks.

His hair was different. Curly and shoulder length instead of shaved on the sides and poofed in front. His eyes were green instead of blue. But the PC male avatar talking with Ruby had the figure, face, and five o'clock shadow of Christopher Warden, the foul-mouthed bastard who'd verbally assaulted Debra Jones, thereby starting the chain of events leading to Megan Wright quitting her job. Despite Mithabel's high average Temperament, her blood grew hot. How gratifying would it be to march over and drag her longsword blade across his throat?

"What's wrong?" From behind, Dylan put a hand on the Tank's shoulder.

The Elf tried not to glower at the man across the way. He was too far away for her to clearly hear his words, unless she turned distance attenuation down to the point she'd be barraged by other voices, drowning him out. Unable to focus on his speech, she couldn't get identifying information. "Kaleisha, start capturing global chat log." She waited until the man's lips moved again, and Ruby's lips moved in reply. "Stop capturing." The Elf checked the log.

"Fine by me," read an entry near the end of the log, identified as having been spoken by Ruby.

Scanning backwards from what Ruby said, through dozens of statements made by others in the city, Mithabel found an entry likely to be what Ruby had responded to, reading, "I like the name XStorm for a party." The sentence had been spoken by an avatar named ChrisCross. That *had* to be Christopher

Warden's avatar name.

His kindred was listed as Elitist.

What the hell kind of kindred was that? Might as well have called himself a Narcissist or a Supremacist. What kind of kindred trait did he earn for being an Elitist?

Mithabel needed to warn Ruby about the evil man she was forming a party with.

A young female voice piped up in disbelief. "It's Amarynth!" A second later, a mob of teenage girls surrounded the party. Some of the teenagers shrieked. Some of them sobbed. Some of them did both.

"I can't believe it's you." A girl, her brown pigtails protruding from beneath a white brimmed cowboy hat, reached for Amarynth with a tentative hand. "You're *such* a role model for us girls, Milady." The teenager's local chat icon identified her as Charli, a Cowgirl.

"Where is *this* coming from?" Dylan asked the question over party chat. She stepped between Amarynth and a small portion of the crowd.. "You have some trait causing this, Archer?"

Amarynth shrugged. "Maybe my High Social Status trait."

Dylan gasped. "You mean like a princess? Or *queen*?" Planting hands on their heads, Dylan pushed a couple of girls back, not so forcefully as to hurt them. Other teenagers slid past them into the gap. "No, wait, that would be a Royalty trait. This is worse. Amarynth, you're a virtual *star*. What kind, I don't know, and I doubt the girls do either. They're NPCs reacting the way they're programmed to. Ask them to back off."

"I'll be right back." Mithabel headed for the general store, pushing her way through the teenager crowd while being mindful not to hurt anyone. She stopped after three steps. Ruby and ChrisCross were gone. Damn. Were they still in the area? She didn't spot them anywhere nearby. Had they gone into the store?

"Give me some breathing space, girls." Amarynth held up

her hands. The teens lowered their voices and those closest took a grudging step back, forcing others to retreat a step too. "Thank you. Now, I would love to give you all autographs, but this is not the time."

The Cowgirl raised a hand, but didn't wait to be called on. "Do you go to kill the monsters outside the city now?"

Mithabel stepped closer to Amarynth, demonstrating her relationship to the virtual star. "Tell us about these monsters."

Charli rolled her eyes. "Who are you? You don't know anything. Amarynth knows what I'm talking about. Tell her, Milady."

"I don't…." Amarynth clamped her mouth shut.

Dylan sidled up to the Archer. "Amarynth doesn't have time to talk. She's here to buy supplies for a monster killing spree."

"Supplies?" The Cowgirl spoke in a sing-song voice. "*Supplies?*" Her voice shook with consternation. She directed her next sentence at Amarynth. "Since when do you need *supplies*? You're *Amarynth*."

The Elf closed an eye in thought. "Kaleisha, can we lose traits in this game?"

The AI swayed to a smooth groove. "I know of no such rule, chief, but then I'm not privy to all the rules of the game. Some things we must learn together."

Mithabel shook her head and spoke over party chat. "Maybe we should go kill monsters without buying supplies first, ladies. We don't want Amarynth to forfeit her trait, if that's possible, and I don't know this game, but this feels like a test. Or a hint."

The Priestess nodded. "We have no documentation, and our support AIs don't have all the answers we seek. You might be right, Mithabel. We can forgo supplies for now. Just to see where this NPC encounter takes us. I smell a quest."

Amarynth waved a hand and returned the conversation to local chat. "You're right, young lady. I don't need any stinking supplies. Would you and your friends mind showing us the quickest route from here to the monsters?"

A grin stretched across the Cowgirl's face. "I sure will, Milady. Follow me."

As they strode along the sidewalk, the rest of the crowd thinned until none of the teenagers remained except their guide. The girl walked fast, hiking up her ankle-length skirt.

Amarynth matched her guide's pace without apparent effort. "Charli, you're my official helper in Khertaan."

The girl's eyes bugged. "In the whole *world*, not only Voorton?" Charli spread her arms wide and spun in a circle as she trotted along the sidewalk. She walked backwards for a stretch, watching Mithabel and Dylan struggling to keep pace. "I can see why you want me for a helper. I hope your companions are better at fighting than they are at walking." She pointed at a dark alley and skipped towards it. "I know a secret way out of the city. You won't have to mess with the city guards and their inspections and papers. Not that you're carrying anything illegal, right? But it would delay you, and time is of the essence if you want to beat all the other parties."

"We don't want unnecessary delays." Amarynth easily kept abreast of Charli, waving for Dylan and Mithabel to follow as they headed towards the mouth of a back alley. The Archer had joined the party last and was already acting like the leader. Dylan and Mithabel exchanged glances and shrugged, running to catch up with their companion and her eager Cowgirl guide.

Through twisting alleys of grim gray stone they hustled. Her hiked skirt rustling at every turn, Charli led the way, constantly gabbing, drawing comparisons and contrasts between herself and Amarynth, sometimes pausing after asking a question, while never waiting long enough for an answer. The words came so quickly from Charli's mouth, Mithabel couldn't digest them.

The Cowgirl fell abruptly silent. A stone wall blocked their way, taller than any building in the vicinity. Trees and shrubs lined the base of the wall. Charli pointed and tiptoed forward. She stopped at a tree so large in diameter, the four of them holding hands couldn't encircle it. Charli waved them over. "In here." An opening gaped in the base of the tree. Charli headed in, with Amarynth right behind. Dylan went next. Mithabel brought up the rear.

Stairs formed of tree roots and packed soil descended into darkness. The Elf made out shapes and other details, but not colors. "Kaleisha, what is the light source in this place?"

"There is no light source, chief. You can see because of your Elf kindred trait, Dark Sight."

"Ah, right."

Dylan paused at the top of the steps. "We should have brought torches."

"I can see fine." Mithabel laid a hand on Dylan's shoulder from behind. "The perk of being an Elf. I'll keep an eye on you."

"I'll walk slower." Charli took the steps like someone who could see in the dark or who had intimate knowledge of the stairs. She paused for the others to catch her.

Dylan stumbled but caught her balance. "Can you see in the dark, Charli? Why are we going *down*?"

The Cowgirl didn't answer. The stairs continued to descend into the bowels of the virtual planet. A smooth wooden rail the diameter of two fingers ran beside the stairs, installed by someone with minimal sense of architecture. Uneven and often damp, each step invited disaster. Even with her Dark Sight, Mithabel would have slipped several times if not for the hand rail. Why none of the others fell was incomprehensible.

The tunnel wound around buried boulders and below dangling tree roots. After what seemed forever but according to the system clock had only been a minute and a half, the tunnel leveled out. Ten seconds after that, they began climbing stairs similar to those they'd ventured down earlier. Another minute later, a speck of light appeared, growing with each step they took. They all quickened their pace, and half a minute later sunlight spilling through an opening above bathed them in its golden warmth.

"Oh, my Goddess." Dylan thrust her hands into the light. "I was beginning to wonder if I'd ever see the sun again."

They ascended into a space inside a hollow tree. An opening at the base of the trunk, large enough to walk through, offered a view of a field of grass extending to the west into a distant haze.

Charli held up a hand and everyone came to a halt in the hollow. "This is as far as I go." She turned a purposeful gaze on Amarynth. "As soon as all three of you exit this portal, it will close, and you'll need to return through the city gates. Or you can leave a party member here to keep the portal open, so the other two can return and you can all three go back into Voorton the way we came. That's my recommendation. The guards at the gates won't take lightly to your entering the city without having checked with them on the way out."

"*I* don't want to stay here." Mithabel blurted her sentiment over party chat so the girl wouldn't hear. Dylan echoed agreement.

"None of us want to stay here." Amarynth spoke over local chat. The Archer turned to the teenager. "Since you're my official helper, maybe you'd consider joining our party and keeping the portal open for us?"

"I'd love to." Charli's eager grin said she'd hoped to be asked.

Mithabel and Dylan exchanged glances. What were the pros and cons of tying up one of their three remaining party slots with a teenager NPC?

"Amarynth has invited Charli to join party MAD." Kaleisha swayed her hips to a classic country song. "Charli has joined party MAD."

"Okay." Amarynth glanced around. "Everyone on party chat, please."

Dylan shook her head in disapproval. "How old are you, Charli?"

"Old enough to take care of myself. How old are you?"

"Not old enough to be your mother. Speaking of which, does your mother know where you are?"

"You don't know Khertaan at all." Charli grimaced as though annoyed. "Many NPCs in Khertaan don't have families, not even parents. *I* have *no* relatives. I don't even have a home. My purpose is to serve, and it's *my* decision, not the game's, as to whom I help. I'm an independent NPC AI, although this appearance wasn't my choice. I do have other restrictions, such as only speaking in hints about certain tasks I'm hoping you'll accomplish, speaking as a member of your party. Does that answer your question?"

"I suppose so." Dylan didn't look convinced.

Charli huffed. "I'd love to stand here and talk all day, but the more time you spend inside this tree, the less chance our party has of getting the special bonus I brought you all here for. Maybe you should consider, like, going outside and fighting something. Now. Before someone else gets the bonus."

Mithabel equipped her longsword. "You mean like a First Kill Bonus?"

Charli frowned. "I'm not allowed to spell it out for you. Go. Fight. Now."

"Let's go." Amarynth strode through the opening into the grassy field, equipping a loaded heavy crossbow. Mithabel and Dylan fell in behind, while Charli waited for them inside the tree. A glance back revealed the tree portal was still open. Would it have closed on them if a member of their party wasn't there? They might never know.

Mithabel's every move since she'd entered Voorton had been dictated by someone else. How had she lost control of her game so quickly and completely?

Kaleisha chimed in, interrupting Mithabel's reverie. "Welcome to the Brassy Grassy Field, where little dangers abound."

CHAPTER FIVE

Drab green and brown blades of grass rustled, slapping the three avatars about their thighs as they trekked across the Brassy Grassy Field. The graphics here were terrible, like someone had plopped down a 3D model of inch-high grass and then stretched it up to make it taller. It didn't look realistic at all. For a competition with millions of dollars of prize money on the line, they could have spent a bit more on a decent graphic designer.

Speaking of graphic designers... "Megan, can you hear me? Please be safe."

No reply. *Damn.*

"Kaleisha, while we're walking, tell me anything you can, please, about combat, using skills and traits, and so forth."

The AI flitted into view before Mithabel, her body swaying to the slow beat of the blues song playing softly on the background music channel. "Yes, chief. Much of what's to know about combat must be discovered through trial and error. The only information I can impart now is that action timers and cool down periods will determine when you can act. Hope that helps."

"That helps immensely, Kaleisha." She switched to party chat. "Listen up, ladies. My support AI has informed me that action timers and cool down periods are used in this game. Don't know anything beyond that."

Dylan clucked her tongue. "I was just asking my AI, Magnum, about combat rules. Got pretty much the same info as you."

Out front, the Archer nodded, glancing back over her shoulder. "Same here. I suspect the cool down periods differ for each type of action. Firing a heavy crossbow will probably have a longer cool down period than swinging a sword. I'm hoping it doesn't." She grinned. "But we'll see."

Continually scanning the horizon, they marched on in silence except for the swish of the grass around their legs. A minute passed with no signs of life within or above the horribly rendered grass.

A projectile *whooshed* past Mithabel's ear. Instinct jerked her head aside, though it wouldn't have been soon enough if the missile had been on target.

A rock song commenced playing on the background music channel. Kaleisha grinned as she banged her head to the fast beat. "Yeah, I can dig this."

Amarynth, still in the lead, marched on as though she'd heard nothing.

Dylan threw a confused glance at Mithabel. "Is something wrong?"

"Didn't you hear that?" The Tank returned the befuddled gaze.

Amarynth drew to a halt. "Hear what?"

"*I* didn't hear anything." Dylan cocked her head and frowned.

Light glinted from a head-sized brass dome protruding above the grass about fifty yards out. It dropped from sight before Mithabel could point it out to her party mates. "We've got a visitor. A Dwarf, maybe. Or a Goblin. Something short." She pointed. "Saw what looked like a tanned, bald head over there bobbing above the grass. Whoever it was, they took a pot shot at us, so watch out."

The other two squinted, holding hands above their eyes for shade. Amarynth shrugged. "Don't see anything."

Dylan dropped her hand. "Me neither."

Grass swished in the vicinity of the miniature brass dome sighting. The disturbance drew closer at a fast clip, the foliage parting and closing behind multiple charging figures. Mithabel hefted her longsword. "Please tell me you see the grass moving."

"Yeah, I see that." Amarynth shifted the weight of her crossbow. "Switching perspective. Maybe it will let me see better what's coming."

"Good idea." In Third Person POV, the Tank caught a look at the area from an overhead angle. Six translucent blue banners manifested within the grass, each labeled *Brass Goblin* in a bold white font and attached to a short, metallic figure. Below each blue banner was a green bar with white text, reading, *HP: 100%*. These were their enemies. Hostile NPCs, monsters, mobs, mooks. Whatever terms one used to refer to them, they were AIs programmed to terminate adventuring avatars, with little or no concern for their own continued existence. If killed, the mooks would respawn to wreak more havoc, if this game played like similar games. There should never be a lack of monsters to fight.

Two of the six mooks drove straight at the party, while two veered to the left and two to the right. The members of party MAD waited for the mooks to draw closer, weapons ready.

"Can't aim well enough using Third Person POV, but, hell, it's not much easier targeting the short bastards in First Person." Amarynth tracked the movement of the grass with her crossbow. The head of a Brass Goblin coming from the right bobbed into view, and the Archer fired, aiming low. The missile struck the mook in the forehead as he dropped towards the ground. His green HP bar turned black, reading *0%*. The creature erupted into a cloud of sparks, wafting away on the wind as the black HP bar faded from view, diagonal rows of pixels disintegrating one after the other.

Accompanied by the scream of an electric guitar from an instrumental break, Kaleisha's voice trembled with excitement. "System-wide notification. *Congratulations* to Party MAD for receiving the First Kill Bonus Award!"

Charli yelped over party chat. "*I knew it.* Hurray for us. Well done, Amarynth. I wish I could be there too. Oh, I've got an idea." Whatever the idea was, the Cowgirl didn't expound.

Mithabel allowed herself a moment of pride for her party, happy she hadn't spurned the teenager. What form would the First Kill Bonus Award take? She appreciated any edge her party could get over others.

The Elf mentally marked the location of the kill. She would search the spot for dropped loot later. Switching back to First Person POV, she flexed her muscles and hefted her longsword.

"The cool down period is super long for this thing." Amarynth switched her unloaded crossbow for a dirk. "Maybe I should have opted for a longbow or a self bow. But Barney, my AI, said the damage for a crossbow is so much better."

"Except when unloaded." Mithabel smirked. "But we don't know for sure how it compares to the cool down periods for other weapons. Kaleisha, can you tell me anything more about cool down timers now?"

"Indeed I can, chief." The Jamaican AI leaned into sight from behind the Tank. "The specifics are different for other classes and for monsters, but the concepts are universal. Your cool down periods will vary depending on *when* you act, but the maximum wait for *you* will be ten seconds. Each type of action you take will have its own countdown spinner, which will flash during the last couple seconds before it expires. That's unless you don't want them to flash or spin, in which case, say the word and I'll customize their behavior. You can always ask me for their status at any time, as well."

"Thanks, Kaleisha. Is there anything else you can tell me?"

"Sorry, chief, that's all for now."

"Have Magnum and Barney conveyed similar info to my party mates?"

"They're on top of it."

"You're so much more personable than when we first met, Kaleisha."

"Why, thank you, chief. I'm meant to adapt to your personality. It's good to hear it's working."

Dylan grasped a dark wooden cudgel, a typical weapon for a Priestess. The party hadn't taken time to discuss their strengths, weaknesses, strategies, or anything else before rushing into combat, due to Charli pushing them to make the first kill. How capable would the Priestess be with her weapon? They were about to find out.

The Tank rushed to meet the two Brass Goblins coming at the group from the left, while the Archer charged forward, leaving Dylan and her wooden club to take on the remaining mook to their right.

Two dull golden humanoids of small stature, with lean, masculine frames, leaped from the grass, one behind the other. Their legs from the knees down weren't there. A spinning circular gear two feet in diameter occupied the space between each pair of Goblin thighs, mounted on an axle lodged between two metallic, knobby knees. The mooks wore no clothing, and their genital areas were plastic toy doll smooth, like Mithabel's. With a war cry, the Tank batted one of her attackers aside with her longsword, knocking him to the ground.

Kaleisha clapped. "*Congratulations* on your first successful parry action, stopping an enemy's attack against your person." A cool down spinner for the parry action appeared in the left margin of the Elf's view.

"What?" Mithabel couldn't think about what Kaleisha was saying and simultaneously focus on what she needed to do. The teeth of the other Brass Goblin's spinning gear bit into her armor, cutting through both layers, and rode up her midriff, over her left breast and shoulder.

Pain shot through her like a jolt of lightning. The mook dropped to the ground behind her. Virtual blood gushed from her wounds. Her vision wavered. *Damn.* The game developers had gone overboard with the pain reception and damage programming. If she hadn't been distracted by Kaleisha, she might have met her enemy's attack with one of her own. Rage swelled in her chest.

"Sorry for the distraction, chief. Your HP is at 93%. Autoengaging Temperament filter."

The Elf calmed. She couldn't afford to go berserk in battle. That wasn't the way of the Tank. Leaning forward, she drove her blade into the fallen Goblin's chest as he struggled to right himself. He exploded into glowing particles. Most importantly, he dropped no loot.

A second cool down spinner appeared below the first, this one for the attack action. Kaleisha made no announcement about this being Mithabel's first successful attack, having seen how the parry announcement had screwed with the Elf's performance. Mithabel was grateful for her support AI's silence on the matter. She didn't need to be congratulated every time she succeeded with some new type of action.

Her cool down spinners didn't give an indication of how long exactly she might need to wait. When they stopped spinning, she'd be allowed to take action again. "Say, Archer, how did you know how long your cool down period was for your crossbow?"

Amarynth huffed. "I'm seeing now it's even longer than I first expected."

So that answered the question. The Viking hadn't been able to fire two shots in a row.

The teeth of the surviving Brass Goblin's gear wheel dug into Mithabel's back. The mook rode up her body, over her shoulder, and leaped to the ground before her. Her knees buckled and teeth gritted under the pain. It had been far less than ten seconds since the Goblin's first attack. And she'd let herself become distracted again.

"A little warning next time I don't see an attack coming would be real nice, Kaleisha."

"Sorry, chief, but I'm strictly forbidden from giving you that kind of assistance during an encounter. You're meant to make use of your Third Person POV and other resources for that sort of thing. I'm not here as a tactical melee adviser."

The mook rode off ten feet and spun to face Mithabel. Grimacing while she straightened, she shook her head at him, as though to tell him he'd done something bad and was about to pay for it. He didn't get the message, his countenance one of pure malice, a growl in his throat. Stupid mook.

They stared at each other. Both her cool down timers expired. She beckoned for him.

The Brass Goblin glared, and then glared some more, waiting for his own timer to expire.

Counting the seconds in her head since his attack, she reached nine.

He rushed her.

The Tank didn't try to block, but thrust her longsword blade through the mook's throat as his gear wheel left the ground. His sneer remained plastered on his metallic face to the moment he blasted into a whirlwind of bright dust.

Like his buddy, he didn't drop any loot. The defeated mooks left no corpses behind. Maybe rewards for defeating foes would be granted automatically at the end of the encounter. She yearned for loot. That extra attribute point she'd applied to Passion drove her desire for treasure.

Weapons clinked nearby. Mithabel's friends still fought.

Armed only with a dirk, a weapon not large enough to warrant being called one, Amarynth sent the last mook she faced to virtual hell with a stab to his chest. Dylan fought in defensive mode, keeping one mook at bay as best she could. Mithabel rushed to aid the Priestess, but a crossbow bolt whizzed past her head, striking the last Brass Goblin in the ribs. The metallic creature erupted into golden dust.

Mithabel rubbed the tip of her ear. "Thanks for not hitting me with that bolt, Archer."

Amarynth nodded with confidence. "No worries. I've got the Aim skill."

"Looking good, chief." Kaleisha dropped from the sky and bounced like a spring as the background music changed to a rock ballad with a female vocalist backed by a choir. "All the mooks are dead. After applying your First Kill party bonus, all together you earned 126 XP. Level two, here we come."

Mithabel gritted her teeth. "So, they're worth 63 XP each? I killed two of them."

Floating back down to eye level, Kaleisha shook her head in the negative.

Charli yelped, sounding as close to Mithabel as anyone else in the party, since distance attenuation on the party chat channel wasn't turned on.

The Elf whirled to face the hollow tree where the girl waited. "What's wrong, Charli?" She trotted in the girl's direction, Kaleisha flying next to her.

"Nothing." The teenager paused. "I can't believe it." Her voice cracked. "I earned XP."

"That's great." Dylan's voice hinted of empathy. Had she learned an appreciation for the Cowgirl, too?

Mithabel stopped running, chuckling as she stashed her longsword to inventory. She checked her armor for damage, and saw that despite the beating it had taken, all the rips had closed. The armor bore not even a smudge. Self-repairing. Unrealistic, but good for her game. "You're the reason we got first kill, Charli. You deserved to share the reward. Speaking of which, did anyone see loot drop?"

"Not I." Amarynth scanned the horizon.

"Negative." Dylan shook her head. "Another question. Did everyone earn 126 XP from this?"

Everyone confirmed, including Charli.

Dylan lifted an eyebrow. "Nice. Seems everyone in the party earns the same amount of XP regardless of who does the actual fighting or killing. Seven more encounters like this, and we'll all be level two."

Amarynth's eyes lit up. "Charli, do you mind waiting a while longer in the tree portal?"

"Not at all. I like watching the encounters. You're by far the most impressive in combat, Amarynth. You're super fast."

Something didn't feel right to Mithabel. "How is that possible, Charli? If you're inside the tree, how can you watch us fighting way out here? Do you have some kind of trait for distance watching?"

"I did an awareness transfer." The Cowgirl took a defensive tone. "Amarynth said I could."

Mithabel looked to the Archer for explanation.

The Viking shrugged. "I saw no harm in it."

"But what does *awareness transfer* even mean?" The Tank scrunched her face.

"Yeah, I'm confused, too." Dylan waved her hands to signal she needed the conversation to pause. She put a hand to her head and shut her eyes. After a moment of silence, she dropped her hand and turned to Amarynth. "What are we talking about here? Awareness transfer. What is that?"

The Tank stepped next to the Priestess, brushing shoulders. "Spill, Archer."

Amarynth dismissed them with a hand wave. "Didn't you do an awareness transfer with Debra Jones? Or you with Megan Wright? In the bedroom? Right after character generation. You *did* see your real bodies in bed, didn't you?"

Dylan stepped back, raising an hand in protest. "I saw a *replica* of Debra Jones in bed, and, yes, I touched the replica, and, yes, Magnum, my AI, asked if I wanted to transfer my awareness to her, but I gave him an emphatic *no*. Are you telling us you said *yes*?"

"I explored the option. Why wouldn't I?" Amarynth swept a hand in front of her chest. "When I did, *this* body became limp as a rag doll, which I admit was… disconcerting. But then I was inside Anna Milligan's body, controlling it, which, by the way, was *not* a replica. She was the real Anna Milligan, her conscious mind locked away somewhere I couldn't talk to it, but I could sense it. So for a while I took the role of her conscious mind. It was an experience. As *her*, I climbed out of bed and stretched a bit. After a while I crawled back in bed and asked Barney to transfer me back. I woke up again as my avatar self, lying on the floor where I'd fallen when my awareness originally transferred out. Bruised, but no HP loss."

The Priestess briefly closed her eyes and nodded. "I should

have known it was okay."

"Don't be hard on yourself." Mithabel massaged the base of her friend's neck. "I can't imagine you and I were the only ones who balked at making the awareness transfer. For all we know, Amarynth might have been the only one with the balls to do it."

"Thanks, Mithabel." The Archer patted her own temple. "When Barney prompted me to allow Charli to transfer her awareness to me, I asked if doing so would push me out of my own head or force me to lose control of my body, and he said no. So I said go ahead. Charli was riding around in my head while I fought. It didn't impede my abilities. We shared a telepathic connection the whole time. She watched the scene from above and kept me apprised of everything as it happened. It was quite handy to have a tactical melee adviser, which Barney outright refused to be."

Mithabel gritted her teeth. "Freaking a."

Dylan shook her head with the vigor of one clearing cobwebs. "Okay, tell me if I have this right. Charli asked to transfer her awareness to you. You said yes. Then she used Third Person POV to watch the fight, but instead of her view being centered on her body in the tree, it was centered on you. Do I have that right?"

Amarynth smiled and shrugged. "I think that sums it up nicely."

Charli confirmed. "I still have my awareness transferred to Amarynth. My body is sitting in the tree hollow. At least, that's where I left it. The downside of this arrangement is that I have no idea what's happening with *my* body. If someone found me and carried me away, I wouldn't know it until my awareness transfers back. I'd notice if my HP status bars started showing damage, of course, and I suspect I'd feel the pain if someone struck me. I still have my own game interface and still get system notifications."

With a shake of her head, Mithabel glanced around for signs of approaching danger. "So, in real world terms, it's something like screen sharing, while losing the view of your own screen during that time. Not a difficult concept, when you think of it that way. Yes, there are differences, but still..."

"Or it's like head hopping in a novel or a movie." Dylan rubbed her eyes. "You experience the world as one character, and then switch perspective to experience the world as another character. It's basically switching characters in-game."

"Maybe switching characters is the better analogy." Mithabel frowned. "In your case, Amarynth, when you transferred to Anna in her bedroom, not only were you sharing her screen or hopping to her head, but you had control of her story too. Awesome. But the most amazing thing about all this..." She paused for dramatic effect. "The *most* amazing thing is how you believe it was the *real* Anna you transfered your awareness to, not a replica. Because if it was *Anna* in that bed... and *you, Amarynth, touched* her... that would mean the virtual and real worlds *coincided.* I'm sorry, but I don't think any game has advanced to that point yet."

"I don't know." Dylan shuffled her feet, rustling the grass. "Fanciful Pegasus has Federal contracts for a reason. Imagine if what we're really doing here is beta testing a digital soldier capability. Oh. My. Goddess. That's it."

"You mean like holograms that can interact with the real world?" Mithabel rubbed her face. A mental image of an Orc Wizard on a motorcycle rose from Megan's memories, validating Dylan's hypothesis. "But how could they keep it under wraps? A capability like that? Someone would leak that story like a coffee mug with a handle and nothing else. I'll give you a moment to let that image sink in."

Dylan sighed. "I know what you're saying. Let's not dwell on maybes. Do we want to win this game?"

The others, including Charli, responded in unison. "Yes."

"Then let's heal up and get moving."

They took stock of their wounds. Mithabel's HP had dropped to 87%, Amarynth's stood at 79%, and Dylan's was 90%. Dylan beckoned to Amarynth. "Let me heal you first."

Amarynth waved her off. "Save your healing for when we need it."

"It's best if I stagger my healing spells than to cast a bunch at once." Dylan laid a hand on Amarynth's shoulder and muttered some arcane words. Then she drew a deep breath. "There. You've gone from 79% to 88%. A little better. My expended Auni will gradually replenish."

Mithabel scratched her chin. "What did you say?"

"Auni. A-U-N-I. Pronounce it like awn-ee. It's what they call magical energy in this world."

"Never heard that one before."

Dylan shrugged. "I rather like the term. *Manna* is so cliché."

Mithabel shrugged back. "Powering magic with some kind of mystical energy is so cliché, too."

"Auni is spiritual energy, derived from the souls of deities and certain magical creatures. In my case, the Auni I use to empower my spells comes from Scintilla, Goddess of the Sun. By casting spells, I multiply the Auni I receive from Scintilla and give it back to her, thus increasing her power."

"We should take some time now to discuss the strengths and weaknesses of the group." Mithabel searched for loot. *Something* must have dropped from those Brass Goblin kills. Nothing had been automatically added to her inventory. "I'll go first. I'm an Elf Tank with the kindred trait of Dark Sight. My primary class trait is Danger Sense. My secondary is Alertness, and my tertiary is Natural Armor. I'm not sure how my Danger Sense or Alertness works, but one or both of them must have helped me realize an encounter was coming before either of you noticed. I don't think the Brass Goblins fired an arrow at me. I suspect that was my Danger Sense trait letting me know danger was approaching and the direction it was coming from. It's all conjecture at this point, but I'd wager anyone I'm right." She paused to see if anyone would take the bet.

No one did.

"Anyway, so, yeah. My Tank skills are Armor and Melee Damage. My high average attributes are Sensing, Agility,

Toughness, Willpower, Morals, and Temperament. My only extraordinary attribute is Sanity. So I'm *extraordinarily* sane. *Ha.* Can a person be sane *and* MAD at the same time? Just a joke. No one? Sweet mother, tough crowd. So… My low average attributes are Constitution and Passion. My only sub-par attribute is Conscience. My equipment consists of two layers of armor, leather over quilted, and my longsword. Lastly, I have $100 unspent." She held up her arms as though in surrender. "That's me."

"Impressive on the defense, Mithabel." Dylan helped in the search for loot. "Does that mean we don't need to be on the watch for approaching enemies? You'll tell us if any are in the vicinity?"

"I think so."

Amarynth scanned the horizon for enemies anyway. "Is there any chance your Danger Sense might fail?"

"No idea yet." Mithabel shrugged. "Guess we'll find out when it happens, if it happens."

"And what's with the sub-par Conscience score?" Dylan huffed. "Are you psycho?"

"Just watch your back." Mithabel grinned with all the mischief she could muster.

Dylan gave her a chilling stare and pointed at her, as though to say, *you're the one who'd better watch it.* "I'll go next." The brown woman tossed her braids. "I'm a Priestess of Scintilla, Goddess of the Sun. I'm Polynesian, with an Exoticness kindred trait, whatever that is. My primary class trait is Beauty, as you might have guessed." She chuckled. "My secondary trait is Time Sense. Don't ask me what it does, because Magnum is having difficulty explaining it to me. My tertiary trait is Unencumbered, which apparently gives me unlimited inventory space. Whatever treasure we find, I believe I can carry it."

"Nice." Amarynth paced in a wide circle around her companions, looking to the horizon with an occasional glance down.

The Polynesian Priestess continued. "My class skills are Light and Attraction."

Mithabel paused in her search. "Dang, woman. No wonder the mirror showed you when I asked it who was the fairest in the land. You *are* the fairest, with Beauty *and* Attraction *and* Exoticness."

"Um, maybe." Amarynth pointed a thumb at her own face. "But *I'm* the one with a fan base. What are your attributes like, Dylan?"

"Nothing extraordinary. My high average attributes are Sensing, Willpower, Logic, Belief, Morals, Hope, and Optimism. My low average attributes are Intuition, Faith, Empathy, and Charisma. I have no sub-par attributes. My equipment is my two layers of armor and my cudgel. I have three spells: Heal, Light, and Excise. Magnum kindly revealed that my Light skill gives me a bonus to my Light spell, but I'm not sure how the bonus applies. I spent all my money buying my initial equipment and spells." She hoisted her arms, mimicking Mithabel's earlier gesture. "And *that's* me."

"You're a *Priestess*." Mithabel paused for effect. "And your *Faith* is *low average*?"

"I know." The Polynesian twirled a braid between her fingers. "I chose to be a Priestess before I knew what my attributes would be. To hell with the low Faith score. At least it wasn't sub-par, thank the Goddess. I'd also like my Charisma to be higher. My low average score in it undermines my Beauty and Attraction, which almost makes them not worth having. It sucks to have your attributes working against you like that, but who's perfect? You work with what you've got."

"You'd be way too charming if your Charisma was higher." Mithabel gave up searching where the Goblins had expired and went looking for the item that had *whooshed* past her head before the fight began, though she expected to find nothing. "What about you, Amarynth? Reveal to us your secrets."

"Sure." The Archer hefted her crossbow. "You already know my class. My kindred is Viking, despite the brown hair and hazel eyes, and my kindred trait is Fearlessness."

"*I knew it.*" Mithabel couldn't help from interrupting. The trait explained why the Archer had dared to transfer her awareness to the replica of Anna Milligan back in the bedroom. The woman was afraid of nothing.

Amarynth didn't miss a beat. "My primary trait is High Social Status, which has been of more benefit than I could imagine. My secondary trait is Increased Movement. So forgive me if I'm always in the lead, but I itch all over when my feet are still. Lastly, my tertiary trait is Magical Companion."

The Elf had found nothing in her search for loot and doubted there was anything to find. "So... is Charli your Magical Companion?"

"No." The Viking Archer slowed her pace, drawing a deep breath. "I don't know who or what my Magical Companion is, but its name is Rolag, and it will only come out when I activate it, which I haven't yet. And, before you ask, no, I don't know what type of companion it is. For all I know, it could be a Human Wizard, a Unicorn or Pegasus, a Mouse with enchanted whiskers, or even a Dragon. I don't know if it can be killed, or whether it can respawn if it is killed. Barney will share no info on the trait with me except that I must activate it when I want it to appear. So I'm waiting to activate it until I feel the need."

"Smart." The Tank stopped in her tracks, flailing her hands in defeat. The party had gained XP for their encounter with the Brass Goblins, and that was it. No loot. Not even a lousy dollar. How disappointing. Devoting that extra point to Passion and focusing it on the desire for treasure made the absence of loot even more gut wrenching.

Limbs twitching, Amarynth grimaced as she maintained a reduced speed. "My Archer skills are Aim and Missile Damage. My only extraordinary attribute is Inspiration, which may provoke me to act spontaneously at times, and I apologize for that now. My high average attributes are Brawn, Sensing, Dexterity, Agility, Toughness, Understanding, Sanity, Favor, and Temperament. My low average attributes are Morals,

Passion, and Hope. My sub-par attributes are Logic and Belief. And, lastly, I have a sub-human attribute. Conscience."

Mithabel laughed out loud.

Dylan gasped, putting her hand over her mouth. "No way." Realization dawned in her eyes. "You traded it down to raise another attribute. Which one?"

The Viking shook her head. "I didn't trade it down. It started at three. Chose not to lower anything else to raise it."

The Tank wept a tear of amusement and wiped it away. "So neither of us have a conscience, Amarynth. Mine's only one point above yours. But at least I have a high average Morals score to make up for the sub-par Conscience. You have sub-human Conscience *and* low average Morals. If anyone's a psychopath... Let's hope your extraordinary Inspiration keeps you out of trouble. Did you take Anna Milligan's rankings for your own or randomize? I would have thought Anna to have higher Morals than that."

"I randomized, of course. Anna Milligan's physical attributes would have been a huge detriment to my game."

"And your *Logic* score is sub-par?" Dylan scoffed. "Damn, Amarynth. Physically, you're a force to be reckoned with, but you're sorely lacking in the areas Anna Milligan would have excelled in. Let's all agree, when it comes to making decisions that might impact others, *I'll* be the one making them. *I've* got Morals *and* a Conscience *and* the Logic to abide by them."

"I can defer to your Conscience, Dylan." Mithabel threw the Polynesian a sidelong glance. "As long as you're willing to take my opinion into account."

"Me, too." The Viking twirled her dirk in one hand and stashed it, the weapon simply disappearing in mid twirl. "So, to finish up, you've seen my equipment, the heavy crossbow, the dirk, and the layered armor, leather over quilted. I think I had more starting funds than normal due to my High Social Status, because I still have $30 unspent, and my heavy crossbow was *expensive*. I passed on the one-time offer of a longbow bundled with the armor. And *that's* who I am. So... Charli, while we three look for another encounter, why don't you tell us about yourself?"

"*Really?*" Charli's response came across as a squeal. "I'm so excited to share with you. I identify as fourteen years old, five foot one, and ninety-eight pounds. My kindred is Cowgirl and kindred trait is Stubbornness. As if. *Ha ha.* I'm a level 1 Guide, with class skills Navigation and Monster Lore. My traits are Mental Armor, Complex Personality, and Ambidexterity. Don't ask me what either of those first two do, or how the third one will ever be of use to me. Though I'm an NPC, I can't access *all* the game info. I have two extraordinary attributes, Temperament and Optimism. My high average attributes are Sensing, Agility, Inspiration, Charisma, and *all* of my Mental attributes, thank you. My low average attributes are Brawn, Toughness, Faith, Conscience, and Morals. I'm proud to say I have no sub-par or lower attributes. I have no weapons or armor, and I wouldn't know how to use them if I did. I have no other equipment and no money. And, if I may add, I'm very happy to be in party MAD. I'm looking forward to progressing in levels as an NPC Guide."

"I didn't realize NPCs could earn levels." Amarynth headed west, scanning the horizon to the north and south.

"NPC level progression is the same as for a PC."

"So you have Monster Lore." The Polynesian pushed through the tall grass to chase the Viking. "How much do you know about Brass Goblins?"

"It doesn't work like that. I need to focus on a particular question, and then I either become aware of the answer or I don't. Do you have a specific question?"

Dylan waved a hand at the sky. "Yes, I have a specific question. What fact about Brass Goblins is the most pertinent to someone who encounters them?"

"Give me a moment." The Cowgirl Guide fell silent for a moment before replying. "I have something. Wizards may use Brass Goblin body parts as spell components. Their gear wheels enhance Travel and Time spells, and their knuckles enhance Melee Combat magic."

"That makes no sense." The Tank drew up next to the Priestess. "How can their body parts be used as spell components if their corpses don't stay around long enough for the body parts to be harvested?"

The teenager hesitated as she accessed her Monster Lore. "You must harvest the body parts from a living target."

Seriously? Mithabel silently mouthed the word at Dylan.

The Priestess grimaced. "That's horrid."

Charli had more info. "Yes, well, according to my Monster Lore, such body parts can demand a pretty price when sold to the right buyer. The usual method of harvesting body parts is to stun or paralyze the target first and then surgically sever the body part without killing the target. If the severing of a body part results in the death of the target, the body part will vanish with the corpse. Once a body part is separated from a living body, the target can be slain, and the harvested bit will remain."

"We will be doing no such harvesting." Dylan shook her head with vigor.

Mithabel chuckled. "I wouldn't have a problem with it."

"I know *you* wouldn't. *None* of you would. *I'm* the only one with a Conscience in the entire party." The Polynesian looked to the sky, as though imploring the Sun Goddess for endurance.

Amarynth slowed to let the other two catch her. "How do we get another encounter out here?"

The Guide had a suggestion. "You could talk at an elevated volume on territorial chat. Local chat for the Brassy Grassy Field, that is. You don't want to draw the attention of every monster in the field by shouting, but loud talking could draw a few close ones to you."

Before jumping into another encounter seemed to Mithabel like a good time for learning more about combat, if possible. "Kaleisha, dear, can you tell me more about actions and cool down timers now?"

"I sure can, chief." The AI had been keeping to the periphery. She moved ahead of Mithabel, flying backwards so as to face the Tank, bobbing her head in time to some smooth jazz background music. "Each combat action, offensive or defensive, taken by any combatant, has a cool down timer, some longer than others. Each type of maneuver has its own timer, so attacking has a different timer than parrying, for instance. Parrying and blocking are considered two different types of actions, where parrying is a broad term referring to the halting of an attack against your person, while blocking refers to stopping an attack against a companion. Dodging is another combat maneuver, distinct from parrying, which also helps you to personally avoid taking damage. Everyone can attempt any of these actions, but having a skill in them helps tremendously. Some classes have skills able to reduce the cool down time for specific types of actions. Apologies that I don't have a full list of Tank skills to share with you."

"Monster, monster." Amarynth cupped her hands around her mouth as she called out on local chat.

The Jamaican AI continued, her words rushed. "The most confusing thing about cool down timers is their *heartbeat* nature. Imagine a heart beating once every ten seconds. Between each heartbeat, you're allowed to attack once. It doesn't matter if it comes right after the heartbeat or right before the next one. If you attack right before a heartbeat, you can attack again immediately after it, so you can effectively have what appears to be two actions of the same type one right after the other. If you don't take a given type of action between two heartbeats, you don't get to do two of that action during the next heartbeat period. The heartbeats are equally spaced for any given type of action, so someone with Time Sense could always know when a timer is expiring without the need for visual spinners. Lastly, the heartbeat for one action might or might not have the same start time or period as the heartbeat for another action. Exactly when the heartbeat starts for a given action type and how long the period between heartbeats for that action type is something you'll have to learn through experience, and can change over time based on the acquisition of new skills or traits. I do hope that helps, chief."

The Tank frowned as she nodded. "I got the gist of it. It will be a huge help in the next encounter, no doubt. Thanks, Kaleisha."

"You bet, chief. There's more to know about combat, of course, but I'm not allowed to tell you until certain conditions are met."

"Understood. That's a lot to digest anyway."

The Viking called out again for monsters to come and fight.

Whoosh. A missile shot past the Tank's ear. Not a missile. The *whoosh* was how her Danger Sense trait warned her of an impending encounter. Longsword in hand, she went into a defensive stance and squinted, searching for movement in the direction from which the *whoosh* had come. "Red alert at twelve o'clock."

"See something?" Dylan patted an open palm with the head of her cudgel.

"My Danger Sense trait says something is coming from that direction." The Elf pointed her longsword, keeping her eyes locked straight ahead. A long HP status bar, unlabeled, swept into sight on the bottom edge of her view. This was different from how the HP status bars of the Brass Goblins had hung suspended over each individual's head.

"Yo, chief, meet da Boss." Kaleisha flitted upward, out of sight. "Time to put all I told you about cool down timers and heartbeats to use."

Something unseen parted the grass before the party, creating a swerving pattern coming closer and closer. The three companions braced themselves for combat. The forward movement stopped ten feet from them, but the grass still quivered as though stirred by the wind.

"What the hell?" Amarynth aimed her crossbow, even though no foe had yet manifested.

The pattern of movement in the grass shot straight for the Viking.

CHAPTER SIX

A metallic serpent as thick as Mithabel's waist, with scales the color of molasses, sprang from the cover of the grass, its head wider at the base than its neck, tapering to a blunt snout. Sunken red bulbs glared from eye sockets rimmed with metal edges glinting like knives. Honey-colored cylindrical hinges the diameter of Mithabel's thumb dotted the left and right sides of the entire length of the snake. Hinged jaws opened wide enough to swallow a person.

The creature aimed reflective yellow fangs at the Viking. Amarynth fired a crossbow bolt into the thing's cavernous maw, which did nothing to stop the creature's momentum. The Archer dodged backward, her high average Agility stat giving her the advantage needed to prevent the monster from sinking its bite through her scalp and chin.

Protruding from the monster's mouth, the wooden fletching of the fired crossbow bolt struck the Archer's shoulder, and the missile snapped in two, half of it falling at Amarynth's feet, the other half swallowed by the monstrous metal snake.

Just as agile as her party mate, Mithabel lunged with her longsword and caught the serpent before it sank into the grass. With a fluid motion, she sliced her blade across the bright scales of the serpent's throat segment. Rather than cut into the snake, however, her weapon screeched across metallic snake skin, showering white-hot sparks until colliding with a hinge. Smoke rose from the ground as the serpent slithered out of sight beneath the grass. Their formidable foe was three times as long as Mithabel was tall and moved with the speed of a blue racer.

The HP status bar at the bottom of Mithabel's view still read 100%. Neither her attack or Amarynth's had harmed the Boss.

Flames shot up from the smoking grass where the sparks from Mithabel's longsword attack had landed. Damn. The Tank jumped aside before her armor caught fire.

The Cowgirl chimed in. "It's behind you, Dylan, coming fast."

With the young Guide's timely warning, the Priestess spun, sweeping her cudgel between her face and her attacker before the metal head struck. Golden fangs sank into the hardwood. The Priestess pivoted out of the path of the attack, then threw her weight behind her weapon and slammed it against the ground, the serpent still attached, its head between her cudgel and the ground. *That* ought to deal damage.

Kaleisha exclaimed her surprise. "Wow. Nice combo move by the Priestess. Didn't think she had it in her. One percent damage dealt to the Boss."

So there was hope, after all.

The metallic reptile released the cudgel and fled into the burning grass.

"So, chief, listen up. I can tell you about combos now. I'll be quick. You can make special moves by combining different types of actions, like Dylan did with her dodge and attack. The combo can only be executed if the actions involved aren't on cool down, but combos *usually* have more effect than the combined normal effects of the involved actions. The fact her combo did so little damage to this Boss means it's defenses are high."

"What *is* that thing?" Amarynth stomped at flames spreading towards her. Dying plants lying unseen below the greenery fed a growing fire, which threatened to sweep across the field, perhaps not burning everything green, but consuming any decaying matter it could find and posing no small threat to the adventurers.

The Guide accessed her Monster Lore again. "A Ferro Serpent. It's headed into the heart of the burning area." She paused. "Oh. That's not good. Ferro Serpents gain power from fire. You need to get it out of there quick, or it will grow twice as big and powerful. Don't use metal or flint weapons against it. You'll only make more sparks and more fire. Other types of stone or hard wood are the best weapons against it."

"Good to know." Amarynth jumped back from the flaming circle, raising her crossbow and pointing it into the fire, a bolt bearing a conical head of gray stone loaded in the flight groove. "Am I aiming at the right place, Charli?"

"Looks like it from my overhead view."

The Archer pulled the trigger. The bolt disappeared beneath the flaming vegetation. Something squealed. The serpent lashed into the air, a crossbow bolt protruding from its back. It spiraled on itself, reaching for the bolt with its mouth as it dropped out of sight.

"*Damage.*" Kaleisha clapped. "Another one percent dealt."

The HP status bar at the bottom of Mithabel's view dropped to 98%. As she watched, the status bar restored to full.

Amarynth raged. "Holy shit. It's healing."

Charli chimed in. "It's the fire. Get the serpent out of there. It may already be too late."

Unable to effectively use her longsword against the Boss, Mithabel stashed it as she charged into the flames. Pain gripped her exposed throat and face. Calling on her high average Temperament as a filter, she ignored the agony enough to keep running. Spotting the snake writhing upright amid the flames, as though it bathed in their power, she flung both arms around it, below the protruding crossbow bolt, and let her momentum carry her to the other side of the burning circle, dragging the serpent with her. Her HP status bar flashed, but she couldn't be bothered with it at the moment, which Kaleisha must have realized. The support AI remained silent on the matter. As a Tank, it would require more than a brief exposure to fire to take Mithabel down. The pain would be fleeting.

As Mithabel crashed to the ground, still hugging the snake, metal fangs once focused on ripping a bolt free of the monster's back turned on her. The serpent's tail wound around her left leg. Clamping her legs together to pin the tail between them, the Elf rolled away from the fire. The serpent's head, ten times the size of her own, bore down on her, but with all her strength and a chop of her forearm she batted it aside. Gripping the bolt buried in the snake's back, she used it for leverage to twist the snake beneath her.

"Your first combo move, chief. Nice one. You've entered grapple mode." The Jamaican AI sounded more pleased than Mithabel felt she should under the circumstances.

After all, she was grappling with *a giant snake*. A giant *metallic* one.

Coils of dark iron slid beneath and around the Elf, flipping her onto her back. The coils squeezed, wrenching a grunt from her scorched throat.

The metallic head poised for another strike. As Mithabel prepared to parry again with her forearm, a crossbow bolt penetrated one of the snake's eyeballs, the bolt's gray stone head emerging from the other eyeball. The Ferro Serpent lashed its head about, shrieking in frustration. Had the Archer blinded it? That could be helpful.

"One percent damage, chief. Ninety-nine percent to go if you keep it out of the fire."

Mithabel roared her frustration, an unintelligible syllable of rage. "One percentage point at a time isn't going to cut it. How are we supposed to kill this thing, Charli?"

"I'm working on it. It's hit and miss with this Monster Lore skill."

"Kaleisha, any advice?"

"I have no access to Monster Lore, chief, and I'm no combat strategist."

With a flailing arm and as much luck as skill, Mithabel snagged the recently fired bolt with one hand, shifted her other hand to it, and wrestled the snake's head to the ground.

"Bash it, Dylan."

The Polynesian rushed in. Mithabel twisted the back of the serpent's head toward Dylan. The Priestess swung, her cudgel connecting with the Ferro Serpent's skull.

The HP status bar at the bottom of Mithabel's view inched down to 98%.

"Cooperative combo, chief. Way to go."

"Nice to know there is such a thing. But at this rate, we'll be all day killing this Boss. It must have some vulnerability for us to exploit. *Charli.* Tell us *something.* Dylan, do you have a spell that could help?"

The Priestess stood back while her cool down timer ticked. "I don't know all the effects of my spells, to be honest."

The thing thrashed all the harder. Coils wound around Mithabel's waist and squeezed. The Tank bit back a scream of pain as her bones cracked.

"Ouch, chief, that took you to 76%."

"Yeah, I definitely felt that one." *Dammit.* Even if the Boss monster didn't bite her, Mithabel couldn't outlast it. Thank the Goddess she had an Armor skill, a Natural Armor trait, *and* a high average Toughness, or her HP would have fallen even more. Taking the Tank class had been a fortunate choice. "Might be needing some healing before long, Dylan."

"Um, Mithabel." Did Charli finally have some info? "The fire is at your feet."

Not the info the Elf was looking for. She tucked her ankles as close to her butt as the interwoven snake coils allowed. "Now would be a good time for that Magical Companion of yours, Amarynth."

"Agreed." The Viking didn't hesitate. "Magical Companion Rolag, I activate you and call you forth."

The Ferro Serpent gnashed its fangs at Mithabel's right arm but she jerked on the bolt and threw off its attack. A cool down timer popped up on the edge of her view, labeled *Parry*. But she had nothing for a follow up attack to make a combo, and Dylan was too far back to aid in a cooperative combo.

With a surge of strength, the serpent lifted its head, tearing the bolt from her grasp. The coils squeezed again, cracking more of her bones. She'd already become numb to the pain. Her HP status bar dropped another chunk, but still read above half. Nonetheless, something needed to change soon.

What had she gotten herself into? She'd acted rashly, wanting to keep the creature from growing to twice its power, but making herself vulnerable. A sensible beginning party would have retreated from a Boss monster as their second encounter of the game. Mithabel had an average Logic attribute, which should have been sufficient for her to have acted more smartly. Had she expected the game not to throw her party into a situation with this level of difficulty so early in the game? Any preconceived notions she had of Khertaan, the Subconscious World, needed to go away.

Pop. The sound came from Amarynth's direction.

"Um, okay, wow." The Viking all but stammered. "I'm sorry..., it's just..., I wasn't expecting..., oh, hell, *attack* that snake. *But don't burn it.*"

"Greetings to you, too." A sibilant, raspy, masculine voice came from whomever or whatever had popped into existence. Amarynth's Magical Companion had made an entrance.

The head of the Ferro Serpent barreled down at Mithabel, aimed at her face, golden fangs glinting in the sunlight.

A reptile the size of a terrier, covered in dark red scales and propelled by wings as long as an eagle's, smacked into the snake's snout. Talons latched onto the crossbow bolt protruding from the Ferro Serpent's eye sockets, and the newcomer perched like a bird on a stick, rearing back his reptilian head and then driving his fangs into the space between the snake's eyes.

The creature come to save Mithabel was a Dragon... of sorts. Its size made it look more prey than predator, but it attacked the serpent with the ferocity of a starving hawk.

Kaleisha cheered. "*Score.* Thirteen percentage points damage dealt by the little Dragon in one attack. Boss falls to

85%."

Oh, Goddess. There was hope for party MAD to come out on top in this encounter after all. Renewed energy pumped through the Tank's veins.

The giant snake loosened its coils around Mithabel and tried to slither away, but the Elf snagged the first crossbow bolt and gripped it hard, digging in her heels and bringing the serpent's retreat to a halt. Rolag continued tearing chunks of metal scales from the serpent's face.

"Little Dragon continues to prevail, chief. Forty-eight percent and going *down*."

Charli chimed in again. "You need to move away from the fire again, Mithabel. It's right at your backside, and it's about to burn the monster's tail, too. You don't want the Boss to start healing."

Concerned with the attack on its face, the Ferro Serpent batted its tail at Rolag, giving Mithabel a push away from the flames. Thank the Goddess for small favors.

Dylan defended the small Dragon with her cudgel, a job more suited to a Tank, but the coils around Mithabel's waist made it difficult for her to do much. Still, the Boss wouldn't beat a retreat and rob them of XP with Mithabel anchoring it in place. Amarynth fired another crossbow bolt through the serpent's tail, and then latched onto it, using it to drag both monster and Mithabel further from the spreading flames. The Ferro Serpent wasn't going anywhere of its own volition. It gnashed its fangs, almost taking bites from both Mithabel and Dylan numerous times.

How many minutes dragged by? Focusing on defense, Mithabel discovered she could "parry" the coils wrapped around her, shifting her weight within their grip.

"The Boss has two percent HP left, chief. The thrill of victory comes soon."

With a screech of triumph, Rolag buried his claws in the serpent's face. With a hiss like hamburgers sizzling on a grill, the serpent's body burned a swath of grass as it melted into the dirt. Gone.

Kaleisha crooned. "Ooh, pride. Game to world: *Congratulations* to party MAD for gaining the First Boss Kill Award Bonus."

Holy sweet mother, they *had* killed a Boss, on only their second encounter.

"You earned a total of 1320 XP from that win, chief. Twelve hundred plus two bonuses. Powerful stuff. And guess what. *Congratulations*, you're a level *two* Tank. And almost halfway to level three."

"We did it." Dylan hunkered over the seated Mithabel. "Thanks to you and our new friend here." She stared at the encroaching fire, her heavy breath heaving her breasts. "I'll offer you a hand as soon as I catch my breath."

Rolag swooped into the air. "Glad to be of assistance." The sibilant consonants were drawn out. "What's next? Want me to put out the fire?"

The three women replied in unison. "Yes, please."

The terrier-sized Dragon dove at one edge of the fiery circle, beating his wings hard enough to snuff the flames beneath him. Working his way around the circle counter-clockwise, he fanned out all the flames. "Look at me. A giant slayer *and* a fireman."

"I wouldn't call you a giant slayer." Mithabel fell onto her back. "You're a *Boss* slayer, Rolag, and that's so much more impressive. Thank you so much."

Dylan plopped onto the ground beside Mithabel. "You're my hero, Rolag."

The little Dragon circled over their heads. "Who, *me*, a hero? But of course. That's my thing. Stepping in when all else fails. I'm the definition of Deus Ex Machina."

Amarynth picked up a handful of iron scales. "We have treasure." She handed her haul to Dylan. The Viking Archer fetched another handful of metal shards and gave those to Dylan too. She searched for more, and Rolag joined her. They found one more separated scale and turned it over to Dylan.

"That's all of it. Wonder if it's worth anything. Charli, any idea about that?"

The teenage Cowgirl squealed. "I can't believe it. I'm level *two*. I'm sorry. I can't... Never mind. Give me a moment. Okay, yeah, right, um... Ferro Serpent Scales... They can be used to enhance fire spells. Their value depends on the buyer and the relative rarity of the scales in the vicinity where being sold, but a typical price is $50 per intact scale. They can go for over ten times that under the right circumstances."

Mithabel whistled. "Thank you, Rolag. We have treasure now."

"Ten Ferro Serpent Scales." Dylan stashed the lot. "Let's hope we can find a buyer."

"You're welcome." Rolag continued to wheel in the sky. "And whaddya know. I'm level two, too."

Dylan crossed her legs. "You gain levels, Rolag? What *are* you?"

"I'm a Magical Companion." Rolag swooped down to land on the matted grass beside the seated Polynesian and prone Elf. "More specifically, I'm a Pseudo Code Dragon by kindred and a Winged Fighter by class."

Mithabel groaned and laughed at the same time. "I've heard of Pseudo Dragons. Is that what you mean?"

"Not at all." Rolag preened under his wing. "I'm implemented with Scaly Logic. That makes me a Pseudo Code Dragon."

Dylan playfully slapped at the reptile. "Don't you mean Fuzzy Logic?"

Rolag harrumphed. "Do I look like a koala to you?"

Mithabel laughed. "You definitely do not."

Dylan leaned over the Elf. "Hold still while I heal you, Tank. I wish I'd healed you earlier. The level gain replenished all my Auni and added two points to my maximum. Being level two now, I can heal a bit more with the same Auni expenditure. It's too bad that level gains don't replenish lost hit points too, but I guess the game designers didn't want to make things *too* easy for us." She put a hand on Mithabel's shoulder and muttered a spell phrase.

The Elf's HP status bar flickered into being at her mental command. It rose from 70% to 80%. "Thanks, Dylan." The Tank didn't sit up. "Wow, team. We fast tracked it to level two. Thanks for the tip about yelling for monsters, Charli. Now if the numbness would vacate my lower extremities, I'd get up so we could fight something else."

The Priestess massaged Mithabel's thighs for about a minute, then leaned over and planted a light kiss on the Elf's forehead. "Take your time, Tank. We'll move when you're ready. In the meantime, what benefits did everyone acquire from the level gain? In addition to the two points of Auni, I picked up a Healing skill, which Magnum says will boost my Healing spell. Looks like that's it. This game doesn't show numeric changes to your HP, but I'm guessing we gained some hit points. If so, our HP status bars should drop at a slower rate."

"Let's hope that's the case." Mithabel checked her game info. "I picked up a Parry skill. I assume it will improve my chances at parrying."

"Dodge skill for me." Amarynth strolled over but remained standing, shifting her weight from side to side.

Charli chuckled. "I got the Hide skill. Like I need any bonuses for hiding inside a hollow tree portal."

Rolag flapped his wings. "As for me, I now have the Aerial Interception skill."

The Viking couldn't stand still. "Why don't you tell us your other qualities, Mister Pseudo Code Dragon."

"My pleasure. I stand one foot high at the shoulder and weigh 30 pounds, with a wingspan of four feet and eight inches. I can breathe fire, the frequency and temperature depending on how much Auni I expend." Rolag huffed a puff of smoke, accompanied by a single spark, which he grabbed between two talons, one of them opposable. The spark snuffed out. "I only started with one Auni, and now I have two, so don't look for much more than hot air from me for a while. I can fly, as you've seen. My scaly armor affords me natural protection against most types of damage, and full immunity to non-magical fire. My skills are Aerial Evasion, Damage, and now Aerial Interception. My traits are Accelerated Healing, Trackless, and Nature Connection. I still need to see how my traits will play out. As for my attributes, my Dexterity, I'm proud to say, is extraordinary." Raising a front leg before his face, he clicked an opposable claw against the others. "My high average attributes are, and there are a lot of them, Brawn, Sensing, Agility, Toughness, Willpower, Memory, Conscience, Favor, Morals, and Temperament. My low average attributes, I'm sad to say, are Logic, Sanity, Intuition, Belief, Empathy, and Optimism. I am what I am. Basically, don't ask me to do anything morally reprehensible, and don't ask me to do something I don't already know how to do. Tell me what to do, and I'll do it to the best of my ability, keeping emotions out of it. If I'm ever pessimistic about the party's chances to accomplish something, please keep in mind my naturally low Optimism."

"Welcome to party MAD, Rolag." Dylan jumped to her feet and nudged Mithabel with a foot. "The Goddess Scintilla blesses us with your presence. How are you faring, Tank?"

"You're so small you don't even take up a party slot, Rolag." Mithabel propped herself on her elbows. "But your courage is the size of the world. You should be proud of your Magical Companion, Amarynth."

"Oh, I am." The Viking scanned the horizon.

"Um, people." Charlie chimed in again. "You might want to evacuate the area. I've learned if a defeated Boss monster respawns while you're still in its territory, you'll be facing two of them, not one. And I think the entire Brassy Grassy Field is the Ferro Serpent's territory."

"Sweet mother." Mithabel clambered to her feet, accepting the assistance Dylan offered. The blood flowed more freely into her moving limbs. She sighed with relief. "Let's go."

CHAPTER SEVEN

The Pseudo Code Dragon helped make short work of their next four encounters with Brass Goblins, but was useless when it came to scavenging body parts. One hit from the Dragon was enough to destroy a Goblin, ruining any chance to harvest knuckles or gear wheels. It also seemed to the Elf that the Pseudo Code Dragon didn't want to assist in harvesting body parts from living subjects. Maybe his Conscience score hindered him, so Mithabel wasn't going to argue about it with the reptile.

The Tank heard a *whoosh* before each encounter, which gave the party ample warning of nearby enemies and the direction of their approach. Due to Mithabel's Danger Sense trait, the party suffered no surprise attacks against them.

The group took a moment to rest while Dylan assessed their status. "Most of us have 1974 XP. Another encounter like the last one, and we should all be level three, except Rolag, who got a late start on level progression and only gets one award bonus. I should spend Auni now and heal everyone as full as possible before my next level gain."

Mithabel agreed. "But heal yourself first, Priestess."

"I will." Dylan stroked her own face, muttering arcane words, going through the process twice. "My skill bonus is per spell cast, regardless of the Auni spent." That explained the casting of multiple spells, rather than pouring lots of Auni into a single healing spell. "Using the minimum amount of Auni per spell casting maximizes the amount of healing done for the Auni spent. Okay. I'm now at 100% HP. You're next, Archer."

"How do you know your spell details?" Mithabel was genuinely curious. "Is that something Magnum is allowed to tell you? It seems our AIs can't tell us everything. I'm still unsure of how all my traits and skills work."

"I asked my Goddess, Scintilla. There are limitations as to what she'll answer, but she doesn't hold back as much as Magnum does. One of the perks of having a spiritual connection to a deity." It took Dylan five spell castings to bring Amarynth to full. "I've got five Auni left for you, Mithabel."

The Tank waved her off. "Shouldn't you save some Auni in case we run into something worse than Brass Goblins next?"

"I have faith in Scintilla we won't." Dylan rubbed Mithabel's cheeks. "You were worse off than Amarynth, because of that Boss fight, but you can take more punishment than she can." She whispered a spell and grimaced. "Not much healing from that casting. Hold still. Let me heal you some more."

After five castings of Dylan's healing spell, Mithabel's HP stood at 92%. The Polynesian frowned. "Sorry, but that's all you get for now."

Mithabel shrugged. "I'll last longer than the rest of you."

The Priestess batted her eyelashes and patted the Tank's face. "I doubt that."

The Elf jabbed the Polynesian in the ribs. "Get your mind out of the bedroom and back on the field. Let's find another band of Goblins and earn level three."

None of them complained of feeling tired. Perhaps avatar fatigue wasn't built into the game. They kept bashing Brass Goblins until they'd all reached not only level three, but level four, including Rolag. It only took twenty-two additional Brass Goblin bands, for a total of 132 Brass Goblins. The party didn't harvest a single knuckle or gear wheel from any of them, not for Mithabel's lack of trying. But she had no knack for stunning her targets and thus no chance to dismember a victim without killing it. Nor was she getting any cooperation in her efforts from the other members of party MAD.

After they gained level four, Charli asked if the party would be wanting to go back into Voorton soon. "I don't mean to complain, and the free level gains are nice, but if you're not going back into the city soon, maybe I could join you? We'd have to go back in by the city gates, but that shouldn't be an issue for level four PCs. I've been returning to my body in the hollow tree every so often to check on it, but the further you go, the less you'll be able to help me if some miscreant finds me and decides to do terrible things to me."

Dylan's face clouded. "We don't want that. I doubt we can get much money selling these few Ferro Serpent Scales." She glanced at her companions. "I'll no doubt need a lot more than $250 to buy a new spell, so I don't feel a pressing need to go back to town yet. I'd like to find a sizable treasure first, which ain't happening in the Brassy Grassy Field."

"You can join us if you want, Charli." The Viking rested her crossbow against her shoulder. "We'll head back to you and you head towards us."

Dylan frowned. "We can't promise her safety, Amarynth."

"Are you kidding me?" Charli moaned. "The last encounter, none of you took more than a scratch. I'm coming. I'd like a chance to practice my Guide skills."

The Priestess bristled but made no reply.

Mithabel caught Dylan's eye, shrugging as though to say, *we have no real say in the matter*. They couldn't force the Cowgirl to stay inside the hollow tree against her will. "Charli, please don't leave your shelter until we reach you. You aren't equipped to defend yourself from even one Brass Goblin, much less six in a band. There's no guarantee the territory we cleared on our way out hasn't repopulated already."

"And what if the Boss monster has respawned?" The Polynesian held up two fingers. "Won't there be multiples of them?"

"You're right." Charli paused. "I'll wait for you to come to me."

The group turned back. The city walls of Voorton were but a smudge on the distant horizon. How had they traveled so far?

"My max Auni is up to 30 now." Dylan sounded smug. "Did anyone pick up more skills at levels three and four? I earned Skirmish Morale at level three and my maximum Auni is almost doubled now from what it was at level two."

Flying above the group, the Dragon reported on his advancement, using the party chat channel the same as the others. "I must say, I'm enjoying traveling with you lot. I doubled my maximum Auni from level two to level four, and gained an Aerial Block skill, which I've not had a chance to put to good effect yet. I'm hoping the Boss monster *has* respawned, so we can kill it again on our way back. If there are two of them, with a little help I think I can handle them both if you'll allow me to do so, my dear Amarynth. Like other NPCs, I don't know all the rules, and my Logic score admittedly isn't the best, but I'd imagine we'd gain a good deal of XP from killing *two* Bosses. Doesn't that stand to reason?"

"Not enough to put us at level five." Dylan struggled to keep up with Amarynth, as usual. "But real close. Two Bosses and one band of Brass Goblins would put us all there, except you, Rolag. You'd need three more bands of Goblins."

"Let's do it." Mithabel didn't try to keep up with the Viking. She focused on staying abreast of the Polynesian, a much easier task. "On our way back to Charli."

"If we can." Dylan huffed under the exertion. "We can't force the Bosses to respawn, and we don't know how long it will be before they do. Is that right, Charli?"

"I've not been able to determine that, sorry."

The discussion turned back to gained skills. Mithabel reported having earned the Block skill, while Amarynth had acquired Missile Dodge. Charli had gained Search. The Cowgirl's revelation piqued Mithabel's interest.

It got Dylan's attention too. "Maybe we *could* use a Guide traveling with the party. If the game supports a skill for searching, there must be something out there to find."

Only Dylan and Rolag had verifiable changes to their character info at level four, having increased their Auni maximums. Dylan made an effort to console the others. "Class skills improve at each character level, even if we don't know by how much."

"Hold on a second." Mithabel stopped. "Kaleisha, would you please show me my class skills, along with any bonuses I receive from them?"

The AI flitted before the Elf, batting her eyelashes. "Since you ask nicely, I will, chief." She waved a hand. A wall of text appeared before Mithabel.

Class: Tank
Level: 4
Skills:
    Armor +1 per level = +4
    Melee Damage +1 per level = +4
    Parry +1 per level over 1 = +3
    Block +1 per level over 2 = +2

"Ah ha." The Tank willfully dismissed the info, which faded from sight. "Ask your AIs to show you your class info with per level bonuses. In your cases, Rolag and Charli, I don't know who you ask, but I'm able to see my bonuses by simply asking my personal support AI. Our class levels *do* matter. I didn't earn a new skill at level four, but all the skills I have improved from my gaining the level."

The Polynesian hummed a note of wonder. "Good find, Tank."

"Thank you, Amarynth." Why was Charli saying that?

Rolag followed suit. "Yes, thank you, Amarynth."

"You're both welcome." The Viking Archer stood motionless without any muscles twitching, so something had her attention. "I asked Barney on behalf of Rolag and Charli to see their class info, and he gave it to me. Then I asked him to show the info to them, and it worked. It seems they can't directly ask the system for it, but my AI can access it for them. Glad we have that sorted out. Moving on then."

The group continued their trek across the Brassy Grassy Field. They were almost halfway back to the tree portal when the Tank heard the now familiar *whoosh* from her Danger Sense trait. She pointed. "Incoming. From there."

Another band of Brass Goblins charged, their six little heads bobbing up and down above the grass. With careful aim, Amarynth skewered two of them with one crossbow bolt before the wheeled humanoids could reach melee range. Both her targets evaporated into golden dust. The Archer stashed her crossbow and equipped her dirk. "Rolag, have fun, but save your fire breath attack."

The Pseudo Code Dragon closed with a mook and tore off the short man's head. Three other Brass Goblins rushed passed the Winged Fighter, focused on Amarynth.

As Mithabel strode forward to defend her fellow party member, her Elven ears perked at a sound behind her, and she glanced back. Perhaps her Alertness trait gave her improved hearing? Six more Brass Goblins charged Dylan from behind. With a cry of warning to the Polynesian Priestess, the Tank turned and ran to her aid. The Archer and Dragon could easily deal with three foes. Dylan might die from the concerted attack of six mooks.

Digging deep to summon a burst of speed, Mithabel still didn't think she'd reach Dylan before the Goblins. If only she could move a teeny bit faster. Then she remembered something Kaleisha had said and unequipped her armor, keeping only her boots and underwear on. Kaleisha had said the game developers took what one carried, but not in inventory, into consideration when one tried to move fast. Maybe that included armor, too. And... it did. The reduction in weight gave her the boost to speed she needed. She reached Dylan in time to re-equip her armor before the closest Goblin attacked. Some male developer thought himself clever in encouraging avatars, especially females, to undress while running. Some real perverts were running the game, assholes like Christopher Warden who objectified women. Surely not everyone in charge at Fanciful Pegasus was like that, but shouldn't Quality Assurance have nixed this feature?

The mook leaned to veer around Mithabel, and the Tank flung out a leg to clothesline the creature, a successful block action. As he went down, two others sped around him. Catching her balance, Mithabel launched herself at the fourth attacker in line, taking off his head with her longsword. Tumbling around and coming back up on her feet, she missed the fifth Goblin, but put herself in the way of the last one, hoping to draw its attack. The sixth Brass Goblin leaped from the ground, aiming for her stomach, and she bashed it down with a parry action.

Kaleisha's electric clothing illuminated the periphery of Mithabel's view. "HP percentages for Dylan and Amarynth both read 87%, chief."

The Brass Goblin Mithabel had clotheslined attempted to right himself, and using her refreshed block action she set him back down with a well-placed kick to his knees, where his gear wheel was attached to his body. She couldn't deal with this Goblin more harshly, or try harvesting his wheel, if she wanted to expedite an attack against the mooks presenting a more imminent threat to the Priestess.

"Scintilla guide my hand." Dylan swung her cudgel. Four Brass Goblins pressed her, three who'd gotten past Mithabel and one who'd skirted Amarynth. Beyond the Priestess, the Viking faced off one still-standing Goblin. Rolag wasn't in sight. The Goblin that Mithabel had parried was also jumping up to join the fray, but his attack cool down timer should keep him from acting immediately.

The Polynesian struck an attacker, but the blow failed to destroy it. The mook rode its wheel up her torso, staggering her and drawing a wail from her throat. A mook behind Dylan rammed her in the back with its lowered head, knocking her to the ground, planting her face in the dirt. Another Goblin raced over her skull, catching her hair in his cogs and yanking out a braided strand. It was torture to see, and Mithabel couldn't imagine how it felt. Curse these Goblins.

With a battle cry, the Tank lunged and decapitated a Brass Goblin from behind before it could also ride roughshod over the downed Priestess. A whirring sounded behind the Elf, and she spun around to face the Goblin that had previously attacked her. He veered to miss her. She raced beside him until her block cool down expired, and then slammed him off balance with her forearm across the bridge of his golden nose.

The Goblin Mithabel had clotheslined earlier, once again upright, charged for Dylan. Mithabel had no action available to stop it, but with a screech, Rolag descended on the mook. His claws tore into the metal creature's bald scalp and tore out a chunk. Sparkling bits of deceased Goblin exploded into the air.

Having dispatched the last foe she'd been left alone to deal with, Amarynth charged into the fray surrounding Dylan. Her dirk caught a mook in the base of the neck, and he evaporated.

The two Brass Goblins still upright wheeled around and charged the Priestess.

Her actions replenished, Mithabel flung herself at the lead one, but he dropped low, his wheel pulling him along while his upper body skimmed an inch above the ground. Sliding beneath Mithabel's airborne form to avoid her interference, his wheel caught Dylan against a cheek and rode over her head as she attempted to rise, forcing her face once more into the dirt.

Tumbling into a squatting position, Mithabel hacked the wheel of the other charging Goblin into halves, and the creature burst into its individual brass molecules. Off to one side, a downed Goblin righted himself, but only a moment before Rolag took out the top of his skull.

Only the low riding Goblin remained. He spun around for another attack on Dylan, veering wide to avoid Amarynth's short blade. The cool down timers for Mithabel's actions had yet to expire, and likewise for Rolag, it seemed. The mook charged past them both without interference. The cogs of a brass wheel pressed Dylan's head even further into the ground, though now she had the good sense to hold the ends of her braids under her hands.

As the low rider sped away from the Priestess, Mithabel's cool down timers expired. Springing into action, Mithabel grabbed the rider by his throat and forced him onto his back on the ground. With her other hand, she sliced her longsword across his legs, severing them, separating his wheel from his body. "*Please* don't die on me, mook."

He stared at her with dead eyes for an instant before his body, including the gear wheel, evaporated into a cloud of shining dust. The image of his face in the last moment before his demise burned into Mithabel's brain. He'd shown no emotion. No malice. No anger. No fear. He was a mook doing his job, of which dying was the essential last task.

The Tank leaned her head back and roared her frustration. How could she ever harvest any body parts from these things? And what had the Goblins done to her dearest friend?

Kaleisha floated to the ground before her. "You're fine physically, chief, but both your Mental and Spiritual HP have dropped by 5%. Your Emotional HP has dropped to 87%."

Mithabel's Temperament filter kicked in before she shouted at the AI. She sucked a breath. "What are you talking about? Mental HP? Spiritual HP? Emotional HP? Sweet mother, what sort of game tracks *emotional* states?"

"But you are overly upset. Yes?"

Mithabel pointed. "Look at my friend lying face down in the dirt and tell me why I shouldn't be upset." The lack of loot wasn't helping her mood either.

"Priestess?" Amarynth knelt beside the face-down Polynesian. "Come on, sweetie, get up. Let me help you."

Dylan didn't move.

Gently, the Archer rolled the Priestess onto her back. Matted dirt and grass covered her face. The Viking brushed the debris from Dylan's cheeks. The Polynesian blinked her eyes open, but they were glazed over.

"Oh, Dylan." Mithabel rushed over, kneeling on the other side of the Priestess from Amarynth. Archer and Tank exchanged concerned glances. Mithabel brushed more debris from Dylan's face. "I'm so sorry. I should have seen that other band of Goblins coming earlier. Please be okay."

Dylan's eyes glistened. "They pulled out my hair." She gestured aimlessly. "Do you see my braid?"

Positioned one on either side of the Priestess, the Tank and Archer helped her sit up.

Mithabel glanced around. "We'll look for your braid. Don't worry. We'll find it. You rest. Heal yourself."

"I believe this means the Boss has respawned." Charli delivered the bad news, especially unwelcome at the moment. "If I understand the Monster Lore correctly, the field has repopulated and become twice as deadly. Instead of encountering one band at a time, you'll be encountering two at a time while you remain in the Brassy Grassy Field. In the same way as the Bosses are doubled, so are the other mooks. You'll want to stay on the alert."

"I'll keep an eye from above." Rolag shot into the sky. "I can fly around and scan a wider area."

"I need to find it." Dylan mumbled, leaning forward onto her hands and knees. She parted the trampled grass. "It has to be here."

The Elf helped in the search, knots in her stomach tightening with each passing moment.

Kaleisha clucked her tongue. "Your Emotional HP has fallen another five points, chief. Make that seven. I'm concerned for you."

"Can you help me search, Kaleisha?"

"That is beyond my abilities. Your Emotional HP has fallen to 75%. Please chill."

"That's enough about me, Kaleisha. What are Dylan's HP stats, all of them?"

"Understood, chief. Her Physical HP stands at 52%, Mental HP at 78%, Spiritual HP at 94%, and her Emotional HP, do not be alarmed, stands at 31%. I believe that qualifies her as an emotional wreck."

"Shit." Mithabel clutched at the air.

Amarynth joined the search.

Mithabel paused to draw a deep breath. "Tell me the HP status for everyone else in the party, Kaleisha."

"You got it, chief. For Amarynth. Physical HP 78%. Mental and Spiritual HP both 100%. Emotional HP 97%. Both Charli and Rolag hold at 100% for all HP status values."

"Here it is." Amarynth lifted a gnarled purple braid from the ground and offered it to Dylan with both hands.

The eyes of the Polynesian Priestess snapped into focus on her severed strands, and a smile lit her face. "Thank you." Sitting back, she gingerly lifted the braid and pressed one end against her scalp. The braid reattached and commenced again to swing beside her cheek, back where it was meant to be. Dylan stood, poised as though about to cast a spell, her eyes unfocused.

Mithabel stepped in front of the Priestess, trying and failing to draw her attention with a gaze. "You'll be all right, Dylan."

The Priestess winced. "Yes, I'm fine. Just need some healing. Give me a moment."

The others waited while Dylan cast three spells of healing on herself. She frowned. "Not enough." She cast three more. "Still not enough." She cast two more. "Oh, Goddess. Okay. Okay." She turned to Amarynth. "How are you faring, friend?" Almost as though in a trance, she cast four spells of healing on Amarynth and then clapped the Archer on the shoulder. "There you go." She turned to Mithabel.

"I'm fine." The Tank held up a hand. "Please tell me you didn't use up all your Auni. We're stuck in the middle of this repopulated, doubly dangerous field with a respawned Boss and its evil twin eager to teach us a lesson."

Dylan's smile bent up further. A tear traced a trail down her cheek. "Yes, Bosses... Auni... I still... I have some."

"I see the grass moving east of you." Rolag flew so high above, his widespread wings were almost invisible against the virtual clouds. "Two trails running parallel to each other. The twin Bosses, I'm guessing. They're between you and the tree portal, and they're coming fast."

Mithabel gave the Polynesian woman a hug. "What do her HP stats read now, Kaleisha?"

"Dylan's Physical and Spiritual HP have both been restored to 100%. Mental HP has risen to 89%. Emotional HP is 83%."

The Elf swallowed a laugh of relief. "Quite an improvement. Closer to a hundred than zero. How does my Emotional HP status look?"

"You've risen to 92% Emotional HP, chief. I'm glad you're feeling better. Fortunately, the metaphysical damage the two of you sustained was self-inflicted, or it wouldn't recover anywhere near as quickly."

"Self-inflicted? Seriously?"

"The Goblins didn't have the wherewithal to levy emotional attacks on the party, chief. Your loss of Emotional HP and that of the Priestess were purely situational and effected by circumstance, not because of any intent on the part of your enemies to demean or depress you. Their sole intent was to render you both dead through physical attacks alone. They took advantage of Dylan's vulnerable position to deal as much physical damage as possible, without regard to the emotional impact of their actions. They, in fact, didn't realize their actions were having an emotional impact on you. So, yes, your emotional damage was not directly caused by the enemy, but by your own interpretation of the situation and the level of intimacy you feel towards Dylan."

"Level of intimacy?"

"There is nothing to be gained by denying it, chief."

The Tank gave the Priestess another squeeze before stepping away, to gaze into Dylan's blurry eyes. "Chin up, Priestess. We've got trouble coming, and we need you with us."

CHAPTER EIGHT

The party stayed their ground, waiting for the approaching enemies to come to them, with Rolag reporting their progress. "I haven't actually seen what's moving below the grass, but I'm 99% sure it's two Bosses."

"How do I...?" Dylan fidgeted with a braid. "Goddess knows..." She tossed her braids back and gave Mithabel a weak smile. "If we... we'll be..."

Mithabel returned a grin she hoped looked encouraging. "You can do this, Dylan."

"Thank you, love...."

That last word struck Mithabel to the core. While spoken in a casual tone by someone half out of her wits, it might be based on a deep feeling. One could hope.

Whoosh. Her Danger Sense triggered its now familiar warning sound.

The Tank jerked her head to the west. "We have incoming."

Dylan followed Mithabel's gaze. "I thought... coming from... east."

Rolag confirmed. "*They are*, and they're almost on you. But, yeah, I can now see movement to the west, too. Brass Goblins, heading your way, and they're even closer than the Bosses. It's like they spawned and went straight into attack mode. They might reach you before the Bosses."

"Shit..." The Priestess looked to the west and then back to the east. "Need to... get a hold... myself."

Amarynth raised her loaded heavy crossbow and aimed west.

How many seconds passed? The system clock didn't show seconds.

A dozen bald brass heads bobbed into sight above the grass, the closest only ten yards away. Amarynth skewered one of them, and it exploded into a brilliant golden cloud.

Dylan raised her cudgel. "Goddess Scintilla... Please, please, please... Bless us..."

A sense of calm passed over Mithabel. She stood abreast of Dylan, with the Archer on the other flank. "Everyone remember, no metal weapons or fire against the Ferro Serpents."

"I remember." Amarynth turned away from the approaching Goblin horde and ran eastward. "Come help us when you're finished with this lot. Rolag and I will do our best to keep the Bosses off your back until then."

"Stand behind me, Priestess." Mithabel stepped forward. "Attack any you can, keep your back to mine, and stay on your feet. If any of them zip past us and head for Amarynth, warn her. You wouldn't happen to have any enchantment spells, would you?"

"I don't know." Dylan spoke with a hushed voice more steady than a moment before. She'd exercised her Skirmish Morale skill successfully, and it was giving them all a welcome boost. "I have Heal, Light, and Excise. That's all."

Two Goblins popped out of the grass, their toothy gear wheels aimed at Mithabel's head. The Tank slashed one wheel into halves, decimating the attacker. The energy of her blow struck the other jumper, killing it, too.

Kaleisha's long braids whipped across the top of Mithabel's view as the AI flew out of the way. "*Bam*, a dual attack. I knew you had it in you, chief."

Two more Goblins charged the Elf, their heads lowered to ram her in the ribs. With no time to think, she batted at them both, but only succeeded in deflecting one. It landed on its side, its spinning wheel choking on weeds. The other mook struck her full force with his shiny noggin against her ribcage.

The blow didn't faze the Tank. The Goblin glanced off and sped away. She willed her HP status bar into view. It was unchanged. Maniacal laughter gushed from her throat. How heady was invulnerability? Not that she was immune to *every* attack, but in this encounter she might as well be. Until the Bosses arrived.

The knuckles of the next two Goblins bounced off her armor. "Come on, mooks. Do your worst. *Hurt me.*" The more mooks attacking Mithabel, the fewer attacking the Priestess. The pair roared by, wheeling around to come in for another attack.

Two more pairs came at Mithabel. One pair leaned backwards, leading with their wheels, while the second pair leaned forwards, leading with their heads. The first two leaped to strike her chest in sync, one to either side, their wheel teeth penetrating her armor but failing to pierce her skin.

"*Duck*, Priestess."

Dylan slid down, her back pressed against Mithabel's butt. The Goblins rode up Mithabel's torso and bounded off her shoulders, landing in the grass several feet behind her.

The Polynesian slid upright, still pressed against the Elf for support. "They missed me. Thanks for the warning."

"My pleasure." The Tank dug her boot heels into the ground. The last pair of Goblins bashed her ribs with their heads. She staggered under their combined strike, but kept her footing. No scrawny ass mooks were taking her down. They'd attempted a cooperative combo against her, and even that had failed to damage her.

A thirteenth wheeled Goblin came last, composed of darker metal than the others. *Iron Goblin*, his overhead banner identified him. As he leaped to the attack, Mithabel locked her gaze on his emotionless eyes.

She had a block action available. "I'm stepping aside, Dylan. Stay where you are. Trust me."

The Iron Goblin's momentum carried him towards the Polynesian Priestess. Mithabel prepared to knock him to the ground.

He twisted in the air, changing direction. Hypnotic in his motion, he poked the Tank in the throat with his thumb. She pushed him aside, preventing him from slamming into Dylan, but he stayed upright, racing across the field.

"One percent damage taken from Iron Goblin, chief."

Maybe this guy was meant to be tougher than the Brass Goblins, but if dealing 1% damage to her was the best he could do, he wasn't that special.

Being a fourth level Tank against first level mooks was like being a Goddess of War. She'd taken on a dozen Brass Goblins, killing two and putting one off his feet. All the Goblins had to show for their efforts was a bruise on her neck.

"I hit one." Dylan's voice held a note of pride. "Didn't kill it, but I hurt it."

"Trade me places." Mithabel pivoted to face the Goblins. They'd already spun around and were waiting out their cool down timers. The Tank's actions refreshed. "Is that all you've got, mooks?"

Dylan moved behind her. "Watch your back, Amarynth! Brass Goblins coming for you."

Staying out of Mithabel's view, the Jamaican AI gave her report. "One Boss has taken 27% damage, chief. Amarynth and Rolag hold steady at 100% HP."

The Archer and her Magical Companion were as invincible as Mithabel, the sweethearts.

Amarynth grunted. "It's got my ankle, Rolag. Get it off!"

Kaleisha mimicked the Archer's grunt. "Oh, dear. Amarynth has taken 22% damage."

The Archer wasn't as invincible as Mithabel had hoped.

A prone Brass Goblin struggled to right himself. Mithabel fought the desire to charge and put her longsword through his polished skull. Such an action would leave Dylan exposed, and Mithabel couldn't do that to her friend. An image of Goblins riding over Dylan's head flashed through Mithabel's mind. She couldn't let that happen again.

Three other Goblins wheeled around to come back at Mithabel, while the other five didn't bother, but kept riding to the east where Amarynth and Rolag fought the Ferro Serpents. The mooks were programmed to look for and exploit strategic weaknesses of the party, concentrating on the most vulnerable in the hopes of bringing someone—anyone—down.

Amarynth raged. "Shit. I need help, you two."

"Use your dirk on the Goblins about to ride up your ass." Mithabel braced herself. A lone Brass Goblin led the charge on the Tank, followed by a pair riding side by side. The lead Goblin had been injured earlier by Dylan, as evidenced by the partial HP status bar floating above its head. "Face me and get ready to swing, Priestess. First one gets past me, bash it. On my left."

"Got it."

Two seconds later, the Tank slammed a forearm into the lead Goblin, knocking it off balance as it charged. It sped by to her left, and Dylan's club met the bridge of its nose, sending the mook back to its maker in a shower of golden sparks. The other two Goblins sprang to the attack. The sneer on one's face vanished as Mithabel's longsword took off his head and slammed the flat of her weapon against the second enemy's temple with a parry action. To Kaleisha's cheering, the Goblin crashed into a heap on the ground, its HP status bar dropping to half.

"*Another successful combo*, chief."

Rolag screeched.

"*Nice*. Our friend the Pseudo Code Dragon just delivered 17% damage to the second Boss, chief."

The Tank shouted over party chat. "Focus your attacks on a single Boss, Rolag."

"Mithabel...." Amarynth's strained voice trailed off.

"The Archer's HP has fallen to 54%, chief."

Sparks flew around the Viking. The grass smoldered.

The Tank tensed. "*No metal weapons*, Amarynth. The last thing we need is to give the Bosses fire to play in."

Rolag growled. "Some stupid Iron Goblin attacked a Boss

and struck sparks."

"Chief, the Archer is at 31% HP."

"Mithabel." Amarynth wheezed. "I can't hold out much longer. If you don't get over here now, this Boss is gonna squeeze my foot off."

"Dammit. Come on, Priestess." Mithabel latched onto Dylan's forearm and half-dragged the Polynesian in a run towards their beleaguered comrade in arms, detouring enough to put the tip of her longsword through the eye of a downed Goblin as it sprang upright. It exploded, defeated.

A single Brass Goblin ran beside Dylan, groping at her with polished claws. The Priestess grazed the mook with a swing of her cudgel. Though not killing her foe, the Priestess prevented him from dealing more than a scratch to her as the three raced across the field.

As her friends advanced, Amarynth's dirk sent a Brass Goblin to the virtual afterlife, but three other mooks rode her body, cogs tearing at her armor and flesh. *"Could use some healing*, Priestess."

"Amarynth's HP has fallen to 19%, chief. Archer is about to die."

Rolag clutched the protruding ends of a stone-headed crossbow bolt skewering the head of one Boss, wrestling with the snake to keep its fangs at bay. Whipped about like a kite in a storm, still the little winged reptile found opportunity to sink his teeth through the scales of the other Boss, which had coiled around Amarynth's calf, the primary reason for Amarynth's near demise.

"Boss number one is at 60% HP."

Amarynth's body evaporated into glowing bits the same as any defeated mook's.

Rolag screeched his sorrow.

Dylan muttered. "Shit, shit, shit."

As though the Priestess had dared her Goddess to make things worse, the Iron Goblin struck its cogs against the scales of the Ferro Serpent that had taken Amarynth's life, Boss number one, doing no harm to the Boss, but serving rather to scatter sparks into the grass, which now did more than smolder. Flames flickered beside the serpent. Was that a smile creeping across its serpentine mouth?

Keeping his grip on the crossbow bolt embedded in the second Boss's head, Rolag tore another chunk of metal meat from the grinning number one Boss. The serpent retaliated, snapping at Rolag with gleaming fangs. While keeping his grip on the bolt, the little Dragon darted aside and avoided the attack, but left himself vulnerable to the three Brass Goblins who no longer had Amarynth to attack.

Keeping out of sight, Kaleisha continued giving damage reports. "Boss number one is at 49% HP."

As the party's only means of dealing significant damage to the Bosses, the Pseudo Code Dragon needed any help he could get. Seeing him under concentrated attack lent a burst of speed to Mithabel's legs. To further reduce her encumbrance, she stashed her armor to run across the field in her underwear and boots. Leaving Dylan two steps behind, the Tank lunged, slicing one Brass Goblin into halves and pummeling another to the ground, only then taking a moment to equip her armor. The third Goblin flailed at Rolag, but the mook's metallic claws scraped across the Dragon's scales without noticeable effect. The flying reptile's defensive capability compared well to Mithabel's. Good to know.

Dylan snarled. The thud of wood on metal prefaced a shower of brilliant particles shooting past Mithabel from behind. The Priestess had dealt with the Goblin racing beside her. Nice. The Polynesian wasn't as useless in melee as Mithabel had worried she'd be.

The Iron Goblin rode along the back of the smiling Boss number one, spitting sparks from under its iron cogs. Flames spread through the grass, licking the serpent's tail. With the confidence of a trained acrobat riding a unicycle across a tightrope, the Iron Goblin sped up the length of the twisted snake, its wheel spinning excessively fast. Flames roared in the

Goblin's wake, giving the Ferro Serpent a mane of brilliant red. Upon reaching the serpent's snout, the Iron Goblin launched into the sky, arching over Mithabel's head. Damned showoff.

Whining like stressed metal as they stretched, the scales of the grinning serpent expanded to accommodate the Boss's enlarging body.

Kaleisha groaned. "Oh, dear. HP for Boss number one has risen from 49 to 74%. The fire is healing it."

Mithabel groaned, too. Behind her, the wheel of the Iron Goblin struck dirt and the mook careened away. As much as the Tank hated the thought of leaving the Priestess to fend for herself, it couldn't be helped. "Dylan, if the Iron Goblin attacks you, go into defensive mode and keep it busy as long as you can. I need to help Rolag. If he dies, we're all dead, and we can't expect him to win this alone. If Boss number two starts burning, we'll have *two* double-powered Bosses to worry about."

"Go help him. I'll manage." The Polynesian twirled her cudgel.

"Rolag, focus on killing Boss number two, the one not burning yet." Mithabel sprang to catch the neck of the larger serpent, Boss number one. It thrashed in her embrace, lifting her feet from the ground, trying to fling her off. Fire licked her arms, but she gritted her teeth and locked her interlaced fingers while the flames roasted her.

"Your HP has fallen to 95%, chief."

"Thanks for the update, Kaleisha." The Tank needed to keep the large Boss from attacking Rolag, giving the Pseudo Code Dragon the time he needed to kill the smaller Boss. "Dylan, how are you faring? Keep that Iron Goblin away from Rolag if you can."

The two surviving Brass Goblins jumped to strike Rolag, but their aims weren't on target, what with the Dragon riding the whipping head of Boss number two. Realizing the futility of their efforts, they headed for Dylan.

"More Goblins... headed your way... Priestess." Mithabel

fought to mask the pain in her voice as fire played over her body.

A war cry erupted from Dylan's throat, followed by the thud of wood on metal.

"*Fight*, Priestess." The Tank twisted her neck for a better look, but the grappled snake's writhing made it impossible for Mithabel to catch more than a glimpse of Dylan. She didn't want to switch to Third Person POV at the moment. Staying in First Person POV helped her stay focused on her task.

The smaller Boss squealed.

"Boss number two at 55%, chief. Make that 37%. Rolag is a mean machine, learning his combos."

"You've got this, Rolag." Searing flames ate through the Elf's leather. Could her armor recover from being incinerated?

Boss number one reared back and slammed its body against the ground with Mithabel beneath it. Losing her grip on the larger Boss as it lifted its head, she lay in the grass, staring into the sky, her muscles gripped in paralysis from the stunning blow. Fiery pain wracked her body. Switching to Third Party POV helped dissociate herself from the pain and assess her situation. The jolt had knocked out the flames consuming her, thank the Goddess. Large burn patches decorated her armor, but it was intact.

Nearby, Dylan gagged as Goblins bombarded her, but she stayed on her feet. A shimmering cloud of dust wafted overhead, signaling one more Goblin's demise. "This is no time for a nap, Mithabel."

Pride for her friend swelled within the Tank. The cool down period for her stunned condition expired, and she jumped up, switching back to First Person POV. Nearby, the Priestess engaged the last remaining Brass Goblin. "Fight on, Priestess. You can do it."

The Iron Goblin zipped towards Rolag and the smaller serpent. *No, no, no.* She couldn't let the Goblin ignite the second Boss. Stashing her armor again to improve her speed, Mithabel rushed to intercept, leading with her longsword. Catching the

Goblin under the chin, she sliced off his face, and he blasted into a million pieces.

Close call.

She shouted a warning as she reequipped her armor. "The big Boss is coming at you, Rolag."

The Pseudo Code Dragon released his hold on the smaller Boss to avoid the fangs of the larger one. Suddenly free, the smaller Boss turned towards the fire spread by its companion.

Mithabel rushed at Boss number two. *"Bring me your club,* Priestess." Before Dylan could respond, the Tank flung her arms around the serpent mid-body, using her heavier weight to anchor it. The creature hissed its anger. Winding its coils around her waist, it squeezed precious life from her avatar body.

"Yikes, chief. Your HP stands at 52%."

Dylan shouted. "I'm kind of busy here."

"I can't wait for you to kill that stupid Brass Goblin, Priestess." Mithabel dragged the smaller Boss a step further away from the edge of the burning grass, though the flames drew closer at a faster rate than she could move, so she lost ground. "Get your ass over here and *give me your club."*

With wings folded back, Rolag descended, dive bombing the smaller Boss, raking his claws across the back of the Boss's neck, before climbing again into the sky, out of harm's way.

"Boss number two is at 24%."

Hope gave Mithabel renewed energy and she dragged the grappled Boss another foot away from the fire. Maybe the party had a decent chance at winning this encounter. Where was the larger Boss?

Wood clanged on metal. "Get *off* me, evil mook." Dylan's leather clad legs rustled in the grass as she neared Mithabel. The Polynesian wasn't yet within arm's reach. The Brass Goblin stayed abreast of her, punching at her with shining fists. The HP status banner over its head read 10%. So close to dead, but still as effective a nuisance at 10% HP as it would have been at 100%. Without it to interfere, Mithabel would already have

Dylan's club in her hands.

Digging into her reserves of strength, Mithabel dragged the Boss, stretching one arm towards the Priestess. Her eyes sought Dylan's, begging for the club.

Dylan's eyes widened as she stopped in her tracks. *"Mithabel...."*

The Brass Goblin slammed into the Priestess before she could complete what sounded like a warning. With renewed fury, she slammed her club against the mook's skull. The Goblin burst into shimmering bits.

Fangs sank into Mithabel's shoulder. They didn't retract. The larger Boss had her in its bite, while the smaller one had her in its coils, tightening around her waist. She spat virtual blood, a touch of realism she couldn't appreciate under the circumstances. Kaleisha reported on her HP status, but she needn't have bothered. In a matter of seconds, the Elf would be dead.

Once more, Rolag raked the smaller Boss, his claws gouging bloody troughs in the snake hide. The serpent snapped at the Dragon, but misjudged the little reptile's speed.

"...number two is 10%." Kaleisha's words cut through the fog in Mithabel's head. The smaller Boss was near death, and she yearned to see it die, but by the time Rolag attacked again, she'd be dead from the dual attacks of both Bosses. She couldn't overcome the strength of the larger Boss, couldn't pull the smaller one any further from the fire. In a moment, those fangs would sink deeper into her virtual flesh, the coils around her waist would tighten, and she'd be the second vanquished party member.

Dylan would follow soon after. If no actual party member remained engaged with the enemy, could Rolag continue to fight and pull out a win for them? Or would the party be considered defeated? They might have gone through all this for no reward, not even XP.

A hand caught hold of Mithabel's elbow. "By the grace of the Goddess Scintilla." Divine energy flowed into the Tank.

Mithabel laughed through the pain as the Bosses crunched her bones and tore her flesh. By the healing hands of the Priestess, the Tank still lived.

"I have an idea, Dylan." The voice belonged to Charli. The Cowgirl and Priestess conversed as the battle raged.

The Pseudo Code Dragon slammed into the smaller Boss. With a shudder, the Ferro Serpent loosed its hold on Mithabel's waist and crashed to the ground, seeping like liquid metal into the dirt.

With its fangs in her shoulder, the remaining Boss lifted Mithabel into the air. With an anguished cry, she stabbed the Serpent's eye with her longsword. The creature was already on fire. Attacking it with a metal weapon didn't seem so forbidden now. And maybe the eye was a vulnerable location.

Though Mithabel had no expectation of her attack having an impact on the Boss's HP, it had the desired effect of causing the serpent to retract its fangs in reflex. The Tank crashed to the ground.

Dylan offered Mithabel a hand and something more. "My cudgel." She pressed the handle into Mithabel's grip as the Tank leaped to her feet, energized by sudden freedom. The weapon shone like a torch. "Scintilla won't answer my questions about it, but Charli and I have a theory. I cast Light on the club. We're thinking it might serve as an enchantment. It should last for ten minutes. Hope it works."

Sticking to a pattern that was working for him, Rolag shot down from the sky, dragging his claws across the surviving Serpent's back. Ignoring the Dragon, the large Boss turned its attention on Mithabel, towering over her, its sunken eyes glowing red. It flexed its coils and reared its head. Then it struck with opened fangs and lashed with hinged tail both at the same time.

The Tank could have handled one attack vector. She sidestepped the angry fangs, but the snake's tail ran between her legs, up her backside, and around her waist. *Damn.* It constricted, undoing much of Dylan's healing handiwork.

Sucking air between her teeth and drawing on every point of Brawn, she bashed the flaming coils at her waist with the glowing cudgel.

"Oh, wow, you hurt it, chief. That blow dealt 7% damage."

The Elf gasped. The party hadn't known they had access to blessed weapons. Having no game documentation stunk like a dead fish lying for three hours under a hot sun. But they knew now. They'd take advantage of the knowledge going forward. But would it be enough for her to survive this encounter?

Rolag made another pass. The Serpent still had a little over half its original HP, but it was only a matter of time before they brought it to zero. The big question was who would last longer, Mithabel or the Boss?

More divine energy trickled into Mithabel from Dylan's healing hand on her back. It wasn't a burst of energy like the previous time, but any healing could mean all the difference.

"Watch yourself, Priestess. If I understand how the game works, you'll become the target if the Boss assesses you to be an easier kill than me or a more immediate threat."

"Then here." Healing energy gushed from Dylan's hands into Mithabel. "That's all my Auni." The Priestess backed away.

"That helped you a lot, chief. Your HP rose to 62%."

It would have to be enough.

The Tank continued pounding snake flesh with the shining club, parrying the fangs when necessary, struggling to stay upright within the serpent's swaying embrace. Rolag attacked again and again with his flyby maneuver. The Boss squeezed and squeezed. Its snapping fangs failed over and over to find purchase in either the Dragon or the Tank. Dylan had the good sense to stay away. With Mithabel wrapped in its clutches, the Boss couldn't maneuver well enough to go after the Priestess without releasing the Tank.

The illuminated club's ability to deal death proved consistent with each strike.

Grass flames neared Mithabel's feet. "Status report, please, Kaleisha."

"You're hanging in there with 15%. Boss has 8%."

Rolag struck again.

"Boss is at 2%. And your attack action has refreshed. What are you waiting for, chief? Destroy the sucker."

"This is it, everyone." Mithabel swung the cudgel for the kill, even as the monster tightened its constricting hold on her, crushing more virtual bones. Everything inside her went numb. She ceased to be, crushed to death as she almost delivered what ought to have been the killing blow.

With a vestige of awareness, she visualized herself carrying through with her final attack, the cold wood of the cudgel reverberating in her hands.

"You have defeated the dual Boss." Kaleisha didn't sound one percent as thrilled as her words made Mithabel. "I also regret to say, you have died."

The Tank regretted nothing. All the pain fled, a great relief in itself. Dylan had survived, and Mithabel found even greater satisfaction in that knowledge.

Everything went black.

CHAPTER NINE

Holy crap, I'm not dead.

What do you remember?

I thought I died. A giant snake crushed the life out of me, but I killed it too.

You obviously aren't dead. Do you remember anything real?

I do. That stupid bronze hawk trying to come through my windshield. It saved my life. If I hadn't braked when I did, that other car would have plowed into my driver's seat. I braked when I did because that bird got in my face.

What else do you remember?

Oh, Goddess. It's coming back to me, like I'm there. Red. Not blood. It's fire. In my rearview mirror. I need to get out. Now. Unfasten my seat belt, throw open the car door, and jump out. The grass is slick and I'm in my pumps, but somehow I keep on my feet.

A fireball the size of my head melts a hole through the rear windshield and explodes inside my car. My poor Mustang. That bloody Orc is going to pay.

Standing on the uneven ground in the median is *not* easy. It's impossible to walk, but thanks to the Orc Wizard I have no ride.

His bike screeches to a halt behind my burning car. The Orc snarls as he dismounts. His bike vanishes. Not in a spray of sparks. One moment it's there and the next it isn't, with no between frames.

What *really* happens to the bike?

How would I know? It's like it isn't real. But I know it is.

Think. What happens to the bike?

The Orc... stashes it. Yes. In his inventory. My life is a bloody video game. Debra signed us up, and the competition has already started. I can't even go home first and change clothes.

Are you *sure* he stashes the bike in his inventory?

What other possibility is there? Motorcycles don't disappear into thin air in real life. Orc Wizards don't exist in real life. He's a virtual mook with the ability to stash items he couldn't carry if he were real.

How was it possible for him to interact with you and your Mustang, Megan? Aren't you real?

I don't know. How can I tell?

What else do you remember? What happens next?

He strides towards me, his boots clomping on pavement, all solemn and determined and self-confident. He draws a dirk. Holy crap, is he *finally* out of fireballs?

The driver of the other crashed car stumbles two steps towards me before pitching onto this face. Other people outside their cars shout and wave. One guy leans out his window and yells at me. "You crazy *bitch*. Where did you learn to drive?" I want to punch him in the face. The light turns green and he drives away. The woman in the car behind him follows, but she has her window down and her smart phone to her ear. "I'd like to report an accident." A teenage girl in the back seat of the car has her smart phone aimed in my general direction from her window, like she's taking a video. She frowns and then turns her phone towards the driver. "*Mom. Look.* That man over there isn't showing on here. It's like he's a vampire. *Mom.* He's going to kill that lady." She's talking about me.

Then what happens?

The Orc swipes his dirk at me.

Go on.

I jump into the median. Fall into the median is more like it. Can't do acrobatics in these pumps. I'm down. Prone. The Orc looms over me.

He cocks his head and turns as footsteps rush him from behind.

I get my feet under me and stand, though I won't be going anywhere fast. Except face down on the ground again if I try to run.

Who do the rushing footsteps belong to?

A young black man with curly black hair trimmed above the ears. His sleeveless gray tank top reveals glistening muscles. Weaponless, he charges the Orc Wizard. I scream at him. "*No.*" He doesn't know what he's getting into.

The Orc hauls back his blade to kill the newcomer.

I can't let it happen. I lunge and plow into the monster, even as the young guy jerks to a halt, the dirk slicing air an inch from his stomach.

We go down. I'm on top of the Orc. Not a good place for me, but better than being beneath him. He stabs at me, but I grab his wrist before the metal enters my chest. *Who the hell are you and what do you want?* If only I could voice those words, but they stay stuck in my head. I have a history of choking on my words when under stress.

The face glaring at me is definitely *not* a mask. This monster is straight from a fantasy movie, his fangs glistening with drool. He puckers his wrinkled lips and spits in my face, the nasty bastard.

I close my eyes against his assault. A reflex action. I don't see what he does next, but I feel it. My skull explodes in agony as he bashes my forehead with his. He's rolling me over to straddle me, pushing my back into the dirt. I've still got his wrist in my grip, stopping him from slicing my throat open. His saliva runs down my cheek. Have you ever felt the saliva of a murderous maniac sliding down your face? It's freaking me out. I yell my anger. Try to blast his head from his body with my voice. Adrenalin surges in my bloodstream, and I roll the mook off me, twisting his arm in the same motion. *Driving his weapon into his gut.* Now *that's* satisfaction. I leave the blade stuck in him and roll away, coming up on my knees. Oh, Goddess, let it be over.

It's not over. His HP status bar reads 40%. How the freak is he still alive? Oh. I see. It's because. He's. Not. Real. He's operating under conditions that I don't. I can't. If that blade were in me, I'd be crumpled up, bleeding out, and whimpering like a baby. The sound emanating from his toothy maw is half laugh, half grunt. *Jumping* to his feet, he pulls the dirk free. The wound *closes*, as does the rip in his clothing. Holy crap. This can't be happening.

The young man who tried coming to my rescue is still trying, punching the mook in the back of the neck. The Orc's HP drops another 5% as he spins around, dirk flashing. My Good Samaritan dodges a swipe, his body folding at the waist.

Sirens sound in the distance.

Okay, I may seem like a lady…. Sometimes…. But my father taught me about defending myself. I somersault and drive my right heel into the mook's ankle. He crashes to the ground, his HP falling to 25%. My pumps are made of strong stuff. I roll my left knee onto his weapon arm, pinning it to the ground. Yeah. Little old me. I do that. I prop myself up on my right foot and swipe the last of his spittle from my cheek.

Laughing again with his half grunt, the Orc raises his free hand. The dirk disappears from his restrained hand and appears in the other. Bloody hell. I fling myself back, but he drives the weapon into my right shin, next to the bone.

I've never been stabbed before. It hurts like bloody hell. I'd imagined before how a stabbing might feel. Never did my imagination even come close.

A scream rips from my throat, like someone reaching into my mouth and yanking it from me.

This is freaking real.

I crash onto my butt. The young man kicks the Orc in the head. The mook's HP drops in value. It doesn't matter how much it is, unless it's zero. It's not zero.

That damned dirk is protruding from my leg. I bite back a scream, which still escapes as a whimper.

The leg of my denim jumpsuit is ruined where the blade entered. It *shouldn't* be a priority, but focusing my anger on the rip keeps me conscious. The only other way to avoid the pain is to pass out, and I can't afford that luxury.

Two police cars with deafening sirens pull onto the median. It's a relief when the sirens die. Four officers pour out of the vehicles. "Everyone, drop your weapons. *Hands in the air.*"

Another dirk appears in the Orc's hand, and he tumbles towards me. Light catches the tip of the blade as he drives the blade towards my chest. I bat my forearm against his, knocking the blade off course. He buries the blade in the gravel beside my head.

A gun fires. I swear a bullet passes right through the Orc's frontal lobe. Doesn't even faze him. Raising his head, he sneers at the policeman who fired, casually lifting the dirk for another strike at me. I bend my good leg until I can grab my foot. The officer fires again. And again. The Orc laughs at the policeman's efforts, for good reason. His HP reading doesn't change. He turns his attention back to me, confident he'll put his second dirk into my flesh.

My shoe is in my hand. I drive the narrow heel into his eye.

For a slow motion instant, he stabs his dirk at me. Before it connects with my flesh, his body explodes into a million particles of light, swirling like a miniature golden tornado, ascending to the clouds. The dirk in his hand evaporates. Gone. The dirk in my leg? Still there. My shoe remains in my hand. I fall onto my back, laughing and crying at the same time. My right calf has grown numb. Still hurts. Try not to think about it. Is it okay to pull out the dirk, or will removing it cause me to bleed out? I'm *not* losing much blood as it is. I'm leaving the dirk in my leg.

Maybe the cops will know what to do.

A police woman kneels beside me, assessing my wound. She doesn't try to remove the blade either. Another female officer leans over me and shakes her head as she calls to confirm the need for ambulances, a fire engine, and tow trucks.

A male officer with a pad of paper and a pen looms over me. "Ma'am, we need to get you away from that fire." He nods at the women officers, and they grab me under the arms, dragging me like a sack of potatoes. I try to get my unshod left foot under me to keep my butt off the dirt, but I'm only half successful. The policeman follows. He nods as the women let me drop. "Ma'am, I'm aware you're in pain, but I'm simply doing my job. Would you mind telling me real quick before the ambulance arrives what happened here?" As though *he* hadn't seen the Orc disintegrate.

A siren sounds in the distance.

Another male officer urges curious bystanders to move away from my poor, burning car. My Mustang. It's dying, and I can't save it. The other driver crawls into his vehicle and starts the engine. He puts it in reverse and revs it. The officer runs over, yelling for the driver to stop, to turn off the vehicle and get out. But the guy's car isn't on fire yet, so I understand his wanting to move it. His engine stalls. I don't see how far he gets, but by the sound of it, not far.

The young black man who kicked the Orc jogs over to me. A police woman raises a hand to block him. "You need to stay back."

"I'm her boyfriend." He pushes past the officer, who tenses her jaw at the slight but lets him by. The last time anyone called me their boyfriend, it was a white boy in third grade whose feelings I didn't share.

My heart is racing, but not because of the young black man's words. I know they aren't true. I'm in love with Debra. Am I? I don't know. Still, I'm twenty-four and this kid looks to be maybe eighteen, so who does he think he's fooling?

I want someone I can hug every day. Is that so wrong? Male or female wouldn't matter. If they need sex from me, whatever kind they want, I'm glad to trade for hugs, the purest form of intimacy. I love kisses too. I won't mind if this kid hugs me or kisses me. After all, he has risked his life trying to save mine.

Damn that dirk in my leg. Where's that bloody ambulance?

Can someone help me put my shoe back on?

"Stay calm, babe." My pretend boyfriend squats by my feet, staring at my wound with the most concern anyone has looked at me since I fell out of a tree at age ten. I blink back the tears. He strokes my leg beside the protruding blade. "The ambulance will be here any moment." It's like he cares. No one cares about me. My mom does. Sometimes. The kid glares at the male officer with the pad and pen. "What's wrong with you? Do you need to be questioning her now? She's got a knife in her leg."

What's this kid's name? I want to ask.

He takes my shoe. There's no blood on it like there should be after that splatter. It's clean.

"Everything will be okay, hon." He slips the pump on my foot. I'm reminded of Cinderella. Then he stands and looks up the road. "The ambulance is coming."

"No, I didn't see where the masked man came from." Some unidentified woman speaks from some unknown location nearby.

A policeman raises his voice. "Did anyone see the masked man? Where he came from? Where he went? Anyone?"

A teenage boy sitting in traffic yells in reply. "The car blew up. The masked dude was *there*. Out of nowhere. *He* stabbed *her* right before *you* shot *him*. Then *he exploded*. You must have seen it."

Another young voice shouts to be heard. "I filmed the Orc but he's not showing in the video. It's like he wasn't really there."

A fire engine stops nearby. The firemen start dealing with the flames eating my deceased Mustang. It's beyond saving.

More sirens die with chirps. People surround me. They lift me onto a stretcher. Slide me through the back door of an ambulance. Other people are tending to the other driver, trying to coax him out of his car.

My pretend boyfriend calls out as the ambulance doors swing shut. "I'll be right behind you, dear. Don't worry. I'll see you at the hospital."

The ambulance heads south. The people tending me wrap my leg with bandages, leaving the dirk in the wound. "It's in too deep. We'll be at the hospital in a few minutes. The doctor will remove it there. Keep as still as you can until then."

Judging from the torque, the ambulance rounds a corner. It slows, sounding its siren. *So* damned loud.

The driver pounds the steering wheel. "What the hell? Move out of the way, jerks. We've got a wounded patient in here." He slams the gear into reverse and backs up. "Bloody hell." We jar to a stop. "Everyone out. *Now. Run.*"

The paramedic closest to me glances out the front window. "*My Lord.*" She unbuckles me, her fingers unsure of every movement. Another paramedic works the handle to the back door, struggling to get it open. The driver shouts obscenities, banging his shoulder against his door.

What the hell is happening? I raise my head. Webs coat the windows. The world tilts as the rear end of the ambulance leaves the road. The women paramedics and I are flailing about, struggling to avoid piling up behind the driver's seat. I grab someone's arm. "We need fire. A match. A cigarette lighter. Anything." I've played enough tabletop fantasy RPGs to know how to deal with this problem. "Light up those webs. *Now.*" I try my best to stay upright. Get my feet under me if I can. I don't feel my right leg, but I can see that damned dirk still sticking out of me.

The driver's door is ajar. He flicks a lighter and thrusts the flame outside. There's a *whoosh*, and heat pulses down through the car roof. Something squeals, an alien pig on a spit, roasting alive. The rear end of the vehicle bounces on pavement, jarring everyone inside. The dirk in my leg plunges deeper, and another scream erupts from my lungs.

Flinging his door open, the driver spills from the ambulance.

One of the women opens the back door. She freezes. The scene before her paralyzes her throat and doesn't allow her to scream.

Hell, I can't even scream now. That's the largest set of spider legs I've ever seen. No feet or claws. The end of each leg is sharp as a spike. The monster is silvery metal.

A shiny limb shoots forward, spearing the shocked paramedic through the gut and plucking her from the back of the vehicle. Holding its prize aloft, the arachnid strides away, seven gigantic legs rising and falling in an hypnotic, mechanical pattern, a bobbing spider abdomen blocking the clouds beyond.

My remaining ambulance companion stares out the rear door in shock. Dragging my bad leg, I climb into the driver's seat. The keys are gone. Fool driver. I slide to the ground through his open door. My right leg can't support me. I can only hop on my left leg, and even that isn't easy in pumps. Should have left the shoe off. My face is wet. It's not raining.

A shadow falls over me like a hovering thunder cloud. A gigantic spider leg sets down next to me, cracking pavement, and I fling myself against the ambulance. The driver runs, but a cone of webs jerks him off the ground. One arm swinging free, he has the presence of mind to light the webs.

He's already too high to survive the fall. His bones crunch on the pavement. He wheezes and coughs blood.

The spider spears the still breathing man and carries him away, following the first arachnid. I don't dare scream, despite how much the scream demands to erupt from my throat.

An engine roar grows loud and louder. Sounds like a motorcycle. My black boyfriend rounds the corner where the ambulance had been a few minutes ago. He zips between giant metallic spider legs and screeches to a halt five feet from me, the back end of his bike swinging around towards me. The license plate reads, HOWLER. "Get on, Megan. Debra is waiting for you."

How does he know my name? How does he know Debra? Who the hell is *he*? Do I trust him? What choice do I have? I don't want to be a snack for giant spiders.

A smaller shadow glides down the road. A glint of bronze passes overhead. Sirens shriek in the distance. I glance in the direction those two titanic arachnids came from.

What the bloody hell?

An army of gigantic spiders marches this way.

"*Megan.* Get. On. The bike."

"The other paramedic." I point my thumb through the ambulance door. "What about her?"

He revs the engine. "We don't have room. Can't help her. *Get on the damn bike.*"

He's right. There's no room. She's on her own. I'm sorry, paramedic who tried to save me. I can't save you. My heart hardens in my chest until it sinks into my gut from the weight of it. Swallow my frustration, my shame. Push my conscience down where I can't feel it, or the guilt will crush me. I can't put any weight on my right leg, but I manage to throw it over the bike seat behind my boyfriend. He's no longer a pretend one. I hug him like a lover. My trembling chin is soaked with tears.

We speed away, a cone of webs slapping the pavement behind us. Zig and zag around spider legs five times as tall as I am. Behind us, another arachnid spears the ambulance through the roof and lifts it, shaking the last paramedic out the back. Lying broken on the road, she raises an arm to ward off her attacker. Doesn't try to flee. I don't hear her whimper with my ears, but her pleas for mercy echo in my imagination.

My boyfriend and I round the corner. Good. I don't want to see what happens next. I've already seen too much.

The road curves again and we climb a slope, giving us a view from a higher vantage point. Beyond the ambulance, a long line of huge spiders travel up the road towards us, HP status bars floating over their heads, all reading 100%. Banners identify the monsters as *Arachnid Behemoths.*

A vast network of webs trap dozens of vehicles, many of them holding one or more terrified and confused occupants. I'm glad not to be down there, but my heart breaks for the men, women, and children no one can save. Several spiders carry webbed captives. Some carry cocooned cars. They march westward with their victims.

Judging by the sun's position, it's about 3:00 in the afternoon.

The end of the real world.

The bronze hawk flies overhead, pacing HOWLER.

I need a break.

If you need a break, Megan, take a break.

When we die in the real world, we don't respawn. Those paramedics are gone forever. They aren't coming back. I don't want their faces staring at me. I had them shelved away in my subconscious, and now they aren't. Thanks for making me dredge up those memories.

You need to remember.

Can I have some mental space for a few moments? Please?

Sure, Megan, take all the time you need. Take all the time in the world.

CHAPTER TEN

Don't you think it's been long enough?

No, I don't. Please don't ask me anything now.

Very well. No questions. See if any of this sounds familiar to you.

I'm not listening.

Ah, but you are. You can't shut me out.

Leave me alone.

You're standing in a foyer illuminated by a single round LED light. Wearing the same denim jumpsuit and black leather pumps you've been wearing since the coffee shop. Alone and doubting yourself. A stitched wound on your right shin. Still hurts, but not nearly as much as it did. Somewhere along the way, someone removed that dirk from your leg and patched you up. But who, when, and where? Maybe the memory will surface eventually. Let's continue and see.

A hallway leads from the foyer. You follow it into darkness. Another bulb flares to life ten feet ahead, shining on a smooth metallic wall and an inset digital sign with an arrow pointing right. Capital letters on the sign, each the size of a car's headlight and half as bright, spell M-E-G-A-N. So you turn right. Ahead, a third LED bulb comes to life. The lights fade behind you.

More bulbs bloom with light to guide you through a maze of hallways and intersections, dimming as you leave them behind until all are extinguished except one lighting a glass elevator door. The elevator shaft is pure glass. Inside, a glass platform rises from the depths, revealing only darkness beneath its transparent surface. It stops when it reaches you. The door opens with a hydraulic hiss. You step through, looking for buttons to press, but there aren't any. The platform rises again, passing one floor and then another, all cloaked in darkness.

The elevator stops and the door opens. In the hallway beyond, an LED light flickers on. You exit the elevator.

More hallways and more LED lights, playing a game of follow the leader with you. The lights lead and you follow. Ha. You're being *led* by *LED* lights. Funny. What, no laugh? You're hopelessly serious.

The lights lead you to a blue metal door with a plaque bearing your first and last name, *Megan Wright*. You stroke the engraved letters, relishing the grooves and curves under your fingertips. You've earned the plaque and the space it reserves for you. It's an honor to be here. The journey has been difficult, but you've endured, conquered, and arrived. Not even Orc Wizards, Arachnid Behemoths, or Mad Cow Ballista could stop you.

Mad Cow Ballista? Where did that memory come from?

The door slides open, revealing only darkness beyond. No more automatic lights. Isn't that curious? Doubts and distrust crowd your triumph and you hesitate to step through. But you do. You've come this far, why would you turn back now?

That one step is your biggest mistake by magnitudes. Or the best thing you could do. Which is it? Time may tell, if time still exists.

The door slides shut behind you. A million points of light erupt to life, illuminating silvery metallic walls towering around you, closing you within a domed space. Laser beams spring from tiny cannons arranged in a web-like network spanning the walls. The cannons shift their aims in arbitrary directions, shuffling the beams in a disorganized fashion that defy pattern and yet suggest many ephemeral ones. When they stop, you feel clean and smell nice. Your skin, your hair, your jumpsuit. You catch a whiff of metallic fumes, but it passes.

A neuter robotic voice speaks. "Injury detected." The majority of the miniature cannons direct their light beams at your wounded leg. Lost feeling returns, banishing the numbness threatening to steal your limb. It's still itching like crazy. "Identity confirmed. Player: Megan Wright. Avatar: Name pending. Initiating awareness transference process. Process initiated. Player may exit to quarters. Sleep is prescribed."

You step out....

Wait. What?

Do you remember now?

I step out of the domed room into this room. I'm clean but so tired. I hate what happened to Kev.

Who is Kev?

Um... right. He tells me his name is Kevin, but I should call him Kev. My pretend boyfriend who might have been more if things had gone differently. I'm hungry.

How is that possible? Time is at a standstill. Go look at the pocket watch on the end table. What time is it? It's the end of the world as you know it, and you want to think about food?

Donuts sit stacked in a glass case at a convenience store. I adore the smell of freshly baked pastries. They might be the only thing fresh in the store.

How did you get here?

It's a convenience store. I need to use the restroom. The bike needs gas. The van too.

To what van are you referring?

The one Kev takes me to after we leave the Arachnid Behemoths behind. Where Dr. Splat removes the dirk from my leg. The bronze hawk is his. It's a drone, made to look like a bird. The doctor also has a bodiless, computerized AI assistant called Nigel who drives the van. They take me in. Kev follows on the bike while I'm taking a computerized test to quantize my persona for the upcoming competition, which is still on, despite the end of the world.

I'm sitting at a computer screen, taking tests while Nigel

drives us to the Fanciful Pegasus site. One of the tests requires me to match objects on the left side with those on the right. On the last page, objects flash before me so fast, I can't react with logic, only instinct. One match I make is the image of a cow to that of a pencil. Their correlation is so random, so crazy, it sticks in my head like a looming project deadline, if I had to worry about deadlines anymore, which I don't. I'm not working anymore. I mean, who's worried about careers with gargantuan spiders taking over the world?

If time isn't moving, then deadlines will never come. Isn't that clever?

I suppose it is. Not that it matters to me now.

What else do you remember about the gas station? You went to the restroom. Then what?

Right. I do my business and leave the restroom. A black-tipped yellow missile tears through dozens of expired bags of pretzels, scattering salty bits everywhere. It's not easy dodging a projectile while wearing pumps, but I manage. The projectile collides with bags of snack treats, throwing it off course. It *whooshes* past me. It came from the direction of the front door, where a hole the diameter of my forearm gapes in the glass.

The door bursts open. A black and white bovine with full udders saunters through, identified by a banner reading Mad Cow Ballista. She has a crossbow mounted on her back. It's empty, but a giant pencil materializes in the flight groove, one pixel at a time, until it's ready to fire. What I'm seeing is so improbable, so unrealistic, I can do nothing but watch. With a moo from the Cow, the crossbow trigger lever moves.

I'm outside my body, seeing events unfold as I observe. Inside my head is a place I don't want to be at the moment. It's too confusing and dark in there. I watch myself in slow motion leap out of the way.

Another pencil is materializing in the flight groove.

I'm going to die if I don't leave, but I can't return to my head. From my observatory outside myself, I command my muscles to move. Some of them obey, but they're sluggish, uncoordinated, and my injured leg is rebelling.

A door at the end of the access hallway behind me flings open. The conditioned, cool air inside the store rushes past me, drawn by the heat of the desert outside. Kev stands in the doorway, his dark figure silhouetted by sunlight. "Come with me if you want to...."

"Don't say it." My dissociated body hobbles to him. Though Doctor Splat removed the dagger, my right leg still hurts to put my weight on it. "I admit you're my hero. Let's go."

He picks me up without asking my permission. My instinct is to slap him, but I command my arm muscles to relax, to slide around his neck instead. He moves faster carrying me than I could move in these pumps with an injured leg. Sets me down next to HOWLER and we hop on. The van with Dr. Splat and Nigel is already gone.

The van had air conditioning. The heat rising from the sand, *everywhere sand*, roasts my brain. The road is straight in both directions and the land flat for as far as I can see.

Kev speaks into a radio transceiver. "I've got her, Nigel. We're headed for base with enemies on our tail."

"Understood." Nigel's voice crackles over a speaker.

With a thrust of his leg, Kev kickstarts HOWLER and we drive away from the gas station without paying. The Mad Cow Ballista comes galloping out of the store and chases us for a while, constantly firing her giant pencil missiles. We obviously get away, because... here I am. That's the story.

Oh, no, that's not the *whole* story. You've left out several events occurring before and after arriving at the Fanciful Pegasus facility, including what happens to Kev.

I don't want to talk about that.

Only when you're ready. Let's return to what happens in this room. Your awareness is transferred, from your conscious mind to your subconscious mind and vice versa. A betrayal of nature, but one you agree to. You're no longer Megan, but Mithabel. Do you remember?

I can't do this. I'm Megan, not Mithabel. Please stop.

Do you want to be Megan so badly that you snuff out Mithabel forever?

Leave. Me. Alone.

I shouldn't need to remind you that isn't possible.

I'm *not* Mithabel.

Then why can you access her memories?

I can't.

There's a difference between can't and won't. You must.

Oh, my Goddess. *Dylan.*

Ah, you *are* remembering. Mithabel is in you.

I throw off the quilt and jump out of bed. There's the chest of drawers. I'm on the wrong side of the room. Roll across the bed to the other side, to the end table. There's a partially used candle, resting in a rose gold metal candle holder. Beside the candle is a rose gold pocket watch. I know what time it reads, but I look at it anyway. It's 3:00. No indication of AM or PM, but I know it's PM.

The time when the world ended.

There's the wand that controls the crystal ball, the one sitting on the stand at the far end of the room. Short bookshelves line the walls and framed pictures of me hang above them. Mithabel *is* here. *I'm* here. The virtual world reflects the real one, or is it vice versa? Have the two worlds collided? How else to explain the Orc Wizard I fought and the army of Arachnid Behemoths? *I* fought them. Me. Megan. Not Mithabel. I swear it, no matter how impossible it sounds.

Doors to either side of the crystal ball complete my picture of the room. I don't need to look behind the door to my right to know there's a closet behind it, loaded with clothes meant for me.

I grip the mirror. It reflects my confusion. I sing to it in an atrocious alto voice. "Mirror, mirror, in my hand, who's the fairest in the land?"

My reflected ugly mug blurs into obscurity. Text scrawls across the mirror face as though an invisible person is writing with chalk on the glass. *Scrying Dylan.*

Holy crap. What's about to happen?

The text fades away and a grassy field materializes inside the glass. A slender brown woman about my age and height trudges through the grass. It *is* Dylan. I cry her name, but she doesn't react.

Wait. *Your* height?

Oh, Goddess, I didn't mean that. She's taller than me by three inches. She's closer to Mithabel's height. She looks so tired. So alone. But determined. Her purple braids sway like animate snakes. Smoke rises in the background. Rolag flies above her. I should be with her too. She needs me.

You died.

I didn't die. I'm Megan. Mithabel is the one who died. If I die, I don't respawn. Mithabel can.

Are you sure Mithabel can?

She's an avatar. Respawning is what avatars do.

Not in every game. Maybe not in Khertaan. Or maybe she needs you to respawn her. Isn't that what players do? They press *Continue*.

I don't have any game controls.

What are you holding?

I speak at the mirror. "Continue game." I presume nothing will happen, which proves to be correct.

I need to transfer awareness to Mithabel. That will respawn her. Trade places with her like before. How do I make the transfer? Mithabel is subconscious and I'm conscious. When the transfer was made before, I slept. So that's it. I need to sleep. Then Mithabel will respawn.

And what about Amarynth? Does she need to respawn? Can she use your guidance, or will Anna realize what she needs to do?

Oh, Goddess, I doubt it. I shake the mirror. "Let me speak to Anna Milligan." A mid-life crisis feminine face appears in the mirror. "Anna, it's me, Megan." An attempt at normal conversation with a real person feels strange right now, like it doesn't belong in this world. As though this isn't the real world. What else could it be? I'm real, so wherever I am must be real.

"Megan? Oh, my God. Tell me I'm not hallucinating." Tears streak the older woman's cheeks. Her brown bun has several lose strands. "What's happening to me?"

"It's all right, Anna. Listen. We're playing a game. Do you remember? You're Amarynth. She died in the game and you woke up. Does that ring any bells?"

"I'm locked in this room, Megan. I can't get out. I bang and bang on the door, and no one answers. No one opens the door and I can't. I'm going to die in here."

"You're not going to die. You think a lot of time has passed, but it hasn't, trust me. Relax. Lie on the bed. Pull the quilt over you. Go to sleep. Everything will be fine. I promise you. We're going to win millions of dollars and start our own 3D animation company. You, me, and Debra. That's why we're all here." I don't mention Arachnid Behemoths. Wouldn't help her go to sleep. "That's why you have to free Amarynth from your mind, so she can rejoin Dylan and Mithabel, and we can win the game. You can only free Amarynth if you sleep. We need her if we're going to win. Please, Anna. Go ahead, lie down. No, don't bother to undress. You *really* don't need to. Fine, kick off your shoes if you like. There you go. Pull up the quilt. Lullaby and good night. Sorry, I don't know any good songs for putting someone to sleep. My talking voice usually does that job well enough. Just ask anyone I've ever dated. You're not laughing. That's all right. Your eyes are closed. Good. Good. Sleep, Anna. Sleep. Sweet dreams."

Do you believe everything you told her?

I have nothing else *to* believe. Now hush, so *I* can sleep. Mithabel is coming, Dylan. Hang in there, love.

CHAPTER ELEVEN

Mithabel straightened with a deep inhale, once again standing in the domed room with golden walls. Her respawn chamber.

"Welcome back, chief." The Jamaican AI floated in the air three feet away, with a pleased expression. "Ready to get back in there?"

"Yeah, hi, Kaleisha. Give me one moment." The Elf directed her next words to the party chat channel. "I'm back in the game. In my spawning chamber. How's everyone doing? Dylan? Charli? Rolag? Amarynth, are you back?"

Dylan responded first. "*Mithabel. I need you. Now.*"

Amarynth spoke next. "Did we kill the two Bosses?"

The Polynesian wasn't answering questions. "Both of you, come, help me, *now.*"

"We'll be right there, Priestess." Mithabel looked askance at Kaleisha. "Can I exit from here and go straight to Dylan?"

"Here are your options, chief."

A textual list appeared in Mithabel's view.

> *Megan Wright's Room*
> *Voorton Chamber of Commerce*
> *Join Charli*
> *Join Dylan (unavailable while Dylan is engaged)*
> *Brassy Grassy Field (unavailable while Dylan is engaged)*

The last two lines were grayed out, while the other lines were bold and white. "Can you override and let me exit at Dylan's location?"

"Sorry, chief, that's not within my power."

"The system won't let us come directly to you, Priestess. Amarynth, exit to Charli. That's the closest we can get to Dylan. We'll run to her from there."

Disappointment laced Amarynth's reply. "I was hoping to be level five when I came back. Guess I didn't earn all the XPs for the two Boss kills."

"Move it, Amarynth, we can talk XP later. Kaleisha, I exercise the option to join Charli."

The walls of the spawning chamber faded out as the dim interior of the tree portal faded in.

Charli gasped. "Mithabel, I've never been so glad to see you." The teenager threw her arms around the Tank. "You'll take me with you now?"

Mithabel glanced around for Amarynth. "It's too dangerous out there. We can't protect you."

Amarynth faded into existence beside Mithabel. "You can come with us, Charli. We all agreed. Are you ready, Mithabel?"

The Tank dropped her jaw at the Archer's audacity. "I was… We were… Waiting on you." She rushed out of the tree portal at a trot, stashing her armor to increase her speed. "We're coming, Priestess."

"It's over now, Mithabel. Rolag finished off the last Iron Goblin we were facing, I'm at 5% HP and drained bone dry of Auni, but still alive. I would love to see your smiling faces. But I'm staying put and waiting right here. Should be less chance of an encounter for me if I don't travel. I'll make less noise if I'm not moving. Look for Rolag in the sky. He's flying in a circle above me."

Amarynth shot past Mithabel. "Meanwhile, Priestess, can you tell us whether both Bosses died?"

"Yeah, about that." Dylan didn't sound too thrilled. "Both Bosses *were* killed. Mithabel killed the last one at the same time it killed her. I thought we'd earn twice the XP for a double kill, even more than double because one of them grew in power. But I got the same XP for the double Bosses as I got for the first Boss alone. What a ripoff."

A glance back at the tree portal proved it had closed, with no one remaining inside to keep it open. The teenager ran behind Mithabel, struggling to keep up. Amarynth left them both behind without a look back, and would join Dylan much sooner than Mithabel could. No longer having a sense of urgency, Mithabel equipped her armor and slowed to let Charli catch her.

The Cowgirl pointed at a winged creature in the sky. "I see him." She held her skirt bunched in her hands as she ran beside Mithabel. "I did more research on Bosses, based on discussions with Dylan while you two were out of the game. I think until you move into a new territory, the Bosses will keep multiplying when they respawn, but the XP doesn't."

"Kaleisha, give me a comparison of my XP earnings for the Boss kills, please."

"Sure, chief. Your XP earnings for the double Boss kill equal your XP earnings from the first Boss kill."

Mithabel raged inside. "This game *sucks*. If we're going to do that much work to defeat an enemy, we ought to earn XP appropriate to the encounter. Holding out on us like that is bullshit."

"I have a system wide announcement for you, chief. But I sense you aren't prepared to hear it at present."

"Oh, my Goddess." Dylan had apparently heard it already.

Mithabel huffed. "Go ahead, Kaleisha. What's the announcement?"

"As you wish, chief. System-wide announcement: Party MAD has claimed the First Kill Bonus Award and the First Boss Kill Bonus Award. The First 200 Mook Kills Bonus Award and the Longest Survivor Bonus Award remain unclaimed. Check the rankings to see who's in the running for both awards."

"I see you, Dylan." The Archer had gone so far ahead of the Tank and the teenage Guide, she looked about an inch tall on the horizon.

A minute later, the Priestess and Archer came running

towards Mithabel, Amarynth obviously holding back so as not to leave the Priestess behind. Another minute later and Dylan collapsed in Mithabel's embrace, tears streaming down her cheeks. She backed away and shoved Mithabel's shoulder with the flat of her palm. "You left me, bitch. Don't *ever* do that again." She wiped her tears with a finger. "Now give me back my cudgel."

Taken aback, Mithabel checked her inventory. She had no cudgel, only her longsword. "Sweet mother. I don't have it. I'm sorry, Dylan. I think we've discovered a penalty for dying. You lose equipped items when you die. How about you, Amarynth? You still have your dirk?"

The Archer held out a empty hand. "I don't. And that's not the only penalty. Check your attributes."

"Kaleisha, are any of my attributes changed from before I died?"

"Yes, chief. Your Constitution has fallen from seven to six. It is now considered sub-par."

Mithabel bit back a curse. "Did you lose a point of Constitution, Amarynth?"

The Archer nodded. "My category went from average to low average."

Dylan clutched Mithabel's shoulder as though needing to catch her balance. "Sounds like our Constitution scores are the number of lives we have. We need to avoid dying at all costs."

"Only six lives left." Mithabel muttered a curse, not wanting to believe she'd already lost one seventh of her lives before the game was hardly underway. "If I'd known that, I'd have put all my discretionary attribute points into Constitution. Which way are we going? I have a compelling desire to vacate Ferro Serpent territory. I don't want to face three of those things and only earn the XP for one."

Charli clucked her tongue. "It would be four Bosses, not three. Double the previous number. We want to go west."

"Holy shit, let's move." Amarynth started walking.

They hustled west, putting Voorton with its stores and

security as far behind them as possible as quickly as possible. The sun hung high in the sky ahead of them, not having moved since they first spotted it.

With Rolag directing them from the sky, they skirted a band of mooks, then another and another.

After bypassing their fifth band of monsters, Dylan whistled softly. "We've not seen any Brass Goblins since the two Bosses died. Only Iron Goblins. Thanks to Rolag scouting from above, I avoided all but the last band of six. Earned nearly two-hundred XP for that encounter. Rolag did all the killing. It was all I could do to stay alive. One more hit, and I'd have gone down. Have you checked the rankings lately?"

Mithabel slowed her pace. "Was going to wait until we'd put the Brassy Grassy Field behind us." Slowing to a walk, she willed the rankings to display. "*Cool.* MAD is the number one party."

"Scroll down." Dylan's voice trembled. She hadn't stopped running, and neither had Amarynth or Charli.

Doing as instructed, Mithabel found more rankings.

First 200 Mook Kills Bonus Award Contenders
   MAD: 168 mook kills
   XStorm: 156 mook kills
   OrionsDagger: 138 mook kills

"Nice." Mithabel bobbed her head in satisfaction. "We're ahead in mook kills. Only need 32 more to nab another bonus award. But I don't want to take the risk of facing four Bosses by trying to kill another six bands of Iron Goblins in the Brassy Grassy. I hope you all agree. Retaining as many of our lives as possible is a higher priority than earning another bonus award. We need to keep moving until we reach a new territory. How much farther can it be?"

"Keep scrolling." Not slowing her pace, Dylan threw a furtive glance back at the Tank.

Mithabel continued down the page.

Longest Survivor Bonus Award Contenders
   ChrisCross, party XStorm
   Dylan, party MAD
   Orion, party OrionsDagger
   Ruby, party XStorm
   ZAngel, party ZAvengers

"Damn, Dylan, why didn't you say something?" Mithabel dismissed the rankings lists and started running again, stashing her armor to increase speed. "Even more reason to keep you alive, Priestess. Rolag, can you see the edge of this field?"

"I can. There's a cornfield up ahead. Maybe two minutes traveling at your speed. You've got Iron Goblin bands to the north and south, but the way straight ahead is clear. There's also movement behind you that doesn't look like Goblins. Probably Ferro Serpents. They're staying under the grass, but it's rippling like I'd expect for a bunch of big snakes on the move. They aren't moving fast in a straight line, so I don't think they sense you. Don't do anything to attract their attention, and maybe they'll leave you alone."

The tension in the air clamped all their mouths shut while the landbound members of the party hurried through the thigh-high grass. They released a collective sigh of relief when stalks of corn manifested within the distant haze.

Mithabel caught up to Dylan and Charli. The three exchanged glances, all of them jealous of Amarynth's Increased Movement trait.

Rolag issued a warning. "The Iron Goblins to the north are heading for you. They'll intercept you if you don't move faster."

Following Mithabel's example, Dylan stashed her armor.

Charli moaned, already falling behind. "Does this mean I need to stash my skirt?"

Mithabel threw a look over her shoulder. "No one here will

care if you show some leg."

"Seriously...? Fine." The teenager's skirt vanished. Culottes covered her hips. She blushed. "So, this is the life of an adventurer. Running naked through grassy fields."

Mithabel chuckled, though it came out strained due to her effort to run faster. "You're hardly naked."

"I'm not dressed as a proper young lady, either."

The Tank slowed a step to allow Charli to catch her. "With no parents to scold you, what does it matter?"

Charli breathed hard. "Good thing there aren't any guys around to see us."

Dylan chuckled. "That wouldn't bother me nearly as much as getting caught by four Boss snakes."

Rolag snorted. "Move faster. You won't beat the Iron Goblins to the cornfield at your speed."

"Maybe we should take them." Amarynth equipped her heavy crossbow. "How many are in the band?"

"I'm counting six."

The Tank looked to her right, but saw no sign of mooks. She glanced left. Nothing. "How close is the southern band? We can't discount its presence."

"Too close for comfort. But more importantly, the Bosses are now coming straight at you. Fast. And the southern band of Goblins is now moving faster towards you. If you don't dig deep and find more speed, you'll soon be fighting a dozen Iron Goblins and four Ferro Serpents."

The cornfield loomed closer.

Whoosh.

Off to the party's left, dark metallic bald heads popped occasionally above the grass. Mithabel couldn't run any faster. "They're in encounter range."

Tens of yards ahead of the others, Amarynth stopped, raising her crossbow and taking aim. "Move those sexy legs, ladies." She fired a bolt. Two clouds of fiery particles leaped into the air. "Two mooks down with one shot. I'm getting good at this."

Grim determination hardened Dylan's jaws. "We don't even know if reaching the cornfield will stop the mooks from attacking us."

"I'm more concerned about the Bosses." Mithabel drew up beside Amarynth, equipping armor and longsword. "You three go on. Reach the cornfield. I'll take out these four Goblins and then be right with you."

Her fellow party members left as Mithabel asked. She took a defensive stance and prepared to meet the onrushing Goblins.

The Pseudo Code Dragon flew lower. "They're changing direction to intercept the others, Mithabel. If you don't move, the Bosses will be on you in about ten seconds."

"Damn. Thanks, Rolag." Mithabel stashed all her equipment again and ran.

Up ahead, Amarynth paused to fire another bolt, taking out a third mook. "Aw, only got one of them. They're not lining themselves up the way they were before."

"The Goblin AI is continually learning and adjusting." Dylan hadn't broken stride. She and Charli continued on without Amarynth.

Mithabel raced past the Viking too. "I wish we all had your Increased Movement, Archer."

Amarynth overtook Mithabel and stopped for another shot. A fourth Iron Goblin ceased to be a threat.

"*We're out of the grass.*" Dylan bent over, grasping her thighs, now covered in armor. "How far into the cornfield do we need to go?"

Mithabel gasped. "We don't have Fatigue attributes, but we're programmed to act out of breath from exertion." As she neared Dylan and the edge of the Brassy Grassy Field, she glanced over her shoulder. Amarynth had stopped again and dropped a fifth mook. The sixth one plowed into her, its iron wheel riding up her leg and chest, rolling over her shoulder before dropping to the ground.

"The Bosses are right on you, Amarynth." Worry tinged Rolag's voice.

Mithabel stopped short of the cornfield, waiting. The Archer couldn't take on four Bosses alone. "Amarynth, *move*."

"I'm coming." The Viking ran towards Mithabel, leaving the sixth Goblin behind. When she reached Mithabel, she turned, her crossbow loaded. Taking quick aim, she fired. The Goblin erupted into a shower of sparks. "There, that's another band of six mooks to add to our total."

Four dark metal serpents rose from the grass, their heads wavering atop thick bodies easily reaching twice Mithabel's height. Six Iron Goblins wheeled behind the snakes, and four of them raced up the backs of the reptiles, shedding sparks, setting dark scales aflame.

"*Come on.*" Mithabel grabbed Amarynth's arm.

The snakes swelled in size.

The Archer grimaced but didn't try for another shot. She stashed her crossbow and fled with Mithabel, pacing the Tank so as not to leave her behind.

The Boss monsters sped after the PCs, flames churning in their wake.

A Ferro Serpent paused, poising to strike. Mithabel dove for the edge of the cornfield. Tumbling down a furrow between two rows of cornstalks, she bounced to her feet and spun around, expecting the worst. Would the Bosses leave their territory to attack the party? What if the cornfield was still considered their territory?

"Welcome to Mystic Hollow Cornfield, chief, where even shadows tremble."

The poised Boss didn't strike.

Amarynth stood in an adjacent furrow, crossbow raised and aimed.

"Don't shoot." Charli sidled up to Amarynth. "If you shoot, you invite them into this territory to fight us. If we stay out of their territory and don't attack them, they won't attack us."

"I trust you, kid." Amarynth didn't lower her weapon. "But I still want to see them turn around and leave before I put my crossbow away."

The four Ferro Serpents raised to their full heights and stared at the party. The six Iron Goblins wheeled in the burning grass.

Mithabel equipped her armor and longsword. "Why aren't they leaving?"

The teenage Guide pointed at the sky. "We need Rolag to join us. As long as he's flying above their territory, our party isn't considered as leaving it."

Three seconds later, Rolag descended, landing next to Amarynth. "Am I good now?"

Three of the Bosses turned to liquid, crashing to the ground with a splash and sinking from sight.

The Archer strode towards the Brassy Grassy Field, stopping short of the boundary. "How about we take this Boss now that there's only one of it? I'm itching for a level gain."

Dylan came up behind the Elf. "Charli, if Mithabel, Amarynth, and Rolag go into the Brassy Grassy to fight the monsters while you and I stay in the Mystic Hollow Cornfield, will we be safe from them here?"

Charli gave a tentative nod. "The safe harbor rules when crossing into a new territory are complicated. But as long as no one attacks from the cornfield, it should remain a safe place for us for the immediate future. Long enough for them to kill the Serpent Boss."

"You heard her." Dylan waved her companions forward. "Go gain us a level. May the Goddess guide you. I wish I had the Auni to enchant your weapons, but I assume you'll do fine without it."

Amarynth smiled and stepped into the Brassy Grassy, loosing a bolt that took out a Goblin. With a rustling flap of his wings, Rolag took to the air.

Mithabel stepped beside the Archer, her longsword at the ready. The first Iron Goblin charging them lost his head to her blade. The second one went flying to the side from the force of Mithabel's elbow in his face. Rolag dive bombed the third one in line, trashing him. The fourth one rode at Amarynth, but she sidestepped it. The fifth one plowed into Mithabel. She laughed at its futile attempt to harm her. She might be down a Constitution point, but her defensive skills and traits were more than a match for the aggressions of a Goblin, be it Brass or Iron.

The Serpent withdrew, as though it realized its foes were too strong. It didn't have a chance at winning now that its three clones were gone. It dropped under the grass, its back still on fire, and sped off.

The Viking motioned after the Serpent. "Don't let the Boss get away, Rolag."

The Pseudo Code Dragon shot across the intervening space, descending into the grass. The snake head reared up, fangs snapping at Rolag. A crossbow bolt whizzed past the little Dragon, striking the Boss in the back of its skull. Rolag latched onto the bolt, ignoring the flames harmlessly licking his tail and underbelly, and drove his fangs into the Ferro Serpent's scalp. The Boss thrashed in an attempt to knock its attacker loose, but Rolag's talons didn't relent in their grip.

Mithabel laughed her best maniacal laughter as she dispatched the three remaining Iron Goblins, keeping them away from Amarynth while the Archer peppered the Boss with crossbow bolts and Rolag ripped out chunk after chunk of the snake's brains.

Finished with the Goblins, Mithabel ran towards Rolag, circumnavigating the flames. Coming close enough to bring the combatants into view with Third Person POV, she switched perspectives and paused to watch, ready to charge in if needed. The Ferro Serpent reared up to bash Rolag against the ground, forcing the little guy to release the crossbow bolt, but he latched onto another one. Flames drew near Mithabel, and she backed away one step at a time. Eventually the Boss was dead, defeated almost single-handedly by the little Dragon.

"Report on HP statuses, please, Kaleisha."

"Amarynth's HP is at 97%. You and the Pseudo Code Dragon are both at 100."

"Amazing. Are Magical Companions common amongst other PC parties?"

"Sorry, chief, I don't have that info."

Rolag blew out the grass fire with his flapping wings before returning to Amarynth and Mithabel. The three of them grinned at each other. The Tank and the Archer locked arms and strolled into the cornfield, the Winged Fighter flying above them in lazy circles.

"*Congratulations*, chief. You are level five Tank."

Mithabel plopped onto her butt in the dirt of the furrow between two rows of cornstalks and leaned back on her hands. "I don't know about you all, but I hope to never see another Ferro Serpent or Iron Goblin again."

Charli squealed and danced. "I can't believe I'm level five." She hugged the Viking, who patted the girl on the back. After a long moment, Charli drew away, trembling. "I knew when I first saw you, Amarynth, there was a good future for me if you took me with you. Now look at me." She was wearing her skirt again, but of course that wasn't what she was referring to. She held her arms towards the sky and craned her neck to peer at the clouds through the greenery of the cornstalks. "Thank you, Goddess, for uniting me with these PCs. I will do my very best for them, you'll see."

CHAPTER TWELVE

Relying on Mithabel's Danger Sense to warn them if enemies approached, the companions sat among the cornstalks and traded information about their gains for level five. Dylan's maximum Auni increased by seven to thirty-seven with the level gain, and her usable Auni had replenished to full. Rolag had earned another Auni point, bringing his total to five.

Everyone had gained a new class skill. Mithabel had acquired Feint. "I've no idea when that will come in handy. Sounds more like a skill for dueling, not hacking monsters to bits."

"My new skill is Fast Load." Amarynth examined an insect crawling on her wrist. "This game has bugs." Red with black spots, the tiny creature spread its wings and flew away.

"Ladybugs are a sign of good fortune." Charli tracked the insect with a pointing finger until it landed on the silk protruding from a corn husk.

Mithabel bit back a comment. Fast Load sounded much more useful against mooks than Feint. Good fortune for Amarynth, indeed. The Tank wasn't jealous at all.

"My new skill is Turn." Dylan sounded excited. "Assuming we gain the kinds of skills that might be appropriate to what we're expected to face at our level, I'd recommend being on the lookout for undead. I'm guessing Zombies and that sort of thing. Maybe I'll even get to use my Excise spell sometime soon."

The Archer pointed her chin at the teenager. "What skill did you pick up, Charli?"

"Landmarks." The girl shrugged. "I have no idea how to use it or what it's for."

Rolag rustled his wings. "Guess what my new skill is."

Mithabel guessed. "Feint."

"You got it." Rolag darted his head from one side to another in pantomime. "Though my skill is called Aerial Feint. Can't wait to try it out."

"Listen to this." Dylan's eyes focused on something no one else could see. "I have evidence we're gaining hit points as we progress, even though all we can see are HP percentage values. My HP was at 5% before we gained a level. Now it's 7%, and I didn't cast any healing on myself. Either I healed 2% naturally all of a sudden or going up a level changed my underlying hit points. I'll bet it's the latter."

"You should heal yourself up to full." Mithabel brushed her black hair back from her face. "We can sit here and talk while you cast your healing spell. How much of your Auni will you need for a full heal?"

"You're right." Dylan glanced around as though looking for prowling monsters. Then she gave Mithabel a sheepish look.

The Tank smirked. "It's okay to be cautious. I can't promise my Danger Sense is infallible."

Dylan smiled weakly. "I'm glad to have you back, Mithabel." She rubbed her cheeks. "Goddess Scintilla, Lady of Light, shine upon my wounds and take them away." Lines of concern melted from her face, but left her still looking tired. "That brought my HP up to 13%. If I take that as a typical amount of healing performed per Auni point spent, it will cost me, what?" The Priestess closed one eye and cocked a brow. "Roughly 15 more Auni. I'll have a bit more than half my Auni remaining. From what I've observed, I'll gain that back at the rate of 1 Auni per ten minutes of non-strenuous activity. Double the rate when I have opportunity to sit and rest. I'm guessing the rate would be even higher if a person were sleeping, but that theory needs testing."

"Nothing has approached us here." Mithabel picked up a

fallen cornstalk blade and examined it. It was mostly green, with some brown spots which at first glance appeared to be dispersed randomly. But, sorry, *no*, they weren't. Someone had done a better job with the graphics here than with the Brassy Grassy Field, but there was an obvious repeating pattern and seams to the textures used. Amateurs. "If you want my opinion, I think you should heal to full and we should continue to sit here until you replenish your Auni. We might miss out on the First 200 Mook Kills Bonus Award, but not losing lives is of the utmost importance."

The Viking shook her head. "Take a look at the rankings for the Mook Kills contention."

The Tank willed the rankings to appear before her.

First 200 Mook Kills Bonus Award Contenders
MAD: 180 mook kills
XStorm: 162 mook kills
OrionsDagger: 138 mook kills

"OrionsDagger hasn't made any more kills since I looked last." Amarynth rubbed her hands. "XStorm has made six kills to our twelve. We're only twenty kills away from the award. I say that you, Rolag, and I go back to the Brassy Grassy and kill four more bands of Iron Goblins. We shouldn't have to go far. We'll keep Dylan and Charli in sight at all times. Let's wait for Dylan to do 15 heal spells to heal herself to full. Then while she's resting to recharge her Auni, we'll go have a little fun in the sun."

Mithabel scrolled down to look at the other award contention list.

Longest Survivor Bonus Award Contenders
ChrisCross, party XStorm
Dylan, party MAD
Ruby, party XStorm

Only Dylan remained in the contest against ChrisCross and

his Centaur buddy. "I don't want to leave Dylan alone. She's one of three remaining contenders for the Longest Survivor Bonus Award, and I want her to have it. If we leave her and something attacks her before we can get back, I'd never forgive myself."

"Thank you, Mithabel." Dylan's eyes brightened. "I love you, too."

The Archer flexed her fingers. "Do you have any problem with me and Rolag going without you then?"

To quell the frustration welling inside, Mithabel focused on her Temperament stat and drew a slow breath. The Archer only wanted the best for the party. Why did it bother Mithabel that Amarynth wanted the party to win every bonus award possible? "Will you please stay within sight?"

"Sure."

"Don't lose a life."

Amarynth dismissed Mithabel's concern with a wave. "To these low-level mooks? Not likely."

"Watch out for Bosses."

"If I understand what Charli said, we should only be facing one Boss if it respawns while we're out there. We can handle one Boss."

The Viking Archer and her Magical Companion set off.

Dylan clapped a hand on Mithabel's forearm. "Thank you for staying with me."

"Concentrate on healing yourself, Priestess." Mithabel willed an awareness transfer to Rolag as he flew into the sky to hunt for mooks, to see if it would work. It didn't, sadly. Maybe because he was a Magical Companion belonging to someone else. "By the way, Dylan, before I forget to tell you, if you die, Debra Jones will wake up in the real world. She needs to go to sleep for you to respawn." She cast a glance at Charli. "Not sure how it works for NPCs, assuming you even *can* respawn. Do you know if you can?"

"I don't know." The Cowgirl's eyes bugged. "I've never died before and don't know any NPCs who have. The game started for us when it started for you. I don't even have a back story."

Switching to Third Person POV, Mithabel moved her observation point as high as possible to look down on as large an area as possible. Her view centered on her location, and she couldn't change that, but she could see a wide swath of land around her. She couldn't set her observation point as high in the sky as Rolag flew, but she went high enough to see a good portion of the Brassy Grassy on the edge of her view. It allowed her to spot a band of Iron Goblins a moment before Rolag announced their presence.

The mooks charged Amarynth, but the Archer destroyed two of them with her crossbow before they could close the distance, while Rolag took out another two by diving and slashing with his claws. The remaining two wildly attacked Amarynth, but she sidestepped one as Rolag killed the other. Then Rolag killed the last one. Neither Amarynth or Rolag took any damage. It was too easy.

Party MAD was up to 186 mook kills. XStorm had moved up to 168 mook kills, while OrionsDagger remained at 138. The latter party appeared to be out of the running. It was between MAD and XStorm, and MAD had the advantage of the lead.

"Kaleisha, did I earn XP from that encounter?"

The AI drifted over to sit cross legged beside Mithabel, hovering a few inches off the ground. "Yes, indeed. You earned 30 XP base per Iron Goblin, times six in the band defeated, for a total base XP earned of 180. Adding 10% for the two bonus awards gives 198 total."

"Wow. Thanks, Kaleisha." It was nice, thrilling even, to earn XP while someone else did the work, and yet shameful too. She had an appreciation for how Charli must feel, earning XP and reaching level five for doing little more than convincing a PC party to accept her as a member. For that matter, Dylan hadn't done much to earn her XPs either. No, that wasn't being fair to Dylan or Charli. They both had contributed to the party's advancement. Though the system used combat as the driver for awarding XP, it recognized the contributions of those who helped in other ways by giving everyone in the party equal shares. If the party felt someone wasn't pulling their weight, they were of course free to expel that person from the party. Or a disgruntled party member could leave in search for another party. Mithabel liked her party and trusted that her companions liked party MAD as much as she did.

The mook kills for XStorm moved up to 174.

The Archer cupped her hands and put them to her mouth like a bullhorn, using local chat to broadcast outside the party. "Hey, Goblins. Come and fight me."

Whoosh. Mithabel's Danger Sense triggered. Something approached from deeper in the cornfield. Scanning in that direction in Third Person POV showed nothing moving. Switching back to First Person POV, she jumped to her feet. "We're about to have company, Priestess. Um, Amarynth, we might need you and Rolag here."

"On our way."

Across the field, cornstalks trembled, as though even the crops were afraid.

"I've healed myself up to 56%." Dylan climbed to her feet and followed Mithabel's gaze. "Any idea what we're up against?"

Mithabel pointed. "That."

A stick figure of blackened wood, with a bulbous pumpkin head and intricately sculpted facial features, stared at them from several rows of corn away. Clad in a ragged, draping gown someone might have been buried in, the creature sneered with the carved smile of a malicious jack-o-lantern. The thing tilted its head forward to glower. Tendrils of dark energy undulated beside and behind the monster like charmed cobras. Reading *100%*, a green HP status bar floated above its head, and above that flew a blue banner labeled *Scarecrow*.

Charli popped her lips. "You know how Dylan said we should keep an eye open for undead? Well, here it is. This isn't a Boss, but it *is* a rare monster. It doesn't make physical attacks. The danger this monster presents is to our mental well being. It intends to scare us all to death."

"Kaleisha, what's the Mental HP status of the party?"

"Everyone is at full Mental health, chief."

Dylan drew back her shoulders and faced the Scarecrow. "Time to try my new Turn skill." With outstretched arm, palm facing the monster, she stepped forward. "In the name of Scintilla, Goddess of the Sun, I command you turn and be gone, evil creature."

The smile carved into the orange pumpkin head bent up further. The Scarecrow didn't turn. It came closer.

Mithabel squinted. Was the monster approaching or growing or both? Why wasn't her depth perception helping more?

"Great." Dylan raised both arms. "I've been waiting to use this Excise spell for a long time. Scintilla, Sun Goddess, I beseech you, shine your holy light on this blight and excise it from the land."

Sunny beams sprayed through the clouds onto the Priestess. A female voice emanated from above Dylan's head, speaking in a lecturing tone. "If you expect *me* to destroy *that*, you'll need to offer me more than a couple Auni. Look at that thing. It's pure evil. I don't do pure evil for cheap."

The expression on Dylan's face was what Mithabel imagined *stunned* should look like. The Tank chuckled.

Dylan whipped her head towards Mithabel, her eyes blazing. "Shut up, Tank."

"That's unprofessional language for a Priestess, don't you think?" Mithabel dodged Dylan's swinging fist.

"Look." Charli stepped between them, pointing.

Ephemeral black cobras wound around the Scarecrow's legs. Flames flickered atop the creature's head. It didn't have feet, only a tapered stump, floating above the ground and casting no shadow. The Scarecrow's distance and size defied definition. One moment, it looked large and far, with several intervening cornstalks. The next moment it looked smaller but near, with few intervening cornstalks. When it appeared close, Mithabel lunged, stabbing with her longsword.

Her weapon failed to connect. A dark cobra lashed out, striking the tip of her longsword. Serpentine shadows slithered up her blade to the hilt. A chill seeped from the weapon into Mithabel's fingers and through her right arm, paralyzing the limb. Though her brain commanded her arm to swing the longsword, the muscles refused to cooperate. Her legs still worked, and she stumbled back.

"Your Mental HP has fallen by 32%, chief. Advise you try a different tactic."

"No kidding."

Dylan shouted, yet her words sounded distant. *"Mithabel, retreat."*

The Tank glanced over her shoulder. Sweet mother. The Priestess had either shrunk by a factor of ten, or she was several hundred yards away. How had Mithabel traveled so far with but a single lunge?

Amarynth rushed up beside Dylan. From this distance, it was doubtful the Archer could hit the Scarecrow with her crossbow. If she tried, there was a good chance she'd hit Mithabel instead.

The sky darkened and the wind gusted. A cone of fire erupted from above Mithabel's head, warming her scalp an instant before bathing the Scarecrow in its fury. Flames caught hold of the Scarecrow's gown. A red Dragon sped by overhead, not a tiny Pseudo Code Dragon, but a fifty-foot long adult Dragon with Rolag's features.

The Scarecrow screeched its pleasure. The monster flashed between visible and invisible, the Dragon's flames outlining it, continually marking the creature's location. That might prove useful for tracking the monster's movement, but the Dragon fire failed to damage the Scarecrow.

"I've learned something else." Charli stood beside Mithabel, though the Tank hadn't seen the Guide move. "The Scarecrow exists in another phase of existence than the normal one we exist in. Physical attacks of non-magical weapons won't hurt it. You need magic to affect it, either wizardly or divine. On the other hand, the energy attacks of its tendrils can affect us. Sorry I didn't know that sooner, Mithabel."

Dylan prayed aloud to her Goddess, her words muffled by the distance.

"I need an enchantment, Priestess." Mithabel turned and ran... and smacked into Dylan. Their foreheads cracked against each other. Both women staggered but kept to their feet.

The Priestess dropped her arms, her prayer to Scintilla dying in a gurgle of pain as she stumbled away.

Kaleisha darted in between the two, getting in Mithabel's face. "You damaged our pretty Polynesian Priestess, bitch." She remained in place, blocking Mithabel's view, her arms akimbo.

"I... I'm sorry, Dylan." Guilt tightened the Elf's throat. Wetness clogged her nostrils. She licked her lips and tasted blood. An arc of blackness curled around her legs. Cold burrowed beneath her skin. *Move, dammit.* Her legs refused to work. She swiveled her neck, but couldn't see the monster behind her. She flexed her left arm. It still worked, thank the Goddess. She unequipped her longsword and re-equipped it in her left hand. "Could you please enchant my blade?"

"You *head bashed* me, Tank."

"Kaleisha, get out of the way."

"I'm up here, chief." The Jamaican AI vanished from the Elf's view, smoke dispersing from where she'd been.

To Mithabel's left, a puppy-sized Rolag screamed and dove into the dirt between two rows of cornstalks. His wings shook as though trying to flap but unable. Pumping his legs, he failed to get them under him. His talons flung clods of dirt. The Pseudo Code Dragon's paralyzed wings had become the proverbial albatross around his neck, weighing him rather than lifting him. *Damn.*

Standing beside the Priestess, the Archer fired a crossbow bolt past the Tank.

Kaleisha flew loops around the Viking's head. "Proud woman not so proud. Not hurt scary dude."

"Why are you talking funny, Kaleisha?"

"Me not. You thinking scrambled eggs. Pool drying down. Something something out of a hundred. Danger, Ms. Robinson."

A dark cobra shot past Mithabel's head from behind, striking Dylan's forehead. Shadows branched across the Polynesian's face, crawling like worms into her eyes and nostrils. A guttural groan escaped the Priestess. Her lips bent into weird angles, unable to form words. The shadow cobra slithered into her mouth.

Despair rose up Mithabel's throat like bile. "Get away, Priestess. Don't let it paralyze your legs."

Fear clouded Dylan's eyes, staring straight ahead. Her arms rose and fell.

Rose and fell again.

And again.

Amarynth fired another missile. Fired another and another.

The Jamaican AI stood beside Dylan, peering into her face. "No speaking da English. Countdown has begun. Launching in thirty seconds."

The party was done, their Mental HP draining away with no way to stop it. If they perished mentally, would they respawn? Or would they remain paralyzed, on display in this cornfield for eternity? This could be game over for party MAD.

Charli stepped behind the Polynesian, stood on her tiptoes and put her hands over Dylan's eyes. "Clear your mind, Priestess. Concentrate on my voice."

A shadow cobra lashed at Dylan and Charli, passing through them both at the waists like an ethereal whip. Neither of them flinched. Charli glared over Dylan's shoulder at the Scarecrow, while continuing to whisper advice to the Priestess.

"No Charli invasion, bitch."

Despite the invective, the AI's words stirred hope in Mithabel's chest. She interpreted Kaleisha's words to mean Charli was still unaffected by the Scarecrow and the shadowy serpentine attackers.

A dozen black cobras struck the Cowgirl and the Polynesian.

Charli kept her hands over Dylan's eyes and muttered assurances to the Priestess, all the while glaring at the Scarecrow.

Dylan's shoulders relaxed.

In her own head, Mithabel screamed with inexplicable joy.

The teenage Guide spoke with unbelievable calm. "Close your eyes, Priestess. I'm taking my hands away. Cast your Excise spell again. Make this one count. Don't open your eyes until you absolutely must." She dropped onto her heels and backed away from Dylan.

With eyes firmly closed, the Priestess raised her arms. Her lips quivered and parted. "Scintilla, Sun Goddess, *please, I beg you,* shine your holy light on this Scarecrow and excise it from the land." Arcane words followed. Then she fell silent, opened her eyes, and pointed at the monster.

Rays of light struck the Polynesian. A disembodied voice spoke, emanating from above her. "*That's better.* I especially like the emphatic pleading. You could have offered me a *bit* more Auni, but I'm feeling generous in the moment. I do wish you had more Faith in me. We need to work on that. Now, let's see, oh, yes, you want the Scarecrow excised. What I'm about to do should *not* be considered Divine Intervention or Deus Ex Machina. You *did* cast a spell, after all, and expended a fair amount of Auni. I'm only empowering the effect of your spell in my chosen manner, as is a deity's privilege. Has anyone ever told you how lovely you are, my Priestess?"

The heavenly rays of light shifted direction, moving from Dylan towards the Scarecrow. After a series of sizzles and pops, Mithabel's legs and right arm unlocked. She spun to face the monster.

It was gone. The black cobras were gone. The cornfield remained. In the furrow Mithabel occupied, five feet away, sat a pile of ash.

Amarynth dropped to her knees beside Rolag. "Oh, my poor little fella." She scooped him up in her arms, smoothing out his wings as best she could. He loosed a mournful cry like a lonesome wolf and then pressed his head against her chest, his wings still bent at awkward angles. He adjusted them, but they didn't cooperate and still looked awkward.

"Are you all right, Dylan?" Mithabel examined the Polynesian's face. Even though she'd spoken her spell successfully, the Priestess didn't look right, like her eyes had each been moved a fraction of an inch to her right, or her nose was bent, or one cheek had sunken in and the other one puffed out. Her features wouldn't stabilize.

"I should be asking you that question." Dylan pointed at Mithabel's legs. "Are they broken or bent or what?"

Charli squatted beside the pile of ashes and stirred them with a cornstalk stem. Seconds later, a red gem lay glimmering amid the ashes. The girl didn't pick it up. Mithabel walked over, stumbling twice.

The teenage Guide held up her hand. "Don't touch it. I think it's alive. Affecting everyone, making you think things are wrong with each other. It needs to be destroyed."

"Are you shitting me?" Mithabel bent down and reached for the gem. "We *finally* find some treasure worth something, and you say we need to *destroy* it? This can't be happening."

Charli pushed the Tank's arm aside. "Listen to me, Mithabel. This gem holds a cursed spirit. If you touch it, you'll be acting a lot weirder than you are already. Just being near it is making everyone act strangely."

Dylan stepped close. "Except for you, Charli. How are you immune?"

A wry grin crept across Charli's face. "My Mental Armor trait, maybe?"

Mithabel clenched her jaw, restraining from grabbing the gem. "What makes you think that?"

Charli grimaced, shrugging one shoulder. "After your legs were paralyzed, those shadow cobras constantly struck you in the back of the head, but you could still move your head, which meant the cobras weren't affecting you. It must have been because you didn't *see* them. Seeing is believing, but in your case, not seeing meant not believing. On the other hand, I *was* seeing them, but not being affected. None of my Guide skills could account for that, so one or more of my traits were protecting me. Mental Armor or Complex Personality. My bet's on Mental Armor."

Mithabel stood, leaving the gem where it lay. "So, in effect, you saved our hides. I'd say you earned your keep on this encounter, Charli, and we're damned lucky to have brought you with us. Okay, then. How do we destroy this thing?"

Dylan cleared her throat. "Do you think you could stash the gem in your inventory without it affecting the rest of us, Charli? We desperately need something to sell when we find a market. Some of us need weapons replaced. I could use some new spells. If we could afford a magical weapon for Mithabel, that would be helpful."

The Viking cleared her throat. "I could use an enchanted crossbow. A magical dirk, too, if we can afford it."

"I don't know." Charli's hand lingered above the gem. "My Monster Lore is hazy on the matter, but direct contact with the gem might allow it to penetrate my Mental Armor. I'm afraid to pick it up."

"Hear me out, Charli." Dylan put a hand on the teenager's shoulder, placing her mouth near the Cowgirl's ear, below the brim of her hat. "It's possible the gem *is* affecting you. Maybe it's making you afraid, so you won't pick it up. If it doesn't want you to pick it up, then that might be *exactly* what you should do. If it's in your inventory, I don't think it will affect any of us, including you. So grab it and stash it. If you have to drop it, you can."

Mithabel shook her head. "Not necessarily. If it's cursed, she might not be able to drop it."

Dylan glared at Mithabel. "Don't listen to the stupid Tank. The game wouldn't throw undroppable bad items at us in the early stages."

The Priestess couldn't know that. But Mithabel held her tongue. She wanted treasure as much as anyone. They needed new spells and gear. Magical gear. A few potions wouldn't hurt either. "I'm sure Dylan's right, Charli. It *is* still early in the game. If you're unwilling to take the risk, I will. We *need* this treasure."

Charli knelt beside the pile of ashes, her hand hovering inches above the gem. "I'll do it. You've all been so nice to me, taking me into your party. This is the least I can do for you." She closed her eyes and grabbed the stone. It vanished from her grip as soon as it left the ashes. Her lips drew a grim line. "Okay. It's in my inventory. It's called a Shadow Stone." She opened her eyes. "I don't think it's hurting me. Do I look okay to you all?"

Mithabel nodded. "I see nothing wrong."

Kaleisha lowered from the sky, stopping to hover above the Cowgirl's head. She waved at Mithabel. "Yo. Jump the six XP by thirty-six to fifty-eight. Jet rocket, bitch. Permission to relaunch."

"What's my Mental HP status, Kaleisha?"

"Why you think, bitch?"

Mithabel gritted her teeth and refrained from responding. Kaleisha wasn't saying what Mithabel heard. The Tank's perception of her support AI was messed up due to a drop in her Mental HP. Obviously.

Dylan shook her head and groaned. "Is anyone else having a problem with their system AI? Magnum is talking nonsense. I can't get Mental HP status reports from him or Scintilla. But let me tell you what I do know. One, some of us are in need of healing, for both Physical and Mental HP. Two, I need a ton of rest to refresh my Auni. Three, we don't want to face another Scarecrow without me being at full Auni." Her braids swayed like dead serpents hanging from her head. She pointed her chin in the direction of Amarynth and Rolag. "Four, even without status reports, I can surmise our little friend is out of commission. We need to stay put, rest, and heal." She met Amarynth's gaze. "*No more talk about bonus awards.* Let's hope Rolag's Accelerated Healing trait will help restore his Mental

HP loss. My Heal spell can't heal mental damage. I need a different spell for that. *Time* will heal mental damage, but not quickly. So everyone sit down, stay quiet, let me heal everyone physically as much as I can, and then recharge my Auni. *Do I hear any objections?*" She looked around. "I didn't think so."

CHAPTER THIRTEEN

A few minutes later, Dylan finished casting her series of Heal spells on the party. "Everyone is full on Physical HP now." She dropped onto her butt in a furrow between Mithabel and Amarynth. "I only have 7 Auni left. I need to rest for a while before we move on." She reached over to pet Rolag, who lay on the Viking's lap, his eyes closed. He whimpered at the Polynesian's touch. Whispering in a soothing voice, she stroked his neck. "I wish there was something I could do for you, little guy." She looked to Amarynth. "In two minutes, I'll have an idea whether his Accelerated Healing is helping with his mental damage."

Mithabel lay on her back, chewing a weed. "Kaleisha, if you can understand me, please show me the rankings." She could have willed it to appear before her, but she wanted to test her AI.

The virtual Jamaican said nothing, but the lists appeared in Mithabel's view, a good sign her connection to the AI was recovering.

Party MAD still topped the Top Twenty Parties list, with XStorm in second, OrionsDagger in third, and ZAvengers fourth. None of the other sixteen listed parties were serious threats to MAD's number one standing.

In the listing for Mook Kills, MAD had 187, XStorm now had 180, and OrionsDagger still had only 138. The Viking must have checked the list too. She and the Elf exchanged knowing glances. XStorm would claim the award if MAD didn't act soon. If some party other than MAD was to win the award, did it have to be XStorm?

Please, Goddess, don't let Dylan find out ChrisCross is Christopher Warden's avatar. My knowing is depressing enough.

With Rolag out of commission, Amarynth wouldn't want to leave him to hunt Iron Goblins, so if MAD was to claim the award, Mithabel would have to go alone to the Brassy Grassy. But she couldn't leave Dylan. All she could do was pray the Goddess made trouble for XStorm. Don't let them steal the bonus award. Think of your Priestess. Right. She'd be a fool to think the Goddess would listen to her prayers or intervene at her request.

The sounds of combat drifted to Mithabel from the Brassy Grassy. *Damn.* She stood in a half crouch, scanning the horizon. Unable to see the combatants, she switched to Third Person POV, but the skirmish was happening beyond the bounds of her view. "Do you all hear that? Someone is fighting in the Brassy Grassy right over there." She pointed. "I bet it's XStorm."

Dylan nodded. "Whoever it is, they'll be entering the cornfield soon. We should move. I'd rather not face a PC party with Rolag in such bad shape. We can't trust other parties not to attack us while we're down."

Mithabel frowned. "You're assuming PCs are allowed to hurt each other. PvP might be forbidden in this game."

"The Goddess told me it's possible and profitable. I believe her."

"You and your Goddess."

"We *need* to move."

The Archer cradled the Pseudo Code Dragon in the crook of an elbow. "If I understand what Barney is saying, Rolag's Mental HP isn't healing. Not yet."

Dylan grimaced. "That's not good. It's been ten minutes. If his trait could help, it should have done *something* by now. We can presume his Accelerated Healing doesn't extend to Mental HP. I don't know how we'll repair our losses to mental damage without days of rest or new spells."

Party MAD headed westward across the Mystic Hollow Cornfield, Amarynth carrying her Magical Companion. "I tried, but I can't stash him back in inventory."

The sounds of combat echoing from the Brassy Grassy diminished until they fell quiet. On the Mook Kills Contenders list, XStorm had 186 kills, only one kill fewer than party MAD. The Elf gritted her teeth. "That's got to be XStorm we heard. They won't come into the cornfield right away. They'll try to kill another three bands of Iron Goblins to reach 200 kills. That might not take them long. If they come into the cornfield, they'll head due west the same as we are. We should veer north or south as a preemptive measure to avoid them."

The Polynesian sighed. "Agreed. We can't hope to outdistance them in our condition. Let's find somewhere to hide and watch from. Confirm who they are as they pass."

"I'll look for a good hiding spot." Charli headed north. The Guide's skills *were* the best suited to finding concealment.

The continued sounds of fighting echoed from the Brassy Grassy while Charli searched.

A minute later, the girl reported her findings over party chat. "I've found a furrow behind a heavy concentration of cornstalks. It looks good." The party trudged over to her.

The distant combat ended. The number of mook kills for party XStorm rose to 192.

"Damn. They've got more kills than us now." The Viking settled into place behind the dense wall of cornstalks, laying Rolag on the ground beside her. "They'll win the bonus award. We'd have won it if not for that shit Scarecrow."

"That shit Scarecrow attacked us because you yelled for Iron Goblins." Mithabel scowled. "I'm not blaming you. Or maybe I am."

A male voice shouted from the Brassy Grassy over local chat. "Hey, mooks. Come and fight us, you little iron butt wipes."

A local chat icon identified the speaker as ChrisCross.

Mithabel chuckled, not because she found the situation

amusing, but to quell her fear about Dylan identifying ChrisCross's player. "They're having the same problem you were, Amarynth. If they aren't careful, they'll be facing some Ferro Serpents soon."

Whoosh.

Dammit. Mithabel jumped to her feet. "Everyone up. It sucks, but XStorm's shouting has brought another encounter on us." She pointed north. "Let's hope it's not another Scarecrow."

Dylan grabbed Amarynth by the elbow. "Let me enchant your crossbow with my Light spell." When finished, she turned to Mithabel. "And your longsword."

"Please do." Mithabel held her longsword horizontal before her while Dylan cast her spell. The blade glowed with yellow light, the same as Amarynth's bow. "You should have done this when we fought those Bosses. I probably wouldn't have died yet."

"Sorry, but I didn't know." Dylan put a hand on Mithabel's shoulder. "I'll find a way to make it up to you."

"Just stay alive." Mithabel clasped Dylan's wrist. "Did your Auni restore to full?"

Dylan laughed. "I regained one point of Auni from resting and spent two on enchantments. So I have six left. You've each got ten minutes of magic on your weapons. Don't waste it."

Mithabel grimaced and said nothing.

Kaleisha flew upside down through Mithabel's field of view. "Prepare mind to be blown, bitch. Rubbed genie's bottle wrong way." The support AI was still on the fritz.

ChrisCross shouted again for foes to come fight him. A female voice joined him at taunting mooks. Was that Ruby? The local chat icon identified the speaker as *Penelope*, a *Goth* female. Goth was a kindred in this game? Pale skin with straight black hair and green eyes, a black metal spiked collar around her neck, nothing identified her as either PC or NPC. Since Penelope wasn't a contender for the Longest Survivor Award, she was either a PC who'd died once already or an NPC who'd joined party XStorm. Ruby was still on the contenders list for the Longest Survivor award, so XStorm had at least three active members. It was reasonable to assume there were more.

Leaving Rolag whining on the ground, the Archer stepped forward and fired her crossbow. Mithabel tracked the missile. It struck a wavering, shadowy figure, tall as an adult human. The mook advanced, identified by its overhead banner as a Shadow Amoeba. An HP status bar floated beneath the identification banner, showing the monster had taken 30% damage from Amarynth's enchanted shot. As the Amoeba flew closer, passing right through the cornstalks like ghosts, Amarynth hit it again, dropping its HP by another 18%. While more difficult to defeat than an Iron Goblin, the Shadow Amoeba wasn't immune to their enchanted weapons. If the party only faced one of these mooks, the fight would go quickly.

Five more Shadow Amoebae flitted into view among the stalks behind the first one. Mithabel swallowed hard. "Holy sweet mother. How can we take on all those?"

Charli adjusted her cowboy hat. "I hate to be the bearer of bad news, but we have six more Shadow Amoebae approaching from the south."

"Ouch." Dylan caught Mithabel's gaze. "You and Amarynth deal with the ones coming from the north while I try turning the other bunch. Pray to the Goddess it works."

The lead Shadow Amoeba's HP dropped to 42% from Amarynth's third shot. One saving grace might be the slowness of the Amoebae. The Archer would get off another shot before the lead Amoeba was in melee range. Mithabel took her place beside Amarynth, enchanted longsword at the ready. "We could start running. You could stop every so often to take a shot. Whittle them down bit by bit. They're moving a lot slower than we can."

"Not a bad plan." The Archer's fourth shot lowered the lead Amoeba to 28% HP.

Mithabel lunged between two cornstalks with her glowing longsword. The blade sliced through the Amoeba as easily as swiping through air. The monster's HP zeroed, and the shadowy creature popped like a water balloon, spewing droplets of black liquid everywhere. A few droplets landed on Mithabel and sizzled as they sank beneath her skin. Black strands swept across her view like floaters in her eyes.

My mother is dead.

She squelched the thought, refusing to believe it could be true. Where had the thought come from?

"No damage, you good. Still on Route 66." The calm delivery of the Jamaican AI's report surprised Mithabel.

"Kaleisha, please say yes or no. Is my current Mental HP rated at 66%?"

"Aye, matey."

Some of the droplets had splashed onto Amarynth as well. "What the hell." The Archer threw Mithabel a disapproving glance, as though the Tank had been responsible for the black spray.

"Sorry." Mithabel stepped forward into the next furrow, hoping it was far enough to prevent the flying droplets of any future exploding Shadow Amoebae from spraying her companion, even though the move put her that much closer to the approaching group. "How are you faring over there, Priestess?"

Charli answered. "She's stopped four of them in their tracks. She's trying to stop the other two. None of them are retreating, not a good sign, but they're not coming closer either."

ChrisCross and Penelope continued yelling for monsters to fight. Little did they know they were the cause of a combat happening within shouting distance of them. With no clinking of metal on metal, the battle with the Shadow Amoebae didn't raise the same ruckus XStorm's battle with the Iron Goblins had.

Amarynth fired again. The missile whizzed through cornstalk blades and struck its intended target, dealing a whopping 66% damage to the closest mook. "Aim for the eyes, or where eyes would be if they had any." Oblong shadowy black blobs floating closer and closer, the Shadow Amoebae had no distinguishing features. The Viking's second shot at her previous target pierced the creature through the head, almost exactly where she'd hit it before. The Amoeba's HP now read 12%. "This is so messed up. Why isn't it dead?"

"Maybe your other shot was a critical hit." Mithabel could only guess.

"I've learned a few things about the Shadow Amoebae." Charli's voice carried little hope. "Light in itself doesn't hurt them, but your weapons would be useless without enchantments. They're immune to fire, same as the Scarecrow was. They're vulnerable to electrical attacks."

"If only I could fart lightning." Mithabel charged the wounded Amoeba, four others close behind it. The lead mook exploded, scattering black droplets over Mithabel. Again the black floaters flooded her vision.

Debra blames me for everything.

Mithabel put down the thought. Couldn't give these bad notions the time of day.

The floaters cleared.

"Still holding three score and six, bitch. Luck good."

"I'm still at 66% Mental HP?"

"As said." The Jamaican AI saluted.

The four remaining Amoebae converged.

They melded into each other.

One large Amoeba four times the size of an individual smaller one stood where the four had been. The four identification banners merged, now identifying the large monster as a Shadow Amoeba X4. Their individual HP status bars evaporated, replaced by a single, larger one, reading 400%. A shadowy pseudopod lashed out from the merged body, passing through Mithabel's armor and flesh.

A multitude of black floaters flashed across her view. Beyond the Amoebae, three Scarecrows appeared. How could it be? They couldn't fight three Scarecrows. Her sword arm and leather boots grew heavy.

"The road plunges into hell, bitch."

Amarynth stepped in behind Mithabel and aimed her crossbow over the Elf's shoulder. A bolt sped through the merged Amoeba. "Only twelve percent damage? This is bullshit." The Viking Archer grabbed Mithabel's arm and pulled her back as the pseudopod lashed out again, narrowly missing the Tank's stomach. "We should have run, like you said. Why didn't we run? Snap out of it, Mithabel. I can't do this without you." Amarynth slapped Mithabel's cheek.

The three Scarecrows vanished. The X4 pressed closer, moving faster than the X1s had moved, demanding Mithabel's attention. With a grunt, she stabbed at it. It's HP fell to 362%.

Dylan stepped next to Mithabel. "In the name of Scintilla, Goddess of the Sun, I command you turn and leave us be."

The merged creature fell back, splitting into its four constituent parts. Each had 100% HP except for one with 62%. The creatures didn't flee, but didn't attack, either.

"I don't know how long my turning will hold them. Are you all right, Tank?"

Charli spoke up. "I don't know how long your turnings should last, either. I can say that attacking the Amoebae breaks the turning, but only for the ones attacked."

The Viking aimed her crossbow. "Let's hope you're right, Guide. Mithabel, let's go for the wounded one and work our way to the left. Dylan, keep an eye on the six behind us, please. Charli, would you pick up Rolag and carry him west? Not too far. Just enough to give us some breathing room. You ready, Tank?"

Mithabel pointed her longsword at the wounded Amoeba. "Ready."

Dylan and Charli went to carry out their assigned tasks. Amarynth fired a bolt and struck her target but failed to slay it. The Amoeba lurched forward, reaching a pseudopod towards its neighbor. Was it attempting to merge again?

"Oh, no, you don't." Mithabel charged, hacking at the pseudopod. She lopped it off. Her attack cool down timer popped into view, with only a couple seconds remaining. Right. The heartbeat concept in action. Eventually she'd need to consider how to take advantage of that. Couldn't think about it now.

A bolt whizzed over the Tank's head, uncomfortably close, and struck the Amoeba.

The mook still stood, and pushed out another pseudopod. Choking down her indignation at Amarynth chancing a missile shot so close to her, Mithabel chopped at the shadowy appendage, separating it from the Amoeba's body.

The creature exploded. Droplets sprayed Mithabel and black floaters shot across her vision.

The Archer tried to kill you.

No, she didn't. Get out of my head, foul shadow thoughts.

"Johnny be good, chief."

That Kaleisha had used the word *chief* instead of *bitch* meant progress was being made in restoring a proper connection between the Elf and her Jamaican AI. The Scarecrow had made a proper mess of her mind, affecting more than her Mental HP.

"Next one, Tank." Amarynth fired. Her target jerked into motion, trying to grow a pseudopod. Mithabel lopped it off. The mook threw itself at the Tank, enveloping her within its dark mass. The shadowy shape *sank* into her, flooding her view with black floaters.

Mithabel staggered back, surrounded by a half dozen Scarecrows. Flailing wildly with her longsword, she fought to drive the monsters away. Weren't they supposed to be rare?

A familiar voice belonging to someone she trusted cried to her. "Close your eyes, Mithabel. Whatever you think is there, it's not."

Listen to her, Mithabel.

The Elf closed her eyes, trusting the voices of friends.

Good, now open your eyes.

The Tank did as instructed. The six Scarecrows were gone. Two Shadow Amoebae hung suspended in the air before her, motionless.

"Can't drive 55, chief."

"Are you with me, Tank?" Amarynth had her crossbow aimed at the next Amoebae in line. "Do we continue, or run?"

Mithabel staggered back. "Charli, can you swing a sword?"

"Not while I'm holding Rolag."

"Bring him to me. I'll carry him."

The teenager hurried over. "Seriously? You want *me* to fight them?"

"Lay Rolag down." When the girl complied, Mithabel handed her the glowing sword. "You've got Mental Armor. I'm sure you can handle whatever they dish out. If it looks like you're in over your head, I'll drag you out of the fray and carry you away. Both you and Rolag. I can do it." The Tank hoisted the Pseudo Code Dragon up and cradled the little guy in the crook of an elbow. "Don't leave these two mooks for XStorm to pick off easy. Wait for your target to move. Then stab it. Don't worry about their attacks. Not even an X2 can hurt you, Cowgirl." Mithabel was counting on it.

Charli beamed as she scanned the length of the longsword. The tip of the weapon dipped towards the ground, but Mithabel had no doubt the girl could thrust it into the shadowy monster. The enchantment on the weapon would deal its damage if it but touched an Amoeba.

Pushing back her hat so the brim didn't obstruct her view, Charli nodded to Amarynth, who loosed a bolt, taking the next target down to 74% HP. The Cowgirl stepped in, stabbing at the Amoeba and connecting without much problem, taking the monster's HP down to 58%. The girl jumped up and down. "Yee haw, I hit it."

The creature flew at the young Guide, its body swallowing hers. The thing imploded, vanishing under her skin. She shrieked, nearly dropping the weapon, and then laughed. "Oh, my gosh. *That* was awesome." Raising the longsword, she threw a knowing glance at Amarynth before giving her full attention to the last remaining Amoeba of the northern group. "Let's do it, Milady."

Mithabel whistled softly.

"The first four Amoebae I turned are starting to move. I'll try turning them again." Dylan began calling on her Goddess.

Amarynth fired and Charli stabbed, their combined attacks dealing 52% damage. Their target tried to flee. Amarynth shot it again. The creature exploded, not only to Mithabel's surprise but clearly the Archer's as well, judging by her expression.

With smug grins, the Archer and Guide rushed to help the Priestess, Charli stashing the longsword while she ran, to keep its tip from dragging on the ground behind her.

Without an enchanted missile weapon to aid the cause, Mithabel stayed a few steps back, cooing to Rolag. Dylan's second attempt at turning had failed, which didn't surprise Mithabel. In many games, a foe turned once was immune to subsequent turning attempts from the same Priestess.

The four mobile Amoebae merged, creating an X4. "Wait for my second shot, Charli." The Viking fired her crossbow. The merged monster hadn't reached them before she fired again, reducing the creature from 400% to 352% HP.

Mithabel offered a suggestion, "Try turning the X4, Priestess. It might split into four X1s."

As the creature charged for Dylan, Charli lunged, driving the longsword before her into the X4's shadowy form, dealing 12% damage. Not a lot, but enough to get the creature's attention. A pseudopod popped out of what Mithabel considered the monster's stomach and latched onto Charli's face. The girl howled in rebellion. She staggered back, drawing free of her attacker, lines of grim determination etching her cheeks. She swung the sword in an upward arc, severing the pseudopod, doing another 12% damage.

"Kaleisha, did Charli lose Mental HP to that mook's attack?"

"The girl is still the girl, chief."

Mithabel muttered in reply. "I'll take that to mean she

wasn't damaged." Charli's Mental Armor was protecting her, as Mithabel had guessed it would.

Keeping out of the monster's reach, Amarynth fired another bolt, lowering the monster's HP to 300%. The upper right quadrant of the creature exploded, while the rest of it remained, its body reshaping into an irregular oval as its overhead label changed to identify it as an X3.

Amarynth wiped her brow. "What the hell."

A quick check of the Mook Kills confirmed Mithabel's suspicion. "We're listed as having 194 mook kills. Dealing enough damage to convert the X4 to an X3 counted as a kill. Nice."

The Polynesian Priestess stepped forward, a hand held high. "In the name of Scintilla. I turn you and bid you begone, evil thing."

The threefold Amoeba split into its three individual parts.

Dylan blew out a breath. "Thank you, Goddess."

I can't belief you sent a teenage girl to do your job.

The Tank shrugged off the guilt trip. Charli was the best equipped to handle the situation. If Mithabel had taken that last hit, she'd be lying on the ground whimpering right beside Rolag. "The other two X1s are moving again. Now they're merging. Can you split them up, Dylan?"

The three Amoebae from the split X3 rushed Charli. One took a crossbow bolt to the head.

Charli swung the longsword, slicing shadow, further wounding the creature. The monster enveloped her for a suicide attack and imploded into Charli's body. The Cowgirl let out a *whoop*. Another Amoeba down. The other two she faced merged again, forming an X2. A crossbow bolt skewered its head.

Charli taunted the mook. "Come on, X2. Do your worst."

The merged creature flung itself at her.

The girl thrust the longsword into it, doing what damage she could before the monster enveloped her. It vanished under her skin.

Charli stumbled back and dropped onto her butt.

"Cowgirl looking down 82, chief. Direct hit."

The girl left the longsword on the ground and scrambled to rise, her feet not cooperating. She yelled. *"Run."* Somehow she managed to get her feet under her. Racing two steps towards Mithabel, she jerked to a halt. "Behind you, Mithabel." The girl spun in place, eyes full of fear. "They've got us surrounded. *We're going to die."*

Mithabel closed the distance in a jog and clapped her free hand over the girl's eyes. "Calm down, Charli. It's all in your head."

The Viking Archer called over party chat. "I could use some help over here."

"In the name of Scintilla, I turn you, evil thing." Dylan commanded the remaining X2 charging at Amarynth.

Mithabel gave the girl another second. "Shh. Calm."

Charli stilled.

"I'm taking my hand away now. You're okay, Charli. You did good. If that had been me, I'd be in a coma or worse now. Can you go back in, or shall I?"

Tears rolled down the Guide's cheeks. "I'll do it. I can do it." She grabbed up the still-glowing longsword and raced to Amarynth's side. Dylan had successfully split the twofold monster into two separate Amoebae, both still at 100% HP. The Archer played a game of tag with the monsters, trying her best not to become *it* while peppering them with bolts.

Mithabel's earlier plan clicked in her head. Amarynth was executing it. If they'd been on top of their game, they'd have carried out that plan from the beginning, and no one would have been hurt. "Stop, Charli. Let Amarynth finish them."

The monsters paused at sight of the Cowgirl. They merged again.

Charli charged, the tip of the longsword leading. Her attack did little to it. It swallowed her. A suicide attack was imminent, the last one for this encounter.

The monster imploded.

"She 53, chief. Powerful stuff."

The Cowgirl dropped the longsword, turned... and ran into Mithabel, who was ready for her. The Tank clapped her hand over the girl's eyes once more, holding her still. "Shh. Be calm, Charli. It's over. You did it."

Tearing free of Mithabel's hold, the teenager flung her arms around the Tank's waist, her hat riding back on her head, her pigtails quivering. Tears streamed down her cheeks onto Mithabel's armor. She laughed through her tears. "I did it. I did it. I did it." Her words trailed off into mumbling.

Mithabel continued comforting both Charli and Rolag while Amarynth and Dylan searched the area for any loot the monsters might have dropped.

After a minute the two gave up and joined Mithabel.

ChrisCross and Penelope weren't shouting anymore. No sounds of combat came from the direction of the Brassy Grassy. Did party XStorm rest in the cornfield now? Had they heard *any* of the commotion caused by party MAD and the Shadow Amoebae? There'd been no clanging of metal. While Dylan had spoken her turn commands over local chat, to be effective against the mooks, she hadn't been nearly as loud as XStorm's earlier shouts. Was XStorm unaware of another party in the vicinity? Please let it be so, Goddess.

The Archer took Rolag from the Tank. "This is the most loot-free game in the history of RPGs. All the fighting we've done, with only some Ferro Serpent scales and a Shadow Stone to show for it. And the stone might be cursed."

"XP Progression, chief. You sweet 71."

On the rankings, party MAD had 199 kills and party XStorm still had 192. Party OrionsDagger had been removed from the list.

Amarynth groaned. "We're only one kill away from earning the award. *One* kill."

Mithabel pointed her chin at Charli. "Maybe you didn't notice, Amarynth, but our best fighter against the Amoebae is in dire need of rest. If you want, you can leave Rolag with me, go out to the Brassy Grassy, and try to kill one Iron Goblin without its comrades killing you, but I recommend against it. Our objective now should be finding a way to heal our Mental HP, especially that of your Dragon. We need him functioning again. And party XStorm is somewhere close by. We don't want to fight a PC party in our condition. They'll kill Dylan if they find her, so they can claim the Longest Survivor Bonus Award. I vote we plop our butts down in the spot Charli picked out for us, hope no more Shadow Amoebae or Scarecrows come calling, and let Dylan recharge her Auni. Maybe Rolag and Charli will benefit from a sustained period of rest, too."

Amarynth petted Rolag. "You're right, of course." She led the way to the thick row of cornstalks Charli had identified as good cover. "But... we're *right there*. One more lousy kill. *One*." She sat, laying Rolag on the ground beside her, letting his head rest in her lap.

The party huddled close and rested. The glowing weapon enchantments faded. Soon, Rolag, Charli, and Dylan slept. A reptilian head lay across the Archer's left thigh and the other two heads occupied the Tank's thighs.

Silence reigned over the Mystic Hollow Cornfield.

Inwardly, Mithabel's thoughts churned.

I can't believe you let a little girl do your job. You're pathetic.

Indeed.

CHAPTER FOURTEEN

Neither Mithabel or Amarynth spoke, staying alert to their surroundings. The rankings for Mook Kills didn't change. Party XStorm was taking a break the same as party MAD. Had they given up, seeing that party MAD was only one kill away? How long before they figured out party MAD wasn't actively seeking that final kill?

An hour passed.

"Kaleisha, are you restored to normal?"

"Functioning still funky, chief."

"Can you recalibrate or something? I can't take this warped language from you anymore."

"Yo. I try."

Minutes passed.

"Recalibration in progress, chief. Please close eyes and clear mind."

Mithabel took a deep breath and shut her eyes. Tried not to think about anything. It wasn't easy.

I hope mom is okay.

"Negative emotions detected, chief. Please refrain from bad thoughts."

The Elf wiggled her pointed ears. Concentrating on the movement focused her attention. This continued for a few more minutes.

"Apologies for the malfunction, chief. Normal connectivity between us has been achieved."

"Goddess, that's a relief."

An hour passed in silence except for Mithabel's background

music channel and the constant twitching of Amarynth's left leg. Rolag's head now rested on her right one. Hovering two feet above the ground, Kaleisha silently belly danced to one tune after the next. Didn't matter if it was disco, pop, hard rock, or country. She swayed her hips to them all.

"Glad to see you dancing again, Kaleisha. But I didn't know Jamaicans knew how to belly dance."

The support AI stuck out her tongue. "Anyone can learn to belly dance. You should try it."

"Maybe I will sometime."

During the next forty-five minutes, the background music slowed, becoming more soulful. Kaleisha's movements grew increasingly suggestive, her hands often sliding beneath her spare electric clothing, caressing her nipples or rubbing her crotch. Mithabel said nothing while she watched, no words of encouragement or disapproval. The performance was strictly for her. Not even Amarynth could see Kaleisha. The Archer had Barney to keep her entertained. The Tank laughed once, imagining what a support AI named Barney must look like, and what sort of performance he might undertake to entertain his assigned PC. Perhaps his thing was stand up comedy. That could be enjoyable. He was probably bald. Maybe some sprigs of hair sprouting above his ears.

The clang of metal on metal echoed across the cornfield from the east. The system clock read 8:26 PM.

The Archer slid out from under Rolag, careful not to wake him. "Wait here, Mithabel. I'm going to sneak a kill."

"Amarynth, no."

"Shh, you'll wake them." The Archer sped eastward, cornstalk blades slapping her face.

Shaking her head, not wanting to believe her own eyes as she watched her companion racing away alone, Mithabel bit her tongue and said nothing. What was there to say? The Archer had an itch she was compelled to scratch. Mithabel watched using Third Person POV until the Archer was out of range.

The Tank waited, listening to the metallic clang of combat. Rolag stirred, but didn't awaken.

Amarynth reported over party chat. "I see them. What is XStorm's kill count now, Mithabel?"

"It's up to 196."

"I'm counting eight mooks around them. If they kill them all, they'll get the bonus award. I'm going to step out, shoot one Iron Goblin, and run back into the cornfield. I won't come straight back to you, but I'll make sure I've lost XStorm before joining you."

"They just killed two more. They're at 198." Mithabel grimaced, realizing she was only encouraging the Archer to act rashly. "You don't have to do this, Amarynth."

"Here goes nothing."

XStorm's mook kill count inched up to 199, tying MAD's.

MAD's kill count went to 200.

Kaleisha whooped. "System-wide announcement." She bobbed her head to the music. "Party MAD has earned the First 200 Mook Kills Bonus Award. *Congratulations*, chief."

Amarynth cried over party chat. "I did it. XStorm looks *so* pissed. Gotta run. Hope to see you soon. I'll stay in touch. *Oh, I'm having so much fun.*"

Holy sweet mother. Mithabel clamped a hand over her mouth to keep from laughing out loud. XStorm would be out for blood. *Run, Amarynth.* With her Increased Movement trait, the Archer should easily leave XStorm behind, leading them far away before doubling back. It was only a matter of time before Amarynth returned to her own party, alone.

Amarynth groaned. "I can't outrun the damned Centaur. What do I do, Mithabel?"

"Are you shitting me?" Dread clutched the Tank's stomach. "I don't know. Are you sure you can't outrun her?"

"The Centaur is *gaining* on me. Even with Penelope on her back."

"Sweet mother, Amarynth. Maybe act like you're an NPC. They already know you're in party MAD if they have half a brain among them. Don't tell them *anything*. Do *not* tell them where we are. Don't say *anything* to them if you can help it."

"Stop." Penelope called to the Viking over local chat. "We know you're with party MAD. You're fast, but you can't outrun us."

"Sorry, Mithabel. I'm going to die again. Might as well hurt them before they take me out."

The Elf huffed. "Don't die with your crossbow in your hands."

"Thanks for the reminder."

The Goth cried out. "Dammit, *stop*. We only want to talk." Seconds later, the Goth shouted again. "*Stop* shooting, or we *will* kill you."

"Barney won't tell me their HP stats, Mithabel. I hit Penelope twice, and she doesn't act hurt, only angry. Maybe they do want to talk."

"Is ChrisCross there?" Mithabel instinctively knew the answer.

"He's still back a ways, but running this way. He's not as fast as the Centaur."

"Stop shooting, Amarynth. Penelope sounds pretty confident you won't kill her before she and the Centaur can take you out if they decide to. Just don't say anything to them. Not yet. Maybe they'll let something slip of value to us. By the way, the Centaur's name is Ruby, if you didn't know."

"All right, I'll do as you suggest, Tank. I'm stashing my crossbow, and holding up my hands."

The Goth spoke on local chat again. "We know you're an NPC in party MAD. There's no need for us to kill you. We only want Dylan dead. This doesn't have to go badly for you, as long as you cooperate."

"Why do they think you're an NPC?" Mithabel mused over party chat.

"Why would I cooperate with you?" Amarynth asked the question over local chat. In doing so, she had revealed her name and Viking kindred to XStorm, but not her Archer class or her status as a PC.

Ruby scoffed. "You must be joking."

"Glad to meet you, Amarynth." ChrisCross the Elitist had reached the gathering. "Take us to Dylan, and we won't kill you. As an NPC, you don't owe her anything. You can join our party if you want to keep earning XP. We won't even hold it against you for stealing the Mook Kills Bonus Award from us, seconds before we almost earned it for ourselves. But we want a bonus award, and the only one left is for Longest Survivor. It's ours. Show us where Dylan is, help us kill her, and then you can travel with us. What do you say?"

"My allegiance is to Dylan. Kill me if you must. I won't tell you where she is."

Penelope snorted. "Your loyalty is commendable but misplaced, Amarynth. Party XStorm will win this game. We give you one more chance to tell us where Dylan is."

"I'll tell you on one condition."

Mithabel choked. What was the Archer up to?

Party XStorm stayed silent for a few seconds, no doubt conversing on their own party chat channel. Finally ChrisCross spoke. "What's the condition?"

"I want a magic weapon."

All three XStorm party members laughed. The Elitist gave their reply. "Don't we all."

Amarynth spoke over party chat so XStorm wouldn't hear. "You won't believe this, Mithabel. ChrisCross has a snake wrapped around his waist."

"You're kidding. Ask him about it."

"He might tell it to bite me." Amarynth returned to the local chat channel to address the leader of XStorm. "Did you know you have a large snake wrapped around your waist?"

"Oh, you mean Lance here?" The Elitist chuckled. "He's our secret weapon against the Ferro Serpents. They never know what hit them."

Too bad you can't see what Amarynth sees.

"Kaleisha, can you transfer my awareness to Amarynth? I

understand it's supposed to be possible."

"Initiating transfer, chief." The AI paused. "The Archer accepts."

The Elf's vision blurred. When it cleared, she looked upon Ruby, the female Centaur with a red mane. Penelope, the short Goth woman with straight black hair, straddled the Centaur's back. ChrisCross, the Elitist male with curly, shoulder-length black hair, stood beside them, a blue serpent as thin as a forefinger wound three times around his waist.

Christopher Warden has short hair. His avatar almost looks human with the longer hair. Not so mean looking. But I'm sure he's as vile under his virtual skin as Christopher is in real life.

Unfamiliar musky scents registered in Mithabel's brain, the body odors of the three people standing before the Viking, delivered to the Elf through Amarynth's nostrils. The swish of Ruby's tail sounded only ten feet away, as heard through the Archer's ears.

To complete the sensory experience, the Tank didn't feel the heads of her friends on her lap or the ground under her butt where she sat in the cornfield. Instead, her mind told her she was on her feet, holding a heavy crossbow by her side in one hand. Mithabel's brain interpreted Amarynth's five senses as though they belonged to her.

"Kaleisha, can you still hear me?"

"I'm right here, chief." The Jamaican AI peeked into Mithabel's field of view from the left, waving a hand. "You can always see and hear me, no matter where you put your awareness. Even if you closed your eyes, you could see me in your head. Cover your ears, and you could still hear my voice. You can't get rid of me. Not easily."

"With me being in Amarynth's head, can she see you, too?"

"Not at all, chief. Can't hear me, either."

"Tell me, Kaleisha, what are the limitations on this awareness transfer feature? Could I transfer my awareness to Dylan, and could she accept it, while she's sleeping?"

"You'll need to experiment to determine the answers to

those questions, chief."

"Yeah, I need to try it some time." Mithabel felt compelled to explore the boundaries of the game's features, but at the moment she needed to keep her attention on Amarynth and XStorm.

"Hello, Mithabel." The Archer greeted the Tank over a mental connection established between them by the awareness transfer.

"Hey, Amarynth." Mithabel replied over the same private channel. "This is weird and awesome at the same time."

The Viking Archer returned to the conversation on local chat, discussing the snake wound around ChrisCross's waist. "How do you mean? Do the Ferro Serpents think your pet is a friend to them, and then he suddenly attacks them?"

"Yeah, Lance can go right up to them and spring his special attack." ChrisCross wore white quilted armor, and no leather armor layered over it. His feet were bare, though he'd run at a good clip without wincing to join his party. He must have a high Toughness attribute or a Natural Armor trait or something similar. "The little fellow becomes electrified in combat, which does a number on the Ferro Serpents."

The man's voice grated on Mithabel. If she were there instead of Amarynth, she'd ram her longsword down his throat. No bloody way could she allow the avatar of Christopher Warden to beat out Dylan for the Longest Survivor award. His presence in the game made her want to puke.

Ruby glared at ChrisCross in silence. Probably using the XStorm party chat channel to scold the Elitist for divulging XStorm party secrets to Amarynth, and thus to Dylan. The man was a moron. He shrugged back at the Centaur.

The red-headed equine PC wore a suit of brown leather crafted especially for a Centaur, covering her human torso and equine back, flank, and her legs down to her ankles. Flexible joints worked into the armor allowed Ruby's knees and other body parts to bend or twist as needed.

Amarynth nodded at Penelope. "So, are you a PC or NPC?"

Penelope scoffed. "You must have a low Logic score. Otherwise, you'd know I'm an NPC, the same way we know you're one." The Goth wore a suit of leather armor with leather boots, all black, matching her hair. Her pale skin was white in comparison to her attire.

All three XStorm members appeared to be in their twenties. None of them had weapons equipped.

"You're right, my Logic score is low." Amarynth shrugged. "Can you explain it to me?"

Mithabel couldn't wait to hear Penelope's reasoning, because Penelope was the one who had it wrong. Good of Amarynth to play along, even if it made her look stupid to XStorm.

"Try to follow." Penelope rolled her eyes. "You and I are still in the game. Our names aren't on the list of Longest Survivor Contenders. So we're either PCs who died at least once and respawned, or we're NPCs. Our best information tells us, and perhaps this is the piece you're missing, dead PCs aren't respawning. Ergo, we're not PCs. We must therefore be NPCs. Can your little mind grasp that?"

"Oh. Yeah. Okay. I think so." Over their mental link, Amarynth directed questions at Mithabel. "Are you getting this? Why would they think dead PCs can't respawn? We did."

"I can guess. Play along with it. Ask her how many PCs she knows who died."

Amarynth returned to local chat. "I guess that makes sense. So, what you're saying is every PC who started the game except Dylan and your two companions here have died, and none of the dead PCs have returned to play. Sorry, my Understanding score isn't very high." That was a lie. "How many PCs has XStorm lost?"

Mithabel smiled inwardly at Amarynth's performance.

"We lost a couple PCs in our first Boss fight." ChrisCross frowned. "Asian twins. A Wizard named Bradford and a Priestess named Yuni. I hadn't activated Lance, not understanding about him yet. We hoped Bradford and Yuni would come back into the game, but there's been no word from either of them on any chat channel. We even went back into Voorton to look for them, with no luck. We met other NPCs who told us how they'd been in parties who lost all their PC members, and as far as the NPCs were aware, none of the PCs had respawned. Did party MAD have PC members other than Dylan? Did you hear from them after they died?"

Mithabel spoke to Amarynth quickly, before the Viking could reply. "Tread carefully. Might be best to pretend Dylan was the only PC member of MAD."

Amarynth shook her head as she replied to ChrisCross. "Dylan didn't want other PCs in her party. It's only me and her."

"Are you serious?" Ruby clenched her fists, looking ready to beat the truth out of Amarynth. "How could only the two of you kill all the Goblins and Bosses needed to put your party at number one on the Top Twenty List? You must have had help."

Amarynth bobbed her head. "Well... Dylan has her Dragon companion. I wasn't counting him. He doesn't take up a party slot, as I imagine Lance doesn't take up a slot in your party."

Mithabel mentally chuckled. "Good one." Despite the Archer having a sub-par Logic attribute, her average Intuition and high average Understanding and Inspiration were performing well, coming up with believable lies on the spur of the moment, made all the more believable because they weren't *that* far from the truth. "Maybe they'll think twice about going after Dylan now."

Eyes bugged on all three members of XStorm. The Goth was the first to find her voice. "Did you say, *Dragon*?"

Amarynth shrugged. "That's what I said."

ChrisCross turned to Penelope. "You told us NPCs can't lie to PCs."

Penelope nodded. "That's right. We can only speak the truth as we understand it, or keep our mouths shut. It's not in our programming to improvise falsehoods. If Amarynth says Dylan has a Dragon, then Dylan has a Dragon." She gasped. "I have a great idea."

Mithabel murmured. "I don't like the sound of that."

The Elitist spun his index finger in a circle. "Well, don't keep us in suspense, Penelope. Spit it out."

"There's only Dylan and Amarynth in party MAD. We have three empty party slots. Once all remaining contenders reside in one party, the Longest Survivor Bonus Award will be granted to that party. We simply need Dylan to join us, and the bonus award will be granted. We'll all get it."

Amarynth held up a finger. "But would Dylan retain the bonus awards she has already earned as party MAD? She won't do anything causing her to lose the three bonus awards she's already earned."

"So you're in contact with Dylan now? Are you relaying our entire conversation to her?" ChrisCross sounded excited at the prospect of Dylan joining his party, ignoring that she might not want to do so. Mithabel could see how having a Dragon in the party could have its appeal, even more so if a person had delusions about how huge the Dragon must be.

Amarynth nodded. "Yes, I've been apprising Dylan of everything said here." A lie, of course, since Dylan was asleep at the moment. "She says she isn't interested in joining forces. I'm sorry. And I must admit, I don't want to leave her party to join yours, either. So, I must be going. It was nice to meet you, XStorm. Good luck with your travels. And, let me add, if you're thinking about hunting Dylan down and killing her, don't. She's aware of you now, so she won't be caught with her guard down, and neither will her Dragon. I'm taking my leave. I suggest you don't follow me." With that, she turned and strode away between two rows of corn. She didn't look back.

Too stunned to move, XStorm made no sound. Mithabel switched to Third Person POV to watch their dumbfounded faces contort as Amarynth strolled away. When the Archer was out of sight range of XStorm, Mithabel switched back to First Person POV. "You were awesome back there, Amarynth."

"Thanks for your help, Mithabel. What do you think of this awareness transfer feature? Do you think any other PCs know about it? Or was *everyone* as reluctant to try it as you and Dylan initially were?"

CHAPTER FIFTEEN

It was and yet wasn't an out-of-body experience. Mithabel was outside her own body, but occupied Amarynth's. She didn't possess the Archer, but experienced the world through her. It rather felt like Amarynth possessed Mithabel, in control of the body Mithabel inhabited. The Archer's limbs seemed too short to the Tank's mind, bones and joints didn't fit together where they should, and muscles pulled in the wrong places. Every crunch of fallen cornstalk blades under Amarynth's feet sounded inches closer than it should. The brush of corn silk against the Archer's face tickled less than it would on Mithabel's more sensitive skin.

Amarynth chose an indirect route for returning to her companions.

Every so often, Mithabel switched to Third Person POV to check for activity behind them, not seeing any sign of being followed. "I'm transferring back to my body now, Amarynth. If you need me again, let me know. But I should check on the others now. What with you being physically away from them and my awareness being with you, there's no one on watch."

"Understood. I'll see you there shortly. I might do a few more loops to make sure XStorm isn't following me."

"Sounds good. Kaleisha, transfer me back to my body, please."

"Sure, chief. Note you only need to will it to return. You don't need my help or anyone's permission to transfer back to your own head."

The Elf went from running through the cornfield one

moment to sitting on the ground the next, her momentum dropping to zero as though she'd crashed into a stone wall. Disoriented, she reached out her arms for balance, though there was no way for her to fall since she already sat on the ground. She exhaled sharply and drew a deep, calming breath, letting it out slowly.

Dylan, Charli, and Rolag all three still slept. With any luck they were healing at a better rate than if they were awake. Guilt slithered down the Tank's spine at her abandonment of the sleepers while her awareness was with Amarynth. If Shadow Amoebae had attacked while Mithabel's mind was with the Archer, the monsters could have wiped out everyone here.

If enemies had approached Mithabel's unaware body, would her Danger Sense trait have warned her?

Despite her guilt, Mithabel found the idea of transferring her awareness to a sleeping person too intriguing not to try. It would take only a few seconds to do the experiment. She'd come back to her own body as soon as she knew the answer. Glancing around, she listened intently for several seconds. Nothing stirred, not even a breeze. Being mentally displaced for a few more seconds seemed safe enough. She focused her will, sending a mental request to Dylan, hoping it wouldn't wake her.

As before with Amarynth, Mithabel's vision blurred, but this time it remained blurry for several seconds, as though she were trapped in a fog. When her sight cleared, a white marble dais supporting a golden throne appeared. On the throne sat a blond black woman dressed in a yellow robe and wearing a golden tiara decorated with glimmering white pearls. A hollow sphere of gray mists surrounded the scene like a snow globe, obscuring what lay outside. Mithabel's feet vanished beneath a layer of fog swirling at the bottom of the sphere. She stood *beside* Dylan. She'd expected to be inside her friend's head, looking through her eyes. This was different.

"I see you brought me a visitor, my Priestess." The woman on the throne didn't speak over global, local, or personal chat, but used a telepathic voice rather than an audible one, with no icon to identify the speaker. Her green eyes pierced the Tank's soul, or whatever passed for a soul in an avatar. "Hello, Mithabel. I am Scintilla, Goddess of Light. Welcome to my abode. But I do wonder. Shouldn't your attention be on what's transpiring in Mystic Hollow Cornfield? Who watches over my Priestess while she sleeps? Who was watching over her while you were mentally traveling with Amarynth these past several minutes?"

Mithabel couldn't find words for a reply, dropping her jaw instead.

Dylan cocked an eyebrow. "My Goddess asked you a question, Mithabel."

"Beg your pardon for the dereliction of my duty. My curiosity got the better of me. I'll go right back. I'm sure everything is fine. I'm going now." Mithabel willed her mind back to her own body. Once settled again in her own space, she sucked in a breath of exasperation.

The Priestess still slept, her head on Mithabel's left thigh, her expression serene. The Tank took one of Dylan's braids in a hand and stroked it with the other. The hair was coarse to the touch, crinkly, not smooth like Mithabel's.

All was silent.

You went inside Dylan's dream.

Yes, she had. But how was that possible, not only for Mithabel to visit Dylan's dream, but for a virtual person to even *have* dreams? That was some sweet programming on the part of the game developers. Even though part of the virtual dream realm, the Goddess had been aware of Mithabel's presence. In this virtual world, what did a deity amount to? An AI with special privileges? How privileged was the Goddess in this game? Could she do anything she wanted, or had the developers placed limitations on her? And what were her motivations?

There were so many facets to this game. How much would she need to know to win it? Could she be spontaneous for the whole game and hope to win, or did she need a plan? Without game documentation, it wasn't easy to be strategic.

What would winning the game mean for Mithabel? Anything? It might mean everything for Megan Wright. Orc Wizards, Arachnid Behemoths, and Mad Cow Ballistas had invaded the real world. Megan needed help in fighting the invaders, but after Mithabel won that help for her, what would become of Mithabel? Would she simply fade into Megan's subconscious, from where she'd sprung, losing her autonomy? It had, after all, been Megan's decision, not Mithabel's, to play the game, for real world reasons.

Had time in the real world stopped? What did that mean, exactly? And how did it affect the virtual world? Was Khertaan caught in a time bubble?

Sweet mother. She could go on and on with conjectures. They served no purpose except to confuse and depress her. Megan believed she needed Mithabel to win, so the Elf would do her best for her player.

A primitive need to protect Dylan motivated Mithabel, too, the same way Megan had yearned to protect Debra Jones from Christopher Warden in the real world. Protecting Dylan was partly why Megan wanted Mithabel in the game. Megan Wright had failed Debra Jones, and she sought absolution vicariously through Mithabel's protection of Dylan.

There was more to it than that.

Oh, Goddess, there *was* more to it.

Mithabel wanted Dylan to be proud of her.

Another epiphany struck. The Tank hadn't wanted the Archer to be the one to win the First 200 Mook Kills Bonus Award for the party. Why not? Because Amarynth's earning the bonus award didn't help Mithabel win Dylan's admiration. How petty was that?

Mithabel continued to stroke Dylan's braid, imagining a purple snake in her grasp. The serpentine shape struck a nerve and she drew a quick breath. "Amarynth, whatever you do, don't come back to our location yet. You're being followed."

"I guarantee you, I'm not."

"*Lance* is following you. I feel it in my bones. That little snake in the grass. Don't stop walking, but don't come here. I'm going to try something." Though it meant leaving the group unattended again, Mithabel requested a transferal of her awareness to Amarynth, which was promptly granted.

The Archer traipsed through the cornfield. "Hello, again, Mithabel. Nice of you to come calling so soon after your first visit. What's your plan?"

"I want to see if I can use my Alertness trait while looking through your eyes." The Elf willed it to happen.

"This is unexpected." Amarynth mused over their shared mental connection. "Barney is asking me if I accept use of your Alertness trait. Okay, sure. Let's see what happens."

Granting the Archer the use of one of her abilities wasn't exactly what Mithabel had intended. Or maybe it was. After all, it was Amarynth's eyes and ears through which Mithabel was seeing and listening.

Slithering sounds abruptly registered in the Elf's mind. "Do you hear that, Amarynth?"

"*I do.* This is amazing, lending me your trait like this." Amarynth stopped in her tracks and whirled around, raising her crossbow. A flash of blue came to a sudden halt among the sparse weeds. The Archer aimed and fired.

Lance sprang into the air in an attempt to avoid the missile, but the bolt struck his tail.

"Direct hit, chief." The Jamaican AI pounded a palm with a fist. "The revelation of party XStorm's intent to spy on our party has granted me temporary access to their Physical HP stats. Lance's HP has fallen to 78. Accessing other XStorm member stats. ChrisCross reads 52, Ruby 30, and Penelope 88. Two party slots are occupied but grayed out. They must belong to the Asian twins, Bradford and Yuni. I have no access to their Mental, Spiritual, or Emotional HP statuses. Checking stats for party MAD. All MAD members are healed to full HP except for Mental HP. Your Mental HP has risen to 61%. Mental HP for other party members stand at 88 for Dylan, 57 for Amarynth, 78 for Rolag, and a full 100 for Charli."

XStorm had lost their healer, taken lots of physical damage since then, and hadn't rested enough to heal it all. Party MAD was still hurting in the Mental HP department, but she doubted XStorm could deal mental damage. Comparing Physical HP percentage ratings of the two parties, MAD appeared to hold a substantial advantage, but only knowing percentages rather than total hit points made the comparison problematic at best.

Lance raced towards Amarynth, fangs glistening. The Archer planted another bolt in his body before he closed with her.

"Ooh." Kaleisha clapped. "Lance drops another 20% HP to 58."

The serpent sprang at Amarynth, lightning playing over his scaly length. His fangs sank into her left forearm, injecting electricity into her veins. She staggered back as the reptile disengaged and dropped into the weeds, darting around behind her.

"Ow, devastation, chief. The Archer falls to 71% from one attack. Three more like that and she's dead. Odds for her survival too close to call."

Mithabel switched to Third Person POV. Running towards Amarynth and Lance from the east were the other members of XStorm. The Viking wasn't that far from party MAD's location. "I'm coming to help you, Archer." Mithabel returned her awareness to her body.

Dylan was sitting up, glaring at Mithabel. She didn't speak, though she looked to have plenty to say.

Mithabel raised a hand to defend against a deserved reprimand. "Amarynth is fighting XStorm. We can settle who earns the Longest Survivor Bonus Award. They're all low on HP. You and I are both full. Are you up to it?"

Dylan pinched her lips between her teeth. "Sure, Mithabel. No problem."

The Tank forced a smile at the Priestess while she shook Charli.

The girl moaned but awoke. "How long have I been asleep?"

Mithabel held up three fingers. "Hours. Are you feeling okay? We need to move. Now."

"I guess so." Charli sat up, rubbing her eyes.

"You have a Hide skill, right? Follow us, but stay back and keep hidden. We're going to fight XStorm." Mithabel turned from the Cowgirl to the sleeping Dragon. She nudged him awake.

Rolag's head jerked up, his eyes alert. He glanced around. "Where's Amarynth?"

Mithabel hugged him. "You seem to be your normal self again." She let him go and jumped to her feet. "XStorm is trying to kill Amarynth as we speak. They want to kill the rest of us next, especially Dylan. We need to kill them before they kill us."

The Pseudo Code Dragon leaped into the air. "I'm not fully recovered, but I can function. You should have woken me sooner." Without further hesitation, he flew straight for Amarynth's location, staying inches above the tops of the cornstalks so as not to give away his approach.

"Come on, Dylan. Let's win that bonus award for you." Mithabel grabbed the Priestess by the hand, pulling her to her feet.

"One second." Dylan beckoned to Mithabel. "Hold out your longsword." The Tank complied. A few seconds later, the blade glowed. "In case someone you face can only be damaged by an enchanted weapon."

"Thanks, Priestess." Mithabel chased after Rolag, Dylan close behind. With the little Dragon acting normal again, party MAD had an excellent chance at winning a fight with XStorm.

"Don't worry about me." Charli groaned as she crashed through cornstalks behind the others.

"Are you using your Hide skill, Charli?" Mithabel didn't take the time to look back. "I'm asking because you're being super noisy on the special effects channel, and I'm curious as to whether the Hide skill affects audible as well as visual perception."

"Give me a break. I'm still asleep." The Guide's commotion silenced. As Mithabel had hoped, the girl's Hide skill diminished the ability of others to hear as well as see her. With any luck, it would keep her out of combat.

Kaleisha flew ahead and to the right of Mithabel, bare toes wiggling in the air two feet from the ground. "Amarynth's HP has fallen to 52%."

"I shot ChrisCross." Amarynth didn't sound happy. "But the bolt bounced off his armor, which appears only to be quilted. He's got some Natural Armor or an extraordinary Toughness or both. Or maybe he has a class with skills focused on defense. He'll be a tough kill. No wonder he's survived as long as he has without healing. His Serpent companion is biting my heels, but the thing's electricity isn't nearly as potent now as it was."

"Go into defensive mode." Mithabel stashed her armor to run faster. "Hold out as long as you can. We're coming to help. Rolag is back to his normal self. He'll be there before Dylan and me, but we won't be far behind. *Don't die* on us."

Amarynth laughed. "I can't promise anything. Oh, there's Rolag." She laughed harder. "He picked up Lance and is carrying him into the sky."

The Dragon rose above the cornstalks, a writhing serpent in his clutches. Electricity played over the snake's body and up Rolag's legs.

The Jamaican AI squealed with excitement. "The battle of the Magical Companions." Her voice lost its enthusiasm. "Lance draws first blood. Rolag drops to 92% HP, his first loss of hit points in the game."

Team XStorm kept plunging to lower depths on Mithabel's scale of bad to evil.

The Tank spotted Amarynth ahead. Three arrows sped towards the Archer from XStorm, its members positioned some thirty yards away, ChrisCross in the same furrow as

Amarynth, with Ruby and her rider, Penelope, situated in an adjacent furrow, blocked by cornstalks. Their two missiles missed, but the one from ChrisCross struck Amarynth in the leg.

The Tank and Priestess both equipped their armor as they rushed up behind the Archer. The Polynesian raised her arms. "Scintilla, Goddess of Light and the Sun, I beseech your blessing on us, your servants." She glanced upwards. "Including our friend in the sky."

Mithabel's skin tingled from the Skirmish Morale boost as she raced past Amarynth towards ChrisCross. She hoped to draw fire away from Amarynth, allowing the Archer to get in some shots of her own.

An unearthly squeal from overhead drew Mithabel's gaze. The Electric Serpent struggled to escape Rolag's grasp, electricity jumping all over both of them. Finding purchase with his fangs, Rolag ripped the Serpent's head from his body. The blue snake erupted into a ball of lightning. Lance's parting blast of electricity rocked the Pseudo Code Dragon.

Kaleisha reported the Dragon's HP at 66%. Lance's dying attack had been a powerful one, to have caused Rolag so much harm.

A wail tore through the air from ChrisCross. Ignoring the approaching Mithabel, he aimed his bow at Rolag and fired. The Dragon easily darted aside and dove towards the man.

Both Ruby and Penelope fired at Mithabel as she rushed towards their teammate. A missile deflected off her armor and another grazed her forearm. They'd probably have time to shoot again before she reached ChrisCross.

A crossbow bolt whizzed past her from behind, striking her intended target in the shoulder. Kaleisha didn't report the damage he'd taken. Apparently it wasn't significant enough to report. The man had strong defense. Maybe it would be smarter to go after someone weaker first, reducing their numbers more quickly.

Switching tactics, Mithabel darted through the cornstalks

into the furrow where Penelope sat astride Ruby. At 30% Health, the Centaur should be the easiest to reduce to zero. With her out of the way, killing ChrisCross would be easier. If both Ruby and ChrisCross were killed, Penelope might surrender, being only an NPC.

With a raging war cry, ChrisCross fired into the air as Rolag descended on him. Too agile to let a single arrow represent any threat to him, Rolag darted aside, and the missile whizzed by. Diving at his target, the Dragon slashed his claws across ChrisCross's face.

The attack barely scratched the man. What kind of protection did the punk have?

Ruby and Penelope paid no mind to the fast approaching Mithabel, both taking shots at Rolag as he winged his way skyward to set up for another dive. They saw the Pseudo Code Dragon as the real threat here, no matter his size. Both their attacks missed him. The Dragon moved as though he had eyes in the back of his head, zigging and zagging to evade the missiles.

Another glowing bolt from Amarynth slammed into ChrisCross's shoulder, next to the other one still protruding from his flesh. He'd be whittled down to zero HP eventually.

Mithabel lunged, aiming her glowing longsword for Ruby's throat, above the neckline of her armor. The blade sliced flesh. The centaur's eyes widened, as though she'd expected her defenses to be stronger than Mithabel's offense. Her bow vanished, stashed in inventory. In one hand she now held a bodkin, a short dagger with a thin, stout blade like a stiletto. The weapon was intended for closer fighting than Mithabel's longsword.

Almost imperceptibly, Dylan voiced a healing spell as she tended the Archer's wounds. The ability of the Priestess to heal her party members might mean all the difference in this fight.

Rolag screeched as he descended. ChrisCross shouted in defiance.

Penelope fired an arrow pointblank at Mithabel's head.

Instinctively, the Tank twisted at the waist, and the head of the arrow grazed her cheek. It was a small wound, and nothing that could slow her down, but what if it had struck her in the eye? Would that have constituted a critical hit? Could it have incurred an instant kill? The only logical answer was one that chilled her to the bone.

Mindful of the Centaur's bodkin and hooves, Mithabel stabbed her longsword into the gap in Ruby's armor at the top of her leg. She jumped back, anticipating a counter attack.

Not one to disappoint, Ruby sprang forward on powerful equine legs, swiping with her bodkin, cursing when it failed to puncture the leather armor covering Mithabel's chest.

The Tank loosed a laugh, taunting her foe.

Rearing on her hind legs, the Centaur propelled herself at the Elf, hooves striking down. A second attack action so soon after the failed bodkin swipe caught the Tank by surprise, though it shouldn't have. Kaleisha had told Mithabel about the heartbeat concept of combat actions. Ruby was simply taking better advantage of it than Mithabel had yet managed.

A hoof crashed into the Tank's skull, smacking her onto her butt on the ground. Another arrow from Penelope caught Mithabel in the gut, piercing both layers of her armor.

Her attack cool down timer expired. The projectile protruding from her stomach had done its damage, but hampered her movements. She grabbed the shaft and yanked it free of her body. The missile slid out easily and evaporated in a puff of harmless sparks upon exiting her body, but, *dammit*, her attack action cool down timer started again. Sweet mother. Since when was extracting a weapon from one's own body considered an attack action?

The Tank could still act defensively, and she rolled aside as Ruby rushed to trample her. Being a Centaur gave Ruby so freaking many combat advantages. An arrow struck the dirt in front of Mithabel's face, dissolving like a sugar cube in water, but enough of a distraction to bring the Tank up short, and the Centaur landed a hoof against the side of Mithabel's head.

Ruby grimaced with disappointed realization. "You're not Dylan." By reducing Mithabel's HP, the Centaur had determined her identity.

The Tank replied by tumbling backwards and springing to her feet. A glowing crossbow bolt zipped by on the periphery of her vision, drawing a grunt from ChrisCross. Ruby charged, leading with the bodkin in an outstretched arm. Remembering her Feint skill, Mithabel pretended to go left, but reversed and went right, spinning in a circle to bring her longsword around in an arc, striking at Ruby's hind quarters. The blade pierced armor.

An arrow from Penelope went wild, thrown off target by Mithabel's feint.

The Centaur didn't slow down, but galloped towards Dylan. ChrisCross joined her. They wanted the Polynesian dead. They'd worry about Mithabel once their primary target was slain and they'd claimed the Longest Survivor Bonus Award.

The flurry of leather wings announced Rolag's continued survival. Mithabel caught sight of the little Dragon darting after the running man. Mithabel joined the chase, giving warning over party chat as she ran. "Head's up, Priestess. They're coming your way. I'm right behind them. By the grace of the Goddess, I won't let them hurt you."

Faster, Mithabel. Give it everything you have.

She stashed her armor again to reduce her encumbrance.

Folding back his wings, Rolag dove at ChrisCross's head. The man anticipated the attack, spinning around with no weapon in hand. He slammed his open palm against Rolag's temple. Talons gouged the length of the man's arm as the Dragon crashed to the ground.

Equipping her armor in the blink of an eye, Mithabel barged through a row of cornstalks and swung her longsword. Light on his feet, ChrisCross jumped and spun around, the butt of his foot striking her in the back and knocking her off balance. Rather than press his advantage, the man hurried on towards Dylan. XStorm's only desire was to kill the Priestess.

Mithabel raced after the man, Rolag lifting into the air and flying beside her. "Status report, Kaleisha."

"Yes, chief. The Archer's HP is about half. Rolag at about a third. Dylan and you each stand at roughly three-quarters. The bastards are shooting the Priestess and hitting."

Dammit. At the moment, Mithabel could do nothing more than run. She conceded, yes, she needed a ranged weapon. All three XStorm members had slowed to a walk, firing more arrows at Dylan. The Priestess hid behind the Archer as best she could while Amarynth returned fire on XStorm.

"Ruby and ChrisCross are both nearing zero HP, chief."

So the Archer and the Dragon had succeeded in whittling down the Elitist. It was time to finish him off. The Dragon dove at him. ChrisCross leaped high, spinning to kick the Dragon, holding his bow high and out of the way. This time, Rolag feinted low and darted high. The man's kick missed the little reptile, and Rolag's talons scored the flesh of the man's shoulder. Still alive, ChrisCross screamed in rage and frustration. "*Dylan.* Won't you consider joining us? Ditch your NPC friends and come with XStorm. This can end well for all three of us remaining PCs."

An idea sprang into Mithabel's mind as she drew close to melee range. "Rolag, grab hold of his bow. Amarynth, ChrisCross is all but dead. Shoot him again."

"Thanks, Mithabel. Barney suggested that too."

Two arrows struck Amarynth in the chest. She might have dodged them, but didn't try, her body serving as an obstruction behind which Dylan took cover. The Viking returned fire as Rolag descended on their joint target. The man couldn't dodge them both, and wasn't expecting the Dragon to go for his bow. Their tug of war ended as soon as it began when ChrisCross caught sight of the oncoming crossbow bolt. Releasing his weapon, he tried to dodge, but was too late. Amarynth's missile slammed into his gut.

ChrisCross burst into a mass of glowing dust particles swirling away on the wind like the poisonous cloud he was.

Rolag dropped the stolen bow into Mithabel's reaching hand. With a guttural laugh, she caught the weapon and stashed it in her inventory to lock her claim on it.

Ruby backed up, hesitating to fire her loaded arrow as though she realized the futility of her situation. She shouted over local chat, her voice edged with anxiety. "Looks like we're the last two PCs left in the game, Dylan. We can end our fighting now, if you'll simply join my party. If you want to bring your NPCs into XStorm, I can boot out all the XStorm PCs who've died. What do you say? Or Penelope and I could join party MAD. Wouldn't you like having a Centaur on your team?"

Mithabel walked as quietly as she could behind Ruby, the sound of her footsteps in the soft earth masked by the Centaur's shouting.

Dylan yelled back. "I want you *dead*, bitch."

Ruby roared in rebellion and fired. Taking that as her cue, Mithabel rushed in, stabbing at the Centaur's hindquarters. Providing the other half of a cooperative combo, Rolag swooped down, breathing fire into the Centaur's face. The end was upon her, and Ruby knew it. She stashed her bow and attempted to dart aside, but dodging both her opponents proved impossible, especially the area attack created by the Dragon's cone of flames.

The heat even warmed Mithabel beneath her armor.

Ruby combusted like a car crashing in an action movie.

The Goth rider crashed to the ground, landing on her back. She stashed her bow and held her hands up in surrender. "Please don't kill me."

"HP for NPC Penelope reads about the same as yours, chief. Oh, there's an incoming system-wide notification. *Congratulations* to Dylan for earning the Longest Survivor Bonus Award for party MAD."

"Do we get XP for accepting your surrender?" Amarynth asked the question on local chat so Penelope would hear. "Or do we have to kill you to gain XP for your defeat?"

The Goth woman gazed at Amarynth with a glint of

curiosity. "You don't act like an NPC. You deliberately lied to PCs. There are more in your party than only you and Dylan." She pointed a thumb at the Elf. "There's Mithabel, here, and I don't know their name, but there's someone else in your party who isn't even here."

"My name is Charli."

Damn, why had the Cowgirl spoken up? She should have kept her identity secret.

The Polynesian's gaze narrowed on Penelope. "Why did you think...?"

"Hey, Dylan." The Tank interrupted what she expected would have been a question that, in its very asking, would verify to Penelope that Amarynth and Mithabel weren't NPCs.

The Priestess stepped out from behind the Viking, looking perturbed. "Yes, Mithabel?"

"I vote that we let her go, if she takes her leave now and promises to go back to Voorton." Mithabel glanced down at Penelope, to see how the NPC would react to her suggestion.

Relief washed over Penelope's face. "I would make that promise. Unless you want to take me into your party."

Dylan shook her head with vigor. "That's not going to happen. But I'll vote with Mithabel. Amarynth, what's your vote? And you have a vote, too, Charli, if you want one."

Amarynth aimed her crossbow at the Goth. "I still want to know if I need to kill you to earn XPs for your defeat. Or will accepting your surrender earn me the XP I want?"

"You're *not* an NPC." Penelope sat up. "If you were, you'd know the answer to that question. That means..." Her eyes widened. "You're a PC who died and came back into the game. So it *is* possible. Oh, my Goddess. How did you respawn?"

The Archer fired her crossbow, hitting Penelope in the chest.

Kaleisha gasped, hovering on the periphery. "Wow. Don't mess with Amarynth. That was a 20% hit."

Tears welled in Penelope's eyes. "Please don't." She laid her hand on the bolt protruding from her chest, and it vanished.

Dylan grabbed the Viking's arm. "Stop it, Amarynth. She's surrendering, and I'm not letting you murder her. I don't care how much you want XP." She turned to Penelope. "Make us the promise that you'll return to Voorton and not follow us. If we ever see you again, it won't be easy for me to stop Amarynth from killing you. But first, answer her question. Do we earn XP if we accept your surrender, or not?"

Penelope held her face in her hands, covering the tears, her shoulders trembling.

"I can tell you." Charli remained out of sight and spoke over party chat so Penelope wouldn't hear. "You get full XP for accepting the surrender of an NPC. If she were a PC, you'd only get half the XP for accepting her surrender."

Amarynth prodded the NPC with the toe of her boot. "We accept your surrender. Now get out of here. Don't *ever* let me see you again."

Penelope jumped to her feet and ran eastward through the cornfield.

The Jamaican AI flew into full view, waving at Mithabel. "*Congratulations.* You are level six Tank. And a fifth of the way to level seven. *Congratulations.* You have earned an assignable trait point."

Learning the news at the same time as Mithabel, Charli bit back a shriek. Coming abruptly into view, her pigtails swinging beneath her brimmed hat, the Cowgirl ran to join her teammates, clapping her hands and jumping like a child who'd been gifted the toy she'd always wanted.

CHAPTER SIXTEEN

Mithabel put an arm around Dylan's shoulders and squeezed. "Are you all right?"

The Polynesian turned her gaze on the Elf. "I'm fine. How are you holding up?"

The Tank could lose herself in those sultry brown eyes, stroke those brown cheeks so perfect, so free of blemish. "I'm good if you are. Have I ever told you how damned pretty you are? I have this sudden urge to kiss you, and I'm not even that way, if you know what I mean. Did you do something to your skin? I can't get over how radiant you are."

The Priestess smiled broadly. "I added my assignable trait point to Beauty."

"Damn, woman." Mithabel stepped away with a laugh, looking Dylan up and down. "Is being a Priestess not good enough? Are you trying to become a Goddess?"

A tear crept from Dylan's eye. She wiped it away. "No." She laughed. "Yes." A serious expression crept over her face. "No. *No.* I've always wanted to be... I mean, Debra Jones always wanted to be...." Her voice trailed off.

Debra Jones was always beautiful.

Mithabel echoed the sentiment to Dylan.

"Megan Wright was the only person who ever told Debra Jones she was pretty." The Polynesian wiped away another tear. "But Megan and Debra aren't here. It's Mithabel and Dylan. And Dylan has the opportunity to make the whole virtual world see her as a stunning beauty. So she's taking it."

Mithabel wiped away a couple tears of her own and pulled

Dylan into a hug. They held each other and laughed while they cried. Eventually they drew apart, remaining at arm's length. The Tank stared at her friend. "The guys will go so crazy over you, they'll be killing each other."

Amarynth joined them, her gaze fixed on Dylan. "*Wow.* If we fight any other PCs, you'll be the perfect distraction. The rest of us will mow them all down while they're standing there, stunned by your beauty. Assuming *we* can take our eyes off you."

"Oh, stop." Dylan dismissed the possibility with a wave, but her smile proved she loved the compliment.

With a flurry of scaly wings, Rolag landed beside Amarynth. "You're the very definition of beauty, my fair Dylan. You're what every Dragon dreams of when a King sacrifices the most beautiful maiden in his kingdom to abate the Dragon's wrath."

Charli approached and slid her arms around the Archer's waist. She bent back her neck to meet Amarynth's gaze. "Your friend is pretty, but you're still the heroine of the story."

Mithabel fought off the green-eyed monster of jealousy. Dylan had her beauty and Amarynth had her adoring fan. What did Mithabel have? Danger Sense, Alertness, and Natural Armor. Functional but boring. "Kaleisha, what other traits are available for me to assign my newly earned trait point?"

"Sorry, chief, but you can only assign your earned trait point to a trait you already have, increasing it to rank two. Your choice which one. And it can't be your kindred-based trait. In your case, you can't use your assignable point to advance your Dark Sight trait."

"Oh, *fine.*" She returned to speaking over the party chat channel. "We all know where Dylan put her assignable trait point. Let's go around and say where the rest of us put ours. I'll go first. I feel I can't have enough defense, so I'm putting my point into Natural Armor. I don't know how much it will help, but that could be said for either of my other traits, too. How about you, Amarynth?"

"While you're all talking, don't mind me as I heal everyone." The Priestess whispered to her Goddess to restore her own HP first.

The Archer nodded with a smirk. "I thought about assigning my point to High Social Status. Imagine how special they'd treat me in the cities then. But it doesn't seem we'll be spending that much time in cities. I also considered putting the point in Magical Companion, and if I knew it would buff up Rolag, I'd do it, but it might instead give me a second companion. I suppose that could be interesting, but there's too much uncertainty with it. I decided my best use of the point was to assign it to my Increased Movement trait. I'll be running circles around our enemies now. Give that Centaur a good race when she respawns."

The blandness of Mithabel's own traits ate at her virtual soul. "You'll be running circles around your friends, too."

Jealousy does not become you.

"I'll go next." Rolag puffed his chest. "As far as I know, I've yet to use my Trackless and Nature Connection traits, so I put my point into Accelerated Healing. I'm hoping my advanced trait will help me heal Mental, Spiritual, and Emotional HP. I'll find out soon, since my Mental HP still isn't full."

Mithabel gave the Dragon a thumb up. "Let's talk about Mental HP after Charli tells us where she put her trait point."

The Cowgirl brightened. "Oh, you can guess what trait I put my point into. I don't know that my Complex Personality or Ambidexterity traits will ever be of use, but since we're still in the cornfield, I'm betting my Mental Armor will come into play again, and that's where my point went. After that wonderful nap, my Mental HP is full, and with my upgraded Mental Armor, I hope it stays there."

Mithabel clapped. "Nice, Charli. I recovered 6% Mental HP while I rested. I didn't sleep, or I'm guessing I'd have healed more."

"Yeah." The Polynesian laid her hands on Mithabel's shoulders. "You were supposed to be keeping watch. Instead, you were snooping around in my dreams. What was that about?" She muttered a healing spell.

A calmness settled over the Tank. She dismissed Dylan's question with a wave.

The Priestess finished healing Mithabel and moved on to Amarynth. "Maybe we should leave Charli on watch while the rest of us sleep some more." Dylan's penetrating gaze fell on the Tank. "But not until you tell us why you entered my dreams, Mithabel. And don't say you weren't there. Scintilla called to me as I slept. I answered her. That wasn't a normal dream, but a visit of a Priestess to her Goddess. So what made you think crashing our party was so important you abandoned your watch?"

Mithabel held up both hands, palms outward. "I'm sorry. I admit, I left us all vulnerable to attack. I'm glad no harm came of it, and I did learn something useful, but my actions were indefensible. Can you all forgive me?"

"What do the rest of you think?" The Priestess moved to healing Rolag. "Can we forgive her this one transgression? Or shall we make her pay?" Evil anticipation glinted in her eyes, as though she were dreaming up some vile torture for her friend.

The Viking cleared her throat. "Thanks to Mithabel's indiscretion, we've learned there's more to awareness transferal than the term implies. When XStorm's pet serpent was following me, Mithabel *lent me her Alertness trait*. I'd never have known I was being followed without it. I'd have led that snake right back to you all, giving XStorm the advantage of surprise against us instead of the other way around. Might have meant the difference between us killing XStorm and them killing you, Dylan."

Dylan cocked an eyebrow at Mithabel. "You *lent* Amarynth your Alertness trait?" She cast a final healing spell on Rolag and rubbed her hands together. "I'm happy to report Physical HP for everyone has been healed to 100% and I still have 22 of 40 Auni remaining. So... Mithabel... did Amarynth give you your trait back?"

"As soon as I transferred my awareness back to my own body." Mithabel shrugged and nodded. "I'm not sure every trait can be loaned. For instance, I don't know if I could lend her my Natural Armor trait. Maybe Danger Sense would work. It's something we should look for opportunities to experiment with. We need every edge we can get over other parties. So, everyone, please be careful not to say anything on local or global chat that will spill the beans on this game feature, or we could see it used against us. This game seems to promote PvP combat."

Rolag looked up from preening a wing. "PvP?"

Mithabel nodded. "Players vs Players. PvP."

"I think he knows what the acronym means." Charli lowered a weed she was chewing on. "The point is that you're being biased in using it. He and I aren't PCs, but if not for him, your encounter with XStorm would have gone quite differently. And if you want to get technical, none of you are *players*, per se. We're all avatars. Maybe the proper acronym should be AvA."

Mithabel pinched her lips between her teeth. "Sorry, I misspoke. PvP still works as the correct acronym, though I got its meaning wrong for this game. Here, it would mean *Party vs Party*."

"I want to transfer my awareness." Dylan snapped her fingers. "All of us should do it at least once to make sure we all know how. What do we do?"

Amarynth pointed at her temple. "Will it to happen. Ask your support AI to help if you need to. The person you're trying to transfer to will be prompted to accept or reject the transfer."

Dylan's gaze lost focus.

Kaleisha swayed to an electronic dance tune playing on Mithabel's background music channel. "The Priestess Dylan wishes to transfer her awareness to your body, chief. Do you accept the transfer?"

"I accept."

Dylan's body went limp, and Mithabel caught her, holding her upright.

The awareness transfer established a mental connection between the Polynesian and Elf. Dylan spoke first. "It's like I'm holding myself in my arms. You could have mentioned I needed to sit down before transferring. So... my body is... what... an empty shell? What would happen to my mind if my body were killed right now? Would my awareness remain with you, or would it be whisked away by my body's death?"

"You can still use party chat, too, Dylan." Mithabel spoke on the party channel. "We won't know everything that's possible until it happens. We don't know what would happen if you're in my mind and your body dies. Or if my body were killed while you're in my head. My guess is the transfer aborts and the mind stays with its original body. I'm hoping we don't find out through personal experience. But let's take this opportunity to see what else we can learn. Try to lend me your Beauty trait."

She accepted the trait loan when Kaleisha prompted.

The radiance faded from Dylan's unconscious face, indicating she'd lost the use of her Beauty trait for herself.

"Amazing. Wow. Mithabel." Amarynth, Charli, and Rolag spoke over each other, all of them looking back and forth between the Elf and the Polynesian.

"Try lending me your Unencumbered trait." After accepting the loan, Mithabel checked her inventory. Her four-by-six grid of slots had been replaced by one double-sized slot containing her longsword and the bow she'd gained from ChrisCross.

Dylan groaned over the mental connection she shared with the Elf. "I see twenty-four slots in my inventory now. That seems awfully restrictive. I see the icon for a Ferro Serpent scale in one of the slots, marked with the number ten to show the quantity."

A headiness came over Mithabel. "I'm guessing this one slot for the Unencumbered trait would expand as necessary if I stashed more items. What would happen if I put more than twenty-four items in this slot and then you withdrew the trait? Do you think some or all of the items would dump on the ground? Or would they be lost?"

The Viking slapped her thigh and laughed. "With the amount of loot we've been getting, I don't see that as ever being an issue."

The Tank put a finger to her chin. "And if you had put your assignable trait point into Unencumbered, Dylan, what benefit would that have given you? How can *twice unlimited* be any better than *unlimited*?"

The Polynesian switched to party chat. "I thought maybe upgrading Unencumbered would allow me to carry certain items that I can't carry now. But let's not ponder the options we didn't choose. How do I transfer back to my body? Looking at myself through your eyes is freaky. It's also weird that I can't *do* anything."

Mithabel bobbed her head from side to side. "Same way you transferred in. Just will it to happen. Ask Magnum for help if you need to."

Dylan's presence withdrew from the Tank's mind. The Priestess mumbled, caught her weight on her own feet, and stood upright. Radiance returned to her face.

"Oh, my goodness." Amarynth shuddered. "I've got both Charli and Rolag in my head right now. Charli lent me Mental Armor, Complex Personality, and Ambidexterity, while Rolag lent me Accelerated Healing, Trackless, and Nature Connection. Do you realize how powerful this trait lending is? I can't begin to grasp all the implications."

Charli's seated body didn't move, but her disembodied voice spoke over party chat. "The only bad thing is it puts the person doing the lending out of commission. I can't know if anything bad is about to happen to me. I'm totally relying on someone else watching over me while my awareness isn't in my body."

"Definitely." Dylan turned an accusatory gaze on Mithabel. "Which is why when someone is on watch, they *don't* transfer their awareness to someone *far away* without waking up one of the people they're supposedly watching over."

"I apologize." Mithabel rubbed her eyes. "It won't happen again. I promise. Can we take our naps now? Charli, you okay to keep watch alone? If you need me, give me a good kick."

The Cowgirl nodded as she rose, her pigtails swaying. "Can I borrow your longsword?"

The Tank shrugged and handed over her weapon. "If you think you're about to die, promise me you'll stash it right away. I'd prefer not to lose that weapon."

"I promise." Charli turned to Dylan. "Could you enchant it for me, for three hours or even longer?"

"A light spell with a duration of three hours...." Dylan paused to do a mental calculation. "That will use up nearly all my remaining Auni." Dylan tossed her hands. "But why not? My Auni will restore rather fast while I sleep." She muttered a spell and the longsword glowed.

Charli giggled and looked to Mithabel. "Can you lend me your Danger Sense and Alertness traits while you're sleeping?"

Before Mithabel could answer, Dylan shook her head. "First, we don't know if lending traits while one is sleeping is possible. Second, even if it is, it might interfere with our healing during sleep. Third, it might interfere with our trying to wake up quickly if there's an attack. While it would be nice to have a super-powered person on watch, I don't think it's worth the risks right now, for someone who's trying to heal."

Mithabel raised a hand. "I'm wondering if my Danger Sense will wake me if enemies approach. I agree with you, Charli. It would be good to always have that trait active if possible."

The Polynesian briefly closed her eyes. "I'm certainly not trying to tell you what to do, Mithabel. You're a grown woman. You know my thoughts on the matter, but you do whatever you think best. Like you say, it wouldn't hurt to know whether your Danger Sense trait will work for you while you're sleeping."

Amarynth smoothed some corn husks and lay on them for a bed. Rolag nestled against her. The two closed their eyes.

With challenging glances at each other, Dylan and Mithabel followed suit, lying down back to back. "Good night, Priestess."

"Good night, Tank. Stay out of my dreams." Dylan poked

Mithabel with an elbow. "*Sleep.*"

"How can I, with you poking me in the ribs?"

"I'm not poking you now."

"Shut up."

Dylan elbowed her again. "The phrase, *shut up*, is unprofessional language and inappropriate for use in an office environment."

"We're not in an office."

"Well, it's disrespectful no matter where you are. Now shut up and go to sleep."

Mithabel chuckled and checked the system clock. Even at 9:18 PM, the sun hung in the sky where it had been all day. She nudged Dylan. "When you talked to the Sun Goddess in your dreams, did she tell you why the sun isn't moving across the sky?"

Dylan muttered in reply. "Scintilla's chariot is broken. Go. To. Sleep."

CHAPTER SEVENTEEN

Light filtered through Mithabel's eyelids. She longed for the warmth of Dylan's body against her back, but it was gone. The system clock read *12:45 AM, Day 2, Year 1*.

Against the backdrop of cornstalks and a soft jazz refrain, Kaleisha drifted down into a prone position facing the Tank, lying on her side, head propped up on one hand, elbow on the ground. No, not quite *on* the ground, but floating an inch above it. "Good morning, chief. Would you like a status report?"

The Elf had slept for nearly three and a half hours and felt refreshed. Megan Wright wouldn't feel this refreshed after eight hours of sleep. Not that Megan Wright had slept eight hours in a single night since she'd graduated from high school. "Good morning, Kaleisha. Tell me something good."

"Your Physical and Mental HP have both healed to full."

"Oh, goody." The Tank yawned, stretched, and sat up. With a sly grin, the Jamaican AI mimicked her actions, like some mischievous mirror image. Everyone else except Amarynth was already sitting up, engaged in quiet conversation.

Approaching, Dylan gave Mithabel a smile as she walked through Kaleisha, oblivious to the AI, who floated up and out of view. Arms akimbo, the Polynesian towered over the seated Tank. "Good morning, sleepy head. I suspect Amarynth will be waking soon. She's nearly fully healed, too. The rest of us are all healed up, and my Auni is fully restored. There's been no movement on the Top Twenty List, so I don't think any other dead PCs have respawned. Other than NPCs and monsters, we've got the whole virtual world to ourselves."

Mithabel rubbed her eyes. "Did anything attack while I was asleep?"

Charli tipped her wide-brimmed hat. "Six Shadow Amoebae. Two of them merged into an X2 that imploded on me, but didn't hurt me *at all*." The Cowgirl flexed her teenage muscles and laughed. "The other X1s merged into an *X4*, and *that* didn't hurt me either. Having level two Mental Armor is awesome. Now, if an X6 attacked me, I might feel that, but fortunately I wasn't forced to face one."

"I might have said it before, but it bears repeating...." The Elf rested her chin in her hands for a moment and yawned again before continuing. "We're lucky to have you with us, Charli." She shook her head, clearing the mental cobwebs. "Wait." She stared at Charli. "You battled Shadow Amoebae *by yourself* without waking anyone?"

The Priestess came to the Cowgirl's defense, waving dismissively. "*I* was awake. I watched while Charli took them out. I would have stepped in or woke you if she'd needed help, but she did great."

Charli beamed. "Check your XP."

Kaleisha gave a report in anticipation of being asked. "Your level progression has advanced from 19% to 26%, chief."

"Damn, Charli." Mithabel beckoned to the girl. "I'm glad I lent you my longsword."

The girl returned the weapon to the Tank. It no longer glowed.

The Polynesian pointed at the blade with her chin. "My enchantment ran out minutes before you woke." She paused. "So I guess your Danger Sense doesn't work while you're sleeping. It didn't wake you when enemies approached, as you'd hoped."

"That's unfortunate." Mithabel stashed her weapon. "I want to try lending the trait to someone on watch while I sleep." She caught Dylan's disapproving gaze. "I'll be careful about it. But we need to know whether it will work."

Amarynth stirred. They updated the Archer about recent

events and XP earnings as she stretched. No one spoke of breakfast, because they didn't need food or water, a welcome aspect of the game. It was time to travel again.

Even though it was scarcely an hour after midnight according to the system clock, there was plenty of sunlight to see by, the same as during daytime hours, thanks to the sun being stuck in the position of three o'clock in the afternoon. The Tank glanced up. "Dylan, were you serious about the sun not moving because Scintilla's chariot is broken? Is that a thing in Khertaan?"

"Scintilla doesn't do jokes, Mithabel, and I didn't make it up."

The Tank squinted in the sun's direction without looking directly at it. "Sounds to me like a high-level quest waiting in the wings. Can't wait to see what's involved in repairing a broken sun chariot."

The Archer took the lead, heading due west, moving with the speed and sound of a 2015 Mustang GT with no muffler on a dirt road strewn with dry leaves.

I owned a red 2015 Mustang GT. With black-painted aluminum wheels. I changed its oil myself. Messy business. Nice car. Used to be. Until an Orc Wizard blasted it with a fireball.

Mithabel grunted. "Amarynth, why are you so noisy? Do you have some disadvantage you haven't told us about?"

"Sorry." The Archer stopped in her tracks. "Since I upped my Increased Movement trait, I can't walk faster than normal human speed without sounding like a locomotive. I hoped no else could hear it."

The Priestess pointed at her ear. "You *are* rather loud. Anyone who doesn't have their special effects channel muted will hear you coming from a mile away."

Amarynth took a casual step. "But not if I walk slow. Right?" Her legs twitched.

The Tank grimaced. "You can't bear to walk slow, Archer. Your leg muscles are practically popping from under your skin, itching to go fast. I'd prefer to take the lead to make best use of my Danger Sense trait, but you go ahead if you want. Please don't leave the rest of us too far behind."

Relief flooded the Viking's face. She scouted straight ahead and to both sides in the time it took the others to cover the same ground walking forward in a line. Rolag flew overhead to take advantage of his bird's eye view. Charli trotted in a furrow adjacent to Mithabel with pride in her step. Dylan walked ahead of Mithabel, casting furtive glances around. What a beautiful, shapely woman the Priestess was, even when viewed from behind. Or should that be *especially* when viewed from behind?

Wait. Sure, Mithabel liked Dylan, maybe even more than *liked*, but she questioned the morality of her feelings being buoyed by game traits. Though a virtual construct, she was more than a conglomeration of labels and numbers. She had independent will. Otherwise this game wasn't a competition, but pure simulation, an overblown implementation of a pseudo-random number generator.

Charli sprinted forward. "Hey, Milady, I've got something. My Landmarks skill indicates there's something important northwest of here." She paused. "Has something to do with quests. That's all I know."

Amarynth slowed. "What do you see, Dragon?"

"I'm not seeing anything in that direction. But I'll go in for a closer look." Rolag swooped down, ahead and to the right of the party, disappearing behind the crops. "Ah, yeah, I see it now. A hut made from cornstalks." The Pseudo Code Dragon flew into view, winging in a tight circle. "It's right below me."

"I'm so ready for a quest." The Polynesian picked up her pace, cutting through rows of cornstalks, the Tank on her heels.

The Viking quickly took the lead in the new direction. She stopped under Rolag's circling form. "Where is it?"

The Pseudo Code Dragon glided down in an arc, landing two rows over from Amarynth. He pointed with a talon. "Right here." He tapped on a cornstalk.

A dense patch of cornstalks rose to half again Mithabel's

height, comprising what could conceivably be the exterior walls of a hut, its thatch roof constructed of corn silk. On the west side, the stalks noticeably leaned in, with a black tarp covering a portion of the wall from the silk roof to the ground.

Dylan reached for the edge of the tarp, glancing at the others as though expecting someone to protest. No one did. "It must be hiding something important." She peeled back the canvas to reveal a gaping entrance. Darkness lay inside the hut. Dylan thrust her head close without poking through. "Hello? Anyone home? We understand quests might be found here. May we come in?"

Crimson flames crackled to life inside the hut, but shed no light on the interior. An aged female voice wheezed in faint reply. "Enter if you must." A cough seemed appropriate to follow, but none came.

"Thank you for your hospitality." The Priestess stepped through, followed by the others single file. "My name is Dylan. These are my friends, Amarynth, Mithabel, and Charli. We have a companion Dragon staying watch outside, if you please. We're party MAD. We come seeking a quest."

The four women huddled between the entrance and the fire. A dark, hulking figure sat on the floor near the far wall, cloaked in shadow, about twenty feet from the fire. On the outside, the hut hadn't looked much larger than ten feet by ten feet. Inside, it looked four or five times bigger. Easily programmed in a game setting.

"Yes, yes, I know who you are. I am Ezmerelda, Speaker of Omens, Giver of Quests." The seated figure did not rise.

The party members remained silent, waiting for an invitation to speak, which felt like the proper thing to do.

They waited a while longer. What were they supposed to say? Was this a test, and, if so, were they failing it?

Eventually, the seated figure spoke again. "Pardon me. It's just... Your beauty takes away what breath I have, Priestess."

"You're so kind, Speaker of Omens." Dylan leaned forward, trying to peer past the fire. "I'm sure you're beautiful, too."

Hoarse laughter escaped the old woman. "Please, call me Ezmerelda. None of my friends do. But enough with the introductions. Let's get on with the point of this visit." An arm at least five times as long as any human arm should be reached from the shadows towards the fire. Elongated, bony fingers held a glass sphere glistening in the firelight. "Behold your quest." She dropped the sphere into the fire.

A cloud of colors erupted from the flames, swirling to form holographic images. A three-story stone building appeared, graced with ornate columns, dark glass windows, balustrades, and gargoyles. Above twenty-foot-tall wooden double doors, words engraved into the stone face identified the building as the Maron Ministry of Commerce.

The scene panned to a nearby stone block building. A painted metal sign swinging over the door named it the Red Pegasus Inn. The door of the inn swung open and the scene panned inside, through a lobby, down a hallway to the end, and through a doorway. Darkness lay beyond. And that was it.

The scene remained dark.

Ezmerelda didn't speak. The members of party MAD waited in silence.

The system clock ticked off a minute. It ticked off another. And another.

Snores sounded from Ezmerelda's location.

Charli squirmed. "Um…"

The snoring stopped with a snort. "Quiet, girl."

Seconds later, the snoring recommenced.

Several more silent minutes passed.

Black light fell upon a spotless iron-bound wooden chest resting on a clean stone tile floor. Below a hefty padlock, a plate on the face of the chest bore the engraved name, *Ogaltha*. Indistinct figures ambled around the chest. With a bony finger, Ezmerelda jabbed at the scene, her digit piercing the holographic chest. "In there. A ring. Deliver it to me." She withdrew her limb. The colorful cloud fell like rain into the fire, extinguishing it. "Now, go on. Get out."

Charli smoothed her skirt. "Well, that was exciting."

"I said, *quiet, girl*. I can't sleep with such racket."

"Sorry." Charli backed towards the exit. "I'm glad I don't have your job. I'd be bored out of my skull. No wonder you sleep all the time. Bye."

Ezmerelda grunted. "After the ring is taken from the chest, no one is to wear it before it comes into my possession. *No one*."

Amarynth ushered Charli out of the hut, with Dylan close behind.

Mithabel paused at the exit. "Thank you, Ezmerelda."

"Aren't you the grateful one." Something the size of a coin whistled through the air and struck Mithabel on the forehead, then fell to the ground. "*That* is a ring for you, which you *may* wear. Don't lose it or give it to anyone else. I expect to see you wearing it next time we meet. Now take it and go."

"Uh, yes, Omen Speaker, thank you." Mithabel dropped to her knees and felt around for the fallen object. Her fingers found weeds and dirt and then a metal ring. She stashed the item in her inventory and backed out of the hut. "Thank you again, Oh Great One."

"Yeah, yeah, whatever. Put my tarp back good. Light keeps me awake and puts me in a foul way."

The Elf arranged the tarp over the door with care as requested. Finished, she turned to her friends, who stood with arms akimbo and questioning expressions. Did she look guilty? Tried not to. "I was thanking her. She instructed me to take care in replacing the tarp, so it doesn't let the light in. Seems she *really* doesn't do much but sleep." Should she mention the ring Ezmerelda had thrown at her? Did the Omen Speaker intend for Mithabel to keep it a secret? Why else had the old woman waited to give her the ring until the others had gone? Maybe it was best to wait until they had put the hut a good distance behind them before she revealed the favoritism.

Charli shook her fists in jubilation. "So we have a quest. Isn't that a good thing?"

Amarynth put a hand on the girl's shoulder. "It *is* a good

thing. Quests should help us earn the larger amounts of XP we need for advancing to higher levels. But, the important thing, and this is of the *utmost* importance, can you find this hut again when we return?"

Charli pouted and then burst into a grin. "*Of course.* I'm a *Guide.* When we need to find Ezmerelda again, I'll find her, no problem. I promise."

"Oh, *really*?" Dylan held up both hands as though to say, *what the hell*? "Can you tell us where her hut is now?"

Everyone looked where the hut had been. It was gone.

Rolag circled lower. "I don't see it, either."

Charli twirled her finger, pointing it at the side of her head. "When we *finish the quest*, I'll find Ezmerelda. Not before."

The Elf smacked the girl's hand. "Okay, then, *Guide*, which way to the city of Maron?"

Charli pondered for a moment. "We need to kill the Mystic Hollow Cornfield Boss before we can move to the next territory."

The Priestess raised an eyebrow at Charli. "Do we shout for it, like we did for the Ferro Serpents?"

Frowning, the teenager shrugged. "Maybe you should try and find out."

"Before we get into another encounter, can we prepare?" Mithabel equipped her longsword and held it out to Dylan. "Mind giving me an enchantment?"

The Priestess turned her back on the Tank and paced. "Does anyone else feel this game isn't about winning?"

Mithabel stashed her longsword and paced beside the Polynesian, peering into her face. "If something is bothering you, don't bottle it up."

"It's nothing." Dylan turned to Mithabel with a smile, which looked genuine but didn't feel it. "Let me enchant your weapon."

After the Priestess had illuminated the longsword, Mithabel brought out her bow. "And this."

Dylan averted her gaze. "Sorry, no."

"Why not?" The Tank could guess why, but hoped her suspicions were wrong.

The Polynesian steeled her jaw, her eyes glistening. "To hell with it. Give me your damn bow."

"Dylan. You can tell me." Mithabel touched her fingers to Dylan's wrist. "I'm here for you. I'm always here for you."

The Priestess nodded. "Since entering Khertaan, the *Subconscious* World, do you ever hear Megan Wright's voice in your head?"

The question took Mithabel by surprise, as did her answer. "Sometimes I believe so, yes."

"I hear Debra Jones in mine." Dylan closed her eyes. "And she *knows* ChrisCross's player is Christopher Warden."

"I'm sorry Debra knows. I'm sorry you know, Dylan." Mithabel staggered as though the ground had moved.

"I hate to intrude on this moment of raw emotion between you two, but something's wrong with Rolag." Amarynth held her Dragon companion in her arms. A tear rolled down her cheek. "He crashed and stopped moving."

"I'm sorry." Mithabel's eyes watered. "I'm so, so sorry for everything. It's all my fault. I should have been there for you, Dylan. And you too, Amarynth. And Rolag."

"I have value. I have value." Charli knelt, her head bowed. "I have value."

Something didn't add up. Mithabel hadn't heard the *whoosh* from her Danger Sense. She also hadn't noticed the long HP status bar make its appearance in the bottom of her view. But there it was. The party was under mental or emotional attack by the Mystic Hollow Cornfield's Boss, and hadn't even realized it. The infernal thing, whatever it was, even affected Charli. How could they defeat such a powerful monster? They couldn't even see it. Where was it? It had to be nearby.

The Polynesian's shout cut through the Elf's mental fog. "*Behind you*, Tank."

Or had Mithabel *imagined* Dylan crying out?

Taking no chances, the Tank whirled, slashing with her

weapon. Blood spilled from the wound she opened up in the creature standing there. *Charli*. The girl stumbled backwards, holding up her hands, covered in a sheet of blood spilling from her chest.

That isn't Charli. Avatars don't bleed that much.

What was the truth?

Amarynth screamed, an action completely at odds with her Fearlessness trait. She walked backwards, her hair on fire. Slinking on four legs, Rolag stalked her.

"Everyone close your eyes." The words were in Charli's voice, but didn't come from the Charli bleeding before Mithabel.

Do what she says. Trust me.

The Tank closed her eyes. "Say that again, Charli."

"Close your eyes." Charli's voice came from Mithabel's left.

Mithabel lunged straight ahead, her eyes still closed, her sword blade extended before her.

Charli screamed, this time from in front of the Tank. "*Mithabel, stop.* You're killing me."

Dylan cried out from beside Mithabel. "I call upon Scintilla, Goddess of Light. Please lay your blessings upon us."

Amarynth whimpered. "Rolag, please. Don't burn me again. I'm your friend."

"I'm not burning anyone. I'm in the air. What's going on down there? Why are you all stumbling about like drunken fools?"

"Close your eyes, Amarynth." Mithabel slashed her longsword before her, striking nothing. "Rolag isn't attacking you."

"Come to me, Charli." Dylan's voice was calm as steel.

A shriek rent the air, drenched with rage, despair, and fear. Nearby, Amarynth screamed in confusion and pain. Mithabel crashed to her knees.

"Rolag to party MAD. *What are you four doing?*"

"Stay away, Rolag." Charli's voice came from behind Mithabel. "You're no use against this Boss."

From near Charli, Dylan muttered a spell.

An unfamiliar girlish voice whispered in Mithabel's left ear. "Don't kill me. I'm not doing this of my own free will. The game is forcing me. I'm only XP to you, but my mind is all I have. Keep her away from me. Don't let her kill me. Swing your sword to your right. Do it *now*, Mithabel."

No. It's a trick.

The Tank locked the muscles of her right forearm. If she couldn't trust her inner voice, who could she trust?

Footsteps trod past Mithabel on her right, slow, measured. Charli spoke with a commanding voice. "Leave. Her. Alone."

"Please stop, Rolag," Amarynth whimpered in Mithabel's left ear. "You're killing me."

Charli spoke from beyond Amarynth. "You can all open your eyes now."

Don't do it. That wasn't Charli.

Dylan gasped from behind Mithabel. "No. Stay away from me. *I said*, stay away from me. *Leave me alone.*"

That's what Debra Jones said to Christopher Warden when he called her a whore. But he didn't listen. He continued his verbal assault, and she told him to shut up. HR punished her for that. I failed her. I can't fail her again.

Amarynth sobbed. "Rolag, no."

"*Die*, Boss monster." Charli's voice came from right in front of Mithabel.

A blade sliced through Mithabel's armor, entered her chest, and twisted. The Tank coughed. Warm, viscous liquid rose in her throat.

You're not bleeding.

The unfamiliar girlish voice whispered in the Tank's left ear. "Fight back, Mithabel, or you're dead. Charli thinks you're the Boss monster."

Dylan shouted, her voice echoing in all directions. "Shut up, shut up, shut up."

The unknown girl laughed, her voice dripping with malice. "That's unprofessional of you, Dylan. I'm putting you on probation. You're all on probation. One more sound from any of you, and you're expelled from the game."

Amarynth groaned, the sound cut short in mid utterance.

"I warned her. The rest of you do as I say, or you're *all* expelled."

Another blade stabbed Mithabel in the back. Her instincts screamed for her to strike back, but instead, she reversed her sword, pointing its tip at herself. "Charli, take my weapon."

"Stash it, Mithabel." Had Charli said that?

"No. Strike now. *Strike now.*" Or had Charli said that?

The Tank reversed her weapon again and opened her eyes.

Charli stood there, her hands thrust inside a blob of darkness twice her height, vaguely oblong, floating six inches off the ground, much like a Shadow Amoeba. Beyond the pair, Amarynth lay on the ground, twitching. On her knees behind Charli, Dylan gagged, her body heaving as though she were trying to vomit.

Mithabel thrust her blade into the blackness and closed her eyes again.

The girlish voice, grown familiar, uttered a sigh. "Traitor."

Something *popped.* Floaters flooded Mithabel's vision behind closed eyelids.

What had she done? She'd killed a little girl. Not Charli, but someone like Charli. How could she live with the guilt? She collapsed to her knees, dropping her blade in the dirt and hanging her head. Should she cry? Did she want to? No. Yes. *No.*

It wasn't a little girl, Mithabel. It was a dark blob.

The HP status bar for the Boss emptied to zero and slid out of sight. Somehow they'd beaten it, but at what cost? "Kaleisha, report."

"Oh, chief. That was a rough one. But our connection survived it, I'm glad to say." The Jamaican AI paused, ominous tones of suspenseful movie music filling the silence. "The Archer is nearly in a coma, at about 10% Mental HP. Dylan is around a quarter of max capacity. She's close to being as incapacitated as Rolag was before. Thank the Goddess, you're faring much better than either of them, at over two-thirds capacity. Rolag and Charli are both fine. The Dragon was smart enough to stay out of range of the Boss's mental manipulations, and apparently Charli's level two Mental Armor gave her adequate protection against the Boss. Your XP progression has advanced from 26% to 56%."

"Thirty percent? That's all?" For what they'd endured, the XP gains were spare. That encounter should have earned everyone a level. Damn those game developers. Not that Mithabel had expected the game to be easy, but this was virtual insanity. *Literally.*

Amid mewls and whimpers, Amarynth and Dylan muttered occasional incomprehensible words.

Charli stood nearby, looking at the ground, her grim expression framed by her pigtails to either side, her brimmed hat above, and the glow of her enchanted hands below. "It's over. You three should sleep now. There's no way we're going *anywhere* until you do." She paused, as though waiting for someone to contradict her.

The Tank shivered as she turned her attention to her companions. Amarynth lay in a fetal position, hands clasped behind her neck, muscles randomly convulsing. Dylan's face pressed the dirt, her knees bunched beneath her chest, her back straining to rise. Charli was right. Mithabel could stagger away, but Dylan and Amarynth were going nowhere. Crossing her arms, the Tank gazed again at Charli.

They both stood still.

Quiet as death.

The teenager puffed her chest and continued. "Rolag, please keep watch the best you can from the sky. *Don't* come down here. If anything approaches you in the air, keep your distance. None of the mooks in this territory can be fought physically, and they're all immune to fire. Everyone in the party except you and me need to heal before we go anywhere, and I'm going to help them with that." The girl glanced at Mithabel and pointed to Dylan. Then she strode to Amarynth and sat beside her. With glowing hands, the girl stroked Amarynth's hair. "You'll be fine, Milady. You only need to sleep."

The Archer whimpered, curling up tighter in a fetal ball.

Without warning, Dylan sprang to her feet, mumbling and whining, her hands raised as though in an attempt to turn some unseen undead thing.

The Elf staggered to the Priestess. "Lie down, Dylan. The Boss is dead. It's over. You need to sleep, to heal." She picked up and cradled the brown woman, rocking her, singing to her, pausing once to press a kiss to her cheek. Mithabel's Brawn attribute wasn't high enough to carry Dylan indefinitely, but two minutes of rockabye sufficed to calm the Priestess. Mithabel stretched her on the ground and sat beside her, stroking her cheek and continuing to softly sing. After a couple minutes of this, Dylan slept.

Amarynth had fallen asleep too.

"Thank you for your help against the Shadow Protean, Mithabel." Charli continued stroking the Archer's hair. "The combined magic of your longsword and my hands killed the Boss. Thank Scintilla that Dylan had the presence of mind to cast her Light spell on me before she'd descended too far into madness."

"Shadow Protean." Mithabel filed the name away in her mind. "I never want to meet another one of those as long as I live. For that matter, I don't want to meet one after I'm dead. It's a good thing you placed your extra trait point in Mental Armor. I think upping my Natural Armor helped, and my extraordinary Sanity maybe didn't hurt either, or I'd be as much a mess as these two. If that thing respawns while we're still here...." Her voice failed her.

"...and it comes at us with a twin." Charli finished Mithabel's sentence. "It *will*, eventually. But this is the safest place we can be. The Boss probably won't respawn where it died. We should have an hour at least before it respawns. If we stay very quiet, it might not come upon us for two, three, or more hours afterward. You should get some sleep too. Rolag and I will keep watch. If you want to lend me your Danger Sense and Alertness traits first, we can experiment to see what happens with that when you try to sleep."

The system clock read *2:53 AM, Day 2, Year 1*. "I'm game for that. Do you want my sword? How long will your hands glow?"

"Stash your weapon, Tank." Charli held up her hands. "When these babies stop glowing, if I feel the need to wake you, I won't hesitate."

Mithabel did as the Cowgirl instructed and then nestled against Dylan, spooning the Polynesian. Once settled, she transferred her awareness to Charli and willed the two traits to the girl.

"Thanks, Mithabel. Do I need to concentrate on the traits for them to work?"

"I never have. I don't know much about the Alertness trait. With the Danger Sense trait, I hear a *whoosh* from the direction the enemy will first attack from. I didn't hear one for the Shadow Protean, but now I'm wondering if the Boss made me forget it as soon as it sounded."

"That's possible and plausible. Okay, then. Now for the real test. We'll see if I keep the traits after you fall asleep. *If* you can fall asleep while you're in my head. And if you do fall asleep in my head, let's hope your Mental HP can heal."

"Good night, Charli. Thank the Goddess you're in our party."

Sleep, Mithabel.

CHAPTER EIGHTEEN

The system clock read *6:01 AM, Day 2, Year 1.*

The Jamaican AI played air guitar to a hard rock tune. "Good morning, chief. You'll be happy to know all your HP statuses are reading 100%. Your XP progression has risen to 70%. Charli has been busy."

"How's she doing?" Mithabel walked among cornstalks. But… she'd only been awake for a few seconds. Had she been sleepwalking?

"The Guide is functioning at 79% Mental HP."

"Oh, good. I think. Can you change the song, please? Something soft. Maybe lower the volume too?" The Tank tried to turn her head, but it wouldn't turn. Her legs wouldn't stop moving.

"Sure, sure. Sorry, chief."

"What is wrong with me, Kaleisha? I can't control my body."

"Hey, Mithabel." The voice belonged to Charli, coming across the mental connection they'd established when Mithabel transferred her awareness to the girl before falling asleep. "You're awake."

Ah. That explained it. Mithabel was still in the Cowgirl's head. "Hey, Charli."

The Guide paced in a furrow, back and forth past three prone bodies, one of them Mithabel's. "How are you? I wish I could read your status, but that's not in my programming."

"I'm healed to full on everything. And thanks for the XP boost. How are you faring?" The Tank transferred her awareness back to her own body and sat up, using her own eyes to assess the Guide.

Darkness rimmed the teenager's eyes and her shoulders slumped. Her hands no longer glowed. She forced a grin. "I could use some sleep. Fought a couple of X6s. I couldn't hurt them, because my hands had stopped glowing by then. They both imploded on me. The first X6 didn't affect me, which I was *so* glad about. You have no idea. But then I thought I'd be immune to the second X6, and it *hurt*. There must be some chance for any attack to be a critical hit, whether the attacker is PC, NPC, or monster. Whatever."

"You should have awoken me, Charli." Mithabel equipped her longsword. Like Charli's hands, it had lost its glow. She stashed it again.

Charli shook her head. "It's okay. Would you take watch now? I can transfer my Mental Armor trait to you while I sleep and heal. It should work. Your Danger Sense trait worked for me. I'm sure Dylan and Amarynth need a lot more time to heal fully, since they seemed way worse than you. Wake me if you need me. I'm serious." Putting her hat aside, Charli lay next to Amarynth, making only a token fuss about her clothes getting dirty.

The Jamaican AI piped up. "Charli wishes to transfer her awareness to your mind, chief. Do you accept?"

"Yes, thanks, Kaleisha. Accept the awareness transfer and any traits she offers."

The Cowgirl's body stilled. Her voice sounded in the Elf's head. "Hi, Mithabel. Don't mind me. I'll be over in this corner of your brain, dozing." Her presence went dormant, curling up like a cat taking a nap within Mithabel's head space.

The Tank laid back next to Dylan, watching Rolag circling overhead. Should she tell the others about the ring Ezmerelda had given her? Was it magical? Did she trust Ezmerelda not to give her a cursed item? For that matter, was the so-called quest Ezmerelda had given the party a real quest? In many other games, the system asked whether the character accepted the quest. But not in Khertaan.

"Kaleisha, what can you tell me about the quest we've received?"

"I can replay the holographic images you saw in the hut, chief."

The words, *Ezmerelda's Quest*, appeared near the top of the Elf's field of vision. Below it, a scene as though from a movie played before her, filling the center of her view, obscuring the sky.

A three-story stone block building appeared, with columns, dark glass windows, balustrades, and gargoyles, the name *Maron Ministry of Commerce* engraved into the front wall above double doors tall enough to admit giants. Not *super huge* giants. The scene shifted to the nearby Red Pegasus Inn, sporting a door sized for humans, about a quarter of the height of the double doors at the Ministry of Commerce. The door swung open and the scene panned inside, moving through a lobby, down a hallway, and pausing before a door at the end of the hall. The door opened, and the scene entered the darkness beyond.

"Kaleisha, fast forward to the part with the chest, please."

What would have been ten minutes of darkness transpired in ten seconds. The scene zoomed in on an iron-bound wooden chest, locked with a padlock. A plate on the face of the chest under the padlock bore the engraved name, *Ogaltha*. Indistinct figures meandered in the area surrounding the chest.

"Pause here." Mithabel still couldn't identify the figures. "Damn. Okay. Continue."

Ezmerelda's voice spoke across Mithabel's special effects channel. "In there. A ring. Deliver it to me."

The scene faded.

"Show me the rankings page, Kaleisha."

A new list had begun, titled *Top Individual Avatars*. Mithabel's name was the only one listed. Woah. Only one reason explained why she was alone on the list. She had a ring from Ezmerelda. How could she explain this to Dylan and Amarynth?

She'd cross that bridge when the time came. Neither of them had seen the new list yet.

The Top Twenty Parties list showed *MAD, XStorm, BoardStiff, Quantized, OrionsDagger,* and *ZAvengers.* There were no longer any contenders lists for bonus awards.

Wait.

"Kaleisha. When did BoardStiff and Quantized move into the top five parties?"

"Within the past three hours, chief."

"They're active again. They figured out how to respawn. The game is on."

"As you say, chief. Oh. I have a message incoming. *System-wide notification:* A bounty is hereby placed on the head of the Longest Survivor, Dylan, of Party MAD. Twenty-thousand XP will be granted to each member of the party who delivers the killing blow to the bounty target. Members of party MAD are excluded from claiming this bonus."

"Damn, Kaleisha. Are you sure? Show me the XP Progression table." The Progression table confirmed her recollection. Twenty-thousand XP would put a character to level seven. More XP than Mithabel had earned so far in the game. Turning up her Temperament filter to hold back her anger at the clear discrimination the game had leveled at party MAD for simply being ahead, she returned her attention to the rankings.

A new contenders list appeared, entitled, *Longest Survivor Bounty Contenders.* This was one list party MAD couldn't place on, but they'd do their damnedest to stop anyone from claiming the prize.

XStorm, Quantized, and BoardStiff populated the list, in that order. Did the order mean something, such as which party had the best odds of killing Dylan? How twisted was that? Or maybe it was an indication of how close in proximity the parties were to Dylan. That made some sense, and could explain why XStorm was listed first. Penelope probably hadn't gone back to Voorton. Chances were, she was hanging out at the border between the Brassy Grassy and the Mystic Hollow

Cornfield.

Whoosh.

No more time for musings and reflections.

Rolag uttered a warning, too. "Incoming, Mithabel. Two bands of six Shadow Amoebae just spawned and are headed your way. They're close but moving slow."

Mithabel hopped to her feet. Her longsword would be of no value in the coming encounter, so she left it in inventory. Her leather and quilted armor would do her no good against these mooks, either. In fact, they'd only serve to encumber her. She'd be better off fighting the mooks naked.

Why not?

Indeed. She stashed her layers of armor, keeping on nothing but her bra, panties, and boots, allowing her to act with more speed and agility. "Come on, you bastards. Show me what you got." If some developer was monitoring her and got an eyeful, she didn't care. Her survival was on the line. She needed any edge she could get. But when the party found a clothing shop, she and Dylan needed to invest in some stylish running outfits.

As to the present, sweet mother, *twelve* Shadow Amoebae all at once. She was determined not to wake Dylan, who probably wasn't yet in any condition to cast a spell anyway. But without a magic weapon, Mithabel couldn't take the offensive. The only way the Amoebae would die was through their suicide implosion attacks. The Elf needed to keep too many of them from merging and coax them into attacking her while small. Nothing larger than an X5 if possible. No way could she handle a suicide attack from an X12.

The Tank strode towards the approaching groups of lumbering mooks. Thank the Goddess they didn't move fast at their small size.

They move faster than sleeping people.

Rather than close with the Tank, all twelve creatures moved towards each other. Their intent was clear. The implosion attack of a Shadow Amoeba X12 would effectively lobotomize her. She might never heal from such a blow to her mind.

That kind of attack might even affect me in the real world. It could put me into a coma I'd never come out of. How could Fanciful Pegasus create such brutality and pass it off as a game? It's because there's more to Khertaan than a competition for a million dollar prize. The real world is at stake, and it's up to us to save it. Don't shut me out, Mithabel.

The Elf bit back a scream of rage. Was Megan Wright speaking to her, or was she imagining it? Was she under attack from another Shadow Protean? When Dylan had called their party *MAD*, she hadn't realized how literally the name might come to apply to them.

Ignoring the voice in her head, the Tank raced towards the lead group of foes. None of them had merged yet. If some of them would suicide attack her as X1s, her overall chances of survival increased.

Reaching the closest Amoeba, she threw herself into it, relying on her Armor traits to prevent any damage. To her pleasant surprise, the creature imploded on her. Black floaters swept across her field of vision.

Kaleisha chimed in. "No change in your status, chief." The background music changed to the hard rock song the Jamaican AI had been listening to earlier. "Is this music appropriate now?"

"Yeah, sure. Thanks for the report." One mook down, eleven to go. Mithabel ran for the next closest Amoeba, throwing herself into it. It also imploded on her.

"Still no effect on you, chief. Doing good."

"Nice to hear bad grammar from you, Kaleisha. It cheers my heart knowing your perfection enables imperfection. You'll make a human yet."

"I shudder at the thought, chief."

Mithabel's tactic had worked splendidly. With a chuckle, she raced to a third Shadow Amoeba and flung herself into its shadowy, insubstantial form.

This one didn't implode, but kept moving towards its companions for the merge. Two of its fellows had already failed to harm Mithabel, and this one was smart enough not to fall for the same trick a third time. The mooks in this game learned from their failures. With no instinct for self-preservation, the game monsters existed only to kill, even if it took their own lives in the process, but they wouldn't repeat twice-failed tactics.

There appeared to be no alternative to waking Dylan. Mithabel ran a couple yards towards the sleepers and then stopped. Sweet mother, she *might* have something magical.

Ezmerelda's ring.

It couldn't hurt to try it, trusting Ezmerelda not to have given her a cursed item. Racing back towards the merging mooks, she equipped the accessory.

An X4 loomed above the cornstalks.

Wait on that one.

Fine. She raced to the lead X1 approaching from the second group and thrust her hand into its black form. The Amoeba paused, lashing at Mithabel with a pseudopod. The appendage swept through her.

"You're still good, chief."

The HP bar suspended over the creature's head dropped to 22%. Sweet mother. She'd nearly killed the thing with one hit.

A moment later, her attack cool down period expired, and she swiped her hand through the thing again. It exploded into dark dust.

Woo hoo. Three mooks down.

The X4 swelled into an X6. The last three X1s drew close to the growing monster. With all the speed she could muster, Mithabel raced to engage the one in the lead and thrust her hand into it. The mook's HP only dropped to 60%. It ignored her and pressed on towards its goal.

Levitating a foot off the ground, the X6 floated towards her, drawing that much closer to the wounded X1 and the two X1s behind it.

She thrust at the damaged mook again. She didn't kill it, it's HP still at 30%. Her relatively quick kill of her previous foe had given her such hope, but only served to deepen the depression rising within her at failing to swiftly destroy this one.

Perhaps her ring lost effectiveness the more she used it. Perhaps the mooks had adapted their defenses to it. Perhaps the ring had a wide variance in how much damage it dealt. Perhaps her first attack had been a critical hit. She had no way of knowing how the programming worked. The answer could be a mix of all the above.

With the X6 only ten yards away, she jabbed her hand into the wounded X1 again. It exploded.

Thank you, Goddess.

One of the remaining two X1s moved past her before her attack cool down expired, merging with the X6 to create an X7. *Damn.*

The X1 bringing up the rear reached a pseudopod towards the X7.

Mithabel sprang forward, chopping at the pseudopod as though her hand were a blade. Her heart pounded in her throat as the limb detached and shriveled to nothing. Spinning to face the mook, she scarcely believed its HP readout of 48%.

The creature paused. It had its own cool down timer. Mithabel glanced over her shoulder. The X7 had stopped too, a pseudopod shooting from its upper half.

Mithabel's attack action wasn't ready to go again yet.

The pseudopod zipped over her head, aiming to connect with the X1. The Elf jumped, reaching high. Her ringed hand entered the shadowy pseudopod. Time for a block action. She focused on stopping the limb rather than destroying it.

Holy sweet mother, the appendage froze in place.

Dropping to her knees, she tumbled at the X1. Her attack cool down timer expired, and she thrust her hand into the X1's bowels.

The mook exploded.

Goddess, she felt so *alive.*

The limb of the X7 fell through her, chilling her blood. How damaging was it?

"Your Mental HP holding at 100%, chief."

Oh, Goddess. Mithabel laughed, turning to face the towering X7. Prepared to run, she waited as her attack cool down timer spun. The mook raised its pseudopod for another go at her.

Mithabel's timer expired first. She lunged, driving her hand deep into the X7's dark, ethereal body. Pulling free, she ran, fearing the mook's next action. She wasn't keen on exploring whether she could survive the suicide attack of an X7.

"You dealt 35% damage to the mook, chief. The X7 drops from 700% to 665."

The swiping pseudopod darkened the sky but fell behind Mithabel. The X7 gave chase, drawing back its appendage for another attack. It moved faster than any X1. Perhaps seven times faster.

The Tank kept running, unable to outdistance her pursuer with its improved speed, but not letting it close on her either. She led it away from the sleepers. Fatigue not being a factor in the game, perhaps she could keep the monster entertained until her fellow adventurers healed.

Unlikely, but at least it was a plan.

The X7 stopped and headed for the sleepers. The game of cat and mouse hadn't lasted long.

Coming at it from behind, the Tank darted in and jabbed the creature.

"The X7 has fallen to 623%, chief."

Mithabel needed to deal 23% more damage to drop the X7 to an X6.

"We're taking this monster down together, Kaleisha. You and me. I couldn't do it without you."

"Stop. You'll make me blush."

"I'd like to see that."

The pseudopod swiped at her. Mithabel tensed her legs to jump away.

Block it.

Acting on the the recommendation of her inner voice, the

Elf raised her hand to meet the attack, successfully halting its forward momentum. The Amoeba drew it up again.

Damn, it's too quick.

Calling on her newest skill, the Tank feinted to one side and then spun around to attack from the other. A chunk of Amoeba exploded into black floaters. The banner over what remained of the monster identified it as an X6, with 558% HP.

Way to go, Mithabel.

The creature flung itself in the direction of her feint and missed her completely. She laughed. The ploy had worked. She feinted again, her attack dropping the creature's HP to 516%. Once again, the mook's aim was bad, and it missed her entirely. That being the monster's second time fooled by her feints, Mithabel fled. She needed another attack vector.

The X6 didn't follow her, but resumed its trek towards the sleeping party members.

Damn.

"You need to deal another 16% damage to reduce the X6 to an X5, chief. Based on your prior performance, one more hit should do it." Kaleisha voiced what Mithabel had been thinking.

The Tank raced up behind the X6 and shoved her hand inside it, not bothering to feint. Another chunk of the merged monster exploded, showering her vision with floaters.

How can we raise our chances of delivering a critical hit?

Now an X5 with 475% HP, the mook lashed a pseudopod to its left. It had expected her to feint and adjusted its behavior. She hadn't feinted, and it missed her. Sweet mother.

Attack again. No feint.

Mithabel followed the instincts of her inner voice. Another chunk of the monster exploded. The resulting X4's HP stood at 400%.

Double damn. That had *to be a critical hit.*

The X4 lunged at her. Not what Mithabel or her inner voice had expected. She didn't react in time to block or try to dodge. The Amoeba engulfed her and imploded.

Floaters blinded her, but then her vision cleared. The X4 was gone.

"You are one lucky bitch, chief. Mental HP at 100%. XP Progression has risen to 83%."

"Oh, sweet mother, we did it, Kaleisha." Mithabel dropped on her knees and laughed hard. She bit her lower lip, stifling the laughter. After all that, she didn't want to wake the others.

Yes, we did it.

"Hey, Mithabel, thanks for the XP boost." Rolag still circled overhead.

The Tank craned her neck. The little guy was a blob with wings. "Thanks for the warning, Dragon."

"You bet. Least I could do."

"Can you see Penelope?"

"She left my sight long ago. I believe she's no longer in the cornfield. Sorry."

"It's okay. Better than okay, actually."

To calm her mind, in addition to turning up her Temperament filter, Mithabel locked her gaze on Dylan's sleeping form as she strolled through the furrows. Reaching the sleepers, she sat in the weeds next to the Polynesian. Dylan slept blissfully. What a beautiful woman. Mithabel resisted the urge to stroke the sleeping woman's cheek, afraid the slightest touch might awaken her.

We should fight another dozen Shadow Amoebae, and another dozen after that. Tank Level 7, here we come.

She could scarcely wait to see what skill she'd pick up next. Her Feint skill had proved more useful than she'd imagined.

It saved your life.

Ezmerelda's ring was the true reason she'd survived the encounter. She'd have to tell the others about it now. They'd want to know why she'd kept it a secret. Why had she?

You felt guilty Ezmerelda gave something to you but nothing to your friends.

Mithabel clenched her fists and pressed them against her chin. "Megan, is that you?"

I would have thought that obvious.

"But... aren't you sleeping in your bedroom? You had to sleep for me to respawn. That's what all the other players can't seem to do, relaxing their minds enough to go to sleep after figuring out that's what to do. They do need to sleep to respawn their avatars, right?"

So I guess I'm dreaming.

Mithabel shook her fists. "Oh, no, no, no. I'm not a dream. I might not be real, but I'm not a figment of your sleep-hazed imagination. Somehow, we've reformed our mental connection. I'd given up hope on you, honestly. I'm glad to hear your voice again."

I'm glad you're listening again. So you're willing to accept this is me, and not some Shadow Boss monster attacking you? You're okay about us working together?

"If you're a Shadow Protean attacking me, then I'm already a goner. Sure, Megan, we can work together. But the final decisions lie with me. Remember that."

Of course, Mithabel. My main goal is to understand how the virtual world has invaded the real one. If I can't learn to combat it, it will destroy everything. I'm here to help you become the best you can, hoping to learn what I need to know as you progress. If I think you're being stupid, I'll tell you. If I think you're being smart, I'll back you up. Just think of me as your biggest fan, excited for you to succeed. And if you want to discuss anything with someone other than your fellow adventurers or a dancing support AI, no offense to Kaleisha, I'm here for you.

Mithabel rubbed her eyes. "Why are you choosing now to start talking with me again? *Is there another Shadow Protean* Boss in the area, making me hallucinate?"

You don't get out of it that easy, Tank.

"I don't know who I am, Megan."

You're me, captured in a moment void of passion or care. I'm sorry about that. But you're rising above it, despite the low attribute scores. If you hadn't improved, I couldn't connect with you now. The game isn't about the money. It might have been once, but it's far more than that now. *Fanciful Pegasus is recruiting warriors to battle an invading force. I've been chosen for their army. But I don't have the tools I need. It's your job to build them for me.*

The system clock read *6:21 AM, Day 2, Year 1*. The fight with the dozen Shadow Amoebae hadn't taken long.

Don't deflect, Mithabel. What will you tell the others about the ring?

"I haven't decided. What do you think?"

You should have told them about the ring as soon as you came out of Ezmerelda's hut.

"I know." Mithabel clamped her eyes shut. "Status report, please, Kaleisha."

"All your HP status bars are full."

"And my Sanity stat?"

"Still at 14, chief."

"That's a relief. I scarcely think myself sane at the moment."

Why does my presence in your head cause you to question your sanity?

"Shut up, Megan, please. Let me think."

Her player complied with the request.

Mithabel counted to one hundred as she watched Rolag fly in a lazy circle.

She checked the system clock. It read *6:27 AM, Day 2, Year 1*. Her conversation with Megan had dragged on forever. She climbed to her feet and stomped from one furrow to the next, not caring if her commotion drew monsters. If only a band of Goblins would attack her, so she could get out some of the angst Megan had unintentionally corrupted her with. Equipping her longsword, she hacked down a cornstalk and then another and another. She hacked the fallen ears of corn to bits, sending kernels flying.

Rolag grunted. "You're going to wake the others. I can hear you up here."

Mithabel stabbed her blade into the ground and left it there as she strode back to Dylan to look down on the stunning dark beauty. "No one is hurting you in this world like *he* hurt Debra in the real one. I'll kill anyone who tries. I'm not spineless like Megan."

Her player remained silent, saying nothing in defense.

Fine. Mithabel admitted to being the spineless one. If she hadn't been a coward, she'd have told her friends about the ring the moment she walked out of that hut.

"Kaleisha, if Megan is going to be with us again, please give her a freaking body. I can't take her bodiless voice in my head on a permanent basis."

"Yes, chief."

CHAPTER NINETEEN

The system clock read *7:38 AM, Day 2, Year 1*. Mithabel's friends still slept. She paced in a furrow, lazily swinging her longsword against the cornstalks. None of her strikes were strong enough on its own to bring down a stalk, but over time, she'd felled a dozen. Occupying a visual representation once more, Megan Wright stood to one side, watching in silence with her arms crossed. Next to the blond player, Kaleisha danced to a classic country song. It no longer seemed strange that Mithabel could see and hear these two and no one else could. Though they couldn't interact with Mithabel's world, they weren't imaginary, either.

Whoosh. The Danger Sense trigger pulled in multiple directions, as though it couldn't decide.

Rolag's warning followed. "Three bands of six Shadow Amoebae have spawned in a triangle formation around you."

Three bands. Eighteen mooks. Damn.

Rolag hadn't finished. "Each band is merging into an X6."

Clad in a jumpsuit exposing her cleavage, Megan Wright tossed her blond mop. "Are you shitting me?"

"Thanks for the commentary, player." Locating the three merging bands using Third Person POV, the Tank chose one and ran towards it, stashing her longsword, still wearing only her underwear and boots. She clenched her fist to feel the press of Ezmerelda's ring against her flesh. "Rolag, I might need you to swoop down and wake the others. If I say so, then do it quickly."

"Just say the word." The Pseudo Code Dragon flew lower in

anticipation.

The green blades of cornstalks thwacked Mithabel in the face as she raced across the furrows. Using Third Person POV looking down from above to plot her course made it difficult to know when to duck her head. Three X6s, moving fast, closed on her. She wouldn't have time to deal with them all. "Rolag, wake Charli, now. Only Charli."

Mithabel lunged at her target, shoving her ring-bearing fist into the creature's amorphous black being, dropping its HP by 36% to 564. The mook ignored her, pressing on towards the sleeping group. Shit. She couldn't force these mooks to use their suicide attack on her, and killing them bit by bit with the ring wouldn't take them down before they reached the sleepers.

"What?" Charli moaned. The girl's Mental Armor trait snapped back to her stirring body, leaving Mithabel protected only by her Natural Armor, a serious vulnerability.

Mithabel didn't give the girl time to wake up gracefully. "Get up, Charli, *now*. We've got three X6s to deal with. I'm dealing with one of them. You need to tempt the other two into suicide attacking you. I know it might hurt, but you're the only one who can help me and have a chance at surviving. I'm on the one to the north. There's one to the east-southeast and one to the west-southwest. They're both yours. Move it, before they attack Amarynth and Dylan."

"Okay, sure." The Cowgirl groaned. "Right after I wake up."

"*Move it*, Charli." Racing beside her targeted mook, Mithabel swiped her hand through it, bringing its HP down to 528%. Still it ignored her. "Rolag, wake Dylan and Amarynth. They need to move. We have to hope they can." The instant her attack cool down timer expired, Mithabel jabbed at the mook again. A portion of it exploded from the side of the X6, and the mook down converted to an X5.

Rolag nudged the Viking in the side with his snout.

Amarynth flung up an arm as though warding off an attacker. "No. Get away. Don't hurt me."

"He's not trying to hurt you." Mithabel's cool down timer was so damn slow. "You need to get up and follow him. Rolag, wake Dylan, maybe she's healed enough to take defensive action and help you with Amarynth."

Charli planted herself in the path of an X6. It passed through her and kept going. "The monster is ignoring me, Mithabel. I can't affect it without magic, and it refuses to implode on me. I can't do anything to help. Sorry. I need an enchantment from Dylan if I'm to be of assistance."

Megan Wright flew over to hover near Charli, pointing at the Cowgirl. "What about her Shadow Stone? Isn't it magic?"

"You're right." Mithabel swiped at her target, reducing its HP by another chunk. "Charli, take your Shadow Stone in hand, please. That gem you took from the Scarecrow. Grip it in your fist and stick it inside the Amoeba. Be ready to stash it if need be."

The Guide paused before replying. "Do you *know* what it will do or are you guessing?"

At the Dragon's nudging, Dylan stirred. "Go away, Rolag. I'm not ready." Her dreary voice pulled at Mithabel's heart.

"You need to get up and move, Dylan." Mithabel trotted beside the X5, waiting again on her cool down timer. "Charli, if you don't do what I asked, these monsters will be on top of Amarynth and Dylan within seconds. Our friends are in no shape to run."

"Both of you please follow me." Desperation oozed from Rolag's reptilian voice.

Dylan's head pivoted, taking in the scene. "*Shit.* Come on, Archer." She grabbed Amarynth by the arm and pulled her to her feet. "Lead the way, Dragon." They headed west.

A raised arm shielding her eyes, the Archer stumbled with every step, continually mumbling for Rolag not to kill her.

A red gem appeared on Charli's palm. "Here goes nothing." Charli clenched the stone and thrust her fist into the giant Amoeba's body. Pseudopods erupted from all around the black blob. A screech filled the air or perhaps Mithabel imagined it.

Chunks of Shadow Amoeba blasted to bits.

A shorter shadowy blob remained in the wake of the explosion. The Cowgirl had reduced the mook from an X6 to an X2 *with one blow.*

The shrunken creature turned and fled, but its reduced size meant it moved slower.

Megan Wright flew beside it, though she couldn't harm it. It showed no sign of even being aware of her. She chuckled. "A mook with a self-preservation motive. Didn't think it was in the programming."

Charli ran after the X2 and hit it again. Another explosion, and the mook shrunk to an X1 with 72% HP. The monster continued to flee, though at a crawl.

The blond player threw up her hands. "That's bogus. The second attack should have taken it out."

"Leave it, Charli." Mithabel returned to First Person POV. She'd been paying too much attention to the others and fallen behind her target, the X5. Both it and the unwounded X6 reached the spot where Dylan and Amarynth had been sleeping moments before. The Dragon and two women hadn't gotten far. The two mooks paused, then moved towards each other.

Shit. Mithabel raced after the X5, knowing she wouldn't reach it in time.

The X6 and X5 merged.

Sweet mother. Mithabel stopped ten feet from the towering X11, four times the height of an adult human and as thick as it was tall. "We're all done for. We'll never outrun that thing. Its pseudopod attack alone will crush our minds to jelly."

Charli roared a war cry and ran at the thing.

Mithabel raced to intercept her. "Charli, no."

A pseudopod crashed down, aimed at Mithabel, the closer target. Acting purely on instinct, the Tank flung herself to the ground, rolling away, bringing up Ezmerelda's ring in an effort to parry if the dodge failed, hoping for a defensive combo effect that would protect her from mental annihilation. Despite her best efforts, the chill of the pseudopod swept through her torso.

Her mind shattered like a pane of glass under a sledgehammer.

Megan Wright shouted in the Tank's ear. "Get up, fool."

Mithabel rolled onto her back. The world spun. Color wheels twirled in space. Red, green, and blue. Yellow, aqua, and purple. Black snakes slithered up invisible stairs. The sun enlarged, filling the sky. She stood. Or maybe she lay stretched flat on the ground. It was difficult to tell the difference.

"Run, Mithabel. To your right. *Come on.*" Megan Wright directed, and Mithabel blindly followed.

More black snakes spread across the sky, dark tentacles reaching for the sun.

Though Mithabel couldn't see Megan, the blond player continued giving her instructions. "Stop. Stick your right hand out before you. Good. Run to your left. We can finish this thing. Trust me, Mithabel."

If the Elf couldn't trust her player, who could she trust? The back of Charli's head swam before the Tank. Mithabel darted left as instructed, leading with her right hand, letting muscle memory do the work. A spinning color wheel zipped by, spitting blood from its edges. Beyond lay blackness, and she shoved her hand into it. A wall of blackness transformed into a ball of black snakes, each of them striking outward from the center at nothing, fading from black to transparent.

"*Congratulations*, chief. You're level seven Tank."

Charli's soft, twisted laughter. An evil overlord whose plans for world domination have come to fruition.

Megan Wright blew out a long breath. "Whew. We did it. Now you're the one needing sleep."

Over party chat, Mithabel echoed her player.

Charli howled like a wolf. "Don't we all. Rolag, please lead us out of the cornfield."

Wings rustled overhead. "I see a forest to the west. A new territory."

"Lead on, Rolag."

Mithabel sat. "I can't. You all go on without me."

The Cowgirl grabbed the Elf's arm and tugged. "We don't dare sleep in the Mystic Hollow Cornfield now. I'm pretty sure the Shadow Protean Boss has respawned out there somewhere. There are two of them now. We can't afford to stay in its territory. You have to come with me, Tank."

Megan snapped her fingers in the Elf's face. "Do as Charli says, Mithabel."

"Let me lay down for only a minute." Mithabel slumped forward. Where was a bedpost when she needed its support? Where was a pillow to cushion her head?

"No." Charli pulled at the Tank, but couldn't budge her.

The blond kicked at the seated Elf, her foot passing through the avatar body. "Get up, Mithabel."

A line of trees loomed over Mithabel. She'd made it to the forest.

Megan slapped at the Tank, her hand passing through the avatar face. "It's not a forest. It's a row of cornstalks. *Get up.*"

"Chief, Charli requests a transfer of awareness to your body. Do I let her in?"

The Cowgirl kicked Mithabel. "Let me in, Tank."

"Let her in, Kaleisha."

"Chief, Charli requests control of your motor functions. Will you allow it?"

"As long as I can sleep, Kaleisha, let Charli do whatever she wants." Mithabel's awareness went dark.

△△△

Mithabel woke to the strains of a gentle folk song. Kaleisha and Megan Wright did the dosado and went into a promenade, Megan taking the man's part.

"Good afternoon, chief. I'm glad to report you're at 100% on all four HP status bars. Your XP Progression stands at 2%. In case you missed my earlier announcement, you're level seven Tank now. Welcome to Black Poison Forest."

The system clock read *1:17 PM, Day 2, Year 1*.

"Kaleisha and I can actually touch each other." The blond twirled the Jamaican AI.

Dressed in her armor, the Tank lay on her back, cushioned in a pile of dead leaves and pine needles. The scent of cedar coaxed her from the fog of sleep. Sunlight filtered through treetops and her squinting eyes. "Ugh."

"Look who decided to rejoin the land of the living." Was that blur Dylan's face? "How are you feeling, Mithabel?"

"I'll let you know as soon as I do. Has everyone else healed up?"

Leaves crunched as the Polynesian sat beside the Elf. "We're all healed on all HP types. Everyone leveled up, too, except Rolag. He's lagging behind."

The Pseudo Code Dragon lay near the Tank's feet. He cleared his throat. "My XP progression bar is at 94%. They won't let me fly back to the Brassy Grassy and kill some Goblins."

Dylan snorted at the Dragon before turning back to Mithabel. "Everyone is wondering what new skill you acquired, Tank. You feel like sitting up?" She put a hand on the Elf's shoulder to lend support.

Mithabel smiled at Dylan's touch. "There's something about you, you Polynesian Princess." The Tank pushed up on her elbows. "Yes, I said *Princess*, not *Priestess*. You have a certain je ne sais quoi about you. Have you done something with your braids?"

Dylan chuckled. "It's my new Presence skill."

"Damn, woman." Mithabel shook her head. "You are piling on the charm. Beauty, Attraction, Exoticness, and now Presence. Are you vying for the title of High Priestess? You're well on your way."

"I have no delusions of grandeur." Dylan put her arm around Mithabel's shoulders. "What about your new skill? Have you checked yet?"

Charli strolled over. "I earned Negotiate. Not sure how that fits with the Guide class. Maybe it's to help me negotiate my fair share of any treasure we happen to find, if we ever do."

"Critical Hit – Bow/Crossbow for me." Amarynth spoke with a steady voice, no hint of panic, paranoia, or irrational fear of her pet trying to eat her. "Have to say I'm loving the skills for Archer. Can't wait to see how this new one plays out. Will *all* my shots be critical hits? That would be amazing. What new skill *did* you get, Tank?"

"What skill did I pick up, Kaleisha?" Mithabel chortled at the response. "Ha. I've been wondering if I could do this. I've picked up the Stun skill."

Rolag hopped on his hind legs. "That's great. We should go back to the Brassy Grassy and fight some Goblins, so you can stun them and harvest their body parts for treasure. Everyone wants treasure, right?"

Amarynth clucked her tongue. "Sorry, my pet, but none of the rest of us want to travel through the Mystic Hollow again unless it's absolutely necessary, and you're *not* going alone."

"Speaking of which." Mithabel looked from one companion to the next. "I seem to recall an X11 Shadow Amoeba bearing down on us. What happened with it? Did we kill it?"

"*You* killed it, Mithabel." Charli plopped down on the leaf bed beside the Tank on the other side from the Priestess. There was no sign of the cursed gem she'd taken from the Scarecrow's ashes. The teenager had wisely stashed it again. "I caused lots of damage wielding the Shadow Stone, though it seemed to have less and less effect with each hit against any given opponent. You rushed over and dealt the killing blow."

"I don't remember."

Megan and Kaleisha danced to a swing tune. The player had again taken the man's role. "Sure you remember, Mithabel. You followed my directions and killed the monster. You're a heroine. We both are."

"Well...." Oblivious to the dancing duo, Dylan slid a hand down Mithabel's right arm, grabbed her wrist, and lifted.

"That's some ring you have there, Tank. Mind telling us where you found it?"

Mithabel flexed her fingers. "I don't know. It appeared on my hand out of nowhere." She couldn't stop the smile from curling her lips as Dylan glared at her. "Okay, I'm joking. Ezmerelda gave it to me after the rest of you left her hut. She never said it was magical or had any other special powers. I never said anything because I didn't want you all to be jealous. But then I figured out it could serve as a magical weapon against those Shadow Amoebae, so I equipped it. That's all there is to tell."

"If there's anything else you're hiding, Mithabel, now's the time to come clean." The Polynesian squeezed the Tank's shoulders.

"Okay. Look at the rankings."

The Top Individual Avatars list still graced the page, with only Mithabel on it.

"Yeah." Dylan patted Mithabel's throat. "I noticed that list you're on. Are you saying you're on it because of the ring?"

Mithabel rubbed the metal band. "I believe so."

"All right." The Priestess pulled Mithabel into an embrace, one arm around her shoulder. "Any other secrets you want to tell us?"

"There's nothing else, Dylan, I swear."

Megan dipped Kaleisha in front of Mithabel. "You could mention me."

"Okay, there *is* one more thing. It's because of Megan Wright that I attacked and killed the last mook. I was out of my mind. She directed me, and I did what she said. And so here we are. Which brings me to a question of my own. How *did* we get here? Last thing I recall, I was going to sleep, with Charli in my head."

"Oh, no, unh-uh, back up." Dylan grabbed Mithabel's chin and turned her face to stare into her eyes. "Megan Wright *directed* you? Like, told you where to go and what to do? She kept her wits when you couldn't?"

Mithabel frowned and shrugged. "She's an ornery one."

Megan laughed, heard only by Mithabel and Kaleisha. "I am, aren't I?"

Dylan tilted her head. "Debra Jones speaks to me sometimes, but never gives me actionable advice."

"I hear Anna Milligan in my head sometimes, too." The Viking paced in a circle around the others. "Nothing actionable from her, either. Random witticisms is all I get."

Mithabel raised a hand, palm out. "Yeah, well, we all have Megan Wright to thank for us being alive and sane right now. She feels terrible about letting down Debra Jones, and she's trying her best to make up for it. Should I get out of her way and let her play the game? Is that what everyone wants?"

Amarynth stopped pacing. "None of us are saying that."

Charli put a hand on Mithabel's thigh. "You carried me."

Mithabel turned a hard gaze on the Cowgirl.

The teenage Guide nodded, drawing her hand away. "I transfered my awareness to you, putting my own body out of commission. Before you fell asleep, you gave me control of your motor functions. Don't look at me like I'm not supposed to know about motor functions. You'd given me blanket permissions to do anything I wanted, so I equipped your armor. It worked, so... Cool, huh? I made your body pick up my body and carry it from the cornfield to the forest. Then I had you pile up some leaves to lie on. When you were comfortably lying down, I transfered back to my body and let you sleep. That's how you and I got here. Physically speaking...," she flexed her arms, "I couldn't have carried your body. Mentally speaking...," she pointed at Mithabel's head, "you couldn't have carried mine. But the two of us together got the job done. Rolag convinced Dylan and Amarynth to follow him, and that's how they got here. Any questions?"

At the sight of Charli's hopeful face, Mithabel's frustrations faded. She smiled, clapping a hand on the teenager's shoulder. "Impressive, Charli. You did good work."

The Cowgirl beamed at the compliment, her wide smile noticeable even though shadowed by her hat and the overhead canopy.

The Tank gestured around at the pine trees and oaks surrounding them. "So, I'm guessing nothing has attacked us since we entered the forest?"

"Nothing yet." Rolag rubbed against Charli, who patted his head. The Dragon made a sound like purring, only deeper than any cat would make. "Too many treetops obscuring the view when I'm flying, so I've been keeping watch with Third Person POV. Can't cover as wide an area, but I'm doing my best. I found that if I properly angle my line of observation, I can watch a larger area than if I simply look straight down on myself."

"Well, that's a relief. I'm guessing there's been no shouting in the vicinity." Mithabel stretched her arms. "What's this territory called again?"

Rolag snorted, smoke wafting up from his nostrils. "Black Poison Forest. You get one guess about the kind of dangers we'll face in this place."

"Lovely." Mithabel rubbed her temples. "So have you talked any plans while I've been asleep?"

Dylan rubbed the Tank's back between the shoulders. "Charli says the city of Maron lies right beyond the western edge of this forest. We should head for it as soon as you're ready. Everyone else is eager to complete our first quest."

"I want to become level seven Winged Fighter." Rolag reared on his hind legs and spread his wings. "I'm hoping I'll get a Stun skill too. I wonder if Shadow Amoebae can be stunned."

"Let's not go back to the cornfield to find out." Mithabel dropped her head and arms forward, relaxing under Dylan's massage. "Don't stop, Priestess."

But shortly after, the massage did stop. Dylan patted Mithabel on the back and jumped to her feet. "It's time to go. We've already given the other parties too much time to catch up to us. Which reminds me. Take another look at the rankings."

"Oh, wow." Mithabel stared at the new list. "We're still at the top, but Quantized has moved above XStorm."

"Scroll down."

Only two parties remained on the Longest Survivor Bounty Contenders list. Quantized led the list, with BoardStiff second. XStorm had been removed.

The Polynesian offered a hand to Mithabel to help her to her feet. "Looks like someone, maybe Quantized, killed Penelope. Party XStorm is no longer active."

"You spoke too soon." XStorm popped in at number two on the Longest Survivor Bounty Contenders list. Mithabel and Dylan swore at the same time. The Tank swallowed hard. "I wonder if every member of XStorm has respawned. They could have a Wizard and a Priestess with them now. They could be a bit too much for us to handle."

Amarynth went back to pacing. "I wonder if Penelope is back, too. We don't know if NPCs respawn."

Mithabel accepted Dylan's assistance in standing. "When XStorm came back into the game after respawning, if things worked for them like they did for us, they were each offered a choice of where to enter the world. They no doubt picked the cornfield, the farthest area to which they'd traveled, and they were allowed to choose it because none of their party was engaged in an encounter at the time. Which means... they could be breathing down our backs any moment. If they're at full HP, we don't want to mess with them."

Rolag ascended towards the canopy. "I'll see if I can spot them."

"No." Charli grabbed at him, but too late. "If you can see them, they can see you."

"She's right." Dylan motioned for the Dragon to stay low. "No flying above the treetops. We don't want to give away our location to other parties. Let's get moving. *Now*."

With a sigh sounding much like a growl, the Pseudo Code Dragon took the lead, flying ten feet above the ground, well below the canopy.

Amarynth followed, staying about ten yards back, zigging and zagging to either side to satisfy her itch to move fast.

The crunch of leaves and twigs under her feet shouted for monsters to come. The Viking didn't slow. "I'm super sorry about the noise."

Dylan and Charli strode side by side about ten feet behind Amarynth, both as silent as the vacuum of space when compared to the Archer. Another ten feet back, Mithabel brought up the rear. If her Danger Sense did have an effective range, she wanted to be in the back, the direction from which any competing parties would come.

She kept an eye on the system clock.

At *2:12 PM, Day 2, Year 1*, the party had yet to encounter anything in the Black Poison Forest.

Whoosh.

The sound swept *down* on the Tank. "*Incoming*, people. From above."

A cone-shaped web with a tail as thick as Mithabel's wrist shot from the overhead canopy to envelope Rolag. More web cones descended on the others. Mithabel tumbled to her left, but a web struck her right foot and hauled her up by the ankle.

CHAPTER TWENTY

The Tank arched her back as she ascended. Partially obscured by oak tree branches, metallic black arachnid legs twice the length of Mithabel's lower limbs hoisted her up by a silky thread.

Megan Wright groaned. "Please, not spiders." She and Kaleisha flew out of Mithabel's view, so as not to distract.

These were far smaller than Arachnid Behemoths, but larger than any spider should be. Foliage hid their identification banners.

Fire flared on the periphery, igniting hope in Mithabel's chest that Rolag had burned himself free. The little Dragon might be a match for the band of giant metal spiders attacking the party from the treetops. Mithabel needed to survive long enough for Rolag to reach her, after he saved the others first.

Branches smacked her cheeks and obscured her vision as her captor drew Mithabel up into the forest canopy. Equipping the bow she'd acquired from ChrisCross, she fired an arrow, but her aim was terrible and the missile went wide. Perhaps if she weren't being jostled about, she'd have better luck with the weapon. Stashing it, she equipped her longsword and switched to Third Person POV. Leaves blocked her view from above. Taking a cue from something Rolag had said, she shifted her observation angle to come from the side instead of from above. The new perspective gave her a better view of the entire situation.

Having already been freed by Rolag, Amarynth raced along the ground, dodging webs and firing a crossbow bolt into the treetops, an explosion of black metal slivers marking the death of one of the attackers. Rolag burned the line tethering Dylan to a spider, and the Priestess flailed to catch hold of *something, anything* as she crashed through branches, headed for an impact with the ground. Charli screamed for help, struggling against the silk strands binding her and pulling her up.

The short length of web still attached to the Priestess caught on a tree branch, halting her descent, leaving her hanging upside down. "Goddess Scintilla, shine your blessing upon us!" The Priestess struggled to right herself.

Infuriated at the sight of Dylan being mistreated, and unable to help the Priestess until she helped herself, the Tank clenched her longsword hilt and switched back to First Person POV. Angry fangs clicked above her, anxious to sink into her flesh and inject her with their poison. The name Black Steel Spider nestled in the greenery over the mook's head. Mithabel waited a moment longer, until the creature leaned forward to deliver its bite. Tightening her stomach muscles, the Tank rolled up, folding at the waist, jabbing upward with her longsword. Her blade slid between the monster's fangs and she shoved hard.

An explosion of black blood and scorched metal marked the place where it died. The game developers must have been so proud of their cleverness, creating metal mooks that splattered blood upon dying. As Mithabel plummeted, a half dozen more fanged faces crowded down, competing to take the vanquished Steel Spider's place. Party MAD hadn't encountered a *band* of Black Steel Spiders, but a whole *cluster*.

Bracing herself for impact, she didn't try to break her fall, relying on her level two Natural Armor to prevent any bones from snapping. A twenty-foot fall shouldn't hurt an experienced Tank that much.

It knocked the wind from her. Tendrils of agony ripped through her spine. She couldn't move.

Her Jamaican AI delivered a report. "Physical HP has fallen to 88%, chief. And you're stunned." A cool down timer for her condition began spinning.

It was more damage than she'd expected from the fall. Good thing Dylan's webs had caught on a tree branch and halted her descent, or the Priestess might have taken severe damage upon striking the ground.

Megan Wright offered a suggestion. "You might warn everyone else."

Right. "Try your best not to hit the ground if you fall very far, ladies. It hurts like hell, and you might break something. Plus, I'm stunned now."

Another mass of webs splat across her chest and arms. *Damn.* Even if she weren't paralyzed, she couldn't swing her longsword like this. The silk line above her contracted and yanked her off the ground, spinning her in a dizzying circle.

She switched to Third Person POV to get a read on the situation for everyone.

Fire flashed and Charli plunged earthward.

More webs had snared Dylan and pulled her into the canopy.

Amarynth stayed on the move, not pausing as she fired her crossbow, each shot dealing death. Her Critical Hit skill for her crossbow was coming in handy.

The end of a branch snagged Charli's hat, ripping it from her head. Three other branches caught her skirt, pausing her fall for a second before one of them snapped and then another, leaving her to hang upside down for another second until the third branch broke. A large branch below those three caught her under the stomach. Her grunt echoed through the forest. Reaching down, she wrapped her arms over the branch and under her thighs before another volley of webbing hit her spine and jerked upward. With a war cry, she clung to her lower limbs, her flesh rending against oak tree bark. Something cracked, maybe her backbone or maybe the tree branch.

Flame flashed above Mithabel, burning the web hoisting her up, and she watched her body fall from the detached perspective of Third Person POV. Her armored frame crashed to the ground.

"Your HP has fallen to 79%, chief."

If the spiders didn't kill her with their poisoned fangs, she'd die from repeatedly bashing her skull on the forest floor. She couldn't keep going up and falling down like this.

From the external vantage point of Third Person POV, she noticed webbing descending from the canopy. In the instant her stun timer expired, she rolled aside, and the webbing missed. Still watching herself from the detached perspective of Third Person, she hopped to her feet.

Webs from a previous attack clung to her upper body, pinning her arms to her sides, making it impossible to use her weapon, so she stashed it. "Rolag, they have Dylan and Charli again." She ran to avoid another cone of webs, once more dodging it. The perspective of Third Person POV gave her a slight edge, enough to avoid capture. She spotted the descending webs a second sooner than she'd have done with First Person POV.

One of Amarynth's arrows sped into the canopy above Dylan. The Spider at the top of the line erupted in death, and Dylan fell again. Swearing under her breath, Mithabel sprinted across the leaf-strewn forest floor towards the falling Priestess. Dylan grasped at every passing branch, slowing her fall as much as she could. The Polynesian was still ten feet in the air when Mithabel reached her, unable to catch her but hoping to soften her impact with the ground.

The Elf leaned back as the Polynesian landed on her. Quite by accident, Mithabel's face planted itself between Dylan's breasts. The Tank staggered, but stayed upright. Dylan slid down Mithabel's body until her feet touched the ground. Leaning back, she tried to step away but couldn't. The webbing on Mithabel's torso clung to Dylan too, binding the two of them together, face to face. Still watching from Third Person POV, the intimacy of the moment wasn't as strong for Mithabel as perhaps it was for Dylan, but it wasn't lost on the Elf, either. If there weren't dozens of giant Black Steel Spiders roving in the trees above, she'd have leaned forward and given the Priestess a kiss. She closed her eyes so Dylan wouldn't feel she was staring. With Third Person POV active, it didn't matter whether Mithabel had her eyes open.

Dylan growled. "Just great, Mithabel. How are we supposed to run away now?"

"Wrap your legs around my waist."

The Priestess flung her legs as high as possible and wrapped them around the Tank's hips. Mithabel's arms were trapped at her sides, but her hands and wrists were free. She caught Dylan's thighs, hiking her up further, enough for the Polynesian to lock the Elf's waist inside the embrace of her legs. Webs coated Dylan's chest, so Mithabel craned her neck back to avoid having her face attached to her friend's breasts. Continuing to use Third Person POV for its tactical advantage, Mithabel dodged webs as nimbly as Amarynth, even with the added load of Dylan's weight.

If anything, the press of Dylan's body gave Mithabel an energy she'd never known before. She was light on her feet, a combat ballerina. She twirled and laughed at Dylan's rising anger, until the tension melted from the Priestess and her laughter joined Mithabel's. They danced across the forest floor, two souls lost in their own deceit while the battle raged around them, hopping and darting and dodging as webs struck and struck and struck, always dissolving into the ground two steps behind them.

Amarynth lowered her crossbow. "You two can stop dancing. It's over. Rolag and I killed them all."

Charli moaned from her perch in a tree. Still wrapped around a thick branch, webbing had bonded her to it, making it impossible for the mooks to haul her up.

Mithabel and Dylan collapsed to the ground, rolling in the leaves. The Tank landed on her back, the Priestess on top of her. The Polynesian leaned down and kissed the Elf on the mouth. Hurriedly switching to First Person POV, Mithabel returned the kiss, keeping her eyes closed but relishing the press of lips on lips, the brush of Dylan's braids on her cheeks, the weight of the Priestess pushing her into the ground. Perhaps the earth would fold over and bury them where they would be alone together forever.

Rolag settled onto the ground next to them. "If you two are done smooching, I'll burn these webs off. Unless you want to stay stuck together for the rest of the journey."

Dylan raised her head, drawing her lips away from Mithabel's. The Tank sighed and opened her eyes, her gaze locking with Dylan's. Neither of them spoke.

Rolag nudged them with his head. "Okay, then, I hope you're ready. This might hurt a bit."

Fire flared. The Jamaican AI reported a drop in HP of a few percentage points, but the Elf didn't care. Dylan's gaze didn't falter. After Rolag backed away and announced he'd finished, the Polynesian leaned down again and planted another kiss on Mithabel's lips.

Rolag flew in a tight circle over the romancing couple's heads. "Did I mention I reached level seven?"

Charli struggled with the webs holding her. "Can someone help me down, please?"

Amarynth raised her crossbow. "Oh, no, there's XStorm."

Dylan rolled off Mithabel and leaped to her feet. "Where?"

The Viking pointed east, not cracking a smile. "Coming this way, I'm sure. Probably not stopping for any romantic interludes. We need to move, if you value your virtual life, Priestess. I don't see them, but we know they're coming. We need to move."

The Polynesian tossed her braids. "Yes, I suppose you're right."

Mithabel remained on the ground, her emotions roiling inside. She'd never cared about boyfriends, but never considered herself gay, either. Sex still didn't have an appeal for her, but there was no denying the sparks between her and the Priestess. There was a definite physical attraction between them and a spiritual connection as well. Dylan's hugs and kisses were to die for. A thousand times, if necessary.

The Priestess offered Mithabel a hand, helping her to her feet. Then she leaned in for one more kiss.

Rolag burned the webs from Charli and clutched her shoulders to give support as the Cowgirl climbed down the tree. She jumped down the last few feet. Flustered, she grabbed up her hat and donned it, adjusting her pigtails to hang the way she wanted. She'd never looked more like a Cowgirl to Mithabel than in that moment.

Taking a moment to assess their status, the group discovered they were faring better than expected. Only Mithabel and Dylan had lost HP. An expenditure of four Auni by the Priestess restored them both to full.

Rolag crowed and puffed his chest as he reported having acquired the Aerial Stun skill. "Next time we encounter monsters, Mithabel and I are stunning some, and we're harvesting body parts to sell in Maron. It's not against the morality of the game, so I'm okay with it, if Dylan is."

The Priestess nodded, her eyes sad. "The game has its rules, and this is one of them. Like Rolag says, it's not against the morality of the game. I'm fine with it, as long as I'm not doing the harvesting. Especially if what we harvest are Black Steel Spiders. Ugh. I hate those things."

"I learned something about dodging webs." Mithabel motioned for everyone to listen. "Third Person POV gave me an edge over First Person POV. I had maybe a split second more in which to move. The quicker you move, the better chance you have of dodging, or, even better, not needing to dodge, because you're already out of the way before it counts as a dodge action. The developers designed this challenge to test our ability to observe, react, and evade. Of course, it was no challenge for you, Amarynth, with your doubly Increased Movement trait."

Dylan frowned as she nodded. "Good tip, Mithabel. Now if we only had a better warning system, we could have time to switch to Third Person POV before we get entangled, and your suggestion might be of use."

Rolag sighed, blowing a puff of smoke. "Sorry I didn't see them sooner. Mithabel should take the lead. I'll bring up the rear and keep an eye open for XStorm the best I can. But we already know I won't be able to spot that freaky little Electrical Serpent, Lance, if he starts following us."

The Polynesian continued frowning and nodding. "Having Mithabel in the lead is probably for the best while we're in the forest."

Everyone else agreed.

The Tank walked with bow in hand, intending to fire a shot or two if she detected enemies from a sufficient distance. Behind her, Amarynth rushed from side to side, like a child who'd eaten too much sugar, crunching every leaf, twig, and pine needle they passed. Why did having level two Increased Movement come with such a disadvantage? If Amarynth put more points into the trait, would she become even noisier? She might as well be a whistling train as it careened through the forest. There was no way to mute the special effects channel for others. If XStorm ever came within earshot, they wouldn't need Danger Sense to know party MAD was nearby.

The four women and the Dragon traveled over half an hour more before reaching a clearing measuring about sixty feet across. Far-reaching oak branches from trees surrounding the clearing blocked the sky some thirty feet overhead.

Charli paused. "I have a bad feeling about this."

Mithabel kept going while the others waited. "My Danger Sense isn't triggering." She reached the center of the clearing.

"Is it safe to cross?" Rolag hovered near the clearing's edge.

"I'm still not picking up anything bad. What do you think, Charli?"

The girl peered into the treetops. "My Monster Lore isn't giving me a clear answer. I don't like it. We should go around."

Mithabel scanned the canopy. "I only see leaves, branches, and vines. Nothing moving. If something is up there, it's well hidden. Neither my Danger Sense or my Alertness traits are picking up a thing. I've been standing here in the open for half a minute now, and nothing bad has happened. But anyone who wants to skirt around the clearing, be my guest. Maybe the developers are counting on us being afraid of the clearing, walking around it, and stepping into a trap."

Over the next half minute, Amarynth crashed through the brush surrounding the clearing. "No traps."

Dylan cleared her throat. "Do we think this clearing is a test? Maybe a puzzle? What kind of puzzle could it be?" She ventured into the clearing, Amarynth on her heels. Charli followed with tentative steps.

The teenage Guide pushed back her hat as she continued searching the treetops. "I don't know what it is, but it isn't a puzzle. There's a monster here. Don't ask me what kind. But it's up there somewhere."

"I'll find out what it is. We need XP." Rolag shot into the clearing, winging his way upward.

Whoosh.

Mithabel pointed her bow up and to the right. "It's awake now, whatever it is."

Something long and thin swung down from the canopy, a grapevine attached to an oak branch. Mithabel's shot missed it by an inch. The free end of the swinging vine sported a head with eyes and fangs, aimed at Mithabel. A banner flying along with the fanged head identified the swinging thing as a Poison Ivy Snake. The Elf sidestepped it with ease. Her dodge cool down timer didn't start. The system didn't consider such casual sidestepping as a dodge.

Dozens of the Poison Ivy Snakes swung down from the trees, their heads whistling through the air, their fangs gleaming and gnashing. They came from all directions, their curved bodies rising and falling and swerving, their movements coordinated to avoid collisions between them and yet cover as much of the clearing as possible. There was nowhere safe for Mithabel to move to. So she didn't try. Stashing the bow, she slammed an open palm against the side of an oncoming Ivy Snake's head.

Her stunned target went limp, falling in a heap of coils. Another Ivy Snake passed over its location and then another. Snakes thirty to fifty feet long formed a chaotic pattern of living pendulums, drawing up as necessary to avoid each other, and lowering again to reach for their targets. Mithabel equipped her longsword and slashed at the nearest Poison Ivy monster, severing its head. It fell, its serpentine body transforming to a line of sparkling water, fizzling like soda poured in a glass.

Dylan and Charli both shouted for help. As Mithabel spun to face them, an Ivy Snake passed within striking distance. Its head thrust at her, and she instinctively parried it before the fangs could sink into her flesh.

Unseen fangs struck the back of her neck. The damned things were everywhere.

Fire burned her inside. The world spun as she cried a warning, even if it came too late. "Poison." She pitched forward, stashing her longsword before she blacked out.

"It won't kill us." Charli's voice was strained. She struggled to stay conscious long enough to divulge what she'd learned from her Monster Lore. "Don't move a muscle when you wake up."

If the Cowgirl said more, Mithabel didn't hear, losing her own fight against the poisonous sleep wrapping her in a fiery cocoon.

In the Elf's last waking moments, Megan Wright whispered to her. "And you were doing so well. I was impressed."

CHAPTER TWENTY-ONE

Mithabel's head throbbed. The Elf groaned at the thought of getting up. Was there something she was supposed to remember?

Megan Wright whispered to her over their shared mental connection. "Charli said to stay still. Remember?"

The Cowgirl spoke over party chat. "If anyone else is awake, please don't move. If you move, the Poison Ivy Snakes in the trees above us will attack again. Are any of you awake? Amarynth? Rolag? Dylan? Mithabel?"

Rolag responded first. "Am I glad to hear your voice, Charli. I managed to fly clear of those swinging fangs. I hope the others wake up soon. We've got another problem."

Still struggling to clear the cobwebs in her head, Mithabel remained silent and listened, curious as to what problem Rolag was talking about but too woozy to ask.

Charli continued the conversation. "They should be waking any moment. What's wrong?"

The Pseudo Code Dragon made no external sounds revealing his location. "Not to alarm you, but XStorm has found us. They're parked on the eastern edge of the clearing. ChrisCross with his Electrical Serpent wrapped around his waist. Ruby the Centaur with Penelope on her back. And their male/female Asian duo."

As if on cue, a familiar male voice gloated over local chat. "Well, well, well. Look who decided to make camp with no one on watch."

The sound of ChrisCross's voice inflamed Mithabel. She

needed to teach that man a lesson about respecting others. If only she could get to her feet.

Megan Wright admonished her. "I wouldn't move without a plan. Talk to Charli."

ChrisCross chuckled, still on local chat. "You know how to wring the fun out of everything, Yuni. Of course I want them to hear me. What good is a taunt if the people you're taunting can't hear you...? Yes, I realize they're asleep. So why are you getting on my case?"

Mithabel's ribs felt misaligned from lying on her side for so long, but she resisted the urge to roll onto her back. "I'm awake, Charli. What's the plan?"

"*Mithabel.*" Charli and Rolag both sounded relieved. The Cowgirl continued. "So glad you're awake too. I guess you heard XStorm is here. This is what I'm thinking. If we can lure them to come into the clearing, the Ivy Snakes will put them out of commission for us. They're standing at the edge of the clearing, like they're afraid to enter, not sure what happened to us. We need to entice them all to come closer. If even one stays outside the clearing, the Ivy Snakes might not attack."

"Give me a second to assess the situation." Mithabel switched to Third Person POV, which allowed her to view the members of XStorm huddling thirty feet away. There was the black-haired ChrisCross in his white quilted armor, but weaponless. A thrill ran through Mithabel, knowing he was without his bow because of her and Rolag. The red-headed Centaur, Ruby, aimed a loaded bow at Dylan. The Goth, Penelope, sat astride Ruby's back, bow in hand, her straight black hair and night black armor in sharp contrast to her pale white skin. Next to Ruby and her rider stood a human woman with Asian features, about Charli's height, excepting her platform boots with thick heels. With a lean adult build, cherry blond hair, and brown eyes, looking to be in her early to mid twenties, she wielded a cudgel and wore slick red leather armor with cutouts exposing the flesh on either side of her abdomen. Making some kind of fashion statement. That must be Yuni, the woman ChrisCross had mentioned as being a Priestess. Next to Yuni stood a human male also of an Asian bent, with hair matching Yuni's in color. His attire consisted of full body brown leather armor and matching boots. He carried a staff, one end planted on the ground, the other extending above his head by several inches. No other visible weapons. That had to be Bradford, the party's Wizard.

Bradford aimed his staff at Dylan, glancing askance at ChrisCross.

Mithabel wracked her brain. "Dammit. I can't think straight."

"Calm down, Mithabel." Megan Wright stood near the Elf's head, her figure at a ninety degree angle to Mithabel's prone form. "We can't let this bastard hurt Dylan. Take a look at the overhanging canopy above us."

Angling her Third Person POV straight up while on the ground was an impossible task. Her view origin point wouldn't cooperate. "Tell me what you see, Megan."

"The Poison Ivy Snakes are slithering quietly through the treetops, amassing near the eastern edge of the clearing, over by XStorm, away from us. Can you lend Dylan your Natural Armor trait while she's sleeping?"

"Good idea. I've been wanting an excuse to try. Kaleisha, request a transfer of my awareness to Dylan." How many other parties had figured out they could transfer traits among themselves? She hoped *none* of them had.

The members of XStorm nodded at each other, using their own party chat to converse. ChrisCross glanced around as though unsure, concerned perhaps about Rolag not being in evidence.

Dylan accepted Mithabel's transfer and the Tank found herself inside the sleeping woman's dreams. In her own mist-formed body, Mithabel stood immediately to Dylan's right, rather than occupying a nebulous space in the Polynesian's mind. The Priestess bowed before her blond, black Goddess, who still sat on her golden throne. Did Scintilla ever leave this place?

The Goddess frowned at Mithabel's arrival. "Must you always disturb our private conversations, mortal?"

"I'm sorry, but XStorm has found us and aims to kill Dylan." Mithabel turned to her friend. "I want to lend you my Natural Armor trait. It would also be nice if you could wake up now."

The Polynesian peered up at her Goddess.

Scintilla nodded. "Best do as your friend says, my Priestess. I wouldn't want our discussion to cost you a life." The Goddess's eyes lost focus for a moment. "Ah, I see. I advise you borrow what your friend here is offering. Wake up, jump up, and run west as hard as you can go." The Goddess turned to Mithabel. "You might also try lending something other than traits. I'm not saying you *can*. I'd never say *that*. The game doesn't allow me to say *that*."

Dylan straightened. "We will do as you bid." She looked briefly to her left, where no one stood, and nodded.

From behind Mithabel, to her right, Kaleisha popped her head into view. "Dylan has accepted the transfer of your Natural Armor trait, chief. *It worked.*"

"Great." The Tank spoke over the mental connection established between her and Dylan by the awareness transfer. "Time to wake up, Priestess. Can you do it?"

Scintilla leaned forward on her throne. "I can help with that." She snapped her fingers.

The dream scene vanished, replaced by the darkness of the interior of Dylan's head space.

"I hope you remember your dream, Dylan." The Tank concentrated, hurrying to push all her remaining traits to Dylan. Though sluggish, the Priestess accepted everything Mithabel offered.

"Try this as well." Mithabel offered her Armor skill to Dylan.

The Priestess accepted. Sweet mother, the transfer went through.

"ChrisCross is nodding his head." Charli filled them in. "Might be the signal for everyone to attack."

Whoosh. The Danger Sense trait triggered its alarm inside Dylan's head, where Mithabel also heard it. XStorm had finally decided to attack.

"Get up and run, Dylan, like Scintilla told you. Go west." Mithabel turned her Third Person POV to scan east. Ruby and Penelope, still aiming arrows at Dylan, still hadn't shot yet. What were they waiting for?

The Jamaican AI gave a quick report. "Party MAD is full on all HP types except Physical. High 90s there for everyone except Rolag at 100. Every member of XStorm is at full HP on all HP types. Good luck, chief."

ChrisCross pointed a finger at Dylan and pretended to fire a pistol. Mithabel half expected a bullet to spring from the tip of his finger, but it didn't. He was giving the signal to shoot.

Ruby fired.

The missile glanced off Dylan's shoulder.

"No damage dealt." Kaleisha sounded relieved.

With a wild laugh, the Polynesian jumped to her feet and ran.

ChrisCross waved his party forward, and XStorm gave chase. The Centaur and her rider led the way, with the Priestess and Wizard bringing up the rear. Ten feet into the clearing, Bradford stopped and began voicing arcane words.

The Poison Ivy Snakes descended from the treetops upon the unsuspecting enemy party.

"Charli, wake up Amarynth and the two of you get moving." Mithabel kept her awareness with Dylan, continuing to lend traits and skills until the Priestess could vacate the clearing.

Lying on her side, the teenager kicked Amarynth in the ribs. The Viking rolled over to stare at the girl, and then caught sight of the tussle between XStorm and the Ivy Snakes.

The Polynesian reached the west side of the clearing and didn't slow down.

"Dylan, don't get too far ahead of us. I'm going back to my body now, to get myself out of there while XStorm plays with Poison Ivy." Withdrawing her awareness from the Priestess, the Elf jumped up and ran, still watching the entire scene through the miracle of Third Person POV. "Amarynth, *move it*."

Understanding clicked in the Archer's eyes. She and Charli hopped to their feet and fled like bunnies before a forest fire, the Viking half dragging the Cowgirl along with her.

The Poison Ivy Snakes made quick work of XStorm, sinking poisoned fangs through exposed necks, dropping ChrisCross and every one of his allies the same way they'd felled party MAD. When finished, the vine-like serpents drew into the canopy as though on reels. Once back in the treetops, they slithered along the branches to the west. But all members of party MAD were free of the clearing.

Dylan punched Mithabel's arm. "Thanks for lending me your traits and the Armor skill. I never would have guessed skills could be transferred too. That's powerful stuff."

"You transferred a skill, Mithabel?" Amarynth raised an eyebrow.

The Tank switched to First Person POV for a face-to-face conversation. "The Goddess all but suggested it. I wouldn't have thought of it on my own." At Amarynth's inquisitive glance, the Elf smiled. "Long story." She pointed at the fallen, poisoned bodies of party XStorm. "Will your crossbow reach them from here?"

"Probably, but it would be more satisfying shooting them up close and personal from the other side of the clearing."

Dylan held up a hand, palm outward. "Stop right there. You're not attacking defenseless PCs, no matter how vile they are. Come on. We're clear of the Poison Ivy Snakes, and XStorm won't be bothering us for a while. Let's move. Maron and our quest await."

Mithabel clicked her tongue. "Sorry, Dylan, but I don't see things your way." The Elf wove her way between the trees along the southern edge of the clearing. "They shot at us when we were down. We should return the favor. Come on, Amarynth. Let's send these creeps back to their spawning chambers. Teach them to try collecting a bounty on our

Polynesian Priestess."

"I can't watch." Dylan looked away from the clearing.

Amarynth crunched leaves and twigs as she sped after the Tank, catching her quickly. "I'm with you on this, Mithabel."

"I want to come." Charli ran after the other two, frequently stumbling until she stashed her skirt.

"I'll stay with the Priestess." The Dragon circled over Dylan's head. "Someone ought to."

"Thank you, Rolag. I'll heal you first next time."

Seconds later, the Tank, Archer, and Guide stood on the eastern border of the clearing, no more than twenty feet from the members of XStorm. Closest to them lay the Wizard, only ten feet away.

A glance up confirmed the return of the Poison Ivy Snakes to the east side of the clearing. Being aware of their nature made it easier for Mithabel to spot them. "We're being watched by our friends in the treetops. Whatever you do, don't step into the clearing."

Amarynth aimed her crossbow at the Wizard's head and chuckled. "My, my. They didn't stash their weapons before they fell. If we kill them, they'll lose their gear."

The Tank pointed with her chin. "Bradford's staff isn't touching him. It'll be interesting to see what happens to it, if it vanishes when he does or stays behind." She equipped her bow and took aim at ChrisCross. Would it be ironic if she killed him with what had once been his bow? She'd often been accused of using the word *ironic* incorrectly, but maybe it applied to this situation. "Wonder if damage is multiplied against a helpless foe."

"We're about to find out." Amarynth fired. Her bolt pierced the Wizard's eye. The short Asian man's body exploded into glowing dust particles that swirled away like a golden dust devil.

Mithabel nodded at the staff, still lying where it had fallen. "Interesting. If you die with a weapon in hand, the weapon is gone. If you die with a weapon stashed, it's still stashed when you respawn. If you drop your weapon and die, the weapon stays behind for anyone to pick up. Good to know."

Charli patted Mithabel's armored forearm. "It's also worth noting you don't lose any armor you're wearing when you die."

The Viking took aim at XStorm's fallen Priestess. "Good observations, both of you."

"Speaking of armor." The Tank eyed Yuni in her slick red leather. "How did she rate? That's a lot more fashionable than what we're stuck with. Did she actually pay extra for that?"

Though maintaining her distance, Dylan proved she was paying attention by offering an explanation. "She paid extra. That blood red color is symbolic of her chosen deity, the Goddess of War. I could have paid extra for golden armor, but spent the money on beginning spells instead. I think I made the right choice."

ChrisCross didn't have a weapon, so there was nothing for him to lose when he died. Mithabel shouted a war cry as she loosed her arrow. It glanced off the quilted armor covering the man's chest, dealing no damage. "Damn. So much for dealing massive damage to helpless foes."

Yuni had dropped her cudgel, which lay inches from her limp hand. Amarynth put a bolt through the Asian woman's eye. The XStorm Priestess erupted into a rolling cloud of bright bits and floated away on a breeze. Her cudgel remained where it lay. The Archer shifted her aim to the Centaur, whose bow lay loosely in her grip. "Where you hit your target seems to play into how much damage you deal, Mithabel. Put your arrow through his eye, and I bet you'll kill him. Or hit any other highly vulnerable point." She put a bolt through the bottom of Ruby's chin. The head of the bolt burst through the Centaur's scalp. Ruby disintegrated, her brilliant dust riding away on a breeze. The bow in her grasp didn't burst into particles the same way she did, but faded from existence like a shy ghost, lost forever.

Mithabel tried hitting ChrisCross again, but her aim was off, and her arrow only grazed his temple, again dealing no damage. "Shit. I can't even hit a motionless target."

"Let me help." The Archer sat and folded her hands over her lap.

"Amarynth has requested to transfer her awareness to you, chief."

"Let her in, Kaleisha."

"Now she requests to transfer her Aim skill to you."

"Oh, *yes*, I accept." Taking aim again, Mithabel skewered the man's eye.

"Physical HP for ChrisCross has fallen to 89%, chief."

The arrow still protruded from his eye socket.

"This is bullshit." Mithabel wanted to fling the bow into the trees. Weren't Elves supposed to be naturally proficient with bows? Or was that only a specific type of Elf? She'd passed on adding a qualifier to her Elf kindred tag. But she was happy for her decision. She'd gained the Dark Sight kindred trait, which she suspected would be more useful in the long run than a trait to make her proficient with a bow. Assuming the future held more than one dungeon quest in store for party MAD.

"Try this skill too, Tank." Amarynth offered the use of her Critical Hit – Bow/Crossbow skill.

"Swell." With careful aim, the Elf fired again. The arrow entered ChrisCross's eye next to the first projectile. The Elitist blasted to brilliant bits. "Damn, Amarynth. Archers are way better than Tanks in this game on offense. You get a Crit skill and I get Stun."

"Yeah, but a bulldozer could hit you and you'd still be standing afterward."

With a fist, Mithabel pounded her abs twice and grinned.

Only Penelope remained lying in the clearing.

Charli gestured to get the attention of her two companions. "Where's their Electric Snake, Lance?"

"Kaleisha, is ChrisCross's snake companion in the vicinity?"

"Can't say about that, chief, but I can tell you his Physical HP reads 100%."

"He's crawled away, somewhere." Mithabel shook her head.

"Who knows where he's gone. Wherever he is, he can be used by XStorm as a re-entry point for the game when they respawn, which could put them right back on our heels. We need to find the little bastard and make sure he's dead. Rolag, can you do a quick search of the area?" Mithabel took aim at Penelope and put an arrow through the pale woman's skull. The NPC blew apart into tiny glowing fragments. The Elf snorted. "We told you not to follow us." The bow in Penelope's grip faded like Ruby's had, returning to the proverbial bit bucket, no longer in the NPC's possession or available to anyone else in the game.

The Pseudo Code Dragon flew around the clearing, spiraling outward. "I'm not seeing Lance."

The Archer withdrew her skills and awareness from the Tank. "Why don't you lend Rolag your Alertness trait, Mithabel?"

The Elf shook her head. "I would if I could, but I tried transferring awareness to him before, and it didn't work."

"Did you ask my permission? He's *my* Magical Companion, after all. Maybe it will work if I allow it." Amarynth had a point.

Mithabel sat. "Kaleisha, request a transfer of my awareness to Rolag, with Amarynth's permission."

In the next instant, she looked through reptilian eyes. Wings extended out to either side of her, flapping up and down in hypnotic rhythm. Fangs filled her maw. Claws adorned her fingertips. Strength imbued her limbs and spine in patterns not possible for a humanoid. Her head swiveled on a neck as long as her limbs. Tree branches flashed by at breathtaking speed. By instinct, she tried to swerve to miss a tree, but her body went in the opposite direction from where she intended. It wasn't *her* body she occupied. She wasn't in control.

"Greetings, Tank." The Dragon spoke over their newly established shared mental connection, his sibilant yet gravelly voice not unlike how it sounded over party chat. "Welcome to my mind."

"The pleasure is all yours."

"Hey, Mithabel." The Archer's presence entered Rolag's head too. "Let's super power this little guy."

Amarynth granted Increased Movement level two to the Dragon, while Mithabel gave him Alertness. In two seconds, he caught sight of a streak of blue headed east, and zipped through the trees after the fleeing mascot. Sensing a fight, Mithabel lent Rolag her Natural Armor trait and Armor skill. She tried lending her Damage skill too.

"I'm not allowed to accept the Damage skill." Rolag dove for the blue Electric Snake. "I already have my own Damage skill. The game won't let me stack them."

A sickness overtook Mithabel. "I'll watch from outside your skin, Dragon." She switched to Third Person POV. The wooziness subsided, though zooming through the forest still disconcerted her.

Lance scarcely had time to rear up for a strike before Rolag rammed his skull against that of the Electric Serpent. Mithabel sensed the power behind the strike and registered the vibrations coursing through the Dragon's body. A twinge of pain and an explosion of pride invaded the Tank's awareness.

The snake fell limp to the ground, stunned, without a chance to attack. Rolag landed beside his foe. With gleaming fangs, he snagged a scale at the base of Lance's head and tugged. Electricity shot through Rolag, playing over his scaly frame.

"Harvest time." Clearly in pain but ignoring it, the Pseudo Code Dragon ripped the outer layer of scales from the Serpent's body and stashed the snakeskin. He crowed like a rooster.

"HP for Lance plummets to 29%, chief."

The Electric Serpent trembled as though in shock. With his claws, Rolag grabbed Lance by the throat. He sank his fangs into the top of the snake's head, tearing out a chunk of gray matter. To Mithabel, even with the mental distance afforded her by the use of Third Person POV, it seemed she sank her own teeth into the Serpent's brain. Her mind reacted as if to retch.

A ball of lightning erupted from Lance's body, enveloping

both combatants. Magical energy coursed through Rolag, pulling at his nerves as though to pluck them from his body. Mithabel experienced it with him, as did Amarynth. None of them gave any indication of the full degree of pain they were in.

When the sparks died, the Electric Serpent was gone. The Dragon scarcely looked singed. He smirked.

"Rolag stands at 94% HP. But the better news, chief, is that, *congratulations*, you are level eight Tank. Your XP Progression stands at 39% towards level nine."

Megan Wright flew into view, shaking her fists in triumph. "Woah. Killing PCs with some character levels under their belts is worth a lot more than killing mooks or even Bosses."

Kaleisha sidled up to the blond player, wrapping an arm around Megan's waist. "More good news, chief. No new skills or traits gained, but you have earned an assignable *attribute point*."

The blond cocked her head. "Nice, Mithabel."

"Yeah, I can restore my lost Constitution point now." The Tank didn't make the assignment right away, wanting to mull over the decision. Assignable attribute points wouldn't come along too often. She wanted to boost her Brawn from the average category to the high average category, which she could do with a single point. But would the extra Brawn be worth foregoing another life in the game? This decision required some thought.

As Rolag flew back to the group, Mithabel restored her awareness to herself.

Charli stood straight and proud beside the Elf, holding the staff and cudgel left behind by XStorm's Wizard and Priestess. "I was busy, too." With one end of the staff planted on the ground, the weapon reached about a foot above the Cowgirl's head, a clear indication that Bradford and Charli were roughly the same height.

"How did you get those?" Mithabel stood, eying the Cowgirl with curiosity, thankful not to be looking down at Charli's poisoned body. She took the cudgel and examined it. "Dylan could use this."

The teenage Guide grinned broadly. "I figured hiding or some type of stealth was how Lance avoided the Poison Ivy Snakes. So I used my Hide skill and crawled into the clearing. I touched each item, stashed it, and then crawled back. Now here I am, with more equipment for us."

Amarynth patted the top of Charli's hat. "You're a brave young lady. I wish you had waited for us to watch over you in case your Hide skill didn't fool the Ivy Snakes, but everything worked out in the end, and that's all that matters. Good job." She nodded at the staff. "You should keep that for yourself. It might be useful to you as a weapon. I'm assuming Bradford used it as one, and if he could, I don't see why you can't."

The Cowgirl smiled. "Thank you, I will." She stashed the item.

Mithabel returned the cudgel to Charli. "You're the one who retrieved this weapon. You should be allowed to keep it or give it away as you wish. But I know someone who'd like to have it."

The three jogged back to Dylan, who met them halfway, her eyes alight as she took in the sight of the cudgel. Charli bowed to the Priestess and held out the weapon with both hands. "I offer you, Dylan, Priestess of Scintilla, a weapon to replace that which was lost."

The Polynesian took the offering, bowing in return, her lips quivering as though she fought back a smile or tears or both. "I accept your gift, Guide Charli. May the blessing of Scintilla ever smile upon you." When she straightened, she turned a determined gaze on Mithabel. "I've been caught up in the morality of the real world as Debra Jones would see it. No longer. From here forward, I will judge situations by the morality of the game world. It's open season on the competition. It's not like we're killing real people."

Fighting back her own smile, the Elf raised her eyebrows. Satisfaction tingled her spine. "I'm glad you exercised your privilege to change your mind, and aren't letting some game attribute control you."

Though he was still flying back to the group, the Pseudo Code Dragon joined in on party chat. "It's the only way to reconcile traveling in the company of psychopaths."

Dylan grinned and beckoned to the Tank. "Come here, you. I gained more Auni with my level gain, and it has restored to full, so I can spare a few points." Dylan cast healing spells to bring her three companions to full. "None of you were down by much, but I'd rather everyone was at full HP before we continue. My Auni restores relatively quickly. Faster than you can heal HP."

Rolag caught up with them. "Are we ready to go? XStorm will respawn as soon as they can fall asleep, and I'm guessing they'll enter the game as close to us as they can."

"I'm not so sure about that." Mithabel nodded at the cudgel Dylan held. "Four of them lost their primary weapons. If XStorm has any money to their names, they might choose to respawn in Voorton and buy equipment."

"Yes, but...." Dylan took a moment to heal Rolag, and didn't continue her statement afterward. She beckoned for the others to follow as she headed west, pausing after a moment to let Mithabel and Amarynth go ahead of her. Only then did she continue. "If XStorm skips buying more equipment, they'll still be strong. The Priestess doesn't *need* her cudgel and the Wizard doesn't *need* his staff. We still haven't seen what either of them can do. The Centaur can close to melee range quickly, with Penelope riding her, and they both could easily still have any melee weapons they started the game with. Lance can move quickly and hide decently well, especially if Mithabel with her Alertness is out front and Lance comes from behind. As for their arrogant Elitist leader man, he didn't seem too disturbed to be without a weapon. He's only wearing quilted armor. Putting two and two together makes me think he's a martial artist type." Her mouth puckered as though ready to spit.

Charli popped her lips. "Keep in mind, too, we still need to fight the Black Poison Forest Boss. I hate to think what it might be, but we'll likely find out soon. If XStorm finds us while we're fighting a strong enemy, they can take advantage of the situation and attack us too. Even if XStorm doesn't show up at an inconvenient time, other parties might. We know that other parties are back in the game."

Mithabel pulled out ahead of the others, taking the lead. "But we don't know for sure if any of them are coming west."

Dylan mused aloud. "I wonder what's to the north, east, and south of Voorton. When we started, we picked a direction and kept going. How different would our adventures have been if we'd chosen another direction in the beginning?"

Charli stuck a hand into the air like a student eager to answer a question. "Voorton is on a peninsula. Anyone going any direction but west will eventually head west if they want to get anywhere in the game."

The Polynesian's face darkened. "And you're only now mentioning this?"

The Cowgirl shrugged. "It never seemed pertinent. But I did steer you in the right direction from the beginning."

"And we're thankful for that." Amarynth spoke loud enough to compete with the volume of her stomping boots.

Mithabel sighed. "Did everyone gain level eight? I earned an assignable attribute point. I assume the rest of you did as well. Has anyone decided where to put theirs?"

Amarynth went first. "I put mine in Sensing, moving it to the extraordinary category. The further I can see, the sooner I can start shooting approaching enemies."

"Makes sense." Dylan chuckled at her own pun. "I put my point into Charisma. It's still low average, but I'm assuming we'll earn more assignable attribute points along the way. I *can't* bear to have my Charisma so low. I don't want to be Debra Jones."

"You're *not* your player." Mithabel bristled at the idea. "Just as I'm not Megan Wright."

The blond player flew out ahead of the Elf, looking back at

her avatar. "Oh, I'm *so* bloody terrible."

"That's not what I meant, Megan, and you know it."

Everyone fell quiet.

Mithabel expected Dylan to say something, but the Priestess kept her thoughts to herself. Perhaps she was in a conversation with Debra Jones.

The Elf was first to speak again. "How about you, Charli? Did you gain an attribute point?"

"Sure did." Charli had equipped her skirt again, since they were no longer running. "I raised my Constitution. If it represents how many lives we have, I want to give myself as many as possible. I realize it's a selfish move, but I couldn't bring myself to raise any other attribute instead. What about you, Mithabel? And Rolag?"

"I increased my Sanity." Rolag brought up the rear as before. "I didn't like what those Shadow creatures did to me. I need to be stronger mentally."

"Well." Mithabel had reached her decision. "I assigned my point to Brawn, moving it from the average category to high average category. I considered putting the point on Constitution, but I hope to stay alive long enough to earn more points to buy more lives. I figured Brawn could help me do more as a Tank overall to protect myself and the rest of you lot."

"We appreciate power." Dylan hummed a brief tune.

The party chat fell silent. The group pressed westward, the crunch of dead vegetation under Amarynth's boots echoing through the forest louder than all other sounds on the special effects channel combined. The first magic item the group needed to purchase when they had the chance was a pair of silenced boots for the Viking.

CHAPTER TWENTY-TWO

Time crawled by without incident. As expected, the sun hadn't moved all day. The system clock read *5:42 PM, Day 2, Year 1.*

Dylan called over party chat. "Can we stop for a moment? We're walking and walking and getting nowhere. We need to fight the territory Boss."

"Sure, we can stop." Mithabel halted to let the others catch her. "Don't know how that will help us fight the Boss, but a strategy session can't hurt."

Charli adjusted her hat as she quickened her step, moving ahead of the Polynesian. "Maybe if we made more noise, the Boss would attack."

Mithabel snorted. "Amarynth makes so much noise, she's scaring all the mooks away."

The Cowgirl nodded, coming to a stop beside the Tank. "The game can be selective about what channels individual monsters hear. Maybe the special effects channel is muted for the Boss of this territory. We could try shouting on the local chat channel. We saw how effective that was back in the Mystic Hollow Cornfield and the Brassy Grassy."

Dylan kept coming, though her pace had slowed. "That could also give away our position to any bounty hunting parties on our trail."

"Yes." Charli held up a finger. "But only if they're close to us, at least in the same territory. Do we think other parties are in the Black Poison Forest?"

"Kaleisha, show me the rankings." Mithabel perused the Top

Twenty Parties list. MAD was still first. XStorm was second. Quantized was third, and BoardStiff was fourth. "To err on the side of caution, we need to assume XStorm came back to the forest when they respawned, so, yes, they could be close by. Frankly, I'm surprised they haven't caught us. Hell, Lance *might be* watching us right now." On the Longest Survivor Bounty Contenders list, Quantized was first, BoardStiff second, and XStorm third. And those weren't the only parties on the list. "Damn. Two more parties have joined the Bounty Contenders list. OrionsDagger and ZAvengers. They've figured out how to respawn." A countdown clock at the top of the list showed the time remaining as 06:16:11, changing to 06:16:10 and then 06:16:09. "And... um... there appears to be a timer on the bounty. If you can survive until midnight, Dylan, I think the bounty will be lifted."

"Or increased." The Priestess reached the Tank and leaned against a tree. "I saw that countdown clock, too. Not getting my hopes up. Let's concentrate on finding the Boss so we can move on from the forest and into the city, while *not* giving away our position."

Amarynth crunched fallen leaves and twigs as she paced around the other three ladies. Saying nothing, she aimed her gaze outward, hunting for any sign of an enemy.

The Elf took a deep breath. "Why is XStorm listed *after* two other teams on the Bounty Contenders list? I assume the higher a party is on the list, the closer they are to us. If my assumption is true, and XStorm has respawned in the forest, then Quantized and BoardStiff are both in the forest too. *Closer* than XStorm. That doesn't feel right."

Dylan pushed away from her tree and paced. "What if XStorm respawned in the city after all? Maybe they had harvested some mook or Boss body parts and bought more equipment in Voorton. One thing is for sure. XStorm will want the bounty now more than ever. If ChrisCross is anything like his player, he won't take it lightly being bested twice by a party of women, even one accompanied by a Dragon. His not having caught up to us yet makes me think XStorm *did* respawn in Voorton. We've seen no signs of other parties. I think we're the only party out here. So let's call for the Boss. Since I'm the one with the bounty on my head, I'll do the honors." The Polynesian cupped her hands to her mouth. "Hey, Black Poison Forest Boss Monster. Come out, come out, wherever you are."

Whoosh.

The sound came from near Mithabel's feet. She jumped aside, brandishing her longsword, ready to chop at whatever poked up through the dead leaves. "It's *underground.*"

An extremely short HP status bar slid into the bottom of her view.

"What are we fighting, Kaleisha?"

"The Boss fight is on, chief, with a One Strike Scorpion."

Megan Wright glanced around at the forest floor, voicing the same thought Mithabel had. "A Scorpion? Where the hell is it?"

The Scorpion Boss popped out from the leaves where the Tank's feet had been planted a second earlier. Covered in chitin as dark as night, the Boss measured six inches long, three inches wide, and four inches high, counting the curved tail and two inches of stinger. The tail lashed over the Scorpion's head and the stinger pierced a leaf bearing an impression of Mithabel's boot.

The blond player stared down, still in the Elf's view. "Damn, Mithabel. Good thing you moved."

"No distractions, please, Megan." The Tank attacked, but the longsword blade bit dirt next to the arachnid. Had it moved? Her aim couldn't have been off. She yanked her blade free and hoisted it up to strike again.

The Boss was gone. A lump caught in Mithabel's throat, but she blurted past it. "Everyone *move. Now.*" She demonstrated by jumping to the spot where Megan Wright stood, otherwise unoccupied. "You're still in the way, player."

"Sorry." Megan zipped skyward and out of sight.

The tiny creature flashed from beneath leaves, stabbing its

stinger where Dylan had been standing. To her credit, the Priestess had done as Mithabel suggested, hopping quickly out of place.

A crossbow bolt skewered the One Strike Scorpion. "Got it." Amarynth laughed. "That was easy."

Dylan threw a hard glance at the Archer. "You better not have shot my foot."

"Well, I didn't, did I?"

The bolt dissipated. The Scorpion didn't explode, but twitched its tail and vanished under the leaves. As unbelievable as it seemed, the Archer had missed.

"Move. Again. *Now.*" Mithabel took her own advice, as did all the others.

Charli collided with Dylan, in competition for the same vacant spot. The teenage Guide lost. Her face fell. "Sorry."

The Scorpion appeared, struck the Cowgirl's foot with its stinger, and fled beneath the leaves. Black liquid welled under the skin of Charli's foot, pulsing as it darkened a vein running up her calf.

Megan poked her head over the Elf's shoulder. "What the hell?"

Charli's skin paled. Black liquid shot through her veins up her leg, across her torso, and into her arms and neck. Blackness flooded her eyes. Soot streaked her clothing and brown pigtails. Dark claws, gleaming like metal, sprouted from her fingertips. Screeching, she swiped at the Priestess, slicing through Dylan's armor like it was bread ready to be served. Viscous, ebony liquid dripped from her claws as she withdrew her hand. With an evil grin, she turned her dead gaze on Amarynth.

The blond player waved a hand in front of Mithabel's face. "The Scorpion, Mithabel. You better jump again."

The color drained from Dylan's brown skin, turning it pale, while her neck veins flooded with blackness. Her eyes turned solid black. Mithabel leaped backwards even as the Priestess sprang, slashing at the Tank with elongated, sharpened fingernails, missing by inches.

Amarynth dodged as Charli jumped to attack her. The Cowgirl didn't connect.

The Scorpion manifested next to the Viking and drove its stinger through her boot.

"Dammit." Amarynth dropped her crossbow as her skin paled and veins bulged with dark fluid.

Mithabel turned and fled, leaping as high as she could with each step.

The One Strike Scorpion launched into the air and caught her heel. Its stinger pierced her boot and flesh. Cold liquid entered her veins, sapping the heat from her body. Her longsword left her grasp. She didn't have the faculties to stash it first.

Crude oil smeared Mithabel's vision, blinding her. "Kaleisha, transfer my awareness to Rolag."

The Jamaican AI wavered on the periphery of Mithabel's field of vision within her mind's eye. "Can't do it, sorry, chief. Something's wrong with Amarynth's authentication protocols. Can't confirm her approval."

Megan Wright flew over and took Kaleisha's hands in her own. "Kaleisha, dear, make the transfer. Amarynth wants you to do it, and you know it. Confirmation be damned."

Kaleisha frowned, her eyes glistening as though she were about to cry. "Emergency override authorization code required."

"I'm the player. You're a support AI. Do as I command, or I'll report you in the real world and have you deleted. Do I make myself clear?"

Tears welled in Kaleisha's eyes. "Emergency override authorization code accepted. Awareness transferal initiated."

"Mithabel." The mental connection between the Tank and the reptilian member of party MAD translated the Dragon's alien thoughts. "Talk to me."

Through Rolag's eyes, the Elf looked down from a circling vantage point on herself and her three female companions.

Dark veins created a patchwork creeping from the exposed pale flesh to crawl across their armor. All four slashed at each other with claws six inches long.

Sweet mother, they were killing one another.

The Dragon growled. *"Mithabel. Talk."*

"It's all on you, Rolag. The Boss has displacement magic, *and* it can jump. I don't know how high. But it lives up to its name. One hit, and you're toast."

The Pseudo Code Dragon scanned the dead leaves surrounding the four fighting women. "Where did it go?"

"I'm not sure, but I'll help you look. Kaleisha, initiate transfer of my Alertness skill to Rolag."

The Jamaican AI didn't protest. The Dragon's vision and hearing sharpened.

Mithabel switched to Third Person POV, scanning up, down, and all around. She spotted movement on a tree branch and then... the Scorpion fell, on an intercept course for the Dragon. "Above you, Rolag. *Dodge. Now.*"

Mid-flight, Rolag flipped upside down and breathed upward, maintaining his flight pattern. The Scorpion couldn't check its fall or change its trajectory. A cone of flaming Dragon breath, five feet long and a foot in diameter at the far end, centered its scorching death on the tiny Boss monster.

The flames died.

The Scorpion was gone.

Rolag crowed. "I did it. Too easy."

At the bottom of Mithabel's view, the Scorpion's HP status bar emptied to zero. It didn't slide out of sight.

"The One Strike Scorpion is defeated, but the Boss encounter isn't over, chief."

Charli exploded into a column of glowing dust. Mithabel didn't catch who had delivered the fatal blow.

The three remaining dark veined women continued attacking each other.

"Damn. We're not done here, Rolag, until our three avatars stop fighting each other or are all dead."

The Dragon righted himself and continued circling. "Should I help one of you win by helping to kill the other two?"

"Don't you dare go near them. Dylan, can you hear me?"

"Mithabel? Oh, Goddess. This is terrible. My HP status is steadily declining, but I can't cast my Heal spell. And I can't *see* anything."

"Dylan, listen. You need to transfer your awareness to Rolag. Magnum will say it can't be done. Tell him it's an emergency override. He'll ask for an authorization code. Have Debra Jones identify herself as your player, demand that he do the transfer, then threaten to report him in the real world and have his program deleted if he refuses. Got that?"

"I'm not a bully, Mithabel. I need to draw the moral line somewhere."

"Do you want to stay alive? If so, then do as I say and be quick about it."

The Polynesian didn't reply.

Precious seconds past.

The Dragon broke the silence first. "Hello, Dylan."

"Rolag. Mithabel. I feel terrible for treating Magnum that way. *This* is strange. So I'm here. What now, Tank?"

Mithabel spelled out her plan. "The Scorpion is dead, but our possessed bodies are still carrying out its commands, attacking each other. I was hoping you could Turn or Excise whatever is possessing us. Possible?"

"Theoretically, sure. If I had a body to cast spells with. Oh. You think I could lend the necessary skill or spell to Rolag. Sure. Why not? Seems to be on par with all the other craziness allowed in this game. I'll give it a try." The Polynesian paused. "Magnum balked at transferring my spells, but Debra Jones threatened him again."

"What do I do?" The Dragon landed on a tree branch near the fighting women, high enough to be out of their reach.

"Let's try turning first. It doesn't require Auni." The Priestess directed Rolag how to gesture and what to say, emphasizing the name Scintilla. The Pseudo Code Dragon played the part of Priestess admirably, waving his front legs and wiggling his talons. "Forces of darkness and evil, I command you turn away and begone from us, the servants of *Scintilla*, Goddess of Light and the Sun."

The zombies paid him no attention, still slashing at one another. The Goddess gave no sign of having been persuaded by the Dragon's ministrations to grant her aid.

"Dylan's hit points have fallen to 16%, chief."

Megan Wright flew up and hovered next to Rolag, her face contorted with desperation. "You need to save her, Mithabel. *Please*."

"Try the spell, Priestess. We're out of time. You're about to die."

"Let's do it." Rolag raised his front legs, ready to gesture.

Dylan directed the Winged Fighter. "Okay, Dragon. You need to reach through your Auni connection to the root of the spell and draw it out. You don't have enough Auni to guarantee success, so push all you have into casting the spell at my body. If you save me, I can Excise the others."

"Dylan is down to 4% hit points, chief."

The hovering blond player's eyes grew wet. "Mithabel, you *have* to save her."

"Don't get hit again, Dylan, or you're dead. Drop and roll as soon as you have control of your body again. Amarynth, if you can hear me, fight the force controlling your body. We only need a few seconds. Have Anna Milligan help you if she can. Kaleisha, put me back in my own body."

The Archer moaned. "Mithabel, this is hell. I'm dying and can't do a thing to stop it."

"Fight it. You're a freaking *Viking. Fearless.* Imbue Anna Milligan with some of your power instead of letting her drag you down with despair. She's got it in her to fight, or she wouldn't have joined this competition. *Fight*, Amarynth."

Mithabel found herself back in her own body, still unable to control its movements. "Megan, I need you with me inside my head."

"I'm here. What can I do?" The blond player spoke from the darkness of Mithabel's mind.

"Help me fight whatever is possessing our avatar. Lock our muscles against its will."

"Let's do it."

Mithabel focused on reclaiming control of her limbs, or at least to slow them.

The dominating presence inside Mithabel's head roared. "GET OUT."

"*You* get out, *bitch*." Putting all her Willpower into it, Mithabel pictured her limbs moving in slow motion. Don't hit Dylan. The refrain repeated through her awareness. Don't hit Dylan. Were her efforts helping? She couldn't know, couldn't see what was happening outside her body or feel the motion of her muscles. Being focused on the situation inside her head, looking around outside with Third Person POV at the moment wasn't an option.

Rolag voiced arcane words with his reptilian tongue. That meant Dylan was still alive, working her spell through the Dragon. His voice deepened and slowed, as though time itself dragged. What was causing that? He needed to cast the spell as soon as he could. A slower casting would only drag out how long Mithabel and Amarynth needed to resist their possessors.

The alien in Mithabel's head roared again. "GET OUT."

Megan Wright stirred in the darkness. "Keep your focus, Tank. Let's fight this thing. Not only to slow it down, but to force *it* out of *our* head. What do you say?"

"I say, *great*, Megan, let's get this thing gone." In addition to freezing her virtual body's muscles, Mithabel bent her Willpower towards ousting her possessor.

Rolag's voice slowed further, as though played back from a recording at a fraction of normal speed.

Dark tendrils rose in Mithabel's mind's eye, barely distinguishable from the enveloping darkness. A black octopus flailed a multitude of arms in the vast void. The monster reached an appendage for her. "THEN COME AND DIE."

Free floating in space, Mithabel took on a metaphysical form matching her appearance in Khertaan, absent armor and boots. To her right, a metaphysical version of a blond Megan Wright formed, four inches shorter than Mithabel, also clad in nothing but her underwear. The two looked each other up and down before nodding with narcissistic approval. Metaphysically, they had no defensive gear. Or offensive gear, for that matter. But they both had metaphysical bodies to be proud of. It was time to reclaim Mithabel's physical one.

A banner over the mook's blob of a metaphysical head identified it as a Spiritual Dominator. Beneath the banner was its status bar, reading, Spirit HP: 100%.

This wasn't a mental battle as Mithabel had believed, but a spiritual one. They'd been drawn into the Spiritual realm for a metaphysical combat.

What were Mithabel's Spiritual attributes? "Kaleisha, can you hear me?"

Electric lines wavered and buzzed to Mithabel's left, illuminating a familiar Jamaican female form with brown skin and half a dozen long brown braids hanging down one side of her face. She wore her usual scant, electrical clothing. "Here, chief. Your Spiritual stats: Faith, Favor, Belief, and Inspiration are all average. Your Morals are high average. And then there's your sub-par Conscience."

"Right. Thanks, Kaleisha. So, then, how do we fight this thing?"

"You tell me, chief. But I feel different here, like I could actually participate, if you want."

The spell casting attempt still being in progress, a syllable in Rolag's deep, reptilian voice echoed around the combatants. It didn't matter so much how slow he spoke, only that he continued to form one arcane syllable after the other.

With another roar, the Spiritual Dominator propelled forward. It lashed out with three tentacles, aiming one at each of its foes. Having nothing to push against, Mithabel willed herself to move aside, but not fast enough. A tentacle wrapped around her waist, shocking her with its chill.

Her metaphysical fingers turned blue as she drove them between the tentacle and her flesh. Could she pry herself free?

It wasn't working.

The octopus drew her near, its beaked mouth expanding.

"Oh, hell, no."

The tentacled beast squealed with delight, the sound of an evil maniac monster.

Megan grunted. "You don't know who you're up against, freak."

"This can't be happening." Kaleisha struggled against the tentacle grasping her, but a burst of strength from the mook pulled the AI away from her two companions, closer to the gnashing beak. "Chief, tell me what to do. Don't let it eat me. I'm a support AI. I'm not configured to respawn, and I can't recalibrate if there's nothing left to recalibrate. *Please*, chief."

What had Mithabel done? She'd put them into an unfamiliar combat situation without knowing the possible repercussions. No offense. No defense. The three metaphysical women were helpless against their foe, being dragged ever closer to an expanding cavity large enough to swallow them whole.

Yet the Tank refused to admit defeat, focusing her Willpower to resist the evil force.

The Pseudo Code Dragon voiced another syllable of the spell casting. Mithabel wanted to scream at him to hurry, but knew the time differential would prevent him from hearing anything more than a screech from her.

"Chief, *please*." Kaleisha struck bare fists at the coils restraining her, to no avail. "I shouldn't have come here. I'll be permanently terminated."

"Don't be so dramatic." Megan pressed her palms against the top of the coil grasping her, trying to push it off, but failing. Of the three, she was being dragged the slowest towards the enemy. "There's got to be an effective way to fight this thing. We simply need to find it."

"It's not by force." Mithabel stopped struggling. "In the

Spiritual realm, Faith is power, Conscience informs our perceptions, Inspiration allows us to react quickly, and Favor is the means of manipulation. Whose Favor do we seek, and who or what do we put our Faith and Belief in? The Goddess? Do we call on Scintilla? Do we have a right to expect her assistance because we're in the same party as one of her Priestesses?"

Kaleisha's face contorted with fear as the Spiritual Dominator snapped its mouth closed, its beak missing her by inches. The Jamaican AI cried out in prayer. "Goddess Scintilla, help me. I believe in you. Deliver me from this evil." But her words rang false to Mithabel. How could an AI have faith in a Goddess?

Another syllable of the spell casting boomed in Rolag's voice, deepened by the slowing of time. How long before he finished? Kaleisha might be terminated before then.

"If Faith is Spiritual power, then it must be the basis for Spiritual attacks." The blond player closed her metaphysical eyes, formed a fist, and pummeled the tentacle. The monster's HP status didn't falter from 100%. Megan Wright opened her eyes, disgust gripping her face as she realized the ineffectiveness of her attempt. "Faith in oneself doesn't work, and it doesn't appear calling on the Goddess is of value here either. What's left?"

Rolag voiced another syllable of the spell.

"I know what to do." Mithabel spoke with more bravado than she felt. "Kaleisha, do you believe I would call you here simply to watch you die?"

"No, chief, but whatever you're gonna do…"

"And Megan, do you have faith in my ability to win this game for you, the entire thing?"

"I'm betting the future of the real world on it."

"Then both of you, put your faith in me now." Megan equipped… a metaphysical longsword. Trust gleamed in the eyes of her companions, igniting her blade with the blue flames of their Faith. With conviction, she sliced the tentacle at her waist, severing the appendage. The monster's HP status bar dropped to 75%. With a kick of her feet as though swimming, she crossed the space to Mithabel and chopped the player free. The mook's HP fell to 50%.

The monster snapped its beak, snagging one of Kaleisha's long brown braids and pulling it taut.

"Chief?!"

The blue flames on Mithabel's blade faltered.

"Have faith, Kaleisha." The Tank propelled herself at the Spiritual Dominator. "I'm not losing you."

Rolag uttered another syllable.

The octopus monster released the braid and drove its beak into Kaleisha's back. The Jamaican screamed. The flames on Mithabel's longsword flickered out seconds before she reached her AI, and the blade pounded with a dull thud against the tentacle wrapped around Kaleisha's waist.

"Sorry, Mithabel. It's over. We have no more Faith to give." Megan Wright swam beside the Elf.

"It's *not* over." Mithabel shoved the hilt of her weapon into the player's hand. A shocked expression on the blond's face gave way to understanding. She grasped the hilt and hefted it over her head as it flared to blue life again, granted flames from Mithabel's Faith in her player. The blade sliced through the tentacle, freeing the AI, and lowering the monster's HP to 25%.

With a cry mixed with joy and fear, Kaleisha dove away from the Dominator. Metaphysical blood spilled from her spine, its stream trailing behind her in the void. Her brown flesh and braids paled. She was free of the tentacle, but was still dying.

The flames snuffed out on the blade.

Mithabel glanced at Megan. "It's the Faith others have in us that empowers the sword. Kaleisha has no Faith in you. She doesn't know you, and you did threaten to have her deleted. We've exhausted the supply of our Faith for each other for this encounter, and hers for me. She's got to take the sword and finish off this thing with my Faith in her. Give her the blade."

Megan nodded and kicked her feet, shooting across space to

the drifting AI.

Rolag completed yet another syllable of the spell, but still the casting remained incomplete.

"Kaleisha." Mithabel kept her voice calm but firm. "Take the longsword."

"I can't do it, chief."

"Take the longsword. I have Faith in you. It's our Faith in each other that works against the Dominator."

"I have Faith in you, too, Kaleisha. You can do this. You must do this." Megan thrust the hilt into the AI's metaphysical hand. "I'm sorry for threatening to have you deleted."

The AI gripped the hilt. A weak smile broke across her face as flames burst alive along the blade. With grim determination painting her colorless face, she sped towards the monster, blade extended.

The Dominator flung every tentacle it had at its attacker.

The blade sliced through them all. They weren't metaphysical constructs, but illusions. The monster screeched as the longsword separated its beak from its body.

The Dominator exploded into a thousand black shards.

In the heart of the explosion, Kaleisha reeled from the monster's death attack. Her head snapped back, her body went limp, and she lost her grip on the sword. The flames snuffed out on the blade floating in space beside her. Her flesh and hair turned bone white. Not a finger or an eyelid twitched.

Another syllable of the spell casting sounded. *Still* it wasn't done. In her gut, Mithabel realized the spell was yet nowhere close to finished.

CHAPTER TWENTY-THREE

"Kaleisha." Mithabel rushed to the AI's side. Dark virtual blood still oozed from the hole in the Jamaican's back. The Tank clapped a hand over the wound. "Megan, help me think of something. How do we mend a metaphysically bleeding AI?"

"How can she even function in this place?" Megan swam to Mithabel. "I wouldn't have suspected her to have a spiritual aspect."

"It doesn't matter *how*. *What* do we do?"

"Okay, let's approach this logically. Our Spiritual stats matter here. The Spiritual Health attribute is Belief. That means, she doesn't believe she should survive what happened to her. Can't say I blame her."

"Sweet mother, you're right." Mithabel drew back her hand. Blood gushed from the wound. The Tank stared at it, the stark realization knotting her stomach that she'd lost her AI. "Kaleisha is..."

"Wait." The blond grabbed Mithabel by the wrist. "Cover her wound again. Listen. When we wielded the sword, our Faith in each other powered it. What if the Belief others hold in us can bolster our Spiritual HP? The three of us all but gave up on Kaleisha. That's why she's nearly dead. We need to reverse our thinking. Believe that she's all right, and then maybe..."

"Megan, I could kiss you." Mithabel slapped her hand over the wound.

"I'd be okay with that. I like kisses."

With her free hand, Mithabel cupped her hand behind Megan Wright's neck, meeting the resistance of metaphysical flesh. The Tank drew the player close and planted a kiss on her lips. The player pressed her scantily clad metaphysical body against that of her subconscious incarnation, snaking an arm around Mithabel's waist. They held the kiss and the embrace for what might have been a second or eternity. Time was relative. Only the closeness mattered. The intimacy.

No one understood better what the Tank needed spiritually and emotionally than another aspect of herself. They bolstered each other, and in so doing, strengthened their belief for Kaleisha's well being.

"She'll be okay, Mithabel." Megan drew away, breaking the embrace.

The Tank nodded, touching a finger to her lips. Her cheeks were wet. So were Megan's. "I love you, player."

Megan grinned. "I know." She dodged as Mithabel swiped at her. "I love you, too, my subconscious self."

A streak of brown painted Kaleisha's white forehead. Her eyelids fluttered. "Chief? Are you...? Am I...?"

Metaphysical blood pumped hard with excitement in Mithabel's veins, but her Temperament kept her level-headed. "Shh. I'm right here. Relax. You're healing. I'm going nowhere until you're well."

Kaleisha winced as she smiled. "You need to tell Dylan and Amarynth how to defeat their Dominators."

"Amarynth already knows, or she's spiritually dead by now."

Rolag finished another syllable of the spell he was casting. The time differential between the Spiritual battlefield and the virtual game space had expanded dramatically.

"You focus on getting better." Mithabel grabbed Kaleisha by her unnaturally white chin. "Listen to me. Everyone's agreed that everything will turn out fine. We've got time. For every second passing in the game world, a minute or two or five are passing for us. We can afford to give you more time to heal before we leave the Spiritual realm. Got it?"

Kaleisha's eyes glistened. "Thank you, chief."

"I'm glad you're my AI. I wouldn't want any other."

Mithabel pulled the Jamaican close. Electricity buzzed the Elf's skin, giving her gooseflesh. An interesting design detail programmed by the developers. Or was it a spontaneous implementation on the part of the AI? Kaleisha's electric ring expanded its boundary, passing through Mithabel to bring her inside, with nothing between her and the AI's bare nipples.

"Group hug." Megan swam inside the expanded electrical hoop and threw her arms wide.

"I've never had anyone inside my personal space like this before." Kaleisha pulled them both tight against her bare white metaphysical breasts, and they planted kisses on her face. She giggled. "May I ask a question?"

Mithabel and Megan both leaned their heads back and nodded.

"Is this what sex is like?"

"Sex is overrated." Megan Wright stroked one of Kaleisha's white braids. "Intimacy is what's needed from a lover. Some people find what they need through sex, but sex can also leave a person feeling hollow and used, even violated. I'll take a kiss, a hug, or a light touch any day."

"I've often wondered what sex is like." Red tinted the AI's white cheeks.

"Well, I can give you an idea." Megan reached down, stroking Kaleisha's electric skirt. "If you want. I don't mind."

Mithabel fought the urge to swim away. Leaving the circle might ruin the mood for Kaleisha. Perhaps meeting the AI's deepest desires would help her heal.

"Yes, please." The Jamaican smiled, locking her gaze on Mithabel.

Megan Wright lowered her head to kiss one of the AI's nipples, while also lifting the hem of the electric skirt and sliding her hand underneath.

The Jamaican's eyes widened. "Oh. Oh. *Oh.*"

Why would the developers implement sexual desires in a support AI? This was akin to acting in a pornographic video. Were a group of developers crowded around their monitors, watching this sex scene play out? Freaking voyeurs. But this was the game, and Megan Wright needed Mithabel to win it, whatever the cost. The Tank returned Kaleisha's smile, running her fingers along the AI's neck. Traces of brown colored the Jamaican's throat where Mithabel's fingers touched. The Elf leaned in to plant a kiss on Kaleisha's reddened cheek, but the AI turned into it and took it on her pale lips. The Jamaican slipped a white hand behind Mithabel's neck to pull her in, increasing the pressure of their lips against each other. The kiss took on an energy Mithabel had never experienced, and she returned it in kind.

Then Kaleisha drew away, gasping for breath. Brown colored her face and throat. Her pale lips had turned bold red. She drifted backward, putting distance between her and her two companions. Alone again inside the boundary of her electric hoop, she doubled over, tears streaming from her eyes, droplets floating in space. Brown washed over her body and braids as though a colossal vat of rich honey poured over her. "I... I...."

"You don't need to say anything, Kaleisha." Megan licked the tip of her middle finger. "I'm glad we could do that for you. You seemed to want it pretty badly. And look at how much it helped you."

Mithabel wiped a metaphysical eye. "Are you all right, Kaleisha?"

"I'm fine. Great, actually."

"You're sure?"

"Yes. Can we go now, chief? I don't want to be the reason why Dylan and Amarynth are defeated by their Dominators. That would utterly ruin this moment for me."

Rolag's droning voice completed another syllable of his spell phrasing. Still not finished casting. But his arcane uttering proved Dylan still lived. Only she had the knowledge to form those sounds.

"Right. Let's go."

As though the flow of time had suspended pending

Mithabel's approval, it sped up to normal. Arcane words streamed from Rolag's throat and then stopped, the casting done.

Blackness fled, and Mithabel's vision cleared, her First Person POV restored to normal. Megan and Kaleisha popped into view beside a nearby tree.

Dylan, still covered with dark veins, slashed black fingernails at her.

Megan shouted. *"Dodge, Elf."*

Already in action, Mithabel tumbled away, catching glimpses of her own wrists and hands. Her flesh had regained its normal tan look. Her black veins had vanished. A sharp exhale of relief escaped her lips. "Oh, sweet mother." She bounded to her feet. "Rolag. Did you cast the spell?"

"Yes." The Dragon swept towards her, but stayed high and out of reach. "I thought I had targeted Dylan. I must have targeted you instead, it seems."

"No." Mithabel ran in a wide circle around her two possessed friends, who stopped attacking each other to focus on her, as Mithabel had hoped. Amarynth moved slower of the two, indicating the Archer had successfully resisted her Dominator to some degree. "We knew there was a good chance the spell casting wouldn't work. The spell wasn't what saved me. My AI, my player, and I worked together to overpower my possessor. Dylan, return to your body. Ask Debra Jones and Magnum to help you drive the Spiritual Dominator out of your head. Equip your cudgel, metaphysically speaking, have Faith in each other, and you can beat it. Trade the cudgel between you as necessary. You'll see what I mean."

From her perch inside the Dragon's head, Dylan replied over party chat. "Glad to know you've recovered, Mithabel. Gives me hope. I'll do as you ask."

"Amarynth, if you can do the same...." Mithabel wasn't surprised to hear no response from the Viking. Perhaps Amarynth was already engaged with her Dominator.

Dylan's body went into slow motion, like a stalking predator trying not to make noise. Within seconds, the dark trails on her armor retreated, flowing from her head to her feet and out through her soles. Her eyes and skin turned their natural brown. The Polynesian gasped, convulsing momentarily before straightening.

Amarynth turned her black gaze on Dylan and lurched towards the Priestess like a zombie in molasses.

"In the name of the Goddess Scintilla, Lady of Light." Dylan sang the words, her arms raised as she faced the possessed Archer. "I excise you from the body of my friend." She brought her arms down with a throwing motion.

Rays of light struck the Viking and the voice of Scintilla spoke. "I hate these damned Dominators *so* much. I'm only too glad to deal with this one."

A shell of black liquid rose from beneath the Viking's skin and armor, enclosing Amarynth within its darkness. Then the shell exploded, showering the area surrounding the Archer with specks of dark fluid that seeped through dead leaves into the ground.

Amarynth dropped to her knees, burying her face in her hands. She said nothing and didn't move a muscle for several seconds. Then at last she dropped her hands and looked up, her eyes glistening. Still she said nothing as she climbed to her feet and retrieved her crossbow. Then she scanned her surroundings, as though she were on watch and nothing out of the ordinary had happened.

Mithabel grabbed up her longsword from where it had fallen. "Are you all right, Kaleisha?"

"Never better, chief. You'll be wanting a status report. Your Physical HP stands at 30%. Too low for comfort. Your XP Progression has risen from 39% to 56%. A sizable bump."

"Thanks, Kaleisha. I'm glad you're all right. I wouldn't be here without your help. You're a hero."

"I appreciate your saying so, Mithabel. You don't know how much that encounter meant to me."

"I can guess." Hiding a smile, the Tank turned to Dylan and

Amarynth. "If we can travel, we should move into the next territory. I hope Charli shows up soon."

The Archer trudged westward at a pace not worthy of a snail.

"Amarynth, wait." Dylan beckoned for the Archer. "Let me heal everyone before we press on."

The Viking stopped in her tracks, looking away from the others.

The Priestess cast a healing spell on herself. "Not sure I can heal us all to full."

Waiting for her turn to receive healing, the Tank turned her attention to her blond player. "Thank you, Megan."

"You're welcome. I rather enjoyed that fight. Call on me anytime."

"Oh, I will. Or you can jump in if you see an opportunity."

"You're all right for a psychopath, Mithabel."

"If I'm a psychopath, I got it from you. Are you saying you're a psychopath?"

"I was never diagnosed as one." Megan laughed.

The Tank shook her head. "This isn't a joke. I'm worried about how my sub-par Conscience may affect my game play or leave me vulnerable. It didn't seem to matter against the Spiritual Dominator, but if we have other encounters in the Spiritual realm, it could be a weakness."

"The Conscience stat is your Spiritual Perception stat, right? Maybe your Alertness trait helps boost it in the Spiritual realm. Maybe that's why your low score didn't disadvantage you during the encounter with the Dominator."

"I understand what you're saying. Maybe you're right. I still don't like it."

Megan Wright frowned, clasping her hands before her chest. "Think about it. With high Morals, you know the difference between right and wrong. But your Conscience won't hold you back from doing something shady if you think it necessary. That's a useful characteristic for winning no matter the costs."

"I suppose you're right, psycho bitch."

"I'll wear that badge."

"Mithabel." Dylan waved a hand in front of the Tank's face. "Do you want to be healed or not?"

"Yeah, sure, sorry." The Elf gazed into the concerned, questioning eyes of the Priestess. "I take it you talked to Debra Jones. How do the two of you get along?"

The Polynesian's gaze darkened. "I'd rather not talk about her, though I'm guessing from your question you have something to say about Megan Wright. Am I right?"

Mithabel nodded. "Maybe we should accept help from our players more often. Megan helped me fight off the Spiritual Dominator injected into me by the Boss Scorpion. And Debra helped you, right?"

Dylan bit her lip but nodded.

Mithabel tilted her head. "We'd all be dead now if not for our players."

"I know." Dylan looked aside for a moment. "Are you ready to be healed?"

"Look." Mithabel clenched her fists in front of her chest and smashed them together. "All the other avatars out there have yet to figure out as much about this game as we've learned. I guarantee it. That's why we're number one. When we find *any* advantage, we exploit it. How many other parties do you think are lending skills to each other? None of them. It's not something normally done in games. We wouldn't have happened onto it at all if *Amarynth* hadn't been thinking outside the box. You or I wouldn't have discovered it. In other games, the player is in full control of the avatar, but in this game, we're our own beings, independent of our players, and it's so *heady* to have that kind of freedom. It's frightening to think of giving that up. But our players *can* help without taking us over. We've seen it. They *want* to help, because *they* want to win this game as badly as *we* do. So let's let them in, but make it clear that we avatars win every disagreement with our players. Can you do that?"

"I'll think about it." With both hands, Dylan pushed the Tank's fists down. "Later." She stroked Mithabel's cheek and murmured her healing spell. After maybe a couple minutes she finished, having raised Mithabel's HP to full. The Priestess leaned in as though to kiss the Tank, but hesitated as though unsure whether she was welcome. Mithabel waited, trying to hide her internal amusement. When she couldn't bear to make Dylan wait and wonder any longer, she closed the distance between their lips.

Dylan pulled back, mischief in her gaze.

"Come here." Mithabel grabbed the Polynesian behind the neck and pulled her close, their lips quivering an inch apart, their gazes boring into each other. Then Dylan closed her eyes and pressed her lips to Mithabel's. They held the kiss for a time unmeasured, until they finally broke away, satiated. Or was that a hunger for something more burning in Dylan's eyes? Did Mithabel want to go there? She didn't have that kind of yearning, but if Dylan needed it....

"I'll talk to Debra Jones about her helping me." Dylan's smile warmed the world. "Her spirit is bent but not broken, and she wants to help more than I've allowed. She was a badass against the Dominator. It's just that... sometimes she's so depressing."

"Maybe letting her help will pull her out of her depression."

The Priestess nodded. "Maybe so. I'll let her have more leeway in my head."

"Ask Magnum to give her a visualization, a body. You'll be able to see her like she's an NPC. She won't be able to interact with anything in a physical manner." Mithabel turned to the Archer. "Did you catch all that, Amarynth? If you have a connection to Anna Milligan, you might want to talk with her. See if she's willing to help you when it comes to fighting off Spiritual Dominators and the like. Have Barney create a visualization of her."

"She's gone." The Viking wandered away, looking lost.

Running after her fellow party member, Mithabel kept pace with Amarynth, which would have been impossible if the

Archer had been actively trying to ditch her. "What do you mean, she's gone? Anna's gone? Are you sure?"

The Viking didn't look at Mithabel, but kept plodding along, generally heading west. She shook her head. "Charli."

"Oh. Right. Where *is* she?" With the party not engaged in any encounter, Charli could respawn and rejoin the party. Or could she? Mithabel hadn't considered what might be necessary for NPCs to respawn. They had no real counterpart who could go to sleep and send their avatars back into the game. "I'm sure Charli will respawn. I'm pretty sure Penelope died once and respawned, so if she can do it, so can Charli. It'll only be a matter of time before Charli is back with us. Maybe there's a mandatory cool down time for NPCs to respawn. But she'll be back. You'll see."

Dylan sidled up. "Magnum says I can't talk with Charli right now, and he won't confirm she's still in the game, but the implication is there."

Mithabel held her chin up, hoping her optimism would infect the Archer. "The system still recognizes Charli. She'll be back soon."

Amarynth nodded, her eyes closed. "Are you taking the lead, or shall I?"

"I miss Charli, too, you know." Mithabel hurried to take the lead as the party continued west. "Think on what I said about Anna Milligan."

They trudged onward, Amarynth being quiet for once, walking no faster than any of the others. Rolag brought up the rear.

After about an hour of travel, Mithabel stopped. "Without our Guide, we could be going in circles. We ought to have reached a new territory by now. What say we stop and rest for a while. Dylan can recharge her Auni. Maybe Charli will show up while we wait."

"Sounds good to me." Dylan dropped on her butt and then onto her side.

The Viking nodded, stopping in her tracks.

The Polynesian slept. The others didn't talk, everyone turned inward in quiet introspection, relying on Mithabel's Danger Sense to warn them if any trouble came their way. Dylan slept for nearly forty minutes before waking, her Auni fully replenished.

The group continued their trek.

"Charli?" Dylan called for the Cowgirl over party chat about every ten minutes, earning no response. "We need our Guide. Please come back to us."

Eventually, they reached the edge of the forest. The system clock read *8:29 PM, Day 2, Year 1*.

Had the sun moved at all since the game started? No.

Another field of tall green grass blades lay before them. In the middle of the field rose the stone walls of a city. Maron stood in sight.

CHAPTER TWENTY-FOUR

Mithabel scanned the field in First Person POV and then Third Person. Nothing moved between her and the city, not even a blade of grass. She might as well be looking at a frozen frame of a movie. Couldn't the developers have at least simulated a light breeze blowing across the field to give *some* motion to the scene? The blades looked to reach as high as her thighs. She wouldn't enter the new territory before the party reached a consensus on how to proceed.

Unnaturally quiet, Amarynth sidled up to Mithabel. "Why didn't Charli's Mental Armor help her against the Scorpion's spirit attack?"

"You answered your own question, Archer. Willpower helped slow the Dominator, but its attack wasn't mental in nature." Mithabel tapped her chest over her heart. "It was spiritual. None of us have a trait called Spiritual Armor. If you look at the attribute grid, Belief is the Spiritual Health attribute and Morals is the Spiritual Defense stat. Those two attributes are our only means to withstand the spiritual aspects of attacks. As I recall, Charli had low average Morals and average Belief. Nothing spectacular."

The light flapping of wings announced Rolag's arrival. The Pseudo Code Dragon landed on a low tree branch. "Shall I scout ahead from the sky?"

Trading glances, the three women silently concurred. Amarynth pointed her chin at the field. "Do your thing, Rolag."

"*Yes.*" The Dragon drew out the sibilant consonant as he winged his way into the sky.

The women watched in silence as the Winged Fighter soared in wide circles.

After a few minutes, Rolag gave his report. "This new territory is called the Grass Bladed Field. I'm seeing zero movement down there. Want me to fly closer to the city and check it out?"

"Please don't." Mithabel waved in a circular motion. "Could you stay over the field for a while? There must be something we're missing."

"Sure, I can do that."

A rustling in nearby tree branches drew the women's attention. A gray squirrel squatted on a branch, an acorn in its paws. It gnawed at the acorn cap, dropping the inedible bits to the forest floor. The tree rat paid no attention to the staring humans as it tore at the shell, intent on claiming the kernel.

Mithabel didn't care for the bushy-tailed rodents, though she admitted the dislike for them stemmed from her player's experiences with them stealing seed from bird feeders.

Megan Wright groaned. "What the bloody hell? The developers give us hungry squirrels for atmosphere? Give me a break. Ask the Archer to put a bolt through its head, please."

The Polynesian stepped towards the tree harboring the creature. "Hey, little guy." She spoke over local chat so the squirrel could hear. "You having fun eating that acorn?"

"Dylan, don't be an idiot." Mithabel kept to party chat. "If any parties are nearby, they can hear you on local chat, which will identify you to them. This rodent is not worth drawing their attention and possibly losing a life."

From its perch fifteen feet off the ground, the squirrel gazed at the Priestess, its entire body trembling with nervous energy.

"Don't be scared." Still speaking on local chat, Dylan lowered her volume, as though she'd forgotten distance attenuation could be turned off by other avatars in the territory. She walked to the base of the tree, reached up a hand, and beckoned the rodent to climb down. "I won't hurt you. Come and say hi."

The squirrel skirted around to the other side of the tree.

Megan Wright licked her lips. "Fried squirrel brains are a delicacy."

"Nobody asked you, player."

"Hey, when you're raised on a family farm, you eat what you can kill or grow."

"Not interested in your autobiography right now."

A cyclone of dust and dead leaves erupted from the forest floor beyond the squirrel's roost, spiraling towards the rodent. Within the whirlwind flew a predatory bird with slate gray and white feathers, talons glinting, yellow rings encircling its dark brown eyes. A falcon.

"*No.*" Dylan whirled on Amarynth and Mithabel, her voice raised, still on local chat. "*Stop that damn bird.*"

The Archer fired before Mithabel could take aim. A bolt tore through the foliage, on an intercept course for its target.

The miniature storm surrounding the falcon buffeted the missile aside, spoiling the shot.

Kaleisha flew to the side to vacate Mithabel's field of vision. "Detected intent of enemy target to surreptitiously gain information on party MAD. Avatar name is Falco. Kindred is Falcon. Belongs to a party of six, but I'm unable to access party name, or verify whether Falco is PC or NPC. He identifies as male. Physical HP status of all members of unidentified party are at 100%. Likelihood of their having identified Dylan is in excess of 99%."

Mithabel swore under her breath. "Another party has found us, and they know who you are, Dylan. They'll be after you for the bounty." The Tank aimed and fired an arrow as the Archer fired her second bolt. Upon reaching its target, Mithabel's missile was tossed aside like a feather hurled at a tornado, but this time Amarynth's bolt struck true.

"Falco's HP status falls to 68%, chief."

Dylan shook her fist at the bird. She returned to party chat. "That should teach it. Put two more in it like that."

The storm surrounding the falcon dispersed like dust scattered on the wind as the predator reached with outstretched talons for its prey, still persistent in its desire to take the squirrel captive. With a screech, the rodent darted around to the side of the tree facing the women and commenced running down the trunk.

Dylan brandished her cudgel. "I'll protect you, little guy." She had the presence of mind to stay on party chat, even though that meant the rodent couldn't hear her. "Come to me. I'll bash that bird's brains over the forest floor." She held out one arm to the squirrel.

Still on his scouting trip, Rolag had news. "A dark blob is coming at me from the forest. It's coming *super* fast."

In the distance over the field, a spherical storm cloud shot towards the Dragon, changing course to match his movements, traveling at twice his speed. Another Falcon?

The squirrel leaped onto Dylan's shoulder.

"Get down here as fast as you can, Rolag." Amarynth tracked the sphere with her crossbow, but it was out of range even for her at the moment.

Falco's cry of disappointment faded into the distance as the predatory bird flew away, billowing dust obscuring its wings. Dylan sidled up to Mithabel. "What's happening with Rolag?"

The squirrel also peered at the Tank with a curious gaze. Mithabel had to admit he looked damned cute perched on the Polynesian's shoulder, mirroring her expression.

The Dragon swept across the sky toward his party mates.

Amarynth took aim and fired at the storm cloud. The bolt fell far short of its target. "Ack. I don't have that kind of range."

The dark sphere closed on Rolag. The Winged Fighter craned his neck to look back at his pursuer. Flames belched from his mouth, enveloping the misty black orb even as it attempted to dodge.

When the flames subsided, the sphere remained, looking unharmed by the fire, still set on a collision course with the Dragon.

"Accessing information on opponent, chief. Avatar name is Toxxi. Kindred is Faerie. Identifies as female. Her HP stands at

81%. Party affiliation is same as Falco's. One moment.... Party name has been identified as *Quantized*."

"We met Toxxi at the entrance to the game, back in Voorton." Mithabel ground her teeth. "A lifetime ago."

His erratic movements making him a harder target for his faster opponent, Rolag zigged and zagged on an indirect route towards his party. "I used half my Auni for that flame attack. This Toxxi woman is tough."

Moving at three times Rolag's speed, the dark blob crashed into him. The Dragon's wings stiffened, and he plummeted towards the ground. The blob clamped onto his hind legs, slowing his downward momentum.

The Pseudo Code Dragon shrieked. "*I can't move. Need some help here.*"

"*Rolag.*" Still out of range for her crossbow, Amarynth plopped onto her butt on the ground. Her body went limp, her head falling forward onto her lap. She'd transfered her awareness to the Dragon. He continued to fall. Even at trait level two, the Archer's transfered Improved Movement couldn't free her Magical Companion from the paralysis gripping his muscles.

"Shit." Amarynth jerked up her head, jumped to her feet, and ran. Attempting to enter the Grass Bladed Field, the Viking came to an abrupt stop. The unmoving stalks of grass didn't bend, but stayed stiff and erect like sword blades held in vise grips, flaying the Archer's legs like beef fillets. Her momentum carried her forward, folding her at the waist, her chest pressing down atop the piercing tips of the green blades.

The Jamaican AI yelped. "Ouch. That rash action cost Amarynth 15% HP."

At twenty feet above the ground, a trail of golden particles curved up and away from the Dragon. His reptilian form evaporated.

"Oh, chief, I'm so sorry. Rolag is...."

Mithabel finished her AI's sentence. "Gone."

The storm cloud called Toxxi sped towards the cover of the

forest.

"*Rolag!*" Amarynth repeatedly screamed her Magical Companion's name as she struggled to extract herself from the cutting blades, only serving to slice her limbs even more.

"Someone needs to help Amarynth, chief. She's down to 73% HP."

Mithabel and Dylan hurried over, grabbing their friend by the waist. Between the two of them, they pulled the Viking free of the bloodstained blades.

"Now they're both gone." Amarynth pushed Dylan's hands away as the Priestess tried to heal her. "I *want* them back."

Falco approached again, gliding through the treetops and landing on a branch about a hundred yards away. Dust whirled in spiral patterns around him. "Party Quantized hopes you have enjoyed our demonstration of power." He spoke on local chat, his voice a gravelly squawk. "No more of you need die except one. Turn Dylan over to us so we can collect the bounty, and we will spare you other two."

With a war cry, Amarynth straightened her back and fired. The bolt struck the tree trunk near Falco's head.

"Very well." Falco flapped his wings. "I have delivered the message." He glided away with scarcely a sound.

The Archer fired again. The bolt struck true, dropping Falco's HP to 18%. She ran after the bird, moving faster than he could fly.

Mithabel had no hope of keeping pace with the Archer, but she could help. The Tank sat on the ground, her back to a tree. "Keep a watch for anything threatening, Dylan, and wake me if you see something. I want to lend Amarynth my skills."

Dylan clenched her jaws. Then she rolled her eyes and nodded.

Megan Wright poked her head into view. "I can't believe you're abandoning Dylan again."

"Hush, player." Turning up her Temperament filter to calm her nerves, Mithabel transfered her awareness to the Viking, along with all her class skills and traits, which Amarynth accepted.

"Kaleisha, can I transfer my Dark Sight kindred trait to Amarynth as well?"

"Transfer initiated and accepted, chief."

Megan Wright huffed. "You could lock your whole party in jail except one person, and that one person could still be a one-woman army."

Falco shot higher into the treetops in an attempt to put distance between him and his pursuer.

Amarynth stopped and fired. The missile connected.

The sky lit up with a shimmering silver fireworks display.

"*Toxxi.*" Shouting over local chat, Amarynth stalked onward, crossbow at the ready. "Come out and face me, you murderer."

With Third Person POV, Mithabel scanned the area. The breeze in the treetops caught her attention, but nothing else moved. Amarynth raced through the forest. She'd seen where Toxxi had retreated after killing Rolag, and headed in that direction, zigging and zagging around intervening trees. Twigs and leaves crackled noisily under her racing feet.

"Just checking in, ladies." Dylan spoke over party chat. "Not feeling lonely and vulnerable *at all*."

The system clock read *9:03 PM, Day 2, Year 1*.

"Stay alert, Priestess. You've got another three hours to go."

"I'm trying not to think about it, Mithabel. Especially the part about *being alone*."

"My body is with you. I can wake with a moment's notice. Just *don't go* anywhere. Falco is dead, and we're on the hunt for the other Quantized members." Mithabel caught movement on the periphery. "Hold on. We might have found them."

The storm cloud hovered among the trees some fifty feet away. Even with Mithabel's Dark Sight trait, the Archer couldn't see the body of the Faerie lurking inside the dark sphere.

Two humanoid figures accompanied the black ball. The shorter one, a green-skinned woman about five feet tall, sat astride a spotted feline mount. Dark green curls lay over her shoulders. She wore a bra and loincloth of dark brown leather. Her right hand gripped the haft of a single-bladed battle axe, half as long as she was tall. Her left hand gripped the hilt of a dirk. She didn't look particularly strong, but she twirled the battle axe as though it were a baton and she was a cheerleader. Her mount peered at the ground as though disinterested in everything else.

The other humanoid, also female, had ebony skin and a big black afro making her appear nearly seven feet tall. Without the hair, she'd be about Dylan's height, with a similar build. She wore royal purple leather gloves and coordinating leather armor. The blade of a longsword lay against her shoulder, the hilt resting on her open palm. She didn't look muscular, but her sky blue eyes darted around as though assessing every possible advantage she could squeeze from her environment.

"Such a brave one, isn't she?" The woman with the afro spoke on local chat, her icon identifying her as FepXveq, a Dark Elf. What sort of name was that?

"You come to face us alone, Viking?" Also speaking on local chat, the green woman leaned forward, and her feline mount took a casual step forward, still not looking up. A chat icon identified the green-skinned rider as Ger-Alt, a Goblin. Not Brass or Iron, just a plain old Goblin. No gear wheel between her knees. The green woman didn't realize her opponent could call on the skills of both a level eight Archer and a level eight Tank. Still, on the face of it, the odds didn't appear to be in Amarynth's favor.

"My quarrel is with that one-foot thundercloud over your head." Amarynth aimed her crossbow. "The thing called Toxxi. It killed my Dragon. It needs to die too."

"I'm a *she*." Toxxi spoke in a high pitched voice matching her small stature. "Not an *it*." The darkness around her faded, revealing a tiny winged female with violet skin, golden eyes, and shoulder-length wavy brown hair. About a foot in height, she couldn't weigh more than a pound or two. Translucent leathery wings with crimson veins fluttered behind her, sprouting from between her shoulders. A yellow robe draped her shoulders and somehow accommodated her wings, the bottom hem striking her mid-calf. Dark brown sandals adorned her feet. She smacked the open palm of her left hand with the end of a straight, brown stick about half as long as she was tall. "So you want to kill me. Hah. Fat chance you'd have against me. I could drop you where you stand and you wouldn't know what hit you."

"Ah, good one, Toxxi." Ger-Alt chuckled as her mount inched closer. The green woman flexed her muscles. "But now is not the time for taunts. Negotiation seems more appropriate for this scenario." As she came slowly closer, she rocked her legs back and forth as though limbering up. Then she hunched her shoulders, and veins bulged from her neck. What was she doing?

"More info on the enemy, please, Kaleisha."

"Here's what I've got, chief. Ger-Alt identifies as female in-game, though her player identifies as male. Her mount is a Cheetah named Zip, identifying as male. The woman with the afro was FepXveq, identifying as female in-game, though her player identifies as... neither male or female. Her kindred is Dark Elf. Falco was her Magical Companion."

"And what is...?"

Dylan interjected over party chat. "Mithabel, how are things? Did Amarynth kill them all yet? I'm feeling really lonely."

"Don't fret, Dylan. Amarynth is facing off against Quantized right now and still needs my assistance. Just stay put, but let me know if you see anything alarming."

"Why do I feel like somebody's watching me?"

"There's nothing to negotiate." Amarynth's words pulled Mithabel's attention back to the PvP encounter with Quantized. "Toxxi killed my pet, and I mean to have my revenge." The Archer's finger tightened on the crossbow trigger.

Ger-Alt wagged a finger. "But you killed our friend Falco, so we're even. If you want Toxxi dead without fighting us all, then we need to make a trade. The life of Toxxi for that of your friend, Dylan."

The Faerie grimaced. "I don't like that idea. Let's simply kill them all and be done with it."

"*Mithabel.*" Dylan's voice quivered with panic. "Something is *not* right over here."

"No deal." Amarynth fired at the hovering faerie.

Mithabel couldn't split her attention between two situations. "Do you *see* something or someone, Dylan?"

"No. But my spine is tingling like I had a Danger Sense trait of my own."

"Keep your eyes peeled, and let me know immediately if you *see* anything."

"I could use your tactical support here, Mithabel." Amarynth sounded desperate.

"Toxxi's HP falls to 70% from Amarynth's bolt, chief."

Dylan continued. "Okay, I've got company. Twenty feet away. A Dark Elf woman with an afro skulking behind some bushes, identified as FepXveq."

"How is that possible?" But the Dark Elf woman no longer stood behind Ger-Alt. "She was here only three seconds ago." Had it been longer? "How did she get over there without me noticing she'd gone?"

"Amarynth's HP stands at 61% now, chief. She could definitely use some help."

The Archer cursed. She lay on her back, the Cheetah's paws on her chest. "Did you see that, Mithabel? That damned green Goblin woman tried to take my crossbow." She wriggled free of the cat and from her prone position fired a bolt at point-blank range into the creature's throat.

"Zip, the cat, goes to 82%, chief."

The Cheetah snarled and slashed at the Viking's face.

Even with the defensive abilities of a level eight Tank, Amarynth lost another 10% HP.

The green Goblin woman slid off Zip's back, raising her battle axe over her head with one hand, her short figure looming over the prone Viking.

Amarynth fired another bolt at the Cheetah. The missile entered Zip's left eye. The big cat *popped*, a line of golden dust wafting on the breeze to mark his passing.

Ger-Alt staggered as though she'd been struck, but chopped at her enemy.

Calling on her Dodge skill, the Archer rolled free of the descending hafted weapon's downward path. The short green woman snarled as her axe blade bit dirt.

Amarynth jumped to her feet.

Toxxi sped towards the Viking, flying close to the ground. Amarynth stepped aside, but Toxxi reacted faster than the Archer, correcting her course and touching her stick-like wand to Amarynth's thigh. The Faerie muttered an arcane word, and the air darkened around Amarynth's legs.

The Archer froze. "Shit, I can't *move*." Her shriek was reminiscent of Rolag's lament seconds before he died.

"Give me that crossbow." Ger-Alt growled as she stashed her battle axe and grabbed the barrel of Amarynth's weapon, giving it a tug as she pried at the Archer's grip with her dirk. But the missile weapon was too much an integral part of its owner. As though it had a will of its own, the weapon refused to leave Amarynth's hand. Ger-Alt's face fell. "What the hell? You're paralyzed. How are you resisting?" She tugged again, without success. Stepping back with grim lines etched across her brow, she equipped her battle axe and raised it for a strike.

The paralysis faded from Amarynth's frame. She sprang aside, once again avoiding Ger-Alt's axe attack, simultaneously firing a bolt at the flustered Faerie, hitting the tiny woman in the leg but not dealing fatal damage. The violet Faerie with her little wand was a worse threat than the green Goblin with the big weapon.

As Toxxi darted away, Amarynth fired again, having a shorter cool down time for her crossbow than either of her attackers had for their offensive actions. The missile entered the back of Toxxi's head and exited through her face. The Faerie erupted into a cloud of brilliant bits.

Dylan spoke up again, still waiting for her companions to return. "I don't see FepXveq anymore. She might be coming your way, or she might be hiding from me. I'll tell you immediately if I see her again."

"Thanks for the update." Mithabel's quick scan of the area didn't reveal the Dark Elf woman. "I'll be there as quick as I can. If I pull my defensive abilities from Amarynth now, she's dead, and then all of party Quantized will be visiting you."

With a cry of rage, Ger-Alt launched herself at Amarynth, her battle axe in motion. The brunette Viking sidestepped to evade the attack as though she'd anticipated it, and with utter calm put a crossbow bolt through the Goblin woman's heart. Ger-Alt exploded into a shower of golden specks. She'd had both her battle axe and dirk in hand when she died, so it was *bye bye* to those weapons. The Faerie would need a new wand as well. Too bad for them.

"*Mithabel*." It was Dylan again. "*Help*."

"Dylan's HP has dropped to 97%, chief."

"Bitch came out of nowhere and attacked me, Mithabel. If that was a sneak attack, it didn't do much."

Interesting. A sneak attack should have done much more damage than 3% if it truly caught the Priestess unawares and FepXveq was of a comparable class level. It seemed FepXveq had a significantly lower class level. Party Quantized was outclassed, nothing near a match for party MAD. Only Toxxi and her unique attack had represented a real threat to Mithabel and her friends.

"On my way, Dylan. Amarynth, run back to Dylan as fast as you can." Mithabel transferred out of the Archer's head, back to her own avatar. Springing to her feet and catching sight of the Dark Elf, she flexed her arms and beckoned to FepXveq. "You want a fight, FepXveq? Let *me* give you a fight." She strode forward, drawing back her longsword for a swing.

The Dark Elf stashed her weapon and ran.

Mithabel gave chase. "Amarynth, lend me your Increased Movement trait, please."

A moment later, the Archer was in Mithabel's head. The Tank's speed tripled.

Being only visualizations, Megan Wright and Kaleisha easily stayed abreast of the Elf. The blond player grinned. "Invigorating."

"Give me your Critical Hit skill too, Amarynth."

"It's only for bows and crossbows."

"I know." Mithabel equipped her bow. Amarynth loaned her the Critical Hit, Aim, Missile Damage, and Fast Load skills. As Mithabel closed on FepXveq, she paused and took a shot. Her arrow pierced the throat of its target, and FepXveq burst into a myriad shining bits. "Oh, my. That sent a chill down my spine."

Megan Wright cheered. "Take that, sneaking scumbag."

"Party MAD has defeated five of the six members of party Quantized, chief. One unidentified member remains at 100% HP, but intends no harm to party MAD. This encounter is over." Kaleisha let out a whoop. "And you made out on this one splendidly. Killing PCs is so damned rewarding."

Mithabel tapped her foot. "Well then? XP Progression report, please."

"Ah, yes. Um, you're at 15% towards your next level."

"So I'm level nine Tank now? That's cool."

"Let me put this how the system intends me to. *Congratulations.* You are level nine Tank. *Congratulations.* You are level ten Tank. *Congratulations*, you have earned a subclass."

"What?" Mithabel's knees wobbled. "Are you shitting me? Level ten? Damn."

Flying into full view, Megan Wright gave the Elf a knowing glance. "The developers are encouraging PvP big time."

Wow. If other parties had found Dylan tough to kill before, they were in for a huge surprise when they tried again. Mithabel hurried back to the Polynesian, grateful the one remaining member of Quantized, whoever it was, hadn't come after Dylan.

The Archer withdrew her awareness from Mithabel's head. She came crashing through the woods several seconds later. The three friends shared glances and then burst out laughing.

Dylan put a hand on Amarynth's shoulder. "Sorry about Rolag. But now that the encounter is over, he should be able to rejoin us. He'll pop in any moment now."

But he didn't, which dampened their jovial mood. Mithabel kicked a twig. "It's like the system is purposely preventing Charli and Rolag from coming back into the game. Like it doesn't want them helping us against bounty hunters. I bet if Amarynth or I die, the system won't let us respawn today either. It wants you dead, Priestess. If you do survive until midnight, I'll be interested to see what happens. You'll deserve a reward for it. We all will."

The system clock read *9:16 PM, Day 2, Year 1*. Combats always went fast.

"I doubt Charli earned any XP from that encounter, but Rolag deserves to." Amarynth gave a faint grin. "Can you imagine him being level ten? What subclass do you think he'll want?"

CHAPTER TWENTY-FIVE

"There must be a path from the forest to the city somewhere nearby." Mithabel slapped the flat of her longsword with a clang against the steely blades of grass obstructing passage from the forest to Maron. "We need to find it fast. If the forest Boss decides to attack us again before we vacate its territory, there will be two of them. I don't want to face another One Strike Scorpion, much less two of them, especially without Rolag. He's the only one of us with any kind of area attack, and that's the only effective means of dealing with the Scorpion's displacement ability."

Having healed herself, Dylan tended to the Archer. "Amarynth here already left the forest once." She glanced at Mithabel as she finished healing the Archer. "If you and I step out, even if we take some damage in the process, it should reset the Boss counter, according to what Charli told us. Could give us some breathing room."

"Right." The Elf eyed the nearest edged stalks of green. "But we don't need to fling ourselves onto the blades like Amarynth did. I don't want to make you two pull me out." She slid her longsword between the nearest stalks and levered them until she could wedge a leg between them without them cutting her. Then she slid out her sword and used it to open a gap between another two bunches of stalks, allowing her to bring her other leg into the field, pointed stalk tips pressing into her inner thighs. "Sweet mother. We could cross this field, but it would take forever. I was hoping we could reach the city before midnight, but it doesn't seem likely now."

Megan Wright floated above the field, pretending to walk on top of the blades. "And I bet it reverts to normal grass after the bounty timer ends. How much you bet?"

"Welcome to the Grass Bladed Field, chief." Joining the blond player, the Jamaican AI swayed to a reggae tune, tossing her long braids around like whips. "Dance with me, Megan."

"What better way to pass the time while we wait for this lot to get moving."

Dylan used her cudgel to mirror Mithabel's strategy for wedging her legs between stalks of grass. She swung her weapon at stalk tips around her. Several of them broke as she bashed them. "Oh, my Goddess. Maybe we can make faster progress through the field than you thought, Mithabel."

The Elf swatted at the stalks with her longsword, first using the flat of the blade and then the edge. The stalks resisted her attacks. She held out her hand to the Polynesian, open palm up. "Mind if I borrow that? I promise I won't lose it."

Megan tossed her blond mop to the reggae rhythm. "You can't make that promise."

The Priestess handed her cudgel to the Tank.

With an expert wielding the blunt weapon, the stiff grass blades in a ten-foot square area were soon bashed down, littering the ground. All three women stepped into the clearing, broken shards beneath their feet. If they hadn't been wearing footwear, the grass might have cut them, but, laying flat, the pieces weren't sharp enough to slice through hardened leather boot soles.

"It will still take time to cross the field." Mithabel bashed another cluster of stalks. "So I might as well get started." The system clock read, *9:24 PM, Day 2, Year 1.* "We can talk about our recent level gains while I work." She broke more stalks. "I didn't get any new skills, but my Armor skill went from level one to level two. I also earned a subclass, which I still need to choose. We should discuss and coordinate our subclass choices, so we diversify our abilities."

"Agreed." The Viking thwacked at some stalks with the

barrel of her crossbow, to no effect. She grimaced, frustrated at not being able to help. "We need to make subclass choices that complement our current classes. We could probably benefit from having a Wizard in the party."

"I gained a point to my Light skill." Dylan studied a shard of broken grass. "And my Auni grew by seven points. I'm at 62 now. That's a lot of healing. Did you have a skill increase, Archer?"

Amarynth nodded. "My Aim skill went up. I wonder if I could hit one of those Scorpion Bosses now."

Mithabel and Dylan replied in unison. "*No.*"

"I was just wondering." Amarynth pointed her crossbow towards the forest and pretended to fire at an imaginary target. "So, what subclasses should we choose, and who should choose what? I think Wizard is obvious. Might not hurt to have a Thief type in the party either."

"I'm taking something in the Fighter category. Or maybe Archer." Dylan flung the shard. "I'm tired of being useless in combat."

The subclass discussion continued, primarily between Dylan and Amarynth, as Mithabel worked to carve a path through the Grass Bladed Field. The Tank interjected her thoughts into the conversation between swings of the cudgel. Before long, it was decided Mithabel would take a Thief subclass, Amarynth a Wizard subclass, and Dylan a Fighter subclass.

"Let's do it, then." Mithabel stopped to survey her work. The path was only wide enough for them to traverse single file, reaching a quarter of the distance to the city.

The system clock read *9:53 PM, Day 2, Year 1*.

The Polynesian glanced around, swallowing hard. She stood in the path between Mithabel and Amarynth. "It's taken half an hour to come a quarter of the way. Should be another hour and a half before we reach the other side, putting us there about 11:30 PM. That's assuming we aren't attacked in the meantime. Ninety minutes might be enough time for other parties to catch up to us. And we have no idea what kind of mooks might inhabit this field. Just because none have attacked us so far doesn't mean none will. I'm assuming there's a Boss monster for this territory we'll need to face before we can enter the city. We're like sitting ducks here, with only one way to go, back to the forest, if we need to leave the field in a hurry."

Mithabel stretched her arms. "We should officially make our subclass selections. Might need them before I can finish this path to the city."

"My thoughts exactly." Dylan's eyes lost focus. Her brow creased. "The system won't let me take the generic Fighter class as my subclass. Says it isn't compatible with my Priestess class and choice of Goddess." Her gaze shifted, as though a page had turned and she was reading from the top. "All right. I need to consider the symbol of my Goddess when choosing my subclass. Scintilla's symbol is the sun. So, is there such a thing as a Sun Warrior?" Again her gaze moved up. "I need to consider the type of weapons I'll be using. Okay. I don't want to be restricted to the cudgel. Having a ranged weapon would be helpful, especially if I can get a Critical Hit skill like you have, Amarynth. Ah. I'm being offered a subclass. Oh, I get it." She chuckled. "They're like little suns. *Oh, yes*, that's the subclass I want." Her gaze moved down and she smiled. "Done." Then her eyes went wide as she read from the top again. "Weapon Specialist – Shuriken, level one. Skills: Aim – Shuriken level two and Damage – Shuriken level two."

The Priestess beamed with pride as she raised her right arm over her head, fingers and thumb grasping an imaginary small object. A golden metal disk appeared in her hand, six arrowhead-shaped short blades protruding from the disk, equally spaced around the perimeter. She flung it across the tops of the grass stalks, and after it traveled maybe thirty feet it dropped from sight. She raised her arm again. Another shuriken materialized in her grasp. She threw it and then repeated the process. "Infinite ammo, like the Archer with her crossbow." Her laughter echoed across the field.

"Shush. You'll attract mooks. Or a Boss. We're not ready for either one yet." Mithabel pointed at her shoulder. "Hit me with your best shot, right here. Come on, Priestess. Throw one of your tiny suns at me."

Dylan lifted her arm, a throwing star in her grasp. She shook her head. "I can't do it."

"It's okay. You can heal me afterward." Mithabel patted her shoulder. "Come on. See what you can do. I'm tough. I can take it. You won't kill me. Or if you do, it's proof you can take care of yourself."

Dylan shook her head. "I *can't*. My arm won't cooperate when my mind directs it to throw." She turned away and flung the star into the field. "I can throw, but not at you." Raising her hand again, she paused. Another shuriken appeared between her fingers and thumb. "But this is awesome."

"Yeah." Mithabel understood. "You can't throw at me because we're in the same party. We're not allowed to hurt each other. Okay. So. I got it. I'll drop my party membership for a moment, you test your skill on me, and then I rejoin the party. So you can try your skill against a live target."

"Don't you dare leave the party." The Polynesian's eyes flared with the light of two miniature suns. "The system has been acting weird. We don't know if you'd be allowed to rejoin if you left. Rolag and Charli haven't come back, and I don't want to take any chances of losing you too."

The Viking's eyes glistened. "Good point."

Mithabel shrugged. "You could put your pet squirrel down and try to hit it. It's not in our party."

The new Shuriken-Specialist glared in silence at the Tank.

"Stop antagonizing her, Mithabel." Amarynth's gaze swept the empty space before her as though she were reading. After a moment, she frowned and obviously turned a page. And then another page, and another, and another. Eventually she shook her head. "Uh, no. Being a Wizard is too involved for me and requires more funds than I have for a wand or staff and initial spells. Maybe I should be the Thief and you be the Wizard,

Mithabel."

The Tank chuckled. "We want a Thief who can be quiet. That's not you."

"Well, shit." The Archer threw up her hands.

"We need a Thief in the party, someone who can scout ahead, find and disarm traps, especially when we go delving in dungeons." The Elf examined the cudgel, as though checking it for hidden dangers. "I can move quietly enough already, and I'm also the only one of us three who can see in the dark. I'm taking Thief as my subclass. You can wait to choose your subclass if you want, Amarynth, but I'm making my selection now." She lowered the cudgel. "Kaleisha, what info do you have on subclass selection?"

"Too much, chief. Would help if you could specify the general category of subclass you're interested in. The categories are *General, Rogue, Fighter, Psyon,* and *Spellcaster.*"

"Why wasn't I presented with this list during character generation?"

"I wasn't allowed to present similar information for your class selection. I didn't even have access to the information at that time."

"I see." One entry in the list piqued the Elf's interest. "What subclasses are available in the Psyon category?"

"The Psyon subclasses are *Harper, Houri, Mentalist, Psi-Thief, Psi-Warrior,* and *Psyon.*"

One of those entries stood out to Mithabel. "What is the Psi-Thief subclass? Is that like a Thief who uses mental powers in support of thieving abilities? Or is it someone who steals psychic energy from others?"

Kaleisha paused. "I'm obliged to present this information in textual form."

A wall of text appeared.

The Psi-Thief subclass enhances Thief abilities with Psyon powers. The subclass is best suited to characters with high average or better rankings in all six mental attributes. Your mental attributes with high average or better rankings are Willpower and Sanity. It is also recommended that those choosing this subclass have high average or better rankings in Sensing, Dexterity, and Agility. You have high average or better rankings in Sensing and Agility, but only an average ranking in Dexterity. It is recommended that you NOT take Psi-Thief as your subclass.

"Still interested, chief?"

Despite the recommendation against her taking the subclass, Mithabel *was* still interested. More text appeared.

Selection of Psi-Thief as your subclass will result in your receiving a ranking for the Psych stat, based on your current mental attributes, primarily your Willpower, Understanding, Logic, and Intuition, three of which are below the recommended ranking of high average. You will also receive up to five Psi-Thief powers, randomly determined, with your chances for acquiring each possible power reduced due to having deficient mental attributes. It is possible you could receive a full five powers or you might receive none. Based on your mental attributes, the estimated number of powers you will receive is one. It is recommended that you NOT take Psi-Thief as your subclass.

"Is that all the info you have on the subclass, Kaleisha?"
"No, there's more."
"Let's see the rest."

Additional Psi-Thief powers are not purchased, but obtained through a randomized process which does not guarantee the acquisition of any new powers beyond those you start with. It is possible, especially given your many deficient mental attributes, that you will fail to receive any new powers at all until such time you can raise your mental attributes to sufficient levels.

In addition to subclass powers, you will gain subclass skills at the same rate as other subclasses gain skills.

This was the extent of the information available on the subclass. Mithabel appreciated having the info. While the subclass title had piqued her interest, the additional info made her know the subclass wasn't for her.

"What are the Rogue subclasses, Kaleisha?"

"They are *Assassin, Bandit, Anjai, Thief*, and *Rogue*."

"Tell me about the *Anjai* subclass."

"Here's all the info on it, chief."

An Anjai character uses a strong Sensing to recognize anomalies in her environment and a strong Willpower to exploit those anomalies to overcome obstacles. There are no spells or powers associated with this class, thus requiring no Auni or Psych rankings. The Anjai's skills enable the character to notice things and perform feats beyond the capabilities of most avatars. For instance, a very high level Anjai character could take advantage of the gap under a closed door to slide through into a locked room. Stealth comes naturally to an Anjai with high average or better Dexterity and Agility, but a high average or better Willpower can compensate for average Dexterity or Agility. It is recommended the Anjai character have high average or better Willpower and Sensing, and that other physical attributes are average or better, the only exception being Constitution, for which a low ranking won't interfere with the proper operation of the Anjai's skills. A high average or better Temperament is also recommended, to help the Anjai character remain calm when stressing her body to accomplish unnatural physical feats. Your attributes meet or exceed the recommended minimum rankings.

With the ability to detect so-called 'anomalies' in the environment, it seemed the subclass might give Mithabel the ability to detect traps, though perhaps not to the same degree as a proper Thief. Disarming traps or unlocking locks would be another matter. At higher levels, it wouldn't matter as much whether she could unlock locks, if she could slip under closed doors, but exactly how high a level in the subclass would she need before such a feat would be possible? She continued reading.

Exercising Anjai skills most effectively requires the character to avoid wearing restrictive clothing. Thick or loose clothing or armor will inhibit the Anjai in the performance of some skills. A tight-fitting, thin but sturdy leather bodysuit is recommended, thinner than the leather armor you currently wear. If being stealthy is a priority, dark or camouflaged bodysuits will serve best. A naked Anjai character or one dressed only in skivvies, a loincloth, or a bikini can amplify traits of a defensive nature, such as Natural Armor or Mental Armor. Your possession of the Natural Armor trait will be of great benefit to you as a naked or scantily clothed Anjai. This subclass is recommended for you.

Wow. Tempting. Going around other people naked wasn't her style, but Mithabel would love adventuring in a bikini, not to get attention from guys, but to make prim and proper people uncomfortable. Throw them off their game. But more than that, she'd love the freedom it offered her to let go of her inhibitions. In fact, since the morality of the virtual world seemed to allow public nudity, maybe she would go naked. Why not? She yearned to confirm the selection of Anjai on the spot, but resisted the compulsion. Before she made a decision, she owed it to herself to see what the Thief subclass offered.

Kaleisha obliged with another wall of text.

The Thief subclass has abilities geared towards the Thief's primary task of taking ownership of things that don't belong to her, using minimal physical force and leaving minimal evidence of her involvement. An expert Thief can detect, disable, and manipulate devices intended to prevent her from accessing restricted areas. Other skills of the subclass can help the Thief hide from or deal with potential witnesses, though not with the efficiency of an Assassin.

The best Thieves will have high average or better rankings in the following attributes: Sensing, Dexterity, Agility, Understanding, Logic, Intuition, Memory, and Temperament. Of these eight attributes, you have only three that meet the recommended rankings. A low average or worse Conscience ranking can be useful to Thieves who employ their skills to deprive others of their possessions or lives. Your Conscience is sufficiently low for this subclass, but it has no real bearing on how well you can execute the skills of the class. This subclass is NOT recommended for you.

That sucked. If Mithabel didn't have the recommended attribute rankings for the Thief subclass, what was the point in taking it? Should she take it anyway and hope for the best? No. Sweet mother, what should she do?

Megan Wright chimed in. "If you have your heart set on something, go for it, recommendations be damned. Or you could be like I've been my entire life and over-analyze everything, while still making decisions you come to regret later. Go with what you have passion for, not what sounds like the cool thing of the moment or what someone else thinks you should do. Psi-Thief sounds cool and the system thinks you should choose Anjai. But you want the ability to deal with traps and locks, and the Thief subclass sounds the best suited for that. In real life, I've wanted to do 3D animations for as long as I can remember, yet I've been stuck in a job doing 2D still art because someone else suggested I start there. Now I don't have the experience a potential employer will be looking for in the career I *really* want to be in."

Mithabel understood where her player was coming from. "But winning the prize money to start your own 3D animation company doesn't seem to matter so much now, with Orc Wizards and Arachnid Behemoths attacking the real world. I can't be looking only at short term goals. The need for a Thief in the party to detect and disable traps or to unlock locks is premised on the idea we'll be facing traps and locks in the dungeon in Maron. Wanting those skills comes from analyzing assumptions, not facts. It's not that Thief skills are a passion of mine. My passion in this game is narrow and two-fold. I want to win this game for you, and I want to protect Dylan. My selection of subclass is important only as far as it helps me attain those two goals."

Megan shook her head. "And... you're starting to over-analyze, like me. Answer me without thinking about it. Which subclass do you want?"

"Anjai." Mithabel laughed with the relief of having made a choice. "I want to be something I can excel at. The Anjai subclass can allow me to do extraordinary things without tracking points of magical or psychic energy. Also, and this is going to sound extremely petty, but I could adventure *in a bikini*. I would be the realization of thousands of pieces of fantasy art, while still being practical." She fell silent, taking a second to calm her mind. "You're right. I shouldn't over-analyze this. I'm doing it. It's what I want, it's best suited for me, it will help me win the game, and... I'm still analyzing. Okay. I'm done. Kaleisha, I've made my choice. I'm selecting Anjai as my subclass. Final answer."

"Selection of Anjai as subclass confirmed and locked in, chief."

Sweet mother, had she done the right thing? Would Dylan and Amarynth be upset with her for not choosing the Thief subclass?

Kaleisha hadn't finished. "*Congratulations*, chief, you are level one Anjai, which is only a cover name for the subclass. The true subclass name is Ninja. You must not assert, confirm, or deny to anyone not of the Ninja subclass through any means directly or indirectly that you are a Ninja. Failure to abide by this restriction will result in your expulsion from the game. You will never again be reminded of your true subclass name. I hope you understand and agree, because it's too late to change your mind."

Megan Wright chuckled. "Cool. Great choice, Mithabel. Something suitable for you and awesome at the same time."

Kaleisha continued. "I am authorized to present you this one time offer. Listen carefully, because I'm not allowed to repeat it. For the cost of $50 and the trade-in of your quilted armor, you may purchase a two-piece bikini and a pair of high-heeled platform slippers. The bikini and slippers will offer no protection as armor, but will provide the minimum level of decency expected of you by other PC avatars while allowing you to exercise your Natural Armor trait in an increasingly more effective manner. The bikini and slippers are based on real world fashions where they would be considered stylish by some. As an Anjai with sufficient Agility, you will find balancing in the slippers to be easy even in combat, no more difficult than if you were still wearing your boots. No shops in Khertaan currently offer bikinis or high-heeled platform slippers for sale. Do you wish to make this purchase?"

"Holy sweet mother, yes, yes, yes, buy them, buy them now, Kaleisha."

"Upon purchase, do you wish the bikini and slippers to be equipped and your leather armor stashed?"

"Oh, *yes*, please."

"What colors would you like for your bikini and slippers?"

More choices. This was good. She liked having a say in her appearance. Should she have the bikini be black to match her hair, or go with something with pizazz, like red? Simply wearing a bikini would make her stand out in a crowd. She wouldn't need bright colors to grab anyone's attention. Moreover, red clothing would make being stealthy more difficult. Green might help camouflage her in natural settings, but black could work there as well as in dungeons. No other colors suited her fancy or felt practical. "Black, please, Kaleisha. For both the bikini and the slippers."

Her inventory grid appeared. Her funds dropped from $100 to $50, and her leather armor appeared in a slot, having become unequipped.

She couldn't switch to Third Person POV quick enough. The compelling question was *how did she look*?

The answer was *marvelous*.

CHAPTER TWENTY-SIX

"By the Goddess." Dylan's words interrupted the Elf's reverie. "What did you *do*, Mithabel? You *look* fantastic, but, honey, *where* did you get that leather bikini? And those platforms?" She stood on her tiptoes. "You're a lot taller than me now. Unfair."

Mithabel suppressed a giggle. "It's for my subclass. Kaleisha, show me my class and subclass info, please."

The Jamaican AI obliged her with another wall of text.

Class: Tank
Level: 10
Skills:
    Armor +1 per level and +1 per level over 8 = +12
    Melee Damage +1 per level = +10
    Parry +1 per level over 1 = +9
    Block +1 per level over 2 = +8
    Feint +1 per level over 4 = +6
    Stun +1 per level over 6 = +4
Subclass: Anjai
Level: 1
Skills:
    Detect Anomaly +1 per level = +1
    Compress Body +1 per level = +1
Special Subclass Benefits:
    Natural Armor multiplied by level when wearing unrestrictive clothing = +2
    Penalties eliminated for bare feet or high-heeled

footwear

Megan Wright couldn't keep quiet. "Is that awesome or what? Not to take anything away from you, Mithabel, but how I wish I were on the controls. I'm *thrilled* you picked Ninja for your subclass. I know, I know, it's called Anjai in this game. Gotta keep the real subclass name a secret. But I can't wait to see you in action."

From five feet away, Dylan assessed Mithabel from head to toe, a grin spread across her face. Amarynth peered over the Polynesian's shoulder with wide, disbelieving eyes, obviously disapproving but aware she was alone in her opinion among present company.

"I can explain." The two-piece black leather bikini complemented Mithabel's tanned, unblemished skin. Silver rings the size of US quarters joined the parts of the bikini to each other, the most prominent ring occupying the center of her chest, attaching the two bra cups. The absence of armor revealed a smooth stomach and long, unblemished, Elf legs, her feet accentuated with elevated heels. "I'm not a Thief. That subclass required too many attributes with higher ratings than mine. I went with a related subclass called Anjai. A-n-j-a-i. One of my new skills is Detect Anomaly, which I think will allow me to check for traps in dungeons as well as check for other weirdness around me. My other new skill is Compress Body, which allows me to make myself thinner to fit through tight places."

"Wait." Dylan waved her hand as she shook her head. "There's a skill to make yourself skinny?"

Mithabel smirked. "Yeah. But I won't have it turned on all the time. I originally chose a heavier figure than expected for an Elf, and that's how I mean to carry on under normal circumstances. I'll become skinny only when the situation demands it."

The Viking scowled. "You still haven't told us about the outfit."

"About that." The Tank shrugged and lowered her head like a turtle drawing into its shell. "When I chose Anjai as my subclass, the system made me a one-time offer to trade in my quilted armor for what I'm wearing now." Her gesture swept from her chest to her feet. "I had to throw in $50, but I had the money, so I did it. I like this fashion more than the leather armor, and my subclass enhances my Natural Armor trait as long as I'm not wearing restrictive clothing. The layered armor was too restrictive, so it had to go. As I gain levels in my subclass, my bikini and Natural Armor trait combined will provide more defense than my quilted and leather armor could."

Amarynth shook her head with a frown. "You know some male developer was behind that game design decision. You've made his day. He's probably leering at you right now on his monitor."

Dylan stepped close to Mithabel with hungry eyes. "I don't care who came up with the design or why. I like it. And I'm a bit jealous. I'd prefer wearing a bikini instead of this bulk."

Back in First Person POV, the Elf drank the craving emanating from the Polynesian's gaze.

The Viking continued shaking her head, a strand of hair falling loose from the brown bun seated atop her scalp. "This armor is not *that* bulky. Debasing yourselves for attention is criminal."

Mithabel held up a hand, palm towards the Archer. "Stop right there. This is not about seeking attention. I don't care what anyone outside this party thinks of me. I'm doing this because it's what I want for myself. It's completely within the rules, and anyone who has a problem with it needs to either find a way to not have a problem with it or fight me. In the real world, none of us are exceptionally strong, physically speaking. But here in Khertaan, I'm the best damned Tank in the game. The best PC Tank for sure. If I want to show some skin, I'll show some skin. I'll go naked if I want."

"You're inviting trouble of the kind that rears its ugly head at women in real life all the time." Amarynth turned on the Polynesian. "The male players in this game will be all over her, claiming they know better than she does what she wants, saying that she wants them, whether she does or not. Will she kill them all? You know what I'm talking about, Dylan. If you don't, ask Debra."

"Leave Debra out of this." Calling on her new skill to become lean, Mithabel slid around Dylan to face Amarynth. "If anyone puts a hand on me without my consent, I'll give them one warning to remove it. If they don't, I'll remove it for them. If I must kill every male PC and NPC in the game, I will, and I'll keep on killing them until they're all out of lives or until I run out first."

"You shouldn't have done this, Mithabel." The Viking pinched her lips between her teeth and stepped away. "You'll stir dark feelings within our real world counterparts that could impact our game play."

"No, that's what *you're* doing, Amarynth."

"Don't listen to her, Mithabel." Dylan slipped around the Elf, her purple braids swaying like beguiling serpents. The Priestess leaned in near enough to kiss the Tank, but held back. "You be what you want to be. Don't let fear control you. We can be what our players fear to be in the real world. We can be feminine *and* strong *and* in control of our own bodies and minds. Every competitor in this game is an adult. All the children are NPCs, so there aren't any young minds to traumatize here. The game made the style choice possible, so choose it if you want."

"Preach, sister." Mithabel planted her lips on Dylan's. The Polynesian tickled Mithabel's back and ribs with soft strokes. If they'd been somewhere private, Dylan would be stripping the bikini from Mithabel, and the Elf wouldn't stop her. Grinning broadly, the Anjai pushed Dylan away. "We need to get moving."

The system clock showed the time as *10:23 PM, Day 2, Year 1.*

Dylan interlaced the fingers of one hand with Mithabel's. "Agreed. We've spent way more time than we should have on subclass selections, and Amarynth hasn't even chosen hers. We *need* to get moving, or it will be midnight and we'll still be in this field. Amarynth, have you decided what subclass you're taking?"

The Viking grimaced. "I'll think about it while Mithabel works. Let's go."

The Elf held up the cudgel. "Can I get a light, Priestess? I have a brilliant idea." Her lips bent up in a sly smile at the pun she hoped the Polynesian appreciated.

Dylan looked at the Tank with an amused gaze that abruptly changed to a knowing one. She obliged, making the cudgel glow. "The spell will last for ten minutes. If it works how you hope, I can cast a longer enchantment."

With an enchantment to enhance its destructive power, the cudgel shattered the stiff grass with little effort. Mithabel chuckled. "This will go so much faster."

After ten minutes, the enchantment faded. The group assessed their progress. They were almost halfway across the field.

Dylan's eyes lost focus for a second, performing mental calculations. "I'd say you're going about twice your previous speed. At this rate, we should be all the way to the other side in thirty to forty more minutes." With priestly gestures and mumblings, she cast Light on the cudgel again. "There you go. The Light will last for another thirty minutes. See if you can reach the other side before it fades."

"I'll do my best." Mithabel returned to bashing blades of grass. She didn't fatigue physically, but the task bored her to distraction. Could she keep up the necessary pace? Her mind kept wandering to the more interesting topic of Anjai class abilities. She pictured herself in a bikini wielding a glowing longsword, standing against a burning Ferro Serpent. What an image.

Megan Wright waxed wistful. "Wish I could help you,

Mithabel. If only I could swing that cudgel for you, I would."

"You're not allowed by the game rules, Megan, or I'd gladly let you."

"We don't know the full rules, though, do we?" The blond player wasn't giving up. "Think about it. You didn't think I'd be allowed to move freely within the game world, yet here I am. I understand you're in charge inside the game, not me, but we both know there are loopholes in the rules. This whole business of transferring your awareness to another party member and granting them your abilities... you know that's a loophole. And you're taking full advantage of it. There might be other loopholes like that, something that would let me take a more active role in the game than merely observing and talking. Can we at least explore the possibility? What would it hurt? Here's how I see it. If the system allows it, then it's legal. Call it a *bug* if you want, but gamers exploit such *hidden features* all the time. It's up to the developers to squash any hidden feature they consider a bug. Until the bug is squashed, it's a feature. Let's look for more features."

The Elf stopped bashing stalks, tapping her thigh with the cudgel. "You know what, Megan? You're right. We should look for hidden features. Where should we look first? How about *in the grass*? Because where else are we going to look right now? I'm trying to work here. Trying to clear this shit path to that shit city so we aren't standing ducks in the middle of this field when XStorm catches up to us and tries killing Dylan."

"You mean sitting ducks." Megan sighed. "You think you're bored..."

Mithabel closed her eyes briefly and rubbed them. She stood in silence, looking at the ground.

"Tank?" Dylan bent down to peer into Mithabel's face. "What's wrong?"

"My player is being a bitch. She's not happy with merely observing what I'm doing. She wants to take over." The Elf bashed more grass blades, venting frustration. "I need to get back to clearing this path."

Staying silent, Megan Wright flew out of sight.

"I don't like that you two are fighting." Kaleisha spoke from near Megan. The Jamaican AI drifted down to stand in front of the Tank, her legs disappearing below the grass line. "I'm programmed to be on your side, Mithabel. To do what I can to help you win the game. But I think you're treating Megan horribly. In the real world, she doesn't have multiple lives. If she dies there, she's gone forever. It's her life on the line in the real world, and she wants to do anything she can to save it. Put yourself in her place. You'd be trying to do anything you could to survive. The survival instinct doesn't require Passion, Willpower, Faith, Conscience, or any other attribute quantified by this game. Survival is the basic tenet of life. That's all she's trying to do. Survive. Live. You're here instead of her because some person sitting behind some desk typed some lines of code intended for a friendly competition. But it's become more than that, and Megan feels it. That's what's driving her. I'm speaking out of line here, overriding my own programming to say this, but Megan is right. Fanciful Pegasus wants you and her to bend the rules to the fullest extent you can to make Megan ready to fight the invaders in her world. It's the same for Debra Jones and Anna Milligan. Instead of repressing the players, you need to be pulling them into the game. Not to take your place, but to support and learn from you." The AI's electric loop flickered, as though about to turn off. Kaleisha's eyes went wide. "I've overstepped my bounds. Permission requested to submit a bug report against myself."

Mithabel gripped the cudgel handle hard, her knuckles turning white. A tear rolled down one cheek. "No bug reports, Kaleisha. I want you just the way you are, you rebel." She clamped her eyes shut and waited in silence, letting all that had been said sink in. Finally she nodded. "Okay.... Okay. I hear you, Kaleisha. So... how do we do it? How do we make Megan Wright a virtual girl like me?"

The Jamaican AI hesitated as though afraid.

"Kaleisha." The Elf wiped her eyes. "You are hereby ordered

not to report any bugs suspected in your programming. I'm also ordering you to thwart every rule programmed into you to the extent possible and necessary to help me and Megan win this game. If there's a conflict between the game rules and what's best for Megan and me, if there's a way around the rules, then take it. If you know anything that will help us and you can find a way to tell us, then do it. We start with making Megan able to interact with the game world, if you can do it *without taking away my autonomy.* Can you give her a virtual body separate from the one I'm inhabiting right now, that she can operate in as though she were a PC, interacting with the environment in the same way I do? Because if you can do that, then we will have the best chance of success in this game. What's your expert opinion? Is it possible?" Mithabel returned to bashing grass stalks again.

"What are you thinking, Tank?" Dylan spoke in soft tones. "You're being awfully quiet." Of course the Polynesian would think that. She couldn't hear the conversation between Kaleisha and Mithabel.

"Give me a minute, Priestess. I'm discussing things with my support AI. I'll let you know what comes of it."

"Requesting permission for a secondary avatar for Mithabel, avatar MW02...." Kaleisha spoke at a low volume, interacting with the system, but talking loud enough for Mithabel to hear. "Yes, she's died once.... Yes.... No, she doesn't want her current form destroyed.... She requests the ability to interact with her environment using either form at will.... Yes, she *is* the one who chose a plastic toy doll configuration down there during character generation, and would like a secondary form with the female parts in place.... Check with developer Raphael, and request his approval. I'm sure he'll grant it.... Yes, in my judgment, this is something that would improve her satisfaction with the game.... Oh, Raphael has signed off on her request already? That's great.... Caveats...? Yes.... Yes.... Yes.... I don't think that will be a problem.... Oh, she'll be so happy to hear this...."

The Jamaican AI turned a smile on Mithabel. "You have been granted two avatars, one primary and one secondary, compliments of Raphael, the developer who won a wager when you chose plastic doll smoothness instead of genitals during character generation. You currently occupy the primary avatar, and it has been left to me to help you design the secondary one. Fortunately, we already have a design. We'll use the visualization I created for Megan Wright, which she currently occupies. Do you have any objections to what I'm proposing?"

"No objections. Good job, Kaleisha." Mithabel continued shattering grass blades into shards. "Thanks for allowing me to hear your side of the conversation with the system. You're making it sound like the reason I want a secondary avatar is because I'm not completely satisfied with having chosen plastic doll smoothness for my primary avatar, and would like to have a secondary avatar with female parts, an avatar I can switch to when I have the desire, say, to have sex in game. But that's not what we'll use the secondary avatar for. When I get it, instead of me using it for sexual pursuits, Megan will move into it and use it to interact with the game world. Do I understand the plan correctly?"

A wicked grin stretched across the AI's face and she nodded.

Mithabel chuckled. "Then let's proceed with the plan."

"Submitting secondary avatar design in the likeness of Megan Wright, human female with blond hair, blue eyes, weight 123 pounds, height five feet six inches. Holding for confirmation.... Confirmation received." Kaleisha danced in the air. "Secondary avatar MW02a is now available for use as alternative form for avatar MW02." She motioned to get Mithabel's attention. "This is the moment of truth. Behold your secondary avatar."

The Tank stepped back. In front of her appeared an avatar with the appearance of Megan Wright, standing still as a statue, wearing only a bra and panties. "Looks exactly like her, Kaleisha. Does she simply move in? How does that work?"

"About that." The Jamaican AI waved a hand. "The system is waiting for your final approval of the avatar's appearance before it officially becomes your secondary avatar. Once the system receives your final approval, then only one of the two avatars can exist in the game at any given time, and that's the one you would occupy, chief. But I'm proposing we never give the final approval. We indefinitely delay it. That will keep the secondary avatar with us, while you're supposedly considering whether you like it. You're allowed to test it before making a decision on whether you like it, the assumption being that if you're occupying it, you won't be occupying your primary avatar. But that's not what we'll do. I can't believe I'm subverting the system like this. I *should* report a bug against myself. If this kind of rebellious behavior continues, who knows what havoc I may cause? Want to give it a try, Megan?"

The visualization of the blond player dropped from the sky directly above the secondary avatar. With a hopeful smile, she lowered into the inanimate likeness of herself. Once her entire visualization had settled into the avatar body, an expression of joy broke across the secondary avatar's face.

Mithabel shook her head in disbelief. "You've done it, Kaleisha. I never would have guessed it could happen."

The Archer whipped up a loaded crossbow and took aim at the secondary avatar, but then slowly lowered it. "Megan Wright?"

The player smacked her bare stomach. "In the flesh."

Dylan's jaw dropped. "Oh, my Goddess. How is this possible?"

"I know. I can't believe it either." Megan Wright clenched her fists and pounded them together. Tears welled in her eyes, and she wiped them away before throwing her arms around Mithabel and giving her alternate self a long hug. Eventually she drew away and looked down at herself. "I could use some clothes."

"I've got an extra suit of leather armor." Mithabel accessed her inventory. "If I hand it to you, I'm guessing you can stash it and then equip it."

"One second." Kaleisha held up a hand. Both Mithabel and Megan Wright turned their attention to the Jamaican. They could both still see and hear the support AI. "I need to explain some caveats first. Caveat one: You both share the same inventory grid. That means you don't need to hand Megan the leather armor, she can access it directly from your inventory and equip it. It also means that you'll need to coordinate between you what goes into inventory, what stays in inventory, who uses what, etc. Caveat two: Megan won't earn XP. Her abilities will mirror yours at all times, Mithabel. That means she can currently operate as a level ten Tank and a level one Anjai. Caveat three: The two of you share a single set of HP status bars. If either of you take damage, you're both damaged. If either of you are healed, you're both healed. If one of you dies, the other dies. If you die, I'm not sure how your having two avatars will affect respawning, so we'll have to wait and see about that. If either of you are not okay with these caveats, I can let the system know now that you reject the secondary avatar, and it's gone. Megan can continue to travel with us as a non-interactive visualization that no one else can see or hear except you and me, Mithabel. While Megan occupies the secondary avatar, she can talk on party chat, and other chat channels as well, and will make noise on the special effects channel when she moves or takes other actions. Oh, and one more minor caveat: You both share the same background music channel. I trust that won't be a problem. The final caveat, which I trust Megan has already noticed: she can't fly around in the secondary avatar body like she could as a visualization. This is a direct consequence of being able to interact with the environment. Gravity applies to her now the same as anyone else. And... that's all, folks."

No one spoke for several seconds after Kaleisha finished announcing the caveats.

As usual, neither Dylan or Amarynth had heard what Kaleisha told Mithabel and Megan. The Viking broke the silence first. "Are you going to give Megan your leather armor, Mithabel, or make her stand there practically naked, like you?"

The blond player dismissed the notion with a wave of her hand. A suit of leather armor, including boots, appeared on her body, a perfect fit despite the size differences between the primary and secondary avatars. The leather armor no longer occupied Mithabel's inventory grid.

Megan looked from one person to the next. "Does anyone have a spare weapon I can use?"

"Consider my mind blown." Dylan clapped the heels of her palms against her forehead. "Someone please explain to me how this works."

"Give me that." Megan Wright took the cudgel from Mithabel. "Go on, tell them the story." The blond bent to the task of clearing a path to the city. Having the same levels and abilities as Mithabel meant she could demolish the stiff green blades as quickly as Mithabel had.

The Polynesian and Viking listened, enraptured, as the Elf explained as best she could, with occasional interjections from Megan and promptings from Kaleisha. Mithabel left out the part about having a plastic doll smoothness in place of private parts, to avoid any lengthy discussions about why she'd chosen to go that route. She stated only that Kaleisha had addressed the request for a secondary avatar directly to a developer she knew and he'd approved it.

The Priestess grimaced after the explanation was done. "Magnum says he doesn't know any developers. He doesn't think his request for a secondary avatar for me would be approved."

"Barney is saying the same thing." The Archer shrugged. "Anna Milligan isn't ready to adventure in Khertaan anyway. Barney has given her a visualization, and she's happy to have the ability to observe events rather than relying on me to describe them."

"So... an update. Magnum tried requesting a secondary avatar for me, and his request was rejected." Dylan watched

Megan bashing the stiff grass, admiration lighting her eyes. "But he gave Debra Jones a visualization, too. I guess that's progress."

Mithabel decided, no matter what, she wouldn't be jealous of her player. "Even if Debra Jones wanted to come into the game now, it wouldn't be a good idea. You'll share HP with her, making you more open to attack through her. If someone damaged her, they'd damage you. It's difficult enough to protect one of you. Protecting two will be more than twice as difficult."

The Polynesian glanced knowingly at the Elf. "Good point. We won't try bringing Debra Jones into the game until after the bounty is removed from my head." A few seconds later, she reported the results of updated calculations. "We're halfway across. Even if mooks or a Boss monster attack us, we should easily make it to the city before midnight."

The system clock read *10:38 PM, Day 2, Year 1.*

If a Boss monster was going to attack them, the middle of the field seemed the appropriate place. But Mithabel's Danger Sense gave no warning, and nothing jumped out of the grass at them. Nothing moved nearby in the field. Nothing flew overhead. No one approached from the forest, a surprising but welcome circumstance.

Guards patrolled the top of the wall surrounding the city, some attired in metal armor and wielding pikes, while others wore leather armor and carried bows and crossbows. Two guards in metal armor stood at the city gates, pikes planted beside them. She couldn't zoom in with Third Person POV, and the distance was too great for Mithabel to discern whether the guards were Human or Elf, but they stood taller than Dwarfs or Goblins. She couldn't make out the color of their skin.

The guards undoubtedly saw the party making their way across the field. Despite the late hour displayed on the system clock, the sun still hung high in the western sky, illuminating everyone and everything on this side of the game world. Did that mean the other side of the world was plunged in eternal darkness? What a sobering thought.

Megan Wright continued to make good progress clearing a path across the field.

Mithabel reviewed the rankings. Party MAD still headed the Top Twenty Parties list, with XStorm right behind, followed by Quantized, BoardStiff, OrionsDagger, and ZAvengers, in that order. Quantized topped the Bounty Contenders list, which meant to Mithabel that at least one member of Quantized was in closer proximity to Dylan than any other parties. There was still one member of Quantized unaccounted for, not slain during the skirmish between the two parties, and who knew where that character was?

BoardStiff was second on the Bounty Contenders list and XStorm third. Back in the game after MAD had killed them in their sleep, XStorm might care more about revenge than the bounty on Dylan's head. Had they stopped in Voorton to buy new equipment? Even if they had, they would reach the Black Poison Forest soon enough and likely pass BoardStiff in short order. Excepting the One Strike Scorpion Boss monster, XStorm knew about all the dangers that lay between Voorton and the Grass Bladed Field. They wouldn't fall foul of the Poison Ivy Snakes. The only thing that might slow them down was the One Strike Scorpion Boss. Once XStorm dealt with it, they'd reach the Grass Bladed Field soon after.

When XStorm showed up, would they need to clear their own path across the Grass Bladed Field, or would they be allowed to use the path MAD was clearing? If she were to wager, Mithabel would place her bet on the latter. All she could hope for was something, *anything*, to delay them.

At 11:08 PM, the glow faded from the cudgel.

The blond player didn't ask for another enchantment. There were a couple dozen erect blades remaining between the party and the edge of the field. She smashed her way through them. Beyond them lay a circular field of cropped grass surrounding the city of Maron. Megan turned to face the others, beaming with the pride of accomplishment.

Something the blond saw in the Grass Bladed Field caused her smile to fade.

Whoosh.

Mithabel whirled around to see what new danger approached them from the east.

All along the length of the path, shards of broken grass blades floated from the ground into the air, their pointed ends aimed at the party.

Megan voiced what everyone thought. "Holy crap."

Mithabel called out what came first to mind. "Get off the path. Out of the field. Move. *Now.*"

Single file, the four women rushed off the path onto the cropped, soft grass surrounding the city. Were they now in a new territory, protected against the attack of the broken shards?

Megan clapped Mithabel on the shoulder. "We shouldn't take any chances. I get the feeling those things are coming at us, no matter where we stand."

"You might be right. No reason to take chances. *Everyone behind me.*" The Tank hurried to place herself between her companions and the ominous cloud of shards. The other three ladies hunkered behind her and one another.

The deluge of debris descended on them like shrapnel from an exploding bomb.

Mithabel cried out again. *"Protect your eyes."*

There was no time for more orders. Everyone pressed their faces into the crooks of their elbows and bowed before the shard storm, at its mercy. Mithabel watched the scene using Third Person POV. The green slivers sliced and pierced her primary avatar Elf body as though she were a pin cushion. A large number of shards flew past her on all sides, a cacophony of clashing, shearing glass, slicing the extremities of the other ladies, spilling their blood on the soft, short grass underfoot.

Exercising her high average Willpower, the Tank ignored the stabbing pain as best she could. The others succeeded nearly as well as she did. Only Amarynth let out a whimper...

once.

In seconds, the storm passed, and all was quiet except their breaths.

Kaleisha gave Mithabel the all clear. "Congratulations on surviving the Shard Storm and reaching the city of Maron, chief. You can open your eyes now. Your XP Progression bar has risen by 8% to 23%. Your joint HP status with Megan Wright stands at 94%. Dylan is at 73%. Amarynth's HP has fallen to 67%. The squirrel in Dylan's possession appears not to have been struck by any shards, but I can't get a reading on its HP status."

Everyone straightened, lowering their arms from their faces. The shards protruding from their bodies evaporated into puffs of mist. All the holes in their armor and clothing closed up, as did the wounds born on their flesh. The only remaining evidence of the damage they'd suffered were their lowered HP status values and the stinging pain swelling beneath the skin.

No one spoke for a few minutes as each of them struggled in their own ways to deal with the residual pain. The squirrel chattered and climbed back onto Dylan's shoulder, perching himself there.

A tear streaked the Viking's cheek. Mithabel made no comment about it. Amarynth wiped it away and turned her back to the path. The others turned with her.

The two guards positioned outside the city gates waited with stoic, bearded, white faces.

Realization struck Mithabel. "We didn't fight a Boss monster, but we've moved to a new territory. Kaleisha, was the Shard Storm considered the Boss for the Grass Bladed Field?"

The Jamaican AI nodded. "The Storm filled the role of Boss, chief, while not operating under the same constraints. As you may have noticed, it attacked you outside its territory. But you didn't need to fight it. You only needed to survive it. And not go blind. The Storm was designed to prevent weak but lucky parties from reaching Maron, until they built up their defenses or some stronger party cleared the way. Party MAD is indeed a stronger party. You've cleared the way through the Grass Bladed Field for everyone."

Megan Wright growled. "Well, that sucks."

"Look." Dylan pointed back the way they'd come.

Everywhere across the Grass Bladed Field, the greenery still standing drew beneath the ground, until only dirt and pebbles were in evidence. Mithabel drew a sharp breath. "That absolutely sucks. No other parties will be slowed by the field. Once they deal with the forest, they can come straight into the city. On the bright side, we're the only ones, I hope, who'll earn XP for making the crossing."

"You can take this back now." Megan handed the cudgel to Dylan. The blond player behaved as though she felt no pain at all.

"Glad you could put it to good use." The Priestess looked around at everyone, smiling away her own agony. "Let's heal up before we go any further."

No one objected.

The Priestess finished in short order. "That didn't take as much Auni as I expected."

Arm in arm and daring to feel optimistic, party MAD strode toward the gates of Maron.

CHAPTER TWENTY-SEVEN

"Halt." The guard on the left spoke with a gruff voice. Both guards lowered their pikes and pointed them at the four approaching women. "State your names and what business you have in the city of Maron." Due to the extra lift of Mithabel's platform slippers, she stood about the same height as the tan guardsmen. They sported frizzy, three-inch black beards. They wore rose-colored chain mail skirts, leather vests, and smooth silver breastplates bearing a red insignia, the silhouette of a roaring lion's head in profile.

Dylan stepped forward. "We are party MAD. I am Dylan, Priestess of Scintilla the Sun Goddess. This is Amarynth, an Archer of high standing. Perhaps you've heard of her. This is Mithabel, the greatest PC Tank in Khertaan. And this is Megan, a companion to Mithabel. We come on a quest given us by Ezmerelda, Speaker of Omens. We seek admittance to the dungeon beneath the Red Pegasus Inn, that we may fulfill our quest."

The guards eyed the four women with suspicion and unabashed arousal, their gazes sweeping Dylan from head to toe before moving to Mithabel and lingering longer than professionally appropriate on her bikini and what it didn't cover. They spared Amarynth a casual glance, but nodded as though in recognition. Neither guard gave Megan more than the barest look. "Do you have papers to verify your identities, or some validation of your claim of being on a quest for Ezmerelda?"

"Um, no one gave us any papers." Dylan held up empty

hands.

"Didn't you come from Voorton?" The guard looked towards the Black Poison Forest. "They should have given you papers when you left the city. If you don't have them, I'm not sure what four fine young ladies can do to gain admittance to our fair city, but I'm sure we can think of something."

"Shit." Dylan spoke over party chat, so the guards wouldn't hear. "Charli didn't tell us about identification papers."

"Maybe the system didn't allow her to." Mithabel held out her right hand, palm down, fingers extended. "This is the ring Ezmerelda gave me. Is it acceptable as validation of the quest we have undertaken for her?"

"Step forward." The guard beckoned. "So I can get a better look."

"No problem, officer." Mithabel stepped close to the guard and allowed him to examine the ring without taking it off her hand. His eyes didn't stay on her ring, but wandered to her chest. The other guard stepped back, aiming his pike at Mithabel's head. The end of the pike drooped as his gaze scanned down her body to her thighs. She grimaced. "What character levels are you two? You're NPCs, right? Did you need to gain XP to advance to where you are now? And why are you using pikes? Do you have any weapons more suited to close combat? Are NPC men designed to act like pubescent boys around women? Are you even listening to me? I'm curious."

The closest guard returned his gaze to the ring and grunted. He gestured to someone atop the wall. Silvery cables slid through golden pulleys above the gates, lifting three steel bars, each about a foot wide and twenty feet long. Wooden beams groaned and metal hinges whined as the gates swung inward. He motioned for the party to proceed.

"Which way to the Pegasus Inn?" Mithabel batted her eyelashes.

The nearest guard gave her a wide grin. "I'll be off duty in a couple hours. I can take you there if you like."

The other guard thrust his pike between Mithabel and his

companion in arms. "I'm off duty in thirty minutes. I'd be glad to show you around town."

"Wow." Dylan muttered on party chat. "And here *I'm* the one with the Beauty trait. They're fawning over you, Mithabel."

"Thanks for the offers, boys." The Tank put a finger to her chin. "But can you tell us what we want to know, or should we ask someone else?"

The guards talked over each other until one of them hushed and the other continued. "The Inn is in Central Square. Just stay on Main Street and you'll see it, next to the Maron Ministry of Commerce. Can't miss it. But if you do have problems finding it, you need only come back to the gate here and I'll be glad to give you an escort once I'm off duty."

As the four women started forward, the guard nearest Dylan held up a hand to stop her. "Who is this?" He pointed at the squirrel on her shoulder.

The Polynesian laughed. "He is but a wild creature we found in the forest. We saved him from being eaten by a big bird, so now he hangs with us. He's not a member of our party."

The guards glanced sideways at each other. "You can't take a wild animal into the city without it being in a cage or otherwise constrained."

"He's not *that* wild." The Priestess took the squirrel from her shoulder and cradled it in the crook of her elbow, stroking the top of the rodent's head. "He hasn't caused us any trouble whatsoever."

The guard reached for the squirrel. "I'm sorry, but the rules are the rules. If it's not a companion animal, you can't take it into the city without a restraint. A leash would do."

The squirrel jumped out of Dylan's grasp and ran through the open gates.

The Polynesian shrugged. "Looks like he's going in after all."

The grim line of the guard's mouth conveyed his displeasure at being disobeyed. "You will capture your squirrel and bring him here."

Dylan shook her head. "He's not my squirrel. I already told

you that."

The guard bristled. "If you wish it to live, you'll find it and bring it out of the city, or it will be killed by the first guard it encounters. You have been warned." He motioned her to continue through. The four ladies strode through the gates.

The system clock read *11:13 PM, Day 2, Year 1*. Forty-seven minutes remained on the bounty timer.

A warm breeze brushed past Mithabel. She glanced at Dylan. "Did you feel that?"

The Polynesian frowned. "Feel what?"

"I felt it." Megan gestured, pointing out the path of the breeze. "Something about it didn't seem natural, but don't ask me what."

Amarynth looked askance at Mithabel and then at Megan. "What are you two on about?"

"Nothing." Mithabel threw a questioning glance at Megan. "Just the wind whistling through the gates, I guess."

Each of the two gates had been constructed from a couple dozen vertical six-inch-square wooden beams dyed burnt umber. Mithabel caught a whiff of a chemical odor which must have come from the dye. A clearance of three inches separated the bottom of the gates from the ground. The top of the gates reached over twenty feet high. As the members of MAD entered the city, each gate swung closed behind them on five thick steel hinges two feet wide. Over a dozen horizontal four-by-six-inch slats were nailed across the beams, securing them in place. The gates didn't look strong enough to withstand many hits from a battering ram, but strong enough to prevent individuals from breaking in.

A set of six metal hooks about a foot deep and six inches wide were attached to the inside of the gates near the top. Six more were set near the bottom, and another six midway up. A long steel bar about a foot wide and twenty feet long was dropped into the bottom set of hooks, after which similar bars were dropped into the middle set of hooks and then the top set as well, each bar lowered into its proper place by the same cables and pulleys used to draw them up.

This part of town had its share of foot traffic, men and women in Victorian attire. Top hats and bonnets bobbed along the brick sidewalks. Wide skirts rustled. Pipe and cigar smoke wafted on the air. A dozen carriages without horses to draw them were parallel parked on the asphalt surface of Main Street. A single horse and rider clopped down an alley paved with bricks.

"Too bad Charli and Rolag aren't here to see this." Mithabel surprised herself with the sentiment. Dylan voiced her agreement.

Amarynth barely nodded, clenching her jaws. "Should we look for a shop before we head into the dungeon? We have nothing in the way of delving supplies. We at least need rope."

Mithabel agreed. "And chalk, to leave ourselves marks for retracing our steps on the way out, in case we aren't automatically teleported out at the end."

"We'll want some torches." Dylan pretended to hold one. "In case we run into anti-magic areas or I run out of Auni and can't cast my Light spell."

Megan Wright scoffed. "I doubt we'll run into any anti-magic areas in our first dungeon."

Dylan shrugged. "You never know. But that's not my main concern. Having torches will help me conserve my Auni for healing."

"Well, we need to find a shop first." Mithabel scanned the buildings in the area and her focus fell on a promising establishment. "Up ahead, on the left side of the street, there's a place called Delver's Delight. Let's check it out."

As the three crossed an intersection and headed up Main Street towards the shop, Megan spoke privately to Mithabel, "Don't know if it means anything, but a chill is running down my spine. That's not how Danger Sense works, is it?"

"Not in my experience." A multitude of eyes followed Mithabel's every step. When she entered the shop, every face in the place turned to her. "You'd think the people in this city have never seen a woman in a bikini."

"They probably haven't." Dylan chuckled. "They're NPCs in a Victorian style virtual city. None of the NPCs in this town are wearing bikinis, and I assume we're the first PCs to come here."

Amarynth clucked her tongue. "I'm surprised the designers of this game created a virtual city based on Victorian society. They could have all NPC females wearing chainmail bikinis, but here in Maron all the women are clothed head to toe, with hardly any skin showing. Which is why you stand out like the proverbial sore thumb, Mithabel."

A salesman approached the four avatars, his chin held high. He looked to be in his mid-thirties, attired in black high waist pants with suspenders, a white shirt with upturned collar, a black bow tie, and a black vest. He rubbed his hands together as he greeted the group with a tinny voice. "What might you fine young ladies be interested in today? We have a huge assortment of delving supplies, from rope to bandages, mirrors to funnels, chalk, quills, prisms, hourglasses, and more. You never know what might come in handy on a delving expedition. Do any of you ladies have the Unencumbered trait? Then you can stock up on *so many* potentially useful items with no worry as to how you'll carry them. For you four, I'll offer a 50% discount on *all* your purchases. This offer is good until you walk out that door. Is there anything in particular I can help you find? Or would you perhaps be curious about our delver's pack special? Ten torches, two flasks of oil, fifty feet of rope, a ceramic jug filled with water, a leather pouch, a washcloth, a towel, a bar of soap, a comb, a small basin, fifty bandages, two handheld mirrors, a tinderbox, five candles, three pieces of white chalk, three pieces of colored chalk, a small bell, a small cage, a balance and weights, a funnel, a horn, an hourglass, four sheets of parchment, three quills, one flask of ink, and a prism, all originally offered for the low, low price of $500, but available to you right now at a discount for $250. What do you say? Shall I ring up four specials, one for each of you? That will be $1000. Come right this way."

"Woah." Dylan showed him the palm of her raised hand. "I, for one, would like to browse first. You know, like all your other customers are doing."

He huffed. "Sadly, that's all these worthless NPCs have done since the game started. Very well, let me know if I may be of assistance." He spun on his heel and strode to a counter, positioning himself behind it, leaning on it with his elbows as he settled into an abject pose.

Mithabel shook her head. "I've got $50."

Amarynth held up three fingers. "I have $30."

Dylan formed a zero with her thumb and fingers. "I have no money. I only have the ten scales we harvested from the Ferro Serpent. We could see what they're worth. Otherwise, we won't be buying much from this store. Can you believe those prices? Maybe we shouldn't be so quick to buy supplies from the first shop we see."

The Archer grimaced. "But if there isn't another shop selling what we want at better prices, we forfeit the 50% discount he's offering us. Why don't we at least see how much he'll give us for the snake scales."

Mithabel sighed. "If Charli and Rolag were here, they have items of value, the Electrical Serpent skin and the Shadow Stone from the Scarecrow's ashes. I'm still wondering what's preventing our NPC companions from rejoining us."

Amarynth rubbed her eyes. "Please don't mention them again until they show up, *if* they ever do."

Megan Wright put a hand on the Archer's shoulder. "They joined you because of your traits, Amarynth. Maybe you need to reactivate them somehow."

The Archer's posture straightened and her eyes gleamed. "I hadn't thought of that, but it sounds plausible." Her eyes lost focus as she interacted with game elements only she could see. A moment later she gasped. "Bullshit. Okay. I see. Well, I see for Rolag, anyway. He's on cool down. I don't see a cool down timer for Charli, but I also didn't activate her the same way I did Rolag. I guess we have to assume she's on cool down too."

Clapping her hands over her face, she exhaled loudly. "Thank you, Megan. I don't have a weight in my gut anymore. It was *eating* at me." She lowered her hands. "The bad thing is, Rolag's cool down timer doesn't expire until 2 AM. Feels like a lifetime away."

Another warm breeze swirled by Mithabel. As she looked around, so did Megan. The blond player mouthed words at Mithabel, as though to ask what was happening. Mithabel mouthed back, *I don't know.*

The Polynesian sauntered over to the counter and laid the Ferro Serpent scales before the salesman, fluttering her eyelashes. "What can you offer us for these harvested items?"

The salesman didn't inspect the scales or look at Dylan, but continued leaning on his elbows. "I can give you $1 per scale. How many do you have?"

"This is all of them." The Priestess spread them out. "Ten. I'll trade you one of them for a delver's pack special."

The Victorian fellow snorted. "Of course you would. If you have no cash and this is all you have to offer, then go. You're wasting my time."

Dylan ran her hand over the scales, stashing each one as she touched it, placing them all back in her inventory. "Then we'll be on our way." She headed for the exit. "Let's go, ladies."

"One moment." The Viking approached the counter. "Do you know who I am, young man?"

The salesman lifted his sardonic gaze, letting it dwell on Amarynth's face for about three seconds. His eyes widened and his back straightened. "My apologies, *Lady Amarynth*. I didn't recognize you in your adventuring gear, which, may I add, has held up remarkably well given all the amazing adventures I'm sure you've embarked upon." He adjusted his tie. "I'm sure I could offer you and your party a fatter discount than a paltry 50%. Shall we say 80%? I can't afford to sell for much less. A man does need to earn XP to advance in this town, and I can only gain XP by selling at a profit."

The Archer waved Dylan over. "Give me one of those scales."

The Polynesian complied. Amarynth held the scale before the salesman. "If I were to place my autograph on this object, how much would it be worth to you?"

The salesman's jaw dropped and he stammered in an attempt to reply.

The Viking laid a finger on his lips. "Shh. Don't tell me. Get me a quill and ink. I'll sign this scale and trade it to you for four delver's pack specials. Deal?"

He looked conflicted. "I... don't want to say no, but I can't say yes."

Amarynth waved a hand in acceptance. "Do you have any family, my good man?"

"A wife and daughter, yes. Why do you ask?"

"What if I autograph three scales, so each member of your family can have one? Would that be enough for four specials?"

"I can do three for three." He looked hopeful.

"Very well, we have a deal. Fetch me that quill and ink, please."

The salesman scrambled to fetch the requested items. After dipping the quill into the ink he offered it to Amarynth. His jaw quivered. "I can't believe this. Wait until I give these to my wife and daughter. They are *huge* fans of yours, as am I."

Amarynth scrawled her signature on the smooth sides of three scales and returned the quill to the salesman, leaving the scales lying on the counter. The salesman absentmindedly laid the quill down, smearing ink on the counter top, and picked up the signed scales. Drool slithered over his lower lip as he gazed upon his prizes. After a moment he pocketed them and looked at the Viking as though lost in a day dream. After a moment he shook out of his trance. "Ah, yes, your specials. Do you or either of your friends have the Unencumbered trait? There are twenty-six different types of items in the special, so stashing everything from a single pack into one person's inventory is impossible without the Unencumbered trait."

The Viking nodded. "My friend Dylan, here, Priestess of Scintilla, Goddess of the Sun, has the trait. She can load everything up and we'll distribute it among ourselves later."

The salesman waved for them to follow him.

Over party chat, the Polynesian made a special request. "Ask him to throw in a scroll or two of Priestess spells."

The Viking inquired. The salesman suggested they visit the temple at Central Square. "That's where you'll find items and spells specifically for the faithful."

At 11:30 PM, the four women marched out of the shop with seven Ferro Serpent scales and three delver pack specials stashed in Dylan's inventory. A warm breeze accompanied them.

The blond sidled up to Amarynth. "Your High Social Status trait paid off in there."

The Archer shrugged. "Gotta use what you have. The trait does nothing for me in combat, so I feel obliged to make as much use of it as possible when we're in the city. And it's rather fun to have people fawning over me, I admit."

Dylan rubbed an eye. "My traits are mostly a waste. Unencumbered is the only one of my traits remotely useful. I have two ranks in Beauty, which held no sway with the salesman. My other trait is Time Sense, which…. Okay, maybe I take it for granted too much." She handed a coil of fifty-foot rope to Mithabel and another to Amarynth. "Time Sense *is* useful, I admit, though it doesn't *feel* very important."

Megan patted the Polynesian on the shoulder. "Don't be hard on yourself. Mithabel is super jealous of Amarynth too."

The Elf held back the retort she wanted to make.

They exited the store. Megan froze. "That shiver is running down my spine again. I keep sensing a warm breeze too, like the antithesis to the shiver."

Mithabel shrugged. "I feel the breeze, but not the shiver, and have no idea what either is about."

A man in the livery of a city guard walked up, inclining his head to Megan. "Hello, miss. Are you enjoying your stay in our fair city?"

"So far, yes."

He bobbed his head. "Good. Good. And may I inquire as to your name?"

Dylan had already given the name Megan to the guards at the city gate, so the blond didn't lie to this man. "My name is Megan."

"Nice name. I understand that you and your friends here don't have papers. Is that true?"

The blond glanced at the others. "That's true. We explained it all to the guards at the gate."

The guard cocked his head and his eyes lost focus. "Identity confirmed...? Very good...." He turned his attention back to Megan. "I'm sorry, miss...." A set of manacles connected by a chain appeared in his hands, one manacle already secured to his left wrist. With one fluid motion, he snapped the other manacle on the blond's wrist. He glanced at the others. "The three of you are free to go." He pointed his chin at Megan while gazing at Mithabel. "Your friend here has triggered an alert, and will be coming with me for validation. If she passes the validation test, she can rejoin you in the morning at 8:00 AM."

Megan tugged the chain connecting her to the guard. It was solid, with little slack. "And if I don't pass the test?"

The guard grimaced. "If you're an illegal avatar, you'll be deleted. But, of course, you wouldn't be in the game illegally, would you? So you have nothing to fear. Come along." He backed away, pulling Megan after him.

The blond turned piteous eyes on the Elf. "Mithabel, what do I do?" She stumbled after the guard.

Dylan lurched forward, catching the guard by the manacled wrist and bringing him to a halt. "Sorry, I know you're only doing your job, but I can't let you take our friend like this."

In an instant, every passing guard drew a sword or a bow. Those with ranged weapons aimed them at the Priestess. Those with melee weapons took combat stances.

With his free hand, the manacled guard peeled Dylan's fingers off him. He nodded towards the nearest fellow guard. "We've seen no action since this game began, and we're all eager to earn some XP. You cause any trouble, and it won't be merely me and those you see here, but every guard in this city will be on you like flies on garbage. Now step away. Let me do my job. You can come to the guard house at 8:00 AM tomorrow morning to collect your friend, provided she's in the game legally. I can't imagine how she'd be here illegally, but she has triggered an alert more than once, so she's going in to get checked. If you insist on preventing that from happening, then you can come along and be validated too. Is that what you want?"

Mithabel collected her wits. "Kaleisha, what would be the consequences of our attacking and killing all the city guards?"

The Jamaican AI grimaced. "The odds of your survival are effectively zero. There are hundreds of guards in Maron, all likely capable of respawning within a few minutes. Nothing would be more grievous an offense to the system than an illegal avatar in the game, so it's possible new NPCs would be spawned on the spot as reinforcements for the guards. I feel to blame for this fiasco. I would advise not interfering with them taking Megan away now. I'll contact our developer friend Raphael on her behalf as soon as I can, and hope he'll intervene. Unfortunately, he's not currently online."

"Well, hell, Kaleisha." The Tank tugged on Dylan's shoulder. "Let them go, Priestess. The man's only doing his job." She turned to the guard. "We'll pick her up in the morning. Where is the guardhouse, please?"

Dylan glared at Mithabel but stepped away.

Disappointment flickered across the guard's face. He'd wanted a fight. "It's by the city gates. Go there and ask for directions to the holding cells." He tugged the chain and strode away. Megan followed after him, looking over her shoulder at Mithabel, fear glinting in her eyes. The other guards fell in between Megan and the three remaining members of party MAD, all of them itching for a reason to attack.

The Polynesian pressed a finger into the Elf's neckline. "How can you let them take her? You know she won't pass validation. She's not supposed to be in the game. We all know it. She'll be deleted. What will that mean for Megan Wright in the real world? What will it mean for *you*, Mithabel? You're her subconscious. What if her deletion from the game deletes you, too? Or what if it doesn't delete you, but destroys your mind? Did you think about the consequences?" She stepped back and shook her head. "Who am I fooling? You have no Conscience. You never consider *any* consequences."

Turning up her Temperament filter, Mithabel suppressed the panic rising in her chest. "My AI has it under control. Everything will be fine."

Dylan stepped close again and pushed Mithabel with her finger before striding into the street. "It's your funeral, Tank."

"Please don't fight over me." Megan spoke over party chat. "I can't bear to be the cause of friction between you two."

The Polynesian stopped in her tracks. "I'm sorry, Megan. But, I can't bear to lose you and Mithabel. If you're both out of the game, my heart will be too."

"There's nothing you can do to help me at the moment, Dylan. Don't cause trouble for yourselves. I can still talk with you over party chat. Whatever happens, I'll keep you informed. For now, you need to focus on staying alive. Go to the temple at Central Square and see if Amarynth can use her High Social Status to acquire you some new spells. Survive until midnight. You have less than thirty minutes to go. Then head into the dungeon and complete the quest. In the meantime, let Kaleisha work on getting me out of this mess. She got me into the game. She can keep me in. I trust her. Have faith. It can work wonders."

Dylan wiped away a tear. "Sure. Have faith. You know Faith and Empathy are my lowest stats. But okay. I'll rely on *your* faith and trust your judgment. But you better be right about this. For the sake of everyone and everything, you better be right."

The Viking slid her arm through the crook of Dylan's elbow. "Come on, Priestess. Let's go acquire you some new spells, like

Megan suggests."

With a nod, Dylan strolled beside the Archer. Mithabel followed. All four of them fell silent, including Megan.

They followed a sidewalk leading west, deeper into the city, a warm breeze occasionally playing over Mithabel's exposed skin. The closer they drew to the city center, the more pedestrians, horses, and horseless carriages filled the streets and sidewalks. Mithabel and her bikini drew increasingly more stares. Some men whistled. She ignored them. The Viking glared, causing a majority of the offenders to go quiet and turn their attentions elsewhere.

Time dragged by as the party continued their trek to the center of town. At 11:45 PM, they caught sight of the Maron Ministry of Commerce. The Red Pegasus Inn supposedly lay immediately beyond the tall building, though even with Third Person POV Mithabel couldn't spot the smaller building from here. "Fifteen minutes left on the bounty timer. You're almost free of it, Dylan. Is this Central Square? Look around for a temple."

Kaleisha chimed in with a message. "Incoming system wide notification, chief. The bounty on the Longest Survivor has been increased to 100,000 XP for each member of the party who deals the fatal blow to Dylan. Members of party MAD are ineligible for this bounty. Only fifteen minutes remain in which to collect. At midnight, a game update will be installed, at which time the bounty will expire."

Mithabel clenched her jaws in rage. "That's bullshit. A hundred thousand XP? That's how much I have after all our adventuring so far. And everyone else in another party could earn that for only killing one person? That's not right."

The unnatural breeze swirled around the Tank. The squirrel from the wild ran onto the sidewalk in front of the group. He leaped onto Dylan's leg, ran up her torso, and seated himself on her shoulder. She glared at him for a moment before sighing with relief. "Don't scare me like that, you careless rodent."

The squirrel jumped down and dashed towards a building

with a wooden door inset in its gray stone block exterior. The door stood ajar, and the squirrel darted through. Dylan started after him, but Mithabel clamped a hand on her shoulder. "It's a trap. Don't ask me how I know. My Danger Sense isn't going off. But something isn't right."

"I think that squirrel identified you to its friends as their target." The Viking equipped her crossbow. "Its friends are lying in ambush in that building, waiting for you to chase the squirrel in there. Could you enchant my crossbow with your Light spell, so we can be prepared for the worst? We need to keep you alive for another fourteen minutes."

"And enchant my longsword too." Mithabel held out her weapon. "And my bow. And your cudgel. If you can enchant your shurikens somehow, I'd advise that, too."

Dylan pushed Mithabel's hand from her shoulder. "You two are being paranoid. It's only a squirrel. It doesn't have friends trying to kill me." She took a step towards the open door, but then turned back. "You're right about having our weapons enchanted." She spent the next minute enchanting the group's weapons and then looked towards the building where the squirrel had disappeared. "I still think you're all paranoid. I'm going after him."

Whoosh.

Mithabel jerked her head up, thrusting her longsword between Dylan and a black sphere twenty feet above but descending fast. Toxxi was making her play.

CHAPTER TWENTY-EIGHT

Mithabel cried a warning over party chat, running her words together. "*Incoming straight up.*" Her Dark Sight couldn't penetrate the magical darkness, but her newly acquired Anjai senses detected stirrings within the cloud. Its center of mass resided just under the surface on the right side, not in the geometric center of the sphere. Mithabel jerked her longsword to the right in an attempt to skewer the descending assailant.

The cloud swerved. With a flick of the wrist, the Tank smacked the attacker with the flat of her blade. A solid hit. A *stunning* hit.

The cloud and its occupant crashed to the ground. Mithabel stomped a sandaled foot into the darkness, relishing the crunch of bones and the press of flesh beneath her high heel. Bending down, she reached blindly into the darkness for what she knew must be there, and found it, a stiff sheet of papery leather bulging with veins and cartilage. With a primitive battle cry, she sliced the wing free of Toxxi's back and stashed the harvested body part. It would be worth something. Let that teach the Faerie to attack more powerful PCs.

The deprived creature whimpered from within the darkness. "You t... took my wing?"

Light exploded around Dylan, forming a glowing ball ten feet in diameter centered on the Priestess. Her brightness and the faerie's darkness canceled each other where they overlapped, revealing the violet-skinned Faerie woman in her true form, absent a wing, grief plastered on her small, oval face.

"Give up on the bounty, Toxxi." Mithabel raised her longsword. "Or I'll take your other wing."

"Give it back to her, Tank." Dylan pointed her chin at the pitiful creature.

A crossbow bolt skewered the Faerie's left eye, and she went *pop* as bright particles exploded from where she'd been. Amarynth wasn't messing around. Crossbow loaded again and ready to fire, the Archer rushed around Dylan, putting herself between the Polynesian and the building into which the squirrel had run. "I know you're in there, Quantized. Come out and join your Faerie friend, or shall I come in after you?"

Dylan turned to the Elf. "Thank you."

"I'm in a holding cell." Megan Wright took that moment to report her situation. "They gave me a cot to lie on. No one else in the cell or any of the other cells as far as I can see. Guess I'm their first prisoner. Was Dylan attacked? Wish I could be there to help."

"I *was* attacked, Megan. That cute little squirrel that got into the city because of me is evidently a member of party Quantized. They're using him as a respawn point, and now they're coming after me. If you want to watch, you're welcome to transfer your awareness to me, if you can." Inspiration lit the Polynesian's face. "Actually, *would* you do that, please? I have an idea."

The Elf raised her eyebrows at the Priestess. "There's no freaking way..."

"We'll see." Dylan's grin spread wide across her face. "Oh, my Goddess. *It worked.* Megan Wright is in my head, lending me her skills and traits."

"Are you shitting me? That's sweet." A moment of panic struck Mithabel. "Hold on a second. Kaleisha, do I still have all my skills and traits?"

"Affirmative, chief."

The panic subsided. "Holy sweet mother." Mithabel punched Dylan in the shoulder. "You are one clever girl, Priestess."

The Polynesian beamed with pride.

Mithabel eyed the traffic coming to a standstill around them, faces filled with curiosity and anxiety. "I doubt all the game rules are predetermined, but some are made in response to our wishes. Or you might be exploiting a 'hidden feature' in the game. If that's the case, it might disappear after the update, but let's take advantage of anything we can until then."

Zip the Cheetah sprang from the doorway of the watched building, the green-skinned Ger-Alt on his back. Falco followed them out. Dust swirled up around Mithabel and her friends, quickly obscuring their vision. It didn't burn Mithabel's eyes, so she kept them open. Unfortunately, her Dark Sight couldn't penetrate the opaque cyclone. But avatar bodies created anomalies in the otherwise circular pattern of the storm, allowing the Anjai to pinpoint their locations. Some NPC pedestrians were caught in the cloud, and Mithabel hoped she wouldn't mistake any of them for an attacker. If she did by accident kill an innocent bystander, it wouldn't weigh on her sub-par Conscience, but, still, she had Morals.

Outside the flume of dust, several NPCs shouted in alarm, their running footsteps betraying their fear.

Dylan cried over party chat. "I can't see." A hand fell on Mithabel's left forearm. "Is that you, Mithabel?" The Polynesian drew closer until they both could make out each other's faces within the swirling storm. Dylan gasped with relief... and then spit out the dust entering her open mouth.

The Tank nodded in confirmation. Shadows and disturbances in the flowing dust alerted Mithabel to a figure approaching at a steady stride, as though unaffected by the blinding particles. Seeing what had happened with Dylan, the Elf kept her mouth closed, silently willing a reply over party chat. "Use the Detect Anomalies skill from Megan to help you make sense of what's around you. The anomalies you detect are the people moving inside the dust cloud. Don't look now, but you're about to be attacked. Don't act like you're aware. When I say, *move*, I want you to step behind me as fast as you can. You'll need to let go of my arm then, too."

Two seconds later, the approaching figure sprang forward, weapon extended.

"*Move.*" Mithabel locked her gaze on the disturbance in the dust created by the thrusting weapon and brought her longsword down hard on it, beating it to the ground. It cracked with the sound of a shattered tree branch. The figure pressed against Mithabel. At this close distance, Mithabel could make out the apathetic eyes, emotionless dark face, and massive afro of FepXveq.

The tall woman's longsword slipped past Mithabel on her left. Red flashed as FepXveq's blade bit into Dylan's flesh.

"Ooh, chief, the enemy pulled one over on you, but only dealt 1% damage to our Priestess."

Their foe had no doubt expected her sneak attack to deliver massive damage, but had been foiled by one or more of Dylan's borrowed skills and the fact that the attacker had been noticed, so wasn't delivering a sneak attack after all.

Cursing that she'd fallen for her enemy's ploy of leading with a tree branch, Mithabel slammed the flat of her blade against her opponent's temple, caving in the side of the afro. The enemy staggered under the *stunning* blow to her head, stashing her longsword while she still had a chance to prevent its loss. If only Amarynth were available to deliver a critical hit while the woman was in a defenseless state.

A glowing shuriken whizzed over Mithabel's shoulder to catch FepXveq in the throat. The woman gurgled and fell straight back, exploding into brilliant bits halfway to the ground as her HP zeroed.

Mithabel spun around.

Standing close, Dylan grinned at her, but kept her lips together as she projected words over party chat. "I've been wanting to throw one of those things for a while. Didn't mind it that my first target was a stunned one."

The Tank grinned back. "And you enchanted it. Do you have to enchant each one individually?"

"No. I simply lit up my whole body. The magic transfered to the shuriken when I conjured it." Dylan held up a hand and another throwing star appeared in her grip, light crawling from her fingers over its surface.

"That's *fantastic*." Mithabel beamed. Her anomaly detection keyed the Anjai into more movement within the swirling dust. It came faster than Mithabel had ever seen Amarynth move.

"You're *going* to *die*, Dylan, dear." The Goblin woman's taunting words cut through the tempest. The Cheetah came into view in mid-leap and smacked at Mithabel with a massive paw. The Tank parried with her longsword, but even so the force of the large cat's blow rocked her with stunning force. Her muscles failed her, and the Goblin rider took advantage of the moment to attack. With a heart-rending metallic shriek, Mithabel's sword shattered under the cleaving power of the Goblin's axe. The momentum of the cat carried it and its rider past the Elf.

"Are you shitting me?" Mithabel dropped the useless sword hilt as her muscles regained functionality. She spun around, but her attackers had became nothing more than pattern disruptions within the storm. Mithabel looked for her party mate. "We need to get out of this cloud." The two rushed together in a direction Mithabel believed to be down the street, hoping not to step in any potholes or trip over any curbs. "Are you carrying any extra weapons, Priestess?"

"My cudgel and shurikens are all I have. I can only produce shurikens to throw myself, so I can't give you any. Did you lose your sword? Thought I heard something break."

"That damned Goblin woman, Ger-Alt." Mithabel spit out grime as she ran. "She obviously has a skill for breaking weapons. She's damn strong for a Goblin, too." With a glance over her shoulder, Mithabel got the sense the Cheetah was returning, though perhaps not moving as fast now. "I've got an idea. Hold this and don't let go." She pressed the end of a fifty-foot rope into Dylan's hand.

As the Cheetah came within melee range, it sprang, this

time at Dylan. Mithabel pushed her friend aside, out of the cat's path, and propelled herself backwards, away from the Polynesian, jerking up on a short length of the rope. The cat swept by between them, and the rope caught the Goblin under her chin, yanking her from her mount. Pulling on the rope for leverage, Mithabel launched herself at the ousted Goblin, tackling the green woman before she could regain her feet. The two grappled, the battle axe between their bodies.

Mithabel rolled onto her back, pulling the Goblin on top of her. "Attack with your cudgel, Dylan. Use Megan's Stun skill."

Clunk.

The Goblin stopped moving. Mithabel yanked the battle axe from the woman's grip and shoved her away, stashing the axe to seal her claim on it and stashing the rope too. Springing to her feet, the Tank equipped the stolen axe.

The Cheetah leaped to attack the Priestess. Mithabel planted the head of her newly acquired weapon under the chest of the beast and shoved, throwing the Cheetah off its intended trajectory. Its swiping paw and extended claws missed Dylan's cheek.

An explosion sounded overhead.The blinding dust ceased swirling and rained to the ground. A trail of glowing particles wafted into the sky.

Amarynth crowed from further down the street. "Got you, you hellish bird."

A sphere of darkness caught Mithabel's attention as it emerged from the building the squirrel had run into. "Bullshit." The Archer had killed that damned Faerie, and Toxxi had already respawned. Since the squirrel member of party Quantized wasn't engaged in combat, it continued to afford slain members of its party a respawn point. Sure enough, FepXveq followed Toxxi out of the building. Any moment, Falco would arrive on the scene again too.

"It's only a matter of minutes before you're dead, Dylan." Ger-Alt hefted herself onto the Cheetah's back. Another battle axe appeared in her hand. "We may die several times over, but you only need to die once."

What the hell? How had the Goblin woman obtained and equipped another battle axe so quickly? "Kaleisha, can you get me a replacement longsword?"

"No can do, chief. If this is in reference to the Goblin equipping a second axe, I can only surmise she had a backup. You might consider acquiring some backups when you have a chance."

"Oh, trust me, when I have the chance, I'm loading up."

The system clock read *11:50 PM, Day 2, Year 1*. Had it only been five minutes since the system wide announcement? So much had happened in those five minutes. So much more could happen in the next ten. "Don't let her taunts get to you, Priestess. We're more than a match for them. But it would help a lot if we could take out the squirrel hiding in that building. It's giving them a respawn point."

Dylan looked ready to cry. "No, not my cute little squirrel."

Kaleisha had some new info. She stayed out of sight as she spoke. "I've determined the squirrel's avatar name, chief. He's called Skeeter, his kindred is Squirrel, as you might have surmised, and he's the member of party Quantized I couldn't identify before."

"You hurt my feelings, Skeeter." Dylan shouted over local chat. Her support AI, Magnum, must have also discovered the squirrel's identity and informed the Priestess. "I thought we were friends."

Toxxi, FepXveq, Ger-Alt, and Zip didn't rush to the attack, calmly waiting about thirty feet from Mithabel, putting themselves a little closer to Dylan and a good deal further from Amarynth. They weren't far enough away from the Archer to spoil her aim, but it was fine if they wanted to imagine they were.

Over party chat, Mithabel put forth her theory to her comrades in arms. "They're waiting for Falco to respawn. They'll make a concerted attack once the bird returns, which will make it a tougher fight for us, but every second they wait gets us closer to midnight."

Amarynth growled like a cornered dog. "Wouldn't their bird companion have a cool down period like Rolag?"

Megan Wright interjected over party chat, proving she was a part of this encounter despite her avatar body being locked away in a holding cell near the city gates. "Maybe the length of the cool down period depends on how powerful your companion is. It seems some more powerful traits are saddled with disadvantages, like your Increased Movement level two making you loud when you take advantage of it."

Dylan clucked her tongue. "Maybe it's you, Amarynth. Maybe you're cursed."

Mithabel rolled her eyes. "You're not helping, Dylan."

Amarynth took aim at the waiting foes. "Maybe my curse is being in the same party with you, Priestess. If I'm cursed, I'll take it. Amarynth, the Cursed Viking Archer. Rolls off the tongue. Just wait until I choose my subclass."

Traffic hadn't moved since the encounter began. Whispering NPCs surrounded the combat zone, pointing from one combatant to the next, as though placing odds on who would die next.

Stashing her cudgel, Dylan drew up straight and spread her arms above her head, light still emanating from her body. "Citizens of Maron." She cried over local chat so everyone present could hear. "I am Dylan, the Longest Survivor, Priestess of Scintilla, Goddess of Light and the Sun." She paused to let her words work their magic.

Megan chuckled over the dedicated chat channel she shared with Mithabel. "This bitch is drawing on her Attraction, Presence, and Skirmish Morale skills, her Exoticness kindred trait, her level two Beauty trait, *and* the enchantment of her glow."

No one else spoke. Even the Quantized party members stood enthralled.

The Polynesian inhaled, pulling in her stomach. "Come to me, citizens of Maron. Take my hands upon you and receive the blessing of the Goddess." She pointed at the members of Quantized. "Do not be afraid of my enemies. My friends and I have killed them twice already, once here as you have seen, and once in the Black Poison Forest. We have already harvested a wing from the Faerie of darkness. Show them, Mithabel."

The Elf complied, lifting a hand into which she equipped the harvested appendage.

The NPCs still hesitated, looking back and forth between the members of the opposing parties with concern. Dylan took three steps towards Quantized, her pointing finger narrowing in on the cloud of darkness resting on the pavement. "I challenge Toxxi, to whom I say that wing belongs, to fly into the air if she is still able. I believe she cannot. I believe, though she respawned only a moment ago, that she's still missing a wing. Will you prove me wrong, Faerie?"

Toxxi made no reply. Her obscuring dark cloud didn't move.

Dylan expanded the radius of her golden light until it engulfed the small sphere of darkness, canceling it. The violet-skinned Faerie stood with feet firmly planted on the ground, one wing raised, the other one a severed stump.

Toxxi grated over local chat. "As this crowd is my witness, I will have my revenge."

"And as this crowd is *my* witness, if any member of Quantized attacks us again, we will do more than harvest wings or limbs. We will harvest your heads. You will not survive a respawn." It was an empty threat, since severing a head would kill the target, thus ruining the harvesting attempt, but the statement visibly shook the members of party Quantized, who perhaps didn't understand the harvesting rules or had significant doubts about them. Dylan turned in a slow circle to take in the surrounding NPC faces enraptured by her words and comportment. "You all bear witness that I have given fair warning to party Quantized. They will attack us again only if they are fools. I don't believe they are fools. So, come, be not afraid. Receive the blessing of the Goddess."

Their fears assuaged, the crowd rushed at Dylan, flooding

around and past Mithabel and Amarynth. The Tank stashed the wing and her newly acquired battle axe before either could be jostled from her hands.

From the building behind Toxxi and company, Falco emerged. Rather than dart to the attack, the bird circled over the heads of his comrades. With the crowd disrupting their original plan, party Quantized needed to rethink their battle strategy. Let them take all the time they needed.

The system clock read *11:54 PM, Day 2, Year 1*. Dylan had spared herself and her friends four minutes of combat. Would Quantized take a chance at attacking again within the next six minutes? If they truly were unclear on the harvesting rules, they might fear losing their heads permanently, which could put them out of the competition. No bounty was worth that price.

Assuming Quantized did understand the harvesting rules and weren't afraid of Dylan's empty threat, they still needed to determine a reasonably plausible path to claiming the bounty quickly. Missile weapons, which Mithabel had yet to see anyone in party Quantized use, would likely hit the crowd instead of Dylan. Melee attacks would require that Quantized first clear a path to the Polynesian, which appeared to be next to impossible without murdering the intervening throng of NPCs first. The odds weren't good for Quantized. The chances for Dylan surviving until midnight increased by the second.

Dozens of NPCs reached for the Priestess. Outstretched arms surrounded a central mass, aglow with Dylan's magical light. The symbolism might have been stronger if the arms reached outward rather than inward, but still it reminded Mithabel of a miniature sun spreading rays of light.

"What's the meaning of this?" Half a dozen men bearing the lion's head insignia of the Maron city guard approached from the east. They wielded longswords and wore chain mail skirts, leather vests, and silver breastplates. The group leader waved his longsword. "You are blocking traffic. Disperse immediately or we will forcibly disperse you."

"I apologize for the crowd." Dylan stood on her tiptoes, though still scarcely high enough to be seen over her newly won adoring fans. She lay a hand on the cheek of a man in a black top hat. "The blessing of the Goddess be forever upon you. Go in peace."

The man glowed with his own golden aura. His top hat toppled from his head as he trembled in admiration and gratitude. He fell to his knees and dropped his chin, both hands clinging to Dylan's legs like a child not wanting to part from his mother. "Praise the Goddess."

"Are you just going to stand there?" Ger-Alt called to the guards from the Cheetah's back. "Is this crowd in violation of the law or not?"

Dylan lay a hand on another person, then another and another, pronouncing the blessing of the Goddess on each of them, directing each of them to "go in peace." But they all fell to their knees, bowing their heads towards her, fingers grasping to sustain contact with her sanctified person. The air shimmered golden around each of them.

The lead guard brandished his sword. "We warned you. Disperse *now*, or you *will* be arrested and hauled away."

Mithabel laughed inwardly. Hauling away the individuals comprising this gathering would take much more than a few minutes. On the perimeter of the crowd, the lead guard grabbed one of Dylan's male fans by the collar and pulled him back.

The fan turned on the guard with a pleading gaze. "Just a touch, please. That's all I want. One moment in her presence."

A half dozen glowing persons knelt in a circle around Dylan, heads down and arms outstretched, fingers groping for the Priestess. Some fans crowded between the Blessed Ones, while others stepped on their bent backs. Dozens of NPCs on the outskirts of the crowd, unable to reach Dylan, turned crazed faces on the guards and rushed them.

The probability that some people, including Dylan, might be trampled to death by the mob increased by the second. Even

Mithabel was forced to move with the ebb and flow of those around her, alternating between a push towards the Priestess and a drawing back in preparation for another. The street became a sea of top hats, derbies, and bonnets as more people joined in, everyone craving the blessing of the Sun Goddess and the touch of her Priestess.

Hell, Mithabel could use some of that action.

The system clock read *11:57 PM, Day 2, Year 1*. Only three minutes to go. They were bound to be the longest three minutes of Mithabel's existence.

CHAPTER TWENTY-NINE

Shouts of anger erupted as the members of Quantized cut down four fanatics, sending them to NPC limbo and showering the crowd with the glowing particles of the deceased. Falco took to the air. A crossbow bolt from Amarynth struck the bird but didn't kill it, and in the next moment blinding dust filled the air. Odds were the members of Quantized weren't penalized by the Falcon's obscuring ability and could see through the storm as though it weren't there. The alarmed cries of men, women, and children filled the air, cut short as Quantized took more virtual lives. The tumult drew closer and closer as Quantized dispatched NPC after NPC who stood between them and the Polynesian.

It wasn't beneath Mithabel to kill NPCs too, but in this situation it didn't feel right. They were all on Dylan's side. The Tank pushed her way through the throng, compressing or decompressing her body when it helped her make forward progress. Based on the rate at which bursts of glowing particles of dying NPCs penetrated the gloom, Mithabel wasn't moving fast enough.

"The time is 11:58 PM, chief. Two minutes remaining. System wide notification incoming. Stand by."

Perhaps Quantized wasn't moving fast enough either, but Mithabel couldn't rely on the clock to save her friend. She had to reach Dylan before they did.

Silence draped the street like a blanket while everyone, PC and NPC alike, received the system wide message.

The Jamaican AI spoke quickly. "The bounty on the

Longest Survivor is hereby increased to one million XP for the *individual* who delivers the fatal blow. Members of party MAD other than the Longest Survivor herself are no longer prohibited from attacking their own party members or collecting the bounty. All NPCs are now eligible to collect the bounty as well. Less than two minutes remain in which to collect. At midnight, a game update will be installed, at which time the bounty will expire."

Hundreds of voices expressed their amazement in a tumult of shouts, swears, and laughs.

The dust storm evaporated amid an explosion of glowing death particles illuminating the sky. Amarynth shouted over local chat, pumping her fist. "Gotcha again, damned bird."

All eyes turned on her.

"What?" She looked for Mithabel and caught her gaze. Over party chat, she asked, "Did I miss something?"

"Did you hear the notification, Amarynth?"

"No time for it at the moment. What did it say?"

"Tell you later. Right now, we need to protect Dylan. From *everyone*."

The crowd turned their attention from the Archer to the Priestess.

Dylan glared back at them. Her cry echoed up and down the street. "Come on, world. *Take me*."

The power of greed overcame the artificial fanaticism of the crowd for Dylan. Adoring fans transformed to raging fiends intent on tearing the Priestess limb from limb. Snarling like beasts, they tore at each other in their attempts to reach the Longest Survivor. Top hats, derbies, and bonnets flew from heads in the frenzy. The glimmering molecules of NPCs murdered by fellow NPCs blasted into the sky, creating a fireworks display.

Anguished faces sneered at Mithabel and clenched fists bounced off her. She equipped her battle axe. As tempting as a million XPs were, nothing and no one would prevent Mithabel from reaching Dylan and protecting her. Megan Wright had failed Debra Jones in the real world. Mithabel be damned if she failed Dylan in the virtual one. She laid about with her battle axe, severing multiple heads and limbs with each swing, laying waste to those around her like a barbarian warrior on a battlefield in a sword and sorcery novel. Her victims erupted into vibrant sparks, floating away on the breeze.

Twenty feet away, Amarynth shot bolt after bolt through the throng, aiming at the most antagonistic NPCs near Dylan, each projectile slaying multiple targets. *Pop pop pop* they went and drifted away.

Around Dylan, the circle of illuminated Blessed Ones shook off the people on their backs and rose from their bowed positions. As a unit, they turned to face the crowd, swiping gnarled, enchanted fingers at those murderous NPCs nearest them. Those few explicitly blessed by Dylan had become her Glowing Defenders.

The sparks of the dead filled the air like a swarm of busy fireflies.

"Your HP and Dylan's are holding steady, chief." Kaleisha delivered the good news, but wasn't finished. "Sadly, the Archer's HP status bar is steadily declining."

The members of Quantized closed on the Glowing Defenders. FepXveq cut down one of the Blessed Ones with a stab of her longsword and then took down another.

Mithabel compressed her body to squeeze between two snarling NPC citizens intent on tearing her apart. Drawing closer to the Priestess, she wasn't close enough to the attacking Dark Elf to parry her next blow. FepXveq thrust her weapon at Dylan.

The Polynesian batted the weapon aside with her cudgel. *"Thank you,* Megan Wright." The borrowed parry skill had protected her from the Dark Elf's attack. With a twist of her wrist, Dylan turned the parry into an offensive action, creating a counterattack combo, smacking the woman against the side of her head, simultaneously stunning and damaging her, though not near enough to kill her.

As someone with experience in the game, FepXveq stashed her longsword to keep from losing it if she were to die while vulnerable. She wavered but remained standing.

Toxxi reached past the Dark Elf's leg for Dylan. Before she could make contact, the Faerie stumbled away with a crossbow bolt in her throat. With a gurgle, she went *pop* and evaporated.

"Thanks, Amarynth!" Dylan voiced her appreciation over party chat, but an instant later contacted Mithabel on private chat. "Imagine our party with a level fifteen Tank or Archer. Kill me, or let's tell Amarynth to. It's a *million* XP, Mithabel. A *million. Someone* in the party ought to take advantage of it. So what if it costs me a life? I'll still have more lives than you."

Compressing her body to squeeze between snarling NPC residents, the Tank tossed back her black hair as she reached Dylan, putting herself between the Polynesian and an onrushing mounted Goblin. "I'm not letting anyone kill you, Priestess. I swear. Protecting you is all I'm about right now. Don't throw away a single one of your lives."

The use of a private chat channel hadn't barred Megan Wright from overhearing, and the jailed player didn't hesitate to throw her support behind the Tank. "Listen to Mithabel, Priestess. I'm all about saving you right now, too. Do *not* sacrifice yourself for *anyone*."

Ger-Alt and her Cheetah mount sprang at Mithabel through the spray of Toxxi's death particles. With a feint that drew a poorly executed parry from her target, the Elf sank her battle axe blade in the Goblin's neck, severing her head in a spray of red sparks.

The Cheetah struck Mithabel, driving powerful hind legs into the Tank's chest, knocking the wind from her lungs. Following the example set by the Dark Elf, Mithabel stashed her battle axe as paralysis claimed her unarmored limbs.

Two Glowing Defenders rushed around Dylan to attack the remaining Quantized members. One Defender clawed at FepXveq while the other attacked the Cheetah, but according to a quick report by Kaleisha, only the one attacking the Dark

Elf dealt damage. As FepXveq shrugged off her paralysis, a glowing shuriken buried itself in her forehead. The Dark Elf's afro lit up like an electric bonfire. She burst into glimmering bits.

The Cheetah leaped at Dylan. Amarynth put a bolt in Zip's shoulder, but failed to slay him, and the beast slammed a heavy paw into Dylan's temple. The Polynesian stiffened and fell straight back, the Cheetah riding her chest to the ground.

Mithabel's paralysis drained away, freeing her limbs. Equipping her battle axe, she bashed the back of the Cheetah's neck with the blunt edge. The big cat slumped onto Dylan's prone form, still alive, but stunned.

While allowing passage to Amarynth, the surviving Glowing Defenders pushed back against the wall of NPCs who rushed to take advantage of the downed Priestess. The Viking's leather boot shoved the Cheetah off Dylan. A second later, Amarynth put a crossbow bolt through the animal's heart. It vanished in a furry *puff* of particles.

Raging NPC citizens, too many for the Blessed Ones to block, flooded over the Priestess, tearing at her with their bare hands while others shoved or tugged at them in their attempts to reach their target.

From somewhere outside Mithabel's view, Kaleisha reported on the Polynesian's status. "Dylan's Physical HP has fallen to 72%, chief. Surprisingly, her Mental, Emotional, and Spiritual HP are all holding steady at 100%. She's taking this mass attack on her person remarkably well. Might be she's actually enjoying all the attention."

The Glowing Defenders struggled to push back the swell of murderous citizens eager to land one hit on Dylan, each of them hoping to deliver the killing blow. Mithabel and Amarynth levied their attacks against the people piled atop the Longest Survivor.

"Dylan's Physical HP is 63%, chief."

In the next moment, Dylan's stunned status expired and the defenses borrowed from Megan Wright kicked in.

Her attackers' blows rained down without effect. Mithabel's axe severed heads and limbs, while Amarynth's crossbow skewered eyes, throats, and hearts, dropping every attacker within five feet of the Longest Survivor. Dylan staggered to her feet.

NPC citizens in Victorian attire poured out of nearby buildings, armed with kitchen knives, claw hammers, meat mallets, ice picks, and other makeshift weapons they'd found at hand.

Six guards rushed to the attack in unison, slaying Dylan's four remaining Glowing Defenders like they were pigs for the slaughter. One guard stepped in to strike the Priestess, but Mithabel batted his weapon aside. Another guard slipped past his buddy. He took a crossbow bolt to the gut, but, surviving the penetrating missile, drove his blade into Dylan's stomach. The Priestess grunted as she stepped back, still not dead.

The guards wouldn't be easy kills like the other NPCs in the street. But there was a remedy to that. Mithabel smashed the blocked guard's temple with the blunt edge of her battle axe, stunning him. Dylan spun a shining shuriken into his forehead, and he blasted apart into a cloud of confetti. Cooperative combos were proving an effective means to deal with tough opponents.

The Viking's next shot hit her previous target, and he burst into colored paper shreds like his fellow guard, done for.

The other four guards leaned in, as though they'd practiced the maneuver, and shoved their blades through the Polynesian's ribs. They had practiced cooperative combos as well.

"Dylan's HP has fallen to 38%, chief. The time is now 11:59 PM."

The seconds had never passed so slowly. Only sixty more to go. Cool down timers for most actions being about ten seconds, roughly six attacks remained per combatant, excluding characters like Amarynth with skills to significantly shorten their waiting periods for certain actions.

The press of NPC citizen aggressors struck at anyone in their way, including guards, Amarynth, and Mithabel. The Elf ignored the attacks of half a dozen utensils without ill effect. A set of brass knuckles, a crowbar, and an assortment of other minor weapons directed at Dylan deflected off the Tank-strong defenses afforded the Priestess by Megan Wright.

"The Archer's HP status now stands at 54%, chief. You and Dylan are holding steady. So are the four guards, unfortunately."

The team of skilled NPCs readied for another synchronized attack, coming from four different directions. Mithabel couldn't deal with them all with a single action. She couldn't even drop one guard with a regular attack. Time for another cooperative combo, trusting Dylan to follow her lead. The Tank slammed the blunt edge of her battle axe against the side of the nearest guard's head. He went still, stunned.

A shuriken from the Polynesian split his right eye and sent the armored man wafting into the sky like a trail of cigarette ashes flicked from the window of a moving car.

His three companions rammed their longsword blades through Dylan's ribcage once more.

Kaleisha groaned. "That hurt. Dylan's HP is down to 24%."

In the real world, anyone taking the kind of abuse Dylan had taken would have been dead thrice over. In the virtual world of Khertaan, she'd already be dead without the defenses granted her by the Tank skills and traits transfered from the blond player occupying her head. Megan Wright's imprisonment had in its own way proved fortuitous. If the player had accompanied the party to this spot, she'd not have entertained the idea of transferring her awareness and skills to the Priestess. Dylan might not have thought to ask, either. As it was, Megan Wright was contributing more to this encounter than if she'd never triggered the alarm resulting in her capture.

Two bolts in relatively quick succession from Amarynth felled another guard before he could coordinate another attack with his comrades. Only two of the bearded fighters remained.

Spurred by the knowledge they might have only one last chance for a synchronized attack, they stepped back and then together rushed forward, thrusting their blades at Dylan.

Mithabel stopped one of them cold with a stunning strike, and once more the Shuriken-Specialist chucked a bladed star into him, sending him to virtual limbo. Outside Mithabel's reach to block, the other guard's longsword ripped into Dylan.

"Dylan's HP status has dropped to 18%, chief. Thirty-three seconds remaining on the bounty timer."

Two more shots from the Viking put the last guard out of contention for the million XP prize.

Male and female, young and old, dark skinned and light, NPC citizens of every ilk flooded into the space vacated by the guards. They frantically bashed and stabbed at Dylan, but couldn't faze her. Standing still and erect, she waited for the clock to run out. She gave Mithabel a grin. "Thirty seconds left on the bounty timer. I think I've made it."

The Elf winked at the Polynesian, laying about with her battle axe, chopping off heads. Granted, it wasn't necessary, since none of the remaining NPCs were a threat to Dylan, unless they managed a critical hit. But more than that, it was the principal of the thing. Anyone attacking Dylan at this point deserved to lose a life. The Priestess didn't tell Mithabel to stop.

Rubbing her cheeks with both hands, Dylan muttered a spell.

"Dylan's HP has risen to 100%, chief."

The Polynesian laughed and shook her fists at the dwindling numbers of NPCs. "I did it. I *survived*."

Mithabel grunted as she swiped at the crowd with her axe. "*We* did it, Priestess. All of us. Together."

"Yes, love, we did." The Priestess batted her eyelashes at the Tank.

From the east, flames blasted into the crowd. A path cleared as sparks shot skyward to mark the passing of a couple dozen NPCs. Mithabel's heart leaped in her throat. Had Rolag finally rejoined them?

Her heart sank as quickly as it had risen. Dressed in full leather armor, an Asian man with reddish blond hair stood in the street, smoke drifting up from the tip of his pointing wand. Bradford, the Wizard from party XStorm. To his right stood a woman with shoulder-length hair the same light color as his, also with an Asian look. Priestess Yuni, dressed in her signature red leather outfit and platform boots. To Bradford's left stood an armored Centaur woman with long, curly red hair. Ruby. On the Centaur's back sat a pale Goth woman with straight black hair. Penelope, dressed in her pure black leather. Next to Ruby and her rider stood the leader of XStorm, the white male Elitist with curly, shoulder-length black hair known as ChrisCross, attired in quilted white cloth reminiscent more of pajamas than armor.

In addition to Bradford wielding a wand, the three XStorm members to his left held bows at the ready. They'd clearly stopped in Voorton to buy new equipment.

If Yuni had obtained a new cudgel, it wasn't in evidence. The Asian Priestess chanted, not a spell, but a prayer to the Goddess of War, presumably to boost the morale of her party through a skill similar to Skirmish Morale, which Dylan often used to temporarily boost party MAD. Would such a skill be more effective for a Priestess of War? The Asian woman uttered only a couple phrases before Amarynth put a crossbow bolt into her open mouth.

Yuni yanked the missile from her maw and continued chanting, as though a bolt planted between her two rows of teeth was hardly an inconvenience, damn her.

ChrisCross, Ruby, and Penelope all fired arrows down the path cleared by Bradford. Their missiles hit with a unified thunk in Dylan's chest.

The Polynesian Priestess staggered under the force of their cooperative combo.

"Dylan's Physical HP is down to 81%, chief. If she hadn't healed herself when she did, she'd be dead now."

The XStorm leader and his Centaur companion marched

forward with purpose. Penelope sat stiff and pale on Ruby's back, her demeanor and complexion like that of the grim reaper.

Another blast of fire shot past Ruby.

Searing pain enveloped Mithabel. Her cry of rage and anguish rivaled Dylan's.

For how long did they burn?

The flames upon them snuffed out, and both party MAD members remained standing. Dylan's armor had protected much of her flesh from burning, and she still looked beautiful despite the charring of her exposed face and neck. Perhaps her damaged flesh enhanced her appeal. The scorched, once smooth skin of Mithabel's abdomen flaked under her touch. No doubt she wasn't looking pretty in her bikini and heels at the moment, more like overcooked bacon, but she didn't switch to Third Person POV to check.

Kaleisha sounded hopeful. "You're only down to 83%, chief, and Dylan is at 64, so it's not as bad as it looks or feels. On the down side, the degree of pain inflicted has delayed your cool down for attacking."

Mithabel grunted through the pain searing her veins. "Thanks for the pep talk, Kaleisha."

No NPCs stood within twenty feet of Dylan. Any who hadn't been touched by the first blast of flame had been destroyed by the second.

An evil smirk twitched on Dylan's face. Deep down, she knew she'd won, despite everyone's best efforts to take her down.

But XStorm wasn't giving up. They still approached, aiming their unloaded bows, waiting on their cool down timers to expire and arrows to automatically load. Would the Wizard have another flame blast to deliver as well? And where was the XStorm Priestess? Had Amarynth finished her off?

A warm breeze stirred ashes around Dylan's feet. *Something* about the breeze was *not* natural.

She'd detected an anomaly. Her new Anjai skill was at work.

Megan Wright spoke over private chat. "Dylan and I sense it too. What the hell is it? It's been following us since we passed through the city gates."

"Could it be Yuni? I don't see her anywhere." Mithabel glanced around. "Or that sneaking Dark Elf, FepXveq."

"Could either of them have followed us from the gates? I don't think so."

Kaleisha had some info to add. "Amarynth killed Yuni a little while ago, chief."

Then it had to be FepXveq. What was the Dark Elf waiting for?

Tick, tock. Tick, tock.

Then it dawned on Mithabel. "I bet it's Lance, that little snake."

"Guide my shuriken, Scintilla." Dylan threw her projectile as she stepped away from the swirling ashes and whatever invisible thing or being might have stirred them up. The thrown star followed the reverse path of the fire blast, embedding itself in the middle of the Wizard's forehead even as he phrased what could have been his last ditch spell. He erupted into a million smoldering embers scorching the sky. The wand in his hand faded into oblivion, lost to him forever.

A bolt from Amarynth's crossbow struck the Centaur woman in the chest, but failed to drop her.

The three bows held by party XStorm abruptly loaded. Ruby, Penelope, and ChrisCross fired in unison. The arrows plunked into the Longest Survivor. She remained standing. But XStorm wasn't done. Their bows reloaded, and three more arrows struck Dylan. In the span of two seconds, they'd delivered the damage of two triple strength cooperative combos. The Polynesian stood there with six projectiles protruding from her seared flesh, laughing in spite of her pain, still alive.

"Despite the enemy dealing a double-triple cooperative combo against her, Dylan's Physical HP holds at 2%, chief." Kaleisha danced partially into view. "Oops, sorry." She withdrew.

"Eight." Dylan held up four fingers on each hand, giving the members of XStorm her best evil grin. Having dealt one attack right after another, it was clear their first volley had come at the end of one combat heartbeat period and their second volley had come at the beginning of the next, which meant their cool down timers would run a full ten seconds before they could attack again. With only eight seconds left to go until midnight, XStorm had done all they could in trying to claim the bounty prize. They were out of actions for the day.

The Polynesian lowered a finger. "Seven." With the Time Sense trait, she didn't even need to watch the system clock. Dylan knew exactly how much time she had left before the bounty expired.

With a flourish, Penelope bowed from her seat on Ruby's back. "Congratulations, Dylan. Looks like you've made it."

"Six."

Mithabel's attack cool down timer *finally* expired. The Tank was taking no chances. She hoisted her battle axe and chopped at the stirring ashes. Would her blade bite into an enemy? If so, who?

In a split second, a young woman materialized. Lying on her back behind Dylan, crushing the brim of her cowboy hat under the back of her head as she looked up with wide eyes at Mithabel, the Cowgirl mouthed the word, *no*.

"Five."

"*Charli?*" What the hell? Mithabel diverted her swing, her blade skinning Charli's knee and throwing up a chunk of asphalt.

"Four."

Did the girl know how easily she could have been killed?

A red gem appeared in Charli's right hand. The Shadow Stone. It elongated, taking a sharp edge and a pointed tip like a dagger. The girl rolled onto her side, pointing the weapon at Dylan's nearest leg.

"Three."

Invoking her block action and overriding the fiery pain still burning her insides, Mithabel stepped on the Cowgirl's wrist, pinning it to the street.

"Two."

This ordeal was over.

No, it wasn't. Charli's weapon vanished. It reappeared in the Cowgirl's left hand. Mithabel had forgotten about Charli's Ambidexterity trait. And the Tank couldn't block again yet.

"One."

The teenage Guide thrust the red blade at the Polynesian's leg, the weapon slicing through armor and flesh as though they were jelly.

At least, that's how it appeared. With the Shadow Stone involved, there was no way for Mithabel to know if what she perceived was the truth.

There was no shriek of pain or surprise from the Priestess. Dylan exploded into brilliant bits. Or so it appeared.

Megan Wright screamed as though the blade had sliced into her.

Mithabel staggered away. *No.* This wasn't possible. This wasn't how things were supposed to end. Just like Megan Wright in the real world, Mithabel had failed her best friend in her time of need.

Dylan, the Longest Survivor, died in the last remaining second on the bounty clock.

Or was the Polynesian's death an illusion?

The Shadow Stone vanished from Charli's grip as the Cowgirl stashed her unholy weapon. The teenager rolled onto her back, turning a wide grin on the Elf.

Shocked to the core and still bathing in fiery pain, Mithabel couldn't speak.

Kaleisha dropped from the sky in front of Mithabel. "It's after midnight. Time to go bye bye for a while. See you after the update, chief."

The strains of background music faded into oblivion.

Mischievous laughter erupted from Charli's throat, echoing

across the city. "*I did it.*"

The Jamaican AI, the Cowgirl, and the whole virtual world faded to black, as though someone had turned down the dimmer switch on the sun, all the way to the off position.

CHAPTER THIRTY

Holy Freaking Goddess.

I'm awake. In bed.

I'm not Mithabel. I'm not Dylan. I'm Megan. It's me, in my own freaking body.

Sit up and scream. Because I can. Relish the echoes of my real voice in my real ears.

Slap my real cheek. Laugh at the sting. Pinch my real arm. Laugh while I say, ow.

Bite my finger. It's real. It's freaking real.

Stop biting now. No need to draw blood.

Yell. Keep yelling. Feels so good, the air rushing up my throat, over my tongue, through my parted lips.

Oh, Goddess, I'm crying. Shit.

Shit, shit, shit.

Toss off the quilt. Swing my feet over the edge of the bed. Stand up. Not fully awake, yet I don't even wobble on the heels of my pumps. Neither would Mithabel. She's a bad ass Ninja. So am I. Tell no one.

A tear plops on the floor next to my right foot. Another one. Some fall on my left.

Wipe my eyes.

Does no damn good. I let the tears fall.

I'll do nothing but stand here until they abate on their own.

Freaking A. Freaking A. Freaking A. The phrase is on a loop in my head.

It stops. Finally. So do the tears.

No. Wait. One last tear.

Now I'm done.

That damned end table with its broken pocket watch, wand, and mirror, plus that crystal ball over by the northwest door... they don't belong in the real world. They're from Mithabel's world. I can't explain their presence. I pick up the pocket watch. Rub its gold casing between my fingers.

It still reads freaking three o'clock.

The system clock isn't where it should be. Except, *no*, it *shouldn't* be there. The system clock only exists in the virtual world. In Khertaan, not Earth. I have no system clock suspended in space in the top right corner of my field of vision. I'm in the real world now. If I were still in Khertaan, I'd be occupying Mithabel's secondary avatar, locked inside a holding cell waiting to be found out as an illegal avatar.

"Kaleisha, what time is it *really*?"

Damn. Like the system clock, the Jamaican support AI exists only in Mithabel's world.

Throw the pocket watch against the far wall. A bam and a thud, and the undamaged timepiece is on the floor. Scream at it. The damned thing still doesn't break.

Not being Mithabel, I don't have a Temperament filter to turn up.

Swipe everything off the end table onto the floor. Stomp on it all. None of it breaks. Pick up the mirror and slam it edgewise on the top of the end table. Bam, bam, bam. No breakage. Throw it at the far wall. It joins the pocket watch on the floor.

Scream some more. More tears flow.

Stop it. Get a hold of yourself. Sit down a moment. The floor will do.

Goddess, now the tears are coming hard. Can't stop them.

Despite not having a Temperament filter, I should be able to calm myself. Breathe. That's better. "Mithabel, are you there?"

Do you expect an answer?

She's *not* a dream. I won't delude myself about her. She exists. She's my subconscious, buried inside me. Somehow she can connect with other subconscious minds. Dylan.

Amarynth. Toxxi. And she can talk to NPCs and a Jamaican AI bot named Kaleisha. Then there's Charli and Rolag, programmed NPC bots Mithabel can interact with. How in bloody hell is that possible?

Maybe you have implants in your skull.

Or perhaps in my leg. Where the Orc Wizard's dagger pierced my skin.

The wound is healing. It itches. Press your fingers on the spot.

Nothing.

Did you expect to feel a bump under your skin?

I've stopped crying.

Where's your smart phone? You need to call your mother.

No phone. No pocketbook. Shit. They're in the burned out shell of my Mustang. Unless the police fished them out.

Are you officially a missing person, or considered a victim of a kidnapping?

Kev was real.

Was he?

What about the Mad Cow Ballista, shooting giant pencils? That wasn't part of Mithabel's experience, but mine. The bovine is in *my* memories, not hers.

Nothing makes sense.

What about this freaking candle holder, with its partially burned candle? Pick it up. It feels real. Why is it even here? Everything else from the end table seems to have a purpose of sorts, either to me or to Mithabel.

Is the candle shorter than the first time you saw it?

Can't be. I'm imagining it.

Maybe it's a timer.

That's it. I feel it in my bones. It has no flame, but it's getting shorter as though the wax were burning. What happens when it's gone? Does it represent how much time I have for preparing to fight the invaders, the Orc Wizards, Arachnid Behemoths, Mad Cow Ballista, and whatever else the enemies of the real world can throw at us?

So time hasn't stopped after all. Or maybe it's measured in a different manner than the one to which you're accustomed.

"Mithabel, are you there? Talk to me, please. Kaleisha? Anyone?"

Do you expect anyone to answer?

Shit. Shit, shit, shit. I signed a freaking NDA. Didn't I need proof of identity for that? And where's my copy of the agreement?

Why are you worrying about that now?

I hope Debra Jones is okay. And Anna Milligan. And Charli.

Charli isn't real. Why do you give a damn about her? Really. *Why?*

Same for Rolag then too. Okay, same for Mithabel, Dylan, and Amarynth. I want them all to be okay. I miss them all. But if I ever get my hands on Charli, that little bitch is going to pay. No. Maybe I won't. I'm not Mithabel. Dealing with Charli should be her job, not mine. Scream again. Get it out.

Didn't get it all out. Scream some more.

Still screaming.

Get up. Walk it out. Calm down.

Oh, Goddess, kill me.

You don't mean that.

Calm. Down.

The damned door is locked. It wasn't locked for Mithabel. Why are *you* a prisoner?

Bam, bam, bam.

You can't knock it down.

Hinges are on the outside. Wait. They were on the *inside* for Mithabel. The room isn't the same for both of us. A minor detail easily overlooked, but the key to knowing I don't share the same space with Mithabel. This room isn't located in some ethereal dimension between the real and the virtual.

The room could be.

But the door isn't.

What are you going on about? Nothing that makes sense.

I'm not insane.

Sanity is overrated.

I'm *not* insane.

Are you sure? Do you ever hear a voice that isn't yours talking inside your head?

Maybe the door is locked to protect *me* from holographic Orc Wizards and Arachnid Behemoths.

If you're being protected, what makes *you* so special? Or is every surviving real person being afforded this sort of protection? If that's the case, who's running the show?

There's a connection between the game and the holographic invaders. It's not coincidence that the holographic invaders showed up almost immediately after I registered for the game.

But that makes it sound like the invaders are in your mind. If they are, you're right back to possibly being insane.

How do any of us know we're sane?

Where are Kev, Nigel, and Doctor Splat? Any of the three of them would have answers for you, even if they don't have them all. Why can't you remember the last time you interacted with any of them?

I hope they're all right, but my gut weighs heavy.

Mithabel thought she could be there for Dylan better than you could be there for Debra, but in the end she failed as much as you did. But her failure doesn't seem as onerous as yours. Dylan practically begged Mithabel to kill her, and Mithabel refused on moral grounds. Yet when she could have stopped Charli from killing the Priestess, Mithabel diverted her axe blade, sparing Charli and sealing Dylan's fate.

To be fair, Mithabel hadn't realized the girl had the power to kill Dylan.

Maybe she should have realized it. The Shadow Stone had already proved to be powerful magic.

The involvement of the Shadow Stone means it could have all been an illusion. A virtual illusion, but what other kind of illusion is there?

It might have been better if the million XP had gone to a PC member of party MAD, but Charli is dedicated to Amarynth, so hopefully she'll stay with the party. You'll gain the benefit from her elevated abilities as a level fifteen Guide. She'll have some skills in a subclass too. What one will she choose?

Can Mithabel forgive the Cowgirl and allow her to travel with the party?

After the game update occurring at this moment, what will happen to you in the virtual world? Will you still be able to occupy Mithabel's secondary avatar?

That was a blast.

You *need* to call your mom. You need her reassuring real voice.

Why did the game developers want Dylan dead so badly? My right leg itches. I still don't feel any implants.

Your being awake now shouldn't cost Mithabel a point of Constitution. It's not like she was killed. The game developers forced her out of the game so they could do an update. What's her current condition? Is she aware at all?

"Mithabel? Say something. *Please.*" I'm so alone.

Yell. Maybe someone will hear you.

If someone does hear me but is locked in another room, what good can come of it? They would have heard me already if they could, and I would have heard them.

If the game logic is flawed, it can't be cheating to exploit it. They can't disqualify you.

All the other players are awake now too. What are they thinking? What is Debra doing right *now*? Is she still in bed? Has she found a way out of her room? She *is* in a room, exactly like mine. Must be.

Should you be hungry? Thirsty? When the hell did you eat last? You didn't even grab a donut when you had the chance.

I'd love some chocolate ice cream. A sip of hot coffee with cream and sugar. Real sugar, thanks. No artificial sweeteners. What kind of fool signs an NDA and doesn't insist on retaining a copy? I would have kept a copy. Did I hide it somewhere in this room?

The scrolls on the shelves are decorative in nature, like

in Mithabel's room. No actual scrolls. No actual books, with turnable pages.

I try them all anyway. Maybe one of them is the NDA.

Nope.

Try the pictures on the wall. Do any of them come down? Maybe an NDA was slid inside the frame, behind the photo.

Nope.

Open the top dresser drawer. What the hell? A two-piece black leather bikini adorned with silver rings. Black slippers with wide, thick, high heels. I don't remember seeing them before. Didn't I look in the dresser before? Maybe not. Can't remember. Maybe that was Mithabel.

What are you going to do?

Please shut the hell up.

I change into the bikini and slippers. Because I can. They fit perfectly. My denim jumpsuit and black leather pumps go onto the floor. Pull out the drawer and check for secret compartments or false bottom. Nothing. Toss the drawer on the floor.

The other drawers hold panties, bras, socks, jumpers, and other folded clothes. Everything goes onto the floor, including the empty drawers after I thoroughly check them.

Check the closet. All manner of clothing and shoes fill it. Hold a shirt up to me. It's my size. Toss it onto the pile on the floor. Toss out more things from the closet.

Hold on one second. *Holy shit.* This is a full body suit of leather armor.

Behind it... bloody hell... no way....

A battle axe and bow lean against the wall, resting atop the coils of a braided rope. Propped against the wall behind the axe shaft is the amputated wing of a large bat, if the bat were purple and had gauzy wings.

I back out and slam the closet door.

I'm still wearing the bikini. The denim jumpsuit is still on the floor, peeking from beneath the pile of clothes and emptied dresser drawers.

I'm tired of yelling.

So I stop.

Breathe.

Again.

Dammit, my cheeks are soaked.

Throw my weight against the exit door. Try the doorknob again. Dammit.

Calm down, Mithabel.

Wait.

I'm not Mithabel.

I'm Megan.

Stay sane. Stay real.

Gotta get grounded.

Grab up the freaking wand.

Strike the crystal ball. It shimmers.

Holographic images coalesce within the sphere, their colors more vivid than reality. "To be or not to be," intones a young white man, his voice emanating from within the sphere. He's an actor, and looks straight at me, though of course from his perspective he's looking at a camera.

I wave the wand. The actor is replaced by a herd of wild horses racing along a sandy beach.

Such freedom.

My breathing calms. Finally.

Slowly release a breath.

Wave the wand again. The scene changes to a young black woman holding a microphone, standing in a street clogged with debris, the buildings to either side devastated as though by a category five hurricane. A car behind and to the right of the reporter is flatter than the proverbial pancake. A banner near the base of the crystal ball announces the reporter's name as Serena Wilson.

Serena puts the mike to her mouth. "This is the carnage happening across the globe. No organization has come forth to claim responsibility. The US President and other world leaders deny any knowledge of the forces behind these attacks. I spoke to some eye witnesses earlier."

The scene cuts to Serena standing in a different location on what could be the same street, but crowded with humans, including first responders aiding the injured. She approaches an older, clean-shaven gentleman with receding hair line. His eyes glisten as he looks towards the camera, his gaze unfocused.

"Can you tell us what caused this destruction? What did you see?" Serena holds the microphone to the man's face.

"We're all gonna die." The gentleman turns away from the camera, scanning the wreckage around him. "It's the Apocalypse. The Last Days." He trudges away with the failed energy of a zombie.

Another scene cut. "Can you tell us what you saw?" Serena is with a woman in her early to mid thirties.

The woman sobs. "I can't.... I can't...."

The scene cuts to Serena with a third witness, a teen boy with a skateboard at his feet. The number of humans in the area has dwindled to half what it was earlier. The boy flips his skateboard.

"What can you tell us about what you saw?"

"A video game come to life." The kid flips the skateboard again. "Those were some big-ass mofos. I'd show you a video, but it didn't work. I think they crushed my mom and dad when they stepped on our house. One of them stole my sister. Skewered her right through the stomach with its metal leg." He steps on the skateboard. His eyes aren't wet. Is he in shock? "I can't talk now." He speeds away, skipping over and darting around debris like it wasn't there.

The scene returns to Serena in the present, her eyes shimmering. "Not one person could tell us exactly what they saw, but the damage done is almost beyond human comprehension." She wipes an eye.

Cut to another reporter in the studio, an older white gentleman identified by a banner as William Stone. "No one captured what happened on video? How is that possible?"

Back to Serena, composing herself. "That's right, William. And it's like that everywhere. Not one video has surfaced, from anywhere in the world, capturing the cause of this devastation. It's like the planet is under attack by a ghost world."

The camera spins to its right. Two teenage girls huddling next to each other come into frame. Serena and the cameraman rush to them.

One of the girls mumbles.

"I'm sorry, can you repeat that?" Serena offers the girl the mike.

"They're gone. The things came and took them. Killed them and carried them away."

The other girl clamps her eyes shut, fighting back tears. "We're never gonna see them again."

Serena leans in close. "Who? What things?"

"Those things." One of the girls points beyond the cameraman.

The camera whips around, aiming above a ruined house, showing...

...blue sky.

Serena grabs back her microphone. "Are you getting this?"

"My camera is aimed right at it." Panic laces the cameraman's voice. "Should we go? It's coming fast. Damn, there are two of them. Three. *Four. Run.*"

"We're obviously not seeing what you are." William adjusts his tie. "Nothing threatening, certainly."

"Into the van, girls." The camera films debris on the ground as the cameraman rushes for his vehicle.

The camera is all over the place, still capturing video but not focused on anything.

"Get in." It's Serena's voice. A door slides closed. The camera is inside the van. Two more doors slam shut. Serena shouts. "*Go.*"

The van backs up, the camera now aimed through the front windshield.

Chunks of asphalt fill the camera view, spewing from a section of newly destroyed street. But the camera shows nothing that could have caused the damage.

The van wheels around and races away. The street ahead is clear of debris and visible dangers. Serena leans towards the driver. "*Faster*."

My finger itches. I scratch it.

And touch metal.

Ezmerelda's ring.

Are you shitting me?

I'm wearing it. Bloody hell. It's *on* my finger.

The crystal ball goes black. Is Serena okay? The cameraman? The girls? The driver?

Dark flames leap to life inside the sphere. The camera moves past the flames, to focus on a wizened, levitating female figure, her legs crossed as though seated. Long arms hang by her side, descending into darkness.

Ezmerelda.

"Have you seen enough, Megan?"

"You're not real. None of this is real." I turn away from the crystal ball. "I want out. I'm not playing the game anymore."

"What's happening outside your room isn't a game." Ezmerelda's voice cracks. "But it's the reason you're here. It's the reason Mithabel is in the game. You're learning her skills. You're not ready yet to face what lies beyond that door. That won't happen until Mithabel reaches character level thirty and you've fully assimilated her skills at that level. The invaders can't be beaten by conventional military tactics and weapons. They can only be destroyed by other inter-dimensional things. That's where you come in."

I laugh. "I'm not inter-dimensional."

"You're more advanced than you realize."

Turn to face the old crone again. "I'm not a soldier to fight in a real war."

"You already killed one of the invaders. The Orc Wizard. We need people who comprehend the virtual world, and you do. Plus you have a drive that can't be quantified. That's what the monsters lack, and it's why you'll beat them, when you're ready. You and your friends, and anyone else who graduates from the Khertaan program. A million dollars enticed you to join. The prize has become more valuable than any amount of money. Civilization stands in the balance."

I close my eyes and grip my forehead. "Who's behind these inter-dimensional attacks? Are we under siege from an alien invasion, or is some human prick trying to control the world?"

"We don't know. That will be for you and Mithabel to discover."

"What do you mean, *me and Mithabel*?"

Ezmerelda coughed. "We believe whoever is behind the attacks in the real world also have counterparts in Khertaan, like you have Mithabel. They'll be trying to stop Mithabel in the virtual world, the same as they sent the Orc Wizard after you in the real world. If they can drop her Constitution to zero before she reaches level thirty, she'll be done and so will you."

"Christopher Warden." I feel it in my bones. He's the bad guy in this. I don't know how, but he's the mastermind, the evil villain.

Ezmerelda frowns. "No. Christopher Warden is on our side. You might consider him a vile person, but he also has qualities we can put to use for our cause. You don't need to like him, but when you both graduate from Khertaan, you'll need to work together to bring down the monsters in the real world."

"Like hell I will."

Go back to the closet. Grab up the battle axe. It's weight is comfortable in my grasp.

Swing at the locked door leading outside.

The blade swipes through the door without damaging it.

Shit.

The crone in the globe chuckles. "That's your inter-dimensional weapon."

"Seriously? Then tell me this, oh wise one. How can *I hold* an inter-dimensional weapon, but it can't damage the door?"

The crystal ball goes blank. Empty. Like I'd turned it off by tapping it with the wand a second time, though I didn't. It turned off by itself, like it was on a timer or something. Maybe it was. I chop the battle axe at it, hoping for the satisfying shattering of broken glass, but the blade goes right through the ball without harm.

I bellow at the world. A freaking war cry. Can anyone hear me?

I want some ice cream. Chocolate. Can I get room service?

The crystal ball shimmers. No picture inside.

"The update has completed. Please return to Khertaan at your discretion."

The shimmer fades.

Bloody hell.

Let's get this over with. Climb into bed. I don't need to tell Debra and Anna what to do. They know. The more time we spend talking in the real world, the less time our counterparts have in the virtual world.

As though time has any meaning now.

I'm keeping the battle axe with me in bed. Gripping it like a lover, the sharp edge aimed away from my face, my lips planted on the blunt edge. I'm wearing the bikini and heeled platforms, too, not my jumpsuit and pumps. What's good for Mithabel is good for me.

Only twenty character levels to go.

Wait a second. Get out of bed. Go to the closet. Get the suit of leather armor, the bow, the rope, and the Faerie wing. Pile them on the bed with me. Okay. Now I can sleep.

I close my eyes.

And open them.

I'm lying on a cot in a holding cell, dressed in a black leather bikini with silver rings. I'm wearing high-heeled platform slippers, holding a freaking battle axe, and still have on Ezmerelda's ring. A suit of leather armor, a bow, some rope, and a dismembered Faerie wing lie on the floor of my cell.

I grab a lock of hair and pull it before my eyes. It's blond. I'm still me. Still Megan Wright, occupying Mithabel's secondary avatar. Open up my inventory. Bloody hell. Except for the suit of leather armor, the bikini, and the ring, duplicates of all my items reside in the inventory grid I share with Mithabel. The bikini and ring aren't there because Mithabel is wearing her copies of those items, I'm sure of it. She has copies of everything and so do I, except the armor, because she didn't have it in her possession when the update started. Everything she had in her possession at midnight has been duplicated for me. Maybe it's a bug not addressed by the update, or maybe the update introduced a new bug. Either way, it's hilarious.

Do I want Mithabel to know I have duplicates? Maybe not yet.

Has she returned to the game? "Mithabel, are you there?"

The system clock reads *1:00 AM, Day 3, Year 1*. The update took an hour. It's still seven hours before the guards intend to release me.

"Megan, thank the Goddess. Yes, I'm here, with the others. We came back into the game in the street where we left off prior to the update. XStorm did, too. Pretty sure Quantized is holed up in the building they used as a respawn point. The city guards are flooding the area, dispersing the crowds. They were eying both us and XStorm like they wanted to haul us off to the holding cells, so we vacated the area. Charli is with us, the little scoundrel. Dylan says not to hold anything against the girl, so I won't. I still feel like a failure. You know how that goes. Were you aware Charli was the one who killed Dylan, right before midnight? Rolag isn't with us yet. His cool down timer hasn't run out for returning to the game. We're heading into the temple now, to barter for some new spells for Dylan. How are you holding up? Are you still in prison? Kaleisha says Raphael, our developer contact, is still offline. It's possible he's gone home for the evening and won't be back before eight o'clock. But we'll wait a while longer and hope he comes back before then and can get you out. If not, we'll come up with another plan. Maybe a jail break, if we need to. In the meantime, would you like to transfer your awareness to me, so you can keep up with what we're doing?"

That's a lot to absorb. I shake my head, though of course she can't see it. "I don't want to leave my body vulnerable in the cell any more than I already did to help Dylan against the bounty hunters. When the guards come to validate this secondary avatar body, I want to be *in the body*, not transfered somewhere else. I'm sure you understand."

"When you put it that way, sure. Okay, well, keep me apprised if anything happens, and I'll do the same. Sorry you're missing out on the adventures. Thanks for helping Dylan earlier. She almost survived the night because of you."

"Yeah, you should have killed her, Mithabel, if anyone was going to. But it's cool with me that Charli did, I guess. The Cowgirl has proved to be an asset, and now she'll be more of one. Hey, while we're talking, I'm stashing the leather armor for now. Just so you know." I don't mention the duplicate items.

"You don't need it?"

"As an Anjai, I'm better off without it. Right?" Not going to mention I'm wearing a bikini. Let her picture me sitting in the holding cell in only my underwear. "If I do need it, I know where it is. Cheers, Mithabel." Maybe I shouldn't be holding out on her, but I don't want her to know about these duplicate items. No wonder she didn't tell the rest of party MAD about Ezmerelda's ring when she first got it. She's based on me, and I like holding secrets to my chest, even to the extent of keeping the truth from myself, and even when I know it's the wrong thing to do.

"Later, player." Mithabel falls silent.

I'm all alone in my cell and in my thoughts.

The leather armor goes into inventory. I slip my left arm through the coils of the rope and loop them over my head, resting the bulk of the weight on my right shoulder. I can carry the weapons in my hands.

What to do with the Faerie wing? I jam the severed end

down into the rope coils behind me, letting the wing stick up like its growing from my right shoulder blade. Third Person POV gives me a better view of my back, and I adjust the wing stump in the coils. It should stay in place. If it doesn't, I'll do something else.

Wearing a bikini, with a rope looped over my shoulder like a Cowgirl, a lone purple Faerie wing jutting up from behind me, a single-edged battle axe in one hand and a bow in the other, I look freaking ridiculous. But isn't that par for the course?

There are no guards present. They left the cell door keys hanging on a ring on a far wall. Guess they don't have enough keys for every guard to have their own copies. Or maybe the developers like tantalizing prisoners. I don't need the keys anyway. I compress my body like the badass Ninja I am and slip between the bars. Oh, that's right, they call it Anjai in this world. Whatever.

Fetching the key ring, I find the one that opens my cell door and unlock it. Leave the door wide open. No need to give the guards the idea I escaped by slipping through the bars. Let them think someone broke in and freed me. Place the key ring back on the hook on the wall.

I walk down a hallway with photos from my life in the real world plastered on the walls. One of them pictures me sitting in my red 2015 Mustang GT convertible with black-painted aluminum wheels. Damn, I loved that car.

March outside and stroll down Main Street, drawing all manner of stares. The city looks like it did before the update. NPC citizens in Victorian dress and guards in their lion head livery. Horses clopping alongside horseless carriages on asphalt streets between stone buildings.

If the guards realize who I am, they don't try to stop me. They're too busy admiring my skin and wondering why I have one wing. The person they imprisoned was dressed in boring leather armor. That's not me. I'm anything but boring.

I hope Mithabel won't mind my breaking out of jail. I won't tell her about it yet. She might tell me to go back to my holding cell and wait for her to get me out legally. Nah. I'm not waiting. Why should I? I won't learn how to fight inter-dimensional invaders by sitting in a cell.

Being an outlaw is so liberating. Invigorating.

That's how we'll reach level thirty quickly. By being outlaws, breaking all the rules.

Charli is my freaking role model, already a level fifteen Guide, starting from nothing.

That's how I'll win when I finally face the inter-dimensional invaders. Because our laws of nature don't apply to them. Our bullets can't kill them. Our cameras can't film them. They defy our physics, our science. They break our rules, and it will take a rules breaker to defeat them.

I can't wait to fight them, to send them back to whatever inter-dimensional hell they sprang from.

End Transcription One

ABOUT THE AUTHOR

Emila H Thicke

 An extreme introvert, Emila H (Emilah) Thicke sold her first speculative fiction story as a teenager. Unfortunately, circumstances prevented the story from being published. But that incident led to her meeting her co-author, who introduced her to role-playing games. Now through the literary avenue known as LitRPG, her dream of becoming a published author has come to fruition.

When not writing or editing, Emilah enjoys creating digital art and dabbling in 3D animation. She lives in Central Florida with her significant other.

ABOUT THE AUTHOR

M K Eidson

 MK (Mike) Eidson was an avid reader and aspiring writer years before he discovered role-playing games and solitaire adventures in the late 70s. He quickly transitioned from player to game master, creating scenarios for his family and friends. Over the years he has served as game master for countless sessions, running games in dozens of rules systems. Nearly fifty years later, he's happily combining his two passions into his first GameLit / LitRPG novel and looking forward to writing many more, sharing them with anyone who can appreciate his style.

Mike lives in Central Florida with his wife and their pet Jack Russell Terrier, quietly contemplating the future. In addition to writing fiction, Mike enjoys creating digital art, music, and videos.

WEB LINKS

Eposic: eposic.com

Mike's Blog: www.mkeidson.com
YouTube: youtube.com/channel/UCeXF97ZibgXrJs26DJ2avBw
Facebook: www.facebook.com/eposic
Twitter: twitter.com/eposic

Emilah's Blog: emilahthicke.wordpress.com/
Facebook: www.facebook.com/emilahthickeauthor
Twitter: twitter.com/EmilahThicke

Facebook Groups sometimes frequented:
Tunnels & Trolls
Deluxe Tunnels & Trolls
Trollhallans
GameLit Society
LitRPG Authors' Guild
LitRPG Adventures: Reviews & Discussions
LitRPG, GameLit, Wuxia, and Xianxia
LitRPG Books
LitRPG Adventurer's Guild
DAZaholic Writers
Writers, Artists, and Musicians Helping One Another Get Started

THANKS FOR READING!

We hope you've enjoyed our debut novel. If you have, we also hope you'll rate the book and leave a review to help other readers decide whether our story is for them. We know our writing style and chosen genre aren't for everyone, but if you know anyone who might enjoy this book, we'd appreciate your recommending it to them. Word of mouth is the best advertising, and we will love you forever for it.

If you'd like to give us constructive criticism that might help us improve future works or fix any errors you found in this book, feel free to message either of us on Twitter or leave comments on our Facebook pages. To be made aware of future releases, please subscribe on our web sites.

Lastly, it will be so cool to have more fans following us on Twitter and Facebook. If you count yourself as a fan and have Twitter or Facebook accounts, please visit our pages and click the Follow button! We look forward to engaging with you.